Other Regencies from ImaJinn Books

A Regency Yuletide

by

Jo Ann Ferguson

Karen Frisch

Sharon Sobel

IMAJINN

ImaJinn Books

This is a work of fiction. Names, characters, places and incidents are either the products of the author's imagination or are used fictitiously. Any resemblance to actual persons (living or dead), events or locations is entirely coincidental.

IMAJINN

ImaJinn Books

PO BOX 300921

Memphis, TN 38130

Print ISBN: 978-1-61026-086-2

ImaJinn Books is an Imprint of BelleBooks, Inc.

ImaJinn Books was founded by Linda Kichline.

We at ImaJinn Books enjoy hearing from readers. Visit our websites
ImaJinnBooks.com
BelleBooks.com
BellBridgeBooks.com

10 9 8 7 6 5 4 3 2 1

Cover design: Debra Dixon
Interior design: Hank Smith
Photo/Art credits:
background (manipulated) © Almoond | Dreamstime.com
background (manipulated) © Annnmei | Dreamstime.com
Couple (manipulated) © Linda Bucklin | Dreamstime.com
Banner & Snowflakes © Jaguarwoman Designs
Snowflakes (manipulated) © Tiago Fidalgo (DesignFera)

:Lyrd:01:

The Lord of Misrule

by

Jo Ann Ferguson

Chapter One

"WHAT I REALLY need is a rope strong enough to hang a man."

Hearing the words that had struck her servants speechless, Lady Priscilla Hathaway walked into the kitchen of Mermaid Cottage, the home she shared with her husband, Sir Neville, and her three children. She was not surprised to see Gilbert, the major domo, frozen in shock. Both Mrs. Moore, the housekeeper, and Mrs. Dunham, the cook, stared wide-eyed at Neville.

Priscilla smiled as she walked over to her husband. She wondered if she would ever grow tired of his darkly handsome looks or the mischievous twinkle in his brown eyes. Or the love and longing that filled his eyes when he looked at her.

"Do you have any specific man in mind for hanging?" she asked as she paused beside him.

He smiled, and the familiar warmth swirled through her. Since their wedding six months ago, just as summer began, she had only grown more eager to see that rakish smile.

"If you wish me to name a name, then I must say the only man I know who deserves a threat of hanging is Duncan McAndrews."

She laughed. From the corner of her eye, she noticed the servants had regained their composure and were making efforts to look busy. Would they ever become accustomed to Neville's outrageous ways? It might be too much to ask that a household once overseen by a vicar should change quickly. When she saw Gilbert hiding a smile, however, she suspected they already had started to accept Neville as part of the family.

"Do you always imagine inflicting such bodily harm to one of your friends?" Priscilla asked.

"Only to those who have been infected with midsummer moonlight."

"But, Neville, 'tis Christmastide." She wagged a playful finger at him. "If you keep making such comments, you will be the one deemed mad."

He took her by the wrist and bent to press his mouth to the skin half-hidden by the lace at her cuff. Her other hand curved along his face before she brought his lips to hers. Every kiss they shared made her long for another. As his arm slipped around her waist, she leaned into him, savoring the closeness that was still new and full of discovery.

He smiled as he raised his mouth from hers. "Thank you, Pris."

"For what?"

"For saving me from utter madness by curing me with your magical kiss."

She laughed as he struck a pose worthy of the years it was rumored he had been an actor before he had inherited his title. Even though he was her husband, she was uncertain which of the rumors of his scandalous past were true and which were exaggerations. Not that the whispers had ever bothered her, not when he was her late husband's friend—and hers—nor now.

"So you no longer need a rope strong enough to hang a man?" she asked.

"Egad!" He slapped his forehead. "Pris, do you know if there is something like that loitering in the nether regions of Mermaid Cottage? If not, Duncan will be quite beside himself with dismay."

"Duncan needs the rope?"

He nodded.

Priscilla considered if she would be wise to ask why Neville's friend needed such a strong rope. Duncan McAndrews was the complete opposite of a dour Scotsman. He enjoyed good company, good drink, and good music. If a bit of gambling was also involved, he was even happier. Duncan had called during the last week of Advent, and he had remained through Christmas, much to Priscilla's three children's delight, because he entertained them each evening with outrageous stories and songs.

"I did," Neville said, "make sure he had no plan to hang himself with it."

"That is unlikely when he is as merry as mice in malt. I know he is looking forward to seeing Aunt Cordelia for Twelfth Night. They have been enjoying each other's company for over a year now."

"You would have thought by now that he would have come to his senses and seen her as the termagant she is rather than the fantasy he has built for himself." Neville's mouth twisted. "I daresay if I hear him laud your overbearing aunt once more as a—and I quote—a paragon of virtue and beauty with a charming wit and even more charming countenance . . ." He gave an emoted shudder. "I hope he has not decided that putting his head in a noose is a better fate. The man has clearly mislaid his mind."

"Love makes people see in a very different way."

"Really?"

"When I think of the people who urged me not to marry you . . ."

He swept her up against his hard chest again. "And who urged you

3

not to marry me other than your aunt who is as contrary as an old cat?"

"I am sorry, Neville." She kissed him lightly, then stepped out of his arms. "I don't have the time now to read you the whole list."

His arm curved around her and brought her back to him. "I guess I should be grateful that being contrary is a trait that runs through the women in your family."

"And the men we marry." She stepped back as he laughed and went to find the rope his friend wanted.

Priscilla kept smiling while she walked to the small office where she handled household accounts and her correspondence. In spite of his comments, Neville admired Aunt Cordelia. Not that her aunt made it easy for him, because she never wasted an opportunity to remind Priscilla that she had married beneath her station . . . again!

Aunt Cordelia had forgiven Priscilla for marrying a vicar only because Lazarus Flanders had been, in Aunt Cordelia's opinion, far more acceptable than Sir Neville Hathaway whose reputation was too sullied. That the *ton* had gleefully accepted him, along with his wealth, amidst them did nothing to change Aunt Cordelia's mind. He was a rogue and a rake and a rascal, all reasons why Priscilla loved him.

But her aunt refused to acknowledge that he was also warmhearted and generous and loyal and loved Priscilla and her three children. When he had come back into their lives after her mourning period for her late husband was over, it was as if her life had begun anew. No day was boring when Neville was in it, and the nights since she had married her no longer stretched out, empty and lonely.

"Ah, Mrs. Hathaway, always a lovely sight."

Priscilla turned to see Duncan behind her. With his black curls and the freckles across his face, he looked more like a leprechaun than a Scottish sprite. And he had a fair share of blarney as well.

With a smile, she said, "You look quite the dashing blade yourself, Mr. McAndrews." Dropping formalities, she asked, "Duncan, what can I do for you?"

"Actually," he said, his delightful Scottish brogue enveloping every word, "I was looking for Neville. Have you seen him?"

"Yes. He has asked the household to help him find a piece of strong rope for you."

"Good."

"May I ask what you need it for?"

"To lash a gift for your aunt to the cart that will be pulled behind my carriage." His freckled face lengthened. "To own the truth, Priscilla, I had expected it to be delivered to her in time for Twelfth Night, but it is arrived here just now instead." His good spirits would not be smothered long, and he grinned. "Do you think your dear aunt will appreciate it?"

"Appreciate what?"

He took her hand and tugged her at an unseemly pace to the front hall where a huge crate had been wrenched opened to reveal a sculpture of a naked man and woman entwined in an amorous pose. Flinging out his hand with as much pride as if he had carved the lovers himself, he asked, "What do you think?"

"Oh, my!" was the best Priscilla could manage. "Is that a prank gift?"

Duncan laughed. "I can understand why you would think that, because Twelfth Night is the best time of the year for hoaxes, but it is truly a gift that I am presenting to your aunt."

"Oh, my," she repeated, staring at the statue.

He must have taken that as a positive response, because he said, "Cordelia speaks highly of the art of the ancient world, so I obtained this for her from a merchant who plies the waters between England and Greece. I know she has been seeking something to put in the entry hall of her country estate."

"That is true." Priscilla fought not to smile at the thought of how shocked her aunt would be at the idea of having her guests met by two nudes who left absolutely nothing to the imagination. The sculptor had not resorted to a fig leaf, leaving the two forms completely naked. "Duncan, I do wish you had informed me that it had been delivered before you began to uncrate it in *my* entry hall."

"I needed to be certain that it was undamaged in transit."

"True, but you must recall that I have two daughters and a young son."

Duncan's face dropped. "Forgive me, Priscilla. I should have remembered that."

"Remembered what?" asked Neville as he came into the front hall with a length of rope wrapped around his arm. He glanced at the open crate, paused and whistled a single note. "*That* is what you plan to give to Lady Cordelia as a Twelfth Night gift?"

"Yes." Duncan now looked thoroughly chastised.

Neville began laughing, struggling to say, "Promise me that I can be a witness when you present the sculpture to her. I must be there to see her face."

"Behave yourself," Priscilla said as she slapped him lightly on the arm.

"Now, Pris, you must agree that seeing your aunt's face when she first sets eyes on this gift will be a moment beyond price."

She laughed, unable to halt herself. She loved her aunt, but Aunt

Cordelia had set herself up as the arbiter of everything proper. For her aunt to be the recipient of this statue would set off fireworks that might be heard throughout the island from Land's End to John O'Groats.

"Will you two get this recrated and out of here before the children see it?" asked Priscilla.

"A wise suggestion." Neville tossed the rope to his friend. "Shall we give yon lovers a wee bit of privacy, Duncan?"

"An excellent idea." Duncan began uncoiling the rope. Finding one end, he set it on the floor next to the lowered side of the crate. "Help me here, Neville."

A younger voice piped up. "Can we help, too?"

Before Priscilla could halt them, her younger two children came rushing into the front hall. Isaac, who had inherited his father's light brown hair, was already growing tall and thin at ten years old. His sister Leah was a couple of years older, and she could scale trees and swim far better than he could, much to his dismay.

"Look at that!" crowed Isaac.

Leah giggled. As always, her dress was rumpled, and there was a mud stain near the hem. Her hair was snarled. A ribbon hung from her hair like a dead bird in a trap.

"Where have you been?" Priscilla asked. "You're both filthy!"

Isaac continued to stare at the statue as he asked, "Why are you scolding us, Mama? Shouldn't you be dressing down *them* for failing to dress at all?"

The comment sent both children into renewed peals of laughter.

Hearing more smothered chuckles, Priscilla aimed a frown at Neville and Duncan. She put one hand on Isaac's shoulder and the other on Leah's.

"March up the stairs now and get cleaned up," she ordered in her most no-nonsense voice.

It failed to reach Isaac who was still staring wide-eyed at the statue. "Where did you get that, Papa Neville?"

Neville frowned at him, but Neville's eyes twinkled as much as young Isaac's. The children had called him "Uncle Neville" until the wedding. Now when they wanted to tease him, they called him "Papa Neville."

"It is not mine," Neville said. "It belongs to Mr. McAndrews, and it is destined to be a gift for your great-aunt."

"Aunt Cordelia?" Leah began to laugh so hard she had to sit on the stairs.

Giving up on persuading the children to leave, Priscilla said, "If you gentlemen would finish preparing that for shipment, we might be able to put an end to the uproar in this house."

"Your wish is our command, fair lady." Neville bowed deeply. Standing, he grabbed the other side of the wooden panel that had been lowered to reveal the statue. "Shall we, Duncan?"

"Most assuredly." Duncan's good spirits had returned.

Priscilla started to smile, but halted when a tempest in pink rushed into the hall. It was her older daughter Daphne, a young miss who had already attended some events during the previous Season. Her golden hair was swept up in a twist, a few tendrils curling along her nape. When Daphne glanced at the sculpture, Priscilla waited for her comment. Her daughter waited for any chance to jest with Neville.

Instead, Daphne simply arched her brows and turned to Priscilla. She held out a handwritten note. "Mama, you must look at this! The most horrible thing in history has happened."

"In all of history?" asked Neville as he shoved the side of the crate into place with a clunk. "That is quite momentous."

Priscilla waved him to silence. After his time in the theater and his time with her children, he should understand Daphne's need for drama. "What is wrong?" she asked.

"This! How could Lady Eastbridge allow this to happen?" She shook the paper to emphasize each word.

"Is that the invitation to Lady Eastbridge's Twelfth Night masquerade ball?"

Each year since before Priscilla had had her own first Season, the countess claimed for herself the prestigious place as hostess to the year's first social event. It was a harbinger of the Season to come, a chance for the young women to reconnoiter the available men and for the men interested in marriage to take note of eligible women and their dowries. Through the fall, Daphne had been looking forward to this ball with unfettered delight. Now her face was longer than Duncan's had been when Priscilla was shocked by the sight of the sculpture.

"What is wrong?" asked Priscilla. "It is an invitation, isn't it?"

"Yes! But to Lady Symmington's masquerade ball on Twelfth Night." She pressed her hands over her face. "Everything—absolutely everything—in my life is ruined."

Chapter Two

"ARE YOU CERTAIN of the name on the invitation, Daphne?" Priscilla asked, astonished. Everyone in the entry hall had stopped to listen, as astounded as she was that someone along the southern coast of England—other than Lady Eastbridge—would dare to invite guests to a Twelfth Night ball.

"If you do not believe me . . ." Daphne held out the invitation. "Read it yourself."

Priscilla was taken aback by the sharp edge on her older daughter's words. Daphne's moods changed as quickly as the weather, but she seldom was curt.

Accepting the handwritten note from her daughter, Priscilla glanced at it quickly. Daphne was correct. The invitation was from Lady Symmington, who was married to a baron. How presumptuous it was for a baroness to usurp a countess! Even if Lady Eastbridge had not yet sent out invitations to the Twelfth Night masquerade, she oversaw each year with her husband at grand Eastbridge Court. Everyone along the south coast of England knew the honor of hosting the first ball of the new year belonged to her. Why would Lady Symmington—a reputedly reasonable woman—do something this out of hand?

"I am sorry to sound as if I doubted you, Daphne," Priscilla said, putting her arm around her daughter's shoulders and giving her a quick squeeze. "You must own that the invitation is quite extraordinary. Had you heard anything of this, Neville?"

He stepped away from the crate and took the invitation. Reading it, he said, "Not a word. I don't know how the Symmingtons could possibly keep such a coup secret. I daresay the whole Polite World will now be rocked from its moorings, and the very underpinnings of England and the monarchy may be in danger."

As both men laughed and the younger children joined in, Priscilla noticed that Daphne appeared shattered. Nothing in the invitation suggested it was "the most horrible thing in history" as Daphne had asserted.

Taking her older daughter by the hand, Priscilla led her into the parlor. She closed the door, a clear sign that she did not want to be interrupted while she spoke with Daphne.

The room, like the rest of Mermaid Cottage, was simple and comfortable. The house, close to the cliffs in the tiny village of Stonehall-on-Sea, had been the family's home while Lazarus had served as the parish's vicar. When he died, everyone had assumed that Priscilla would sell it and move to Town or to live with her aunt. But she could not bear to lose her home, too.

Going to the settee, she gestured for Daphne to sit beside her. She reached out and smoothed back her daughter's hair that was the same burnished gold as her own. "What is really wrong? You are on edge."

"Forgive me, Mama, for being cross. 'Tis not the invitation or your questions about it. It's just that, when we were in London earlier in the year, I could not help noticing that Alice Symmington had her claws out for Burke."

Priscilla swallowed her sigh. Since Daphne had first danced with Burke Witherspoon in the days leading up to Priscilla's and Neville's wedding, she had been fascinated by the young marquess. The problem—at least in Priscilla's eyes—was that Lord Witherspoon returned Daphne's affection. He had called on the family many times since the Season had ended, but he had not offered for Daphne's hand. Much to Priscilla's relief and Daphne's frustration. Priscilla suspected that Neville had taken the young man aside for a private conversation about the fact that Daphne still needed to wait at least another year before she could consider any marriage proposal.

"I do not believe I know Alice Symmington," Priscilla said.

"She is the only girl in a family of five boys, and she has been led to believe that she is worth far more than any other female in any room." Daphne rolled her eyes. "Mama, you must have seen how rude she was to Miss Wilson at the last party we attended before we returned to Stonehall-on-Sea."

"*That* was Miss Symmington?" Priscilla frowned. She *had* seen how uncivil the young brunette had been to Miss Wilson, who had done nothing but speak a greeting to her. Miss Symmington had cut her direct, then laughed about it with some of the other young misses. When Miss Symmington had repeated cruel comments within earshot of the male guests, Miss Wilson had fled the room in tears.

Priscilla was dismayed, for she had met both the baron and his wife and their older sons. She had found them pleasant, if a bit bland and boring. None of them would have been cruel enough to speak slurs openly.

"If you would prefer that I send our regrets," Priscilla began.

"No! We must go!"

Surprised by her daughter's apparently abrupt change of heart, she said, "I thought you wished to avoid Miss Symmington."

"I told you, Mama. She has her claws out for Burke." Coming to her feet, she asked, "Don't you see, Mama? Lady Symmington is holding the ball in order to lure Burke into attending so Miss Symmington can try to wheedle a proposal out of him."

"Daphne, such talk is not becoming." She frowned. "I trust you will refrain from speaking thus in others' company."

"I will, but I want to be honest with you."

"And I wish you to." Priscilla tried not to sigh. Raising three intelligent children required her to use her wits. She could only be grateful that Leah still considered males a completely different species and barely worthy of her contempt, save for her brother and Neville and a few others who had always been part of her life. Priscilla had great sympathy for women who had more than one daughter suffering from a calf-love.

"You must see why," Daphne said, "you must write to Lady Symmington posthaste and accept her invitation. If you insist on waiting to hear from Lady Eastbridge, the situation may deteriorate to the point that everything will be ruined."

"If Lord Witherspoon's intentions are not constant, surely you would be wise to learn that now."

"Mama, how many people told you that Neville would break your heart?"

"Just your aunt."

"How many *thought* that?" Daphne folded her arms in front of her.

This time, Priscilla let the sigh escape. "What is your point, Daphne?"

"Simply that you went ahead and married Neville because you trusted your heart more than you did the *on dits* that wafted through every party you attended with him." She knelt by the settee and grasped Priscilla's hands. "Mama, you trusted your heart and Neville. I watched that, and I learned. Now I am doing the same."

Priscilla was tempted to remind her daughter how young and inexperienced Daphne truly was, but then Priscilla recalled her aunt speaking much the same words to her. Not when Priscilla accepted Neville's offer of marriage, but when she had wed her first husband. That marriage had lasted through many happy years and given her these three wonderful, challenging children.

"Yet," Priscilla said softly, "that does not preclude me from worrying that you will suffer a broken heart."

Daphne smiled. "I know, Mama, and I appreciate that." She jumped to her feet. "Do accept the invitation. I just know that Burke will be in attendance." She flung out her hands and swirled around the room. "I have not seen him in ages."

"I will consider accepting the invitation."

"Just consider?"

Standing, Priscilla put her hands on her daughter's shoulders. "And I will take your request into consideration. I want everyone to be able to enjoy Twelfth Night."

"But, Mama, how can I enjoy it if I am not there when Alice Symmington stalks Burke?"

She smiled at her daughter. "I know, and I can promise you that I will keep in mind that we want to avoid the most horrible thing in all of history."

Daphne's lips tilted. "I did say that, didn't I?"

"Yes." She kissed her daughter's cheek. "I will let you know this evening."

Even though Priscilla could tell Daphne wanted to ask many more questions, her daughter said only, "I will try to be patient, Mama."

Priscilla appreciated Daphne making the effort, but half-expected her daughter to come into the office to interrupt while Priscilla tended to her household accounts. But the door stayed closed. Even so, Priscilla could hear the efforts of the household to move the large sculpture out of the front foyer. She hoped Duncan had a cart strong enough to tote the statue to Aunt Cordelia's house.

Or mayhap not. Aunt Cordelia might not be pleased to be presented with such a gift.

Shaking the thoughts from her head, Priscilla focused on her work. She wanted to settle her accounts before the new year.

Something tickled her nape. She brushed at her collar, but found no loose thread. As she began to write again, the tickle returned. She looked up to see a sprig of mistletoe dangling over her head.

Neville's mouth covered hers in a slow, sensual kiss that seared her to her toes. He drew her up from the chair and into his arms. As he deepened the kiss until she could think only of the brush of his tongue against hers, she combed her fingers up into his dark hair.

"Ouch!" she said, drawing back as something hit her on the nose. She shook her hand, and white powder rose from it. "Did you pack away the statue or take it apart?"

He raked his own hand through his hair which was covered with plaster dust. "We tried to do the former, but I think half a shattered fresco was shipped along with it. I do hope your aunt does not break the whole thing over Duncan's head."

"He seems to believe she will be happy with his gift."

"Hmm . . ." He put the mistletoe on her desk next to Lady Symmington's invitation that she had set to one side. "This was unexpected."

"It is."

"Do you think it is a Twelfth Night prank?"

Priscilla shook her head. "I doubt Lady Symmington would do something that outrageous."

"True. None of the Symmingtons seem to have been born with an ounce of imagination. Ambition, yes, but no imagination. Which means this is a legitimate invitation. Shall you accept it, Pris?"

"If it had come from Lady Eastbridge, I would accept with alacrity. As it is . . ." She looked down at the handwritten note. "I cannot help wondering if the countess knows of Lady Symmington's ball. I don't want to vex the countess, for she was very kind after Lazarus's death." She sighed. "As was Lady Symmington. Oh, Neville, this is such a muddle."

"You know Daphne will never forgive you if she discovers young Witherspoon attended and danced with the baron's daughter rather than with her."

"I do not make such important decisions based on who will stand up with whom."

He put his arm around her shoulders. "Pris, when you assume such a tone, I know you are letting something unsettle you too much."

"It is bizarre that Lady Symmington would do something that others would deem an unforgivable *faux pas*. You cannot deny that."

He arched his ebony brows. "If Christina Symmington wishes to put an end to Lady Eastbridge's goodwill in such a public way, that is her concern alone."

"You are not often wrong, Neville, but when you are, you make a huge mistake. If we accept this invitation, Lady Eastbridge may take umbrage at *us*." She held up her hand as he opened his mouth. "I know you care nothing for the canons of Society, but—"

"As the stepfather of an eligible miss, I must walk the straight and narrow path that proper behavior dictates." His face became a tragic mask.

With a laugh, Priscilla slapped his arm. "You are wasting your dramatics on me."

"Then let me offer you a different sort of performance, one that I excel at." He tugged her back into his embrace. He gave her a devilish grin before his mouth lowered toward hers.

A knock on the door brought a low curse from him as Priscilla drew back to call, "Come in."

Juster, one of the footmen, entered and held out a folded piece of paper. "This was just delivered for you, my lady."

"Thank you," Priscilla said as she took the page.

The footman bowed and left the room, closing the door after him.

Priscilla opened the page. "It is from Aunt Cordelia."

Neville's nose wrinkled as if the paper reeked. "What does your shrewish aunt have to say?"

"Give me a moment." She was too curious why her aunt had written that she paid his insult to her aunt no mind. "Neville, you will not believe this!"

"Try me."

"Aunt Cordelia wrote to remind me—as if I need a reminder—that as Daphne is not yet officially out, we must be doubly watchful of my daughter during the masquerade ball at Symmington Hall."

Neville gave a short laugh. "There, sweetheart, is your answer. Your aunt is giving Lady Symmington's gala cachet simply by attending, so it is clear that you have carte blanche to attend as well."

Folding the note, Priscilla walked to the window and looked out at the back garden. It was withered and gray in the dim light of the winter afternoon.

"You look bothered, Pris." Neville slipped his arm around her waist and leaned her back against him.

"I am. I had believed that my aunt considered Lady Eastbridge a good friend."

"Have you considered that the countess might have given her blessing to Lady Symmington's plans? Even though I know a gentleman should never discuss a lady's age, I am no gentleman, so I can say that Lady Eastbridge is no spring filly. She may have bequeathed the onus of the Twelfth Night ball to a younger woman."

"A bequest is what it would have to be. I cannot envision Lady Eastbridge relinquishing the first ball of the year unless she was dying or dead."

"Let us hope it does not come to that!"

Chapter Three

THE AVENUE LEADING up to the magnificent Tudor house known as Symmington Hall was flanked by gardens that must have been magnificent when their flowers were in bloom. Hedges and topiaries had been neatly trimmed, and a dusting of snow accented their contours. In the distance, small buildings might be useful or merely garden follies.

Neville drew the heavy, wool blanket more closely around Priscilla. "Symmington has wasted no expense bettering his dirty acres, it would appear."

"The family has lived here for almost a thousand years."

"Ah, yes. I have heard the tales of how the family's Saxon ancestor eagerly bought and sold his fellows to the Normans. In exchange, he was granted a title."

Isaac leaned forward. "Did he toss the other Saxons in his dungeon?"

"Nay, for he had no dungeon." Neville lowered his voice to a rasping whisper. "The word did not exist here until the Normans conquered England." Ruffling Isaac's hair, he laughed. "But I daresay he handled his one-time comrades with a lethal skill and precision because King William did not offer many titles to Saxons."

"Neville, do not be ghoulish," Priscilla said as her son's eyes widened with excitement. "Giving Isaac more ideas in that direction is hardly necessary."

"You did say just a few days before Christmas that he needed to be more interested in his history lessons."

Priscilla was spared from having to reply when the carriage slowed in front of the house's formal facade. A footman in deep blue livery rushed forward to open the door and bow them out. Another was already at the back of the carriage to take their bags from the boot. A third was giving the coachee directions to the stables beyond the house.

Putting her hand on Neville's arm, Priscilla walked with him and the children toward the front door that was swinging open. A single glance at Daphne slowed her older daughter to a sedate walk. The younger two were looking around, wide-eyed, as they entered the house.

Not that they were impressed with the marble floors or the niches filled with fine art. Priscilla knew that. She guessed instead they were more interested in the smooth curve of the banisters of the double staircases. Sliding down them or other mischief would be foremost in Leah's and Isaac's minds. She knew they would not act inappropriately within view or earshot of the baron's guests, but she also was quite aware that they would take any other opportunity to test the speed and sturdiness of those banisters.

A different footman came forward and bowed his head slightly. "If you will come this way . . ." He walked away without looking back.

"He is quite certain we will follow," Neville said. "What do you think he would do if we failed to do so?"

Priscilla smiled and slipped her hand again onto Neville's arm as he offered it to her. Taking Isaac by the hand, because she noticed how he now was eyeing a suit of armor set within the curve of the left-hand staircase, she went with her family after the footman. The girls walked close behind them, and she heard them whispering about the rooms they passed.

She was tempted to remind them that such chambers were meant solely to impress. The finest furniture and the most elegant fabrics had been used to make the rooms look perfect. If Symmington Hall was like other country estates she had visited, the family would use rooms in another section of the house on a daily basis.

The footman paused by a wide door. He motioned for them to enter. It was, as Priscilla had expected, a cozier room with comfortable looking settees and a simple, pale yellow paint on the walls. Also, unlike the other rooms, it was not empty. Several people sat enjoying some tea and conversation.

One woman jumped to her feet and rushed over to the door. Lady Symmington was a woman average in height, weight, and coloring. The only thing not average about her was her sharply pointed chin.

She grasped Priscilla's hands and said, "Priscilla Flanders—"

"Hathaway," Neville corrected gently.

Lady Symmington ignored him as she continued to gush. "It is wonderful to see you and your children. Look how big young Isaac has grown! He'll be as tall as his late grandfather in no time. And your girls. They have your loveliness, Priscilla."

"Thank you," Priscilla said. "You have met my husband, haven't you?" She knew quite well that Lady Symmington had attended their wedding, but it was the only polite way to draw Neville into the conversation.

"Yes. Of course. Welcome to Symmington Hall, Sir Neville," she said in a tone that suggested each word was distasteful. She turned back to Priscilla. "Your aunt is waiting upstairs. She has been told of your arrival."

Lady Symmington gave her a broad smile. "I am sure you are pleased to have this opportunity to celebrate the holiday with Lady Cordelia."

"Words could never express how pleased we are," Neville said in that tone which offered no hint of anything but sincerity to strangers.

However, both Leah and Isaac began to giggle because they recognized his underlying sarcasm. They knew, as well, how their great-aunt had never approved of Neville and had made efforts to keep him from marrying their mother.

Lady Symmington looked puzzled, but recovered enough to say, "I shall have you shown to your rooms so you might relax after your journey."

Thanking their hostess, Priscilla herded her children ahead of her and out into the corridor where the footman waited. Neville chuckled under his breath, and she shot him a stern glare. It had no more effect than any of the others she had ever fired in his direction.

Quietly she said, "You should not take advantage of easy targets."

"It is almost too easy, isn't it?" He took her hand and put it on his sleeve again. "That is what happens when I spend time with you away from the *ton*. I forget that everyone has not been blessed with your quick wits."

"You are quick yourself, Neville. You were wise enough to say everyone rather than every woman."

His eyes widened in feigned shock. "Do you mean to tell me that you have never met a want-witted man among the *ton*?"

"Present company included?"

"Ouch," he said with a grin. "Pluck your dagger from my heart, Pris."

A commotion exploded into the foyer. A hurricane of bags and servants. At its eye, but definitely not as calm as the center of a tempest, stood Lady Eastbridge.

Priscilla bit back her gasp of astonishment. She had not expected to see the countess amidst Lady Symmington's guests.

The countess, a woman who must be in her seventh decade, tapped her foot with impatience. Her silver hair was perfectly accented by the ribbons on her simple bonnet. Beneath her long red spencer, an elegant gray silk dress was edged by muddy lace. More lace adorned the neckline, a thick white lace with a Tudor rose pattern woven through it. A long-ago Eastbridge had been a cousin to the Tudor monarchs, and the family had never allowed anyone to forget that connection.

A man edged out of the throng, followed by an attractive young woman. The man was Lord Eastbridge. Priscilla recognized the earl by his large, hooked nose and his full belly that strained the gold buttons on his red waistcoat. She was unsure who the young woman was, but her simple clothes suggested she was some sort of upper servant.

Lord Eastbridge tried to calm his wife, but she paid him no mind.

"Where is our hostess?" demanded the countess, scowling at the footmen who seemed overwhelmed by her arrival.

Priscilla stepped forward when no one else appeared capable of movement. "Lady Eastbridge! How pleasant it is to see you!"

The portly woman came over to give Priscilla a kiss on the cheek. "And you, my dear! You have no idea how much I hoped you would be in attendance. You look well. Marriage must be agreeing with you." Looking past her, she smiled warmly at Neville. "And it is quite easy to see why." She held out her hand to him.

Neville bowed over it. "My lady, it is—if I may be blunt—"

"I doubt you could be any other way," the countess said with a smile.

"Then I must say that I am surprised to see you here."

"I am sure you are. I can say, without hesitation, that nobody expected to see me here."

Priscilla hid her smile at the countess's answer. It was amusing to watch someone else match wits with Neville.

"Now," Lady Eastbridge went on, "do allow me a moment to speak with your lovely bride."

He nodded, then urged the children to follow the footman up the stairs. She did notice him giving the young woman a curious glance, then another.

"What a charming family," the countess said. Not giving Priscilla a chance to respond, she went on, "You must come and have tea with me tomorrow so we may enjoy a comfortable—and private—coze." She flicked her fingers, and a pretty young brunette rushed to her side. "This is Miss Annalee Baldwin, my companion. She arranges such matters. Annalee, do make arrangements for Lady Priscilla and me to take tea alone tomorrow afternoon."

"Yes, my lady." Her voice was so low that Priscilla wondered how Lady Eastbridge could hear her. Then Priscilla realized the countess was not worried about such small details. She expected her companion to comply with every order.

Lady Eastbridge stepped aside as both her servants and the Symmingtons' began toting the stacks of bags and crates up the stairs to where the earl and the countess and their servants would stay. Her gaze followed her husband.

"I am sure *you* are surprised to see me here, too," the countess said.

"I am," Priscilla said. "Almost as surprised as I was to receive Lady Symmington's invitation for a Twelfth Night."

"As I said, nobody will expect to see me here."

"Including the Symmingtons?"

Lady Eastbridge smiled. "I knew you would see through polite words to the truth, my dear. When Horatio was insistent that I step aside and allow the Symmingtons to host the Twelfth Night masquerade, I did only when he promised that we would attend the one here in spite of our invitation going astray. Or so I was informed when I sent a message here. Lady Symmington's apology arrived back within hours."

"I hope you will enjoy this gathering."

"I do, too. I doubt Horatio will." Her lips grew straight and thin as she squeezed out each word about her husband. "The man has no idea of the importance of tradition or how much the tradition means to me." She sighed. "He has been a bit distracted, and it seemed like a good idea to accede to his wishes. In spite of how much I have enjoyed being the hostess for the Twelfth Night masquerade."

Priscilla felt sorry for the countess, but to express such a sentiment aloud would embarrass Lady Eastbridge and possibly insult their hostess. "Your galas were always a great deal of fun. I first attended the January before my first Season."

"Your only Season as an eligible miss before you lost your heart to your first husband." Lady Eastbridge brightened. "Ah, we shall see how the change in tradition goes, shan't we? I do hope Lady Symmington has planned some amusing Twelfth Night games and charades for her guests. What would Twelfth Night be without some merriment and silliness?

Chapter Four

CORDELIA EMBERLEY Smith Gray Dexter rose from the chair as if she were the queen and her niece and her family were lowly petitioners coming to beg a boon. Her gown was of the latest style. As always. Her hair was perfectly styled. As always. Her smile was warm . . . until she glanced at Neville. Then it became icy. As always.

Turning her back on Neville, a rare feat because he stood next to Pris, Aunt Cordelia said, "My dear Priscilla, I am pleased that you came to see how I fared. I know you and the children must be exhausted after the long journey."

"Mermaid Cottage is not far from here," Pris replied.

Neville knew that Pris continued to hope that the tension between her aunt and her husband would vanish completely. If Priscilla's aunt relented, Neville would, but Aunt Cordelia would never change.

"Ah, yes. I forgot that you had decided to spend Christmas by the sea." Aunt Cordelia shivered. "I have no idea why you would choose to stay in that drafty cottage when you have a perfectly comfortable house in Town."

"You know that we like to attend Christmas Eve services at Lazarus's church."

Neville bit back angry words as he heard the grief in Pris's voice. Dash it! Her aunt had no reason to pick at the barely healed scar on Pris's heart. Even though almost two years had passed since Lazarus's death, the pain was fresh. Just as it was for him. That was something her aunt should understand since Aunt Cordelia had buried three husbands of her own. He had to wonder if any of her marriages had been a love match like Pris's and Lazarus's. Neville did not expect the old tough to understand that his love for Pris was deep, but why couldn't she understand Pris's loss?

Pris's fingers settled gently on his sleeve, a silent acknowledgment that *she* comprehended what he was fighting not to say.

"Well," Aunt Cordelia said, as if unaware of the pain her thoughtless words caused, "at least you are here now, and we can spend Twelfth Night together." She held out her arms. "Come and give your great-aunt a kiss, my dears."

The children inched forward, and Neville noticed Leah giving Isaac a shove toward Aunt Cordelia. Each of them endured a hug and a kiss. He knew the children loved their great-aunt, but she annoyed them even more than she did him.

If possible.

"Yes, Duncan is attending the masquerade," Aunt Cordelia said in response to a question he had not heard Pris ask. "He has a few holiday calls to make, and then he will come directly here. He wants to try some English wassail."

Neville made a mental note not to let his friend empty more than one bottle of whisky into the bowl before it began its rounds.

Walking to the hearth where a fire snapped and crackled, he remained silent as he watched the tableau of his family. It still astonished him that a man who had led a less than reputable life was now married to an earl's beautiful daughter and was the father to her three remarkable children. He hoped Lazarus was pleased, because Pris's husband had been his friend for many years, believing there was something worthwhile in a man who had had to struggle to make his way in the world. When the family's tarnished title descended to Neville, Lazarus had both congratulated him and joked with him about being a legitimate part of the Polite World.

"You were quiet in there," Pris said as they walked toward the lovely suite of rooms where they would stay for the next few days. The children had gone ahead, excused by their aunt while Neville had been lost in thought.

"If a man is silent, his words cannot be used against him."

She regarded him with a half-smile. "Wise words."

"They should be. They were Lazarus's." He put his arm around her waist and smiled when she leaned her head on his shoulder. "I came to learn that listening to his advice was the best thing I could do."

"I thought they sounded familiar." She chuckled softly, her breath brushing his neck above his collar. "I believe I first heard him say them after an early encounter with Aunt Cordelia."

"You are jesting!"

"No, quite the opposite. My aunt did not have a high opinion of him either, as you may recall."

"Until you wed me."

"Ah, yes." She raised her head so he could see her twinkling blue eyes. He adored every part of her, but especially her eyes which revealed every emotion. Now they glowed with good humor and more. It was that— more a promise of pleasure—that drew him even closer. "I do hope you will not covet her good opinion enough to do something beef-headed."

The laugh roared out of him and swept along the empty passage. "Mayhap you might wish to mention to your aunt that if I were to leave you a widow, it would be only another opportunity for you to marry un-wisely."

"That is Aunt Cordelia's opinion. Not mine." She hesitated, then asked, "Why were you staring at Miss Baldwin?"

"Who?"

"Miss Baldwin, Lady Eastbridge's companion. Pretty. Dark-haired."

He smiled. "Jealous, Pris?"

"If you hope so, you will be disappointed. I saw how you were looking at her. It was that expression you wear when you are puzzled about something."

"I am puzzled because Miss Baldwin looks familiar."

"Have you called at the Eastbridge's estate?"

"Never, and not at their house in Town either. That is what puzzles me."

She smiled. "I am sure the answer is simple. Ask her."

"I would rather ask you."

"Ask me what?"

"Where are the children bound and how long will they be gone?"

"Long enough," Pris said with the husky warmth that set his blood afire.

"Then there is no time to waste." He swept her up into his arms and carried her to their rooms, his lips feasting on the sweet flavors of hers.

PRISCILLA HEARD THE raised voices on the far side of the bedroom door. As she brushed her hair into a simple twist, she stood from the dressing table.

"Neville, will you hook me up?" she asked.

He looked up from where he leaned against the pillows on the mussed tester bed. He put the book he was reading down on his bare chest. "You know I hate doing that, Pris."

It would be easy to melt back into his arms, but she asked, "Don't you hear that?"

He cocked his head. "The children are arguing about something. Leah and Isaac probably are trying to decide which prank to unleash first."

"No. I don't think that is the younger ones. I recognize Daphne's voice, but not the other. I should check to see what is wrong."

"Sometimes I wish you were not such a good mother, Pris." He quickly did up the back of her gown. "Shall I come with you?"

"I think not. If I hear correctly, the louder voice belongs to a female as well." She ran a fingertip along his skin. "This is a sight I don't want to share with any other member of the gentler sex."

He smiled. "Call if you need my help."

"I will." She gave him the bawdy wink she had learned from him. "You can be sure of that."

Neville's chuckle followed her out of the bedroom.

Priscilla closed the door quietly behind her, but she doubted either Daphne or the young brunette would have taken note of her arrival if she had been announced with trumpets. The two girls stood almost nose to nose. If they had been cats, their fur would have been standing straight up.

Walking over to them, she asked, "Daphne, would you like to introduce me to your friend?"

Daphne bristled even more at the word *friend,* but she took a deep breath, looked away from the dark-haired girl and said, "Mama, this is Alice Symmington. Miss Symmington, my mother, Lady Priscilla Hathaway."

"Good afternoon, my lady," Miss Symmington said with a polite curtsy. She scowled again at Daphne, then said, "If you will excuse me . . ."

Priscilla waited until the outer door was closed before she asked, "What was that to-do about? You were screeching like fishwives, and I suspect they heard you in the most distant wing of the house."

"*I* was not screeching, Mama." Tears bubbled into Daphne's eyes. "She was."

"I heard . . ." Priscilla realized that she had recognized Daphne's voice through the thick door because she was familiar with it. The other voice—Miss Symmington's voice—had been more strident. She sat on a chair in front of the room's single tall window. "Tell me what—happened."

"Miss Symmington told me that I should leave before Burke arrived because, if I stayed, my heart would be broken when he paid her more attention."

"Miss Symmington sounds quite sure of what Lord Witherspoon's actions will be if he comes here."

Daphne smiled, and her face softened as she sat facing her mother. "He is here. I saw him briefly in the upper gallery. He had just arrived, and he wasted no time letting me know how glad he was to see me."

"You saw him alone?"

"Leah and Isaac were with me, Mama. They only left to visit the kitchen and hope for a treat *after* Burke and I finished talking." Color flashed up Daphne's face. "You used to trust me to do the right thing. Why don't you trust me now?"

"I do trust you."

"Then you don't trust Burke."

Priscilla smiled at her daughter. "I don't distrust Lord Witherspoon either. It is simply that the cost of flouting Society's rules is very high."

"I would never do something that would label me a harlot. A few kisses . . ." She put her fingers to her lips. "I am sorry, Mama. I should not have said that."

"No, I would rather you kept being honest with me." She took her daughter's hand in hers. "Daphne, even a few kisses, if witnessed by the wrong person, can damage a young woman's reputation."

"I know."

"And I know that you will keep that in mind, because you need to worry about not only your reputation, but your sister's. If you are labeled forward and bold, that will reflect upon Leah when it is her turn to have her first Season, as you will this spring."

Daphne's eyes grew wide. "Really, Mama? A real Season?"

"Yes, and you know what will be expected of you."

Getting up, Daphne twirled about the room, her arms outstretched as if she danced with a young man. "I cannot wait! I cannot wait!"

Priscilla smiled, but inwardly she knew that she still must tell Aunt Cordelia of the decision she and Neville had made with the greatest care. She would speak with her aunt—in private—at the first chance she had. Mayhap with her aunt in such good spirits with the anticipation of Duncan's arrival, the time was right. She *must* speak with Aunt Cordelia before her aunt saw that statue.

The bedroom door opened and Neville came out, dressed in prime twig. He smiled. "I see you told her, Pris."

Daphne flung her arms around his neck. "Oh, thank you, Uncle Neville, for persuading Mama to let me have a real Season."

"Actually it was quite the opposite," he said. "Now that I have a daughter of my own, I must say I look at every man with disapproval. She reminded me that girls must become young misses at some point."

Running back to Priscilla's chair, Daphne hugged her as enthusiastically as she had Neville. "Mama, thank you! I am so happy! I am—"

A sharp rap was set upon the outer door. With a glance toward Priscilla, Neville went to open it.

The door crashed inward before he reached it. A maid rushed in. "You must help me!" she cried. "You must!"

"What is wrong?" asked Priscilla, standing and coming over to the maid.

"'Tis the countess! She is dead!"

Chapter Five

"DEAD?" CRIED PRISCILLA. "The *countess* is dead?"

"Yes," the maid said. "So I was told to tell you."

"Who told you?"

"The countess's maid when she sent me to ask you to come posthaste, my lady. Said that you would know what to do, seeing as how you have been around so many dead people already." The maid flinched. "Mayhap I didn't hear her correctly with the last, but I know she wants you there right away, my lady."

Priscilla did not hesitate. Once she had directions to the countess's suite, she pushed past the maid and raced out of the room. Neville would be following close behind. She did not have to look back to confirm that.

Word of the disaster must have exploded through the house with the speed of a lightning flash. By the time she reached the corridor where the Eastbridges were staying, the narrow space was choke-full of people.

Attempts at order failed, as the sad news was confirmed by Lady Eastbridge's personal maid. She stood in the door to the suite, and her own face had no more color than a corpse. Guests erupted into dozens of shrieks and swooned in the corridor. Not just the female guests, but the earl. He toppled over and would have hit his head on a table if Neville had not caught him.

The man, Priscilla realized quickly, must be far heavier than he appeared because Neville strained to hold onto him at the odd angle. She cupped the man's head as Neville lowered the earl slowly to the floor.

"If we leave him here, he will be trod upon," Priscilla said, elbowing aside a guest who was struggling to get closer to the room.

"I will stand guard if you will alert the Eastbridges' servants that he is here. Have someone send his valet to take him to some place where he can recover from this shock."

Priscilla pushed herself to her feet and squeezed her way through the thickening crowd. She apologized when she stepped on feet, but did not slow.

"Aunt Cordelia!" she gasped when she saw her aunt scowling at the crowd trying to surge along the passage.

Somehow she reached her aunt and quickly asked for her help in keeping the tragic situation from turning into a farce.

Aunt Cordelia was always a woman to be reckoned with, and when she had a task that she believed no one else could do as well, she was as formidable as a cannon. Her voice, even though she did not raise it, resonated along the passage. Everyone became silent and turned to heed what she had to say.

Priscilla edged toward the countess's door and hid her smile. How insulted Aunt Cordelia would be if Priscilla spoke her thoughts! With a strong voice that carried well, Aunt Cordelia could have become the leading lady in any London theater. But no lady—most especially Cordelia Emberley Smith Gray Dexter—would consider a life on the boards.

Her smile fell away when she opened the door and slipped into the room, closing it before anyone else could enter. The suite was much like the one her family was using because the main room had a single window and several doors opening off it.

The room was empty. No, Priscilla amended when she heard a soft sound, someone was there. She took another step into the room and saw Miss Baldwin hunched on a bench, weeping. That astonished Priscilla because earlier Lady Eastbridge had treated her companion with barely more than contempt. Now Miss Baldwin sobbed as if she had lost her best friend.

Going over to Miss Baldwin, Priscilla touched her sleeve lightly. "I am here as was requested."

"I did not—" She wiped the back of her hand against her cheeks. "Someone else must have sent for you."

"I did." A steadier voice came from behind Priscilla.

Straightening, Priscilla turned to see a woman who could only be described as gaunt. Her simple maid's dress and apron hung on her, even though the apron had been cinched around her waist. Her lean face was colorless, and her bottom lip quivered with each breath.

"Who are you?" Priscilla asked.

"My name is Jeannette. I am—I was—Lady Eastbridge's abigail."

Priscilla's hope that the tidings might have become mangled faded when she heard the maid correct herself. "Tell me what has happened, Jeannette."

"The countess is dead."

Miss Baldwin began crying anew and hid her face in her hands. When her sobs became a keening, Jeannette motioned for Priscilla to come with her.

For a moment, Priscilla steeled herself for entering the countess's room. The draperies were drawn, but the bed curtains had been left open. On the grand bed beneath the covers, Lady Eastbridge lay unmoving. Her face was gray, and her hands were folded over her chest. The maid reached past her and pulled a sheet up over her lady's face.

Jeannette motioned for Priscilla to precede her out the door. "I should have done that before. I should not have left my lady."

Priscilla blinked back tears. She had known the countess for many years, and she could not help thinking of Lady Eastbridge's generosity and her sense of humor. No hostess would ever be able to match her Twelfth Night galas which left everyone warm with laughter and goodwill on a cold winter night.

Glancing at where Miss Baldwin still sat sobbing, Jeannette opened another door and led Priscilla into a room with a desk and some bookcases. Two chairs faced each other, but neither Priscilla nor Jeannette sat. Leaving the door ajar behind them, the maid waited for Priscilla to speak.

"May I assume from Miss Baldwin's grief that she found the countess dead?" asked Priscilla.

Jeannette nodded. "She went in to wake up the countess and realized Lady Eastbridge would not wake. Miss Baldwin kept trying to rouse the countess. When she could not, she sent for me."

"Miss Baldwin was alone when she found the countess?" asked Priscilla.

"Yes, my lady." Jeannette lowered her eyes as her face became even more ashen. "I have no idea what could have happened."

"Did you see any signs of violence against the countess?"

"None." She stared at her toes. "She looks as if she is asleep, peaceful."

"Did her recent health give you any cause for worry?"

"No. When I left the countess earlier, she was in fine form."

"Was she resting when you took your leave?"

"No. She was—I should not say."

Priscilla took the maid by the arm and drew her aside as the door swung open again. Relief surged through her when she saw Neville.

"Your aunt has everything firmly under control out there," he said, "so I thought I would join you."

Relating what Jeannette had told her, Priscilla turned back to the maid. "Jeannette, whatever Lady Eastbridge was doing when you last saw her, you need to tell us."

"As you wish." The maid took a deep breath, then released it slowly. "When I last saw my lady, she and Lady Symmington were quarreling. My lady was in a miff, and the baroness was ready to fly up to the boughs."

"Was it because of the Twelfth Night masquerade or another reason?"

Jeannette's eyes grew wide. "Should there have been another reason for an argument between them?"

"I have no idea." Priscilla glanced at Neville. "I believe I should speak with Lady Symmington."

"What about Miss Baldwin?" asked the maid.

"Lord Eastbridge has regained his senses," Neville said, "and he offered to sit with her. They share a common loss. In the meantime, I will send for the local vicar."

"That has already been done," Jeannette said. "I have been told he is on his way here now."

"You have served your lady and her husband well." Neville's mouth twisted. "Would you like me to wait with you for his arrival?"

The maid shook her head vehemently. "I would like some time alone with my lady."

"As her companion and husband will." Priscilla put her hand on Neville's arm. "Let us withdraw for now. Send for us if we can do anything to help. Our sympathies to you as well, Jeannette."

Again the maid lowered her eyes. "That is very kind of you, my lady."

Priscilla went with Neville out into the main room. She heard a gasp and spun to see Miss Baldwin quickly removing herself from Lord Eastbridge's arm that had been around her shoulders. The young woman stood and instantly dropped into a swoon.

Neville sprang forward to assist the earl in lifting the senseless companion onto the bench where she had been crying earlier.

Horatio Eastbridge, a burly man who looked more like a teamster than an earl, flushed. "I know how this must have looked, Hathaway."

"No one should ever judge another who is suffering from a great loss."

"A great loss. Yes." The earl tried to stop a sob, and it became a hiccup. "There is some brandy in my room." He pointed at one of the doors. "Will you do me a great favor and retrieve it for me, Hathaway? I believe a small bit of the spirits will bring Miss Baldwin back to her senses."

Neville nodded. As he walked toward the door Lord Eastbridge had indicated, he said quietly, "Go ahead and speak with our hostess. Something about this does not feel right and proper to me."

"Other than the countess being dead?"

His face was grim. "Yes."

NEVILLE LOOKED UP when Pris returned to their rooms shortly after he had. Before she could ask, he said, "I have found the children, and Daphne is reading to them in the girls' room."

"Thank you." She dropped to sit on the settee in the center of the main room. Staring at the fire on the hearth, she added, "At least one of us has achieved something."

"I take it from your words that your discussion with Lady Symmington did not go well."

"What discussion? Both she and the baron and even Miss Symmington have shut themselves away in their private rooms, and none of them will speak to anyone. The only answer I got to my query was that the guests need to remain here on the chance that the coroner might wish to speak with them."

"Why would they send for the coroner?" He frowned, surprised at this turn of events. "But Lady Eastbridge's death was not an unnatural one." Is there any question that Lady Eastbridge's death was an unnatural one?"

"I think they want to make sure they have done everything they can to deflect any hints of guilt from them."

He sat behind her and began to massage her shoulders. Saying nothing, she leaned back against his strong chest. She closed her eyes, then stiffened.

"Relax," he murmured against her golden hair.

"How can I when every time I shut my eyes, I see the dead countess?"

"You saw her?"

"Yes, Jeannette let me see her. Lady Eastbridge looked peaceful. Something she was not in her life. She was always seeking excitement."

"I remember a few years ago that the earl mentioned to me that she planned the events for their Twelfth Night assembly for the whole year leading up to each one."

Pris turned to face him. "Lady Eastbridge mentioned that her husband was pleased to have the Symmingtons take on tradition."

"Mayhap he wished her to focus that attention on him."

"Mayhap, but she said as well that he seemed distracted to her."

"She may never have noticed prior to this year because she was consumed by the planning for the games and pranks that were central to each of her masquerades."

"Mama?" asked Leah from the other side of the room.

Pris held out her arms, and her children rushed to them. Neville caught Isaac and swung him up into his arms as Pris drew Leah onto her lap. Daphne sat on the other side of her mother.

He listened without comment while she answered their questions. She did not hedge, but she offered no specific details either. He had always admired Pris's calm with the children and how she never spoke down to them.

The quiet moment ended when a knock came on the door, and it swung open before anyone could move.

"Burke!" Daphne said as Lord Witherspoon walked in.

The young marquess was tall enough to stand eye to eye with Neville. His light brown hair curled fashionably around his face, and his clothes, as always, had been made by a master tailor. His usual smile was missing, and the nervousness that often filled his voice when he spoke with Neville or Pris had steadied into a taut tone.

"Hathaway, may I speak with you?" he asked in his warm tenor.

"Of course, Witherspoon." He motioned toward a chair next to where Daphne sat, hope vivid on her face. "Make yourself comfortable."

The young lord shook his head. "I would prefer that we speak elsewhere. The ladies, you know."

Normally, Neville would have retorted that Pris would be outraged to be left out because someone feared to ruffle her female sensibilities. But he could not mistake the unusual tension in Witherspoon's words.

As he stood and turned to excuse himself, Neville saw Daphne's despair. He gave her a bolstering smile, then glanced at Pris. She came to her feet and put her arm around Daphne's shoulders. When she gave the slightest nod, he knew she trusted him to share later whatever young Witherspoon had to say.

The marquess led the way down the stairs in the silent house and outside. Neville was not overly surprised because Witherspoon was acting like a thief with the watch on his trail. Whatever he intended to say must be something he wished to keep a secret.

Snow was falling in the thickening twilight, and it crunched under Neville's boots. The gardens were as deserted and quiet as the house's interior. It was as if the earth had drawn in its last breath with the countess and now was unsure when to release it and take in another. Everything waited for *something* to happen.

Witherspoon did not pause until he reached a fake Japanese pagoda in the center of a rose garden. He walked inside.

Neville followed and waited for his eyes to adjust to the darkness. The silence was so deep that Neville could hear Witherspoon's breathing as well as his own. No one could sneak up on them here, because the sound of their footfalls in the crisp snow would announce their arrival.

Witherspoon must have realized that as well because he clasped his hands behind his back, straining the buttons across the chest of his great coat. "Thank you for coming out here." His breath solidified to accent each word.

"I am here, and I am listening." Neville smiled. "And freezing. What is it that you want to tell me where no one else can hear?"

"I ask you this as a favor, Hathaway. Please take your family and leave Symmington Hall posthaste."

"If you fear for Daphne—"

"I do, and I am not afraid to own to that." He shuffled his feet, then met Neville's gaze steadily. "May I speak plainly?"

"I doubt you could do otherwise."

Witherspoon smiled quickly, but his expression grew serious again. "Miss Flanders has inherited her curiosity and determination to right the world's wrongs from her mother. It is well-known throughout the *Beau Monde* that Lady Priscilla has assisted you in solving some rather unsavory crimes."

"The truth is closer that I have assisted her."

"Either way, if Lady Priscilla and her family remain here, she may become involved in solving *this* . . . puzzle."

Neville leaned back against the stone wall and folded his arms in front of him. "I have not heard anyone suggest that Lady Eastbridge's death was not due to natural causes."

"I am sure it was."

"But?"

"I have not solved crimes as you and Lady Priscilla have, but I cannot fail to see the guilty expressions worn by too many in that house."

Neville was intrigued. Daphne had insisted the marquess had depths that neither Neville nor Pris had seen. Mayhap Witherspoon was about to prove that. "Can you give me some examples?"

"You have not seen the looks yourself?" The young man's face showed both his astonishment and a hint of pride that he might have discovered something that Neville had overlooked.

"I did not say that. I simply asked you for examples that *you* have noted."

That was the only invitation Witherspoon needed. His observations, once started, poured out of him. He had chanced to encounter their hosts while on his way to find out what had kicked up a dust in the Hall. Neither of them would meet his eyes nor would they answer his questions.

"They scurried past like frightened rabbits." He paused, then said, "Or someone carrying a vast load of guilt. And they were not the only ones. I daresay no more than two or three people would look in my direction when I spoke to them. Lady Priscilla's aunt was one of them, but she was quite clear that I should stop asking questions and tend to my own concerns."

"That sounds like Aunt Cordelia. She is determined to recreate the world into her own image of common sense and decorum."

Witherspoon smiled again quickly, then said, "She also was quite clear that asking questions might stir up a wasp's nest."

"That is simply her way."

"Mayhap, but I ask you again, Sir Neville, to take Lady Priscilla and her family back to Mermaid Cottage without delay."

Neville pushed himself away from the wall. "Lord and Lady Symmington have asked the guests to stay in case the coroner wishes to speak to them."

"So they suspect something other than a simple death?"

"No death is simple, Witherspoon, but that does not mean that someone put out the countess's lights."

"Still, it is strange to send for the coroner if she simply died in her sleep."

"It is."

"Do *you* believe someone killed her?" Witherspoon asked sharply.

"I only believe what I know to be true. The lady is dead, and we have been asked to remain." He held up his hand before the marquess could bluster back a protest. "However, I promise that I will speak with Lady Priscilla about your concerns, but don't expect her to accede to your wishes."

"Thank you, Hathaway. I trust you to watch out for Miss Flanders."

"Good." He slapped the young man's shoulder. "Now let us get back inside before they find us frozen to death out here."

Witherspoon nodded and walked out into the snow that fell aimlessly. He stopped, turning to face Neville. "But be aware that I will never let any harm come to Miss Flanders. No matter what may occur." He walked away.

Neville cursed under his breath. Such youthful zeal and determination could create problems where there had not been any. Mayhap convincing Pris and the children to leave Symmington Hall might not be a bad idea.

If only he had any idea how . . .

Chapter Six

PRISCILLA LOOKED around the large parlor. The Symmingtons' guests had gathered together in the grand light-yellow room, as their hosts had requested. The guests sat or stood as motionless as the dour portraits on the walls. Every face was taut, and she could have sworn that the whole group breathed in and out as one. The manic curiosity from that afternoon had faded into numb disbelief.

Even Daphne, who stood next to her brother and sister, wore a blank expression. She had not glanced once in Lord Witherspoon's direction.

Priscilla knew her eldest was horrified by what had happened in the midst of what should be merriment, but Daphne also was unhappy about the idea of leaving Symmington Hall immediately. She had not said a word when Neville had returned from his conversation with Lord Witherspoon. In fact, she had not uttered a single word from that moment to this, several hours later. Priscilla suspected that her elder daughter would not have been so reticent if Neville had revealed to Daphne that Lord Witherspoon had vowed to protect her forever, but Neville had wisely not mentioned that pledge. Daphne would have been even more loath to depart.

Even more amazing than that was the fact that Lord Eastbridge and Miss Baldwin had joined the other guests in the parlor. The late countess's companion sat in a shadowed corner among a half dozen large plants while the earl had chosen a chair close to the hearth. The fingers of his right hand twitched, and Priscilla suspected he wished that he had a glass of something mind-quelling in them.

Only one face in the room was not expressionless. Aunt Cordelia sat in a chair beside Priscilla's, and she wore her most outraged scowl. Her eyes shifted from Lord Eastbridge to the door. That warned Priscilla that her aunt was vexed about two matters. Propriety demanded that the widower should be focused on making arrangements for his wife's burial, not for him to be seated among guests who had been preparing for a Twelfth Night assembly. And Aunt Cordelia had no patience with anyone who disregarded the demands of propriety, as Priscilla had learned firsthand often.

When Neville had whispered that Duncan should have arrived before dark, Priscilla assumed the other reason her aunt was annoyed was his failure to appear as he had promised. Priscilla could not try to soothe her aunt because any explanation other than the truth would sound feeble. Telling her aunt about Duncan's gift could start another uproar that Priscilla wished to avoid.

A rumble went through the gathering, and all heads—save for the ones in the paintings—turned at the same time toward the door. Lord Symmington entered with his wife and daughter on either side of him.

The baron was a man who commanded any room he entered. He was strikingly handsome, and his clothes accented his brawny limbs. One look revealed that he was a man who enjoyed a sportsman's life of riding and shooting, as well as other sports. Beside him, his wife and daughter appeared fragile and pale, and they seemed to fade into the background.

"Friends," Lord Symmington said in his booming voice, "thank you for gathering here under these sad circumstances. I know I speak for everyone when I express our sympathies to Lord Eastbridge."

The earl nodded, but said nothing.

"As you have realized," Lord Symmington continued, "Lady Eastbridge's untimely death means that entertainments planned for Twelfth Night must now be canceled. We—"

"Wait!" called a voice from the corridor. "I must speak to Lord Eastbridge. Immediately!"

The Symmingtons turned as one, then stepped back to allow Jeannette into the room. Lady Eastbridge's abigail looked neither left nor right. She walked directly to where Lord Eastbridge sat.

He stared at her as if she were a phantom risen from a grave. His eyes got larger with each step she took toward him.

"May I speak about Lady Eastbridge's dearest last wish?" Jeannette asked.

"Here?" he choked out.

"Yes, if I may, my lord, because Lady Eastbridge's last wish was that the Twelfth Night entertainments not be canceled."

Gasps exploded from every corner of the room, but none louder than from where Miss Baldwin had been sitting. The companion was now on her feet, her hands pressed to her face.

Priscilla jabbed Neville with her elbow and whispered, "Someone needs to be close to that young woman. She has shown a propensity for swooning."

He started to stand, but sat again when Miss Baldwin resumed her seat. "She should not do herself any damage if she loses her senses while sitting."

"Are you certain that my late wife wanted the masquerade to be held, Jeanette?" asked Lord Eastbridge before Priscilla could respond to Neville's comment.

The maid nodded. "Quite certain, my lord." She reached into her apron and drew out a slip of paper. "She asked me to give this to you if you doubted me."

Lord Eastbridge took it in quaking hands. In fact, his hands shook so hard, he could not unfold it. Turning, he held it out. Aunt Cordelia reached for it, but he stretched past her hand and toward Priscilla. "Could you please read what it says? I fear I am too discomposed."

Standing, Priscilla accepted the note. She was glad Neville had set himself on his feet, too. He stood close to the earl, ready to catch the older man in case the widower collapsed again. She gave her aunt a sympathetic smile, but it was to no avail. Aunt Cordelia's vexation was focused once again on Priscilla, even though nothing that had occurred was of her doing.

Priscilla decided she must ignore her aunt's botheration. Later, she would apologize to her aunt, but for now, Priscilla must help the earl as he had asked. She opened the page and scanned it. She sensed everyone leaning toward her as if they could see through the thick paper and read the words themselves.

The note was short and to the point. It stated simply in the countess's florid flourishes that Lady Eastbridge had decided to forgive the baroness for her *faux pas*, and the countess wished for the masquerade to go ahead, no matter what. Priscilla shivered when she read, *If today is my last, I do not want to go to my eternal sleep with conflicts unresolved.*

"What does it say?" asked Lady Symmington, then blushed at her outburst.

Priscilla looked at Lord Eastbridge, and he nodded. She read the few lines aloud, then handed the page to the earl. Stepping back, she watched Neville and Jeannette help Lord Eastbridge to sit in his chair. The earl looked as if he had aged a decade during the moments while Priscilla read.

Neville motioned for Priscilla to sit, then took his place beside her. Bending close, he whispered, "Do you think she had a premonition of her own death?"

Priscilla glanced at him in astonishment. Keeping her voice as hushed as his, she said, "You are being ghoulish again!"

"I thought I was being logical. Clearly the countess believed her time was drawing to a close, so she wrote the note to express her final wishes."

"That is not an image I want in my head."

"Forgive me, Pris. I am simply trying to make sense of these events."

"I am not certain you can. The whole of it seems nonsensical to me."

In the doorway, Lord Symmington shifted uneasily from one foot to the other. "What do you think we should do?"

Nobody answered, and Priscilla understood. Who wanted to be the first to deny a dead woman's last wish? Who wanted to be the first to suggest dancing while the countess's body was returned to her family crypt for burial? Everyone looked at everyone else at the same time they were trying to avoid anyone from catching their eye.

Beside her, Aunt Cordelia sniffed her disbelief. "He is our host," she said under her breath. "Why would he ask *us?*"

Then every voice seemed to find its life at once. Priscilla wanted to put her hands up over her ears. Her face must have revealed her thoughts because Neville stood, took her by the hand, motioned to the children and led them away from the middle of the room. Aunt Cordelia did not notice them leaving because she was trying to explain to several shouting guests that the decision was not theirs. Neville did not pause until they were separated from the arguing guests by a potted plant.

"What a muddle!" he said.

A small gasp came from the shadows, and Miss Baldwin jumped to her feet. Neville started to apologize for intruding on her corner, but Lady Eastbridge's companion rushed away, weaving through the crowd. Her exit was hampered by the fact that everyone had come to their feet.

Priscilla said, "Let her go. Poor thing."

"I had hoped for some answers to explain why she looks familiar," Neville said, "But now is not the time. She is clearly distraught at her lady's death."

"Far more than that maid Jeannette," announced Daphne with a frown. "Do you think she waited until the exact moment when her words could have the greatest effect?"

Before Priscilla could scold her for such cold words, Neville said, "It is quite possible, Daphne. She could not have timed her entrance better if she had been given a cue to step onto the stage. At no time could the revelation of a letter from the late countess have made a greater impact than just now."

"Listen to the two of you," Priscilla said. "You are judging that maid without any facts to support you."

"Except what is happening now."

"Yes, there is that." She looked at her children. "I believe we should withdraw."

"But, Mama," interjected Leah, "it is fun to watch argol-bargol adults."

"Argol-bargol?" Priscilla asked, astonished. "What does that mean?"

Her daughter looked proud that she had stumped her mother. "It's a word from Scotland. Mr. McAndrews taught it to us."

"He said," piped up her son, "that it means having a huge argument." He chuckled. "And they are. Do you think someone will give someone else a facer?"

Priscilla frowned at her husband. She was quite certain where Isaac had heard *that* vulgar cant.

Putting one hand on Isaac's shoulder and another on Leah's, Neville said, "I think your mother is right. We should withdraw immediately."

"And miss the fun?" asked Isaac.

Abruptly Neville was as somber as an old stick in the mud. "Never forget, any of you, that a woman has died." He looked steadily at each one in turn. "Go ahead, Pris. We will follow you out like a group of ducklings."

"No!" Daphne shook her head. "I cannot leave *her* stalking Burke as if he were the fox. Blast her!" She stormed back toward the center of the room where Miss Symmington struggled to make her way to where Lord Witherspoon was trying to calm two older women.

Priscilla gestured toward the door and asked Neville to take the younger children up to their rooms. "I will retrieve Daphne before she does something harebrained." Gathering up her skirt, she went after her older daughter.

If she had not known better, Priscilla would have accused their hosts of arranging for their guests to keep her from catching up with Daphne. She knew it was as simple as nobody was stopping Daphne to ask her opinion. However, each person wanted to know Priscilla's thoughts about Lady Eastbridge's last request and try to persuade Priscilla to share their opinions.

At least a dozen people stood between Priscilla and her daughter when Daphne reached the spot where Miss Symmington was trying to monopolize Lord Witherspoon's attention, taking it away from the two older women. She could not hear what her daughter was saying, but color burst forth on Miss Symmington's face. The marquess looked both embarrassed and amused to be at the center of attention of so many females.

The embarrassment must have won out because Lord Witherspoon said quite loudly, "I have heard enough of this debate!" He strode toward the door. Their host had abandoned it and now could be found at the far side of the room, pouring himself something from a decanter.

The guests faced him, shocked into silence once again.

"May I suggest," Lord Witherspoon asked as he paused in the doorway, "that we retire for the night and consider the lady's last request? Nothing can be done further tonight, for the hour is late."

Miss Symmington edged toward him, but halted when her mother put a hand on her arm.

Lady Symmington said from near Lord Eastbridge's chair, "I will have your supper delivered to your rooms. Please join us for breakfast tomorrow."

There were some uneasy grumbles, but the guests seemed to agree with the suggestions of both the marquess and Lady Symmington. As the guests began leaving the parlor, they spoke in hushed tones.

Suddenly, footfalls came toward the parlor. Duncan McAndrews appeared in the doorway, smiling and wiping snow off the dark shoulders of his greatcoat. He scanned the room, and his smile widened when his gaze alighted on Aunt Cordelia. Ignoring everyone around him, he crossed the room and caught her hands in his. He gave them a squeeze, before lifting one, then the other to his lips.

"You are a sight for loving eyes, my dear," he said in his charming brogue. "Forgive me for being late. I had to arrange for a surprise at your house, a Twelfth Night gift unlike any other. I cannot wait for you to see it. I . . ." As his voice trailed off, he looked around at the crowd staring at him.

Only then did he seem to notice the bleak atmosphere in the room. He glanced at Priscilla and asked, "What did I miss?"

Chapter Seven

NEVILLE OPENED the door to the suite he and Priscilla shared with the children. When he had decided to linger in the sitting room in order to speak to both Eastbridge and Symmington, she knew he had expected to have some questions answered. She suspected, from his grim expression that, after speaking with them, he had obtained no answers . . . and now had more questions.

"Alas and alack," Duncan was saying over and over as he paced in the suite's main room.

"Duncan, do sit down and eat before your supper grows cold," urged Aunt Cordelia, who had obviously elected to join them for the evening meal that had been delivered by several silent maids. "No matter what else I might say about the Symmingtons, they have hired a cook who is a genius." She popped a piece of chicken into her mouth.

"Why didn't you stop me from making an ass of myself?" Duncan demanded, pausing in front of Neville. "How could you just stand there and let me say something beef-headed?"

"We were on the other side of the room." Neville took his friend by the arm and steered him to sit next to Aunt Cordelia where his plate waited, untouched. He glanced at Priscilla, then

looked from her to her aunt and back. She nodded, and he smiled. He now knew that she would curb her curiosity while the rest of her family was present. As if he did not have a care in the world, he said in a jesting tone, "Duncan, you may atone to the Symmingtons and Lord Eastbridge on the morrow, assuming you eat well tonight and don't sicken from hunger."

"'Tis not food I need, but a wee drink." His voice was mournful. "As a proper Scotsman, it is my duty to raise a glass to the late lady's soul. That way, she will know that I meant no disrespect to her or her household."

Neville reached for the bottle of wine that had been delivered along with the roasted chicken.

"Nae," Duncan said, his accent deepening along with his morose spirits. "Froggy wine will not do at a time like this. What a Scotsman truly needs in this situation is a fine mountain-dew." When Neville regarded him, puzzled, he said, "Whisky, my boy!"

Priscilla stood and went to the door. Seeing a servant in the hall, she called to him. The man hurried to ask what she needed. She sent the man to collect the bottle that Duncan always carried with him. "You will find it packed between his shirts." She shut the door.

"How do you know that?" asked Duncan with astonishment.

Aunt Cordelia looked daggers at her.

Priscilla resisted rolling her eyes as if she were no older than her daughters. Her aunt had no reason to be jealous of Priscilla. With a serene smile, she said, "Each time you have paid us a visit at Mermaid Cottage or in Town, Gilbert assures me that he has instructed a footman to unpack your clothes with care. The first time, your bottle of whisky almost was sacrificed for our ignorance of its existence."

"A brilliant woman." Duncan smiled at Neville. "You did well to leg-shackle yourself to her, my boy."

"I think so." Neville took her hand and brought her back to sit beside him. "Now eat up, Duncan, before you fade away."

The shorter man complied only when Aunt Cordelia seconded Neville's request. Silence settled on them, save for a knock when Duncan's bottle was delivered. The weight of the day's events sat heavily on their shoulders and in their hearts. The children agreed to go to their rooms and get ready for bed. Without a protest, they rose, said their good nights and went to the doors to their rooms.

Daphne paused long enough to whisper to her mother, "Did Uncle Neville reveal what Burke told him earlier?"

"No." She smiled at her daughter. "He will explain if he feels we need to know."

"But—" Daphne halted herself and nodded. "I will try to be patient, Mama."

"Good." She hugged her older daughter, as she had her younger ones.

As soon as Daphne closed the door on the room she shared with her sister, Aunt Cordelia cleared her throat. It was a signal that she intended to speak what was on her mind. Priscilla had known this moment was coming as soon as her aunt had announced she would join him for supper.

Priscilla sat next to her husband. When he put his hand over hers on the arm of the chair, she flashed him a quick smile before asking, "Now that the children have left, do you have something you want to say to us, Aunt Cordelia?,"

"Of course I do!" Outrage bristled from every inch of the indomitable lady. "How much longer are you going to participate in this farce?"

"I have no idea," Neville replied. He chose his steadiest voice, and

Priscilla was grateful. There was no reason to give her aunt more excuses to fly up into the boughs. "If young Witherspoon had his way, we would have left for Mermaid Cottage by now." He glanced at Pris.

"That was what he wished to speak of to me when he came here earlier. He wishes to keep Daphne from suffering more despair."

"Really?" Priscilla asked, then wished she had not. The tension etching lines around Neville's eyes warned her that he was telling her only part of what he and the marquess had discussed.

"We should have taken our leave before it got dark!" Aunt Cordelia refused to allow the attention to shift from her.

"There was not enough time to make such arrangements before the sun set, even if we could have found a way to inform our hosts that we were leaving." He reached for the whisky bottle and poured a bit more in Duncan's glass, then a similar amount in three other glasses. He handed one to Aunt Cordelia and another to Pris. Picking up the last, he took a slow sip. "I would not risk traveling after dark. I will not endanger Priscilla and her children. I was thoughtless about that when we set off on our honeymoon, and I will not be careless again."

"Then we must leave as soon as the sun rises," Aunt Cordelia said.

"No." Pris put her glass, untouched, on the table and shook her head. "Lady Symmington looked close to tears, and it behooves us, as her guests, to help her during this uncomfortable situation."

"We can help by leaving." Aunt Cordelia pressed her point. "She does not need us underfoot."

"She asked that we join the family for breakfast on the morrow."

"We could offer our regrets."

Neville noticed how Pris's fingers were digging into the arm of the chair. In spite of the number of times her aunt had tried to instigate arguments, Pris hated each one. Yet she loved her aunt and longed for the chance to spend some pleasant time with her.

"Too late," he said.

"Why?" Aunt Cordelia reaimed her scowl at him.

"I told Lord Symmington," Neville said, "that I would speak with him on the morrow."

"And you always keep your word." Sarcasm dripped from Aunt Cordelia's words.

"Whenever it involves Pris and the children, yes." He gave her no time to make any further comments as he asked Pris how the children were faring with the countess's death.

Even though he said nothing of his desire to speak with her alone, Pris again seemed to read his mind. A short time later, she sent her aunt and Duncan on their ways with a graciousness he could never aspire to learn.

Taking her hand, he led her into their bedchamber. He drew in the scent of her hair and wished he could forget about everything going on beyond their door. When she turned to face him, he saw that she was torn, too. She felt an obligation, as she had said, to help the Symmingtons through this unsettling time. Even so, as she slanted toward him, he knew she longed to toss aside concern and lose herself in the ecstasy they could share as man and wife.

It took every bit of his willpower to walk away and sit on the deep windowsill. He heard her soft sigh as she sank to sit on a bright blue chaise longue.

"You spoke with Lord Symmington?" Pris asked.

He nodded. "And with Eastbridge as well."

"I hope you did not bother the earl with too many questions. He seems as fragile as a newborn bird. That is no surprise after the shocking news of his wife's death, but I fear for his health as well."

"As I do. I asked Symmington to have one of his footmen sit in the earl's bedchamber and keep a close eye on Eastbridge. The shock of one spouse's death can lead to the other's."

"And Miss Baldwin and Jeannette will be watching over him closely, too." She laced her fingers together tightly, as she often did when she was unsettled. "I don't think either young woman took her eyes off him during the debacle downstairs. Do you think they will leave in the morning?"

"I don't know. It appears that he is staying for the masquerade."

"Don't you find that odd?"

"It *was* his wife's last wish that the ball be held."

"Or so we have been told."

A slow smile edged along Neville's lips. Not a humorous smile, but his predatory one. "I do believe your aunt would suggest, as Shakespeare wrote for Northumberland's character, 'Before the game is afoot, thou still let'st slip.'"

"Aunt Cordelia might say that, but I suspect your response would be closer to Hotspur's. 'Why, it cannot choose but be a noble plot.'"

"Pris, I had no idea that you were familiar with *Henry IV, Part 1*."

"Only bits and pieces." She clasped her hands on her lap. "But you are right, Neville. I do believe there is a game afoot, a game that has nothing to do with the revelries of Twelfth Night."

"Revelries?" His mouth became a straight line. "Aunt Cordelia is right about one thing. We should have been urged to leave as soon as it is light tomorrow."

"What were the Symmingtons thinking to gather us altogether and then tell us that they expect us to join them for breakfast?"

"In their defense, I suspect that, when they asked us to meet them downstairs this afternoon, they planned to bid us farewell because they knew the coroner had no need to speak with us."

Pris's eyes widened. "Oh, my! You are most likely right. They had no idea that Lady Eastbridge's maid would come in with such an announcement. I have been nettled by the Symmingtons' actions when I should have sympathy for them."

"Do not waste your sympathy on our hosts. They are hiding something."

"Neville, you more than anyone else should recall that everyone has something to hide."

"Ah, but, Pris, I hide my secrets openly. The Symmingtons are trying to act as if the only thing amiss is the countess's passing." He leaned forward, and his voice hardened. "When *they* called the coroner in to investigate. Why? Do they believe there is something out of the ordinary about Lady Eastbridge's passing?"

"*You* spoke to Lord Symmington. What did he have to say?"

"Remarkably little." He did not add the oath that burned on his tongue. Pris never chided him for swearing when they were alone, but he tried to curb any vile cant in her company. She had been married to a vicar. "He avoided answering me when I asked about the coroner's visit."

"Why? There would be no reason not to speak of the coroner's comments unless . . ."

"Unless he believes there was some foul play." He stood and drew the draperies closed to shut out the cold light of the waning moon. "I believe I should pay a call on the coroner on the morrow—after we make our appearance at breakfast."

"On what excuse? You are not part of Lady Eastbridge's family, so he will be suspicious of why you wish to speak with him about her death."

"I am sure I can come up with some tale that will satisfy him, Pris." He rubbed his chin. "There is something decidedly not right with the whole of this. It is more than Lady Eastbridge's unfortunate death just before Twelfth Night. Could it be because she died amidst the celebrations were closely connected to her after her years of hosting a masquerade renowned for the excitement of its pranks and the silliness of its jokes?" A shiver ran its icy finger down his spine. "The irony is the joke now is on us."

"Which joke?"

"That we can continue on as Lady Eastbridge requested." He glanced up at the ceiling. "Do you think she is laughing at us even now?"

Pris came to her feet and slipped her arms around him. "I don't want to think of that." One hand came up to guide his mouth down to hers.

"Nor do I," he barely managed to say before their lips touched. He tasted the desperation in her kiss, but he thought only of holding her in their bed.

He lifted her into his arms, When he placed her on the pillows, she held her arms up to him. It was the only invitation he needed to drive away the cold thoughts.

Tomorrow would come soon enough.

THE DINING ROOM must have been built within the walls of the original hall. Thick rafters, stained with smoke, created an ornate pattern far above Priscilla's head as she walked into the room with her family. A long table cut the room into two equal parts. Life-sized portraits covered the stone walls, the Symmington ancestors marching along in chronological order. Three hearths held large fires, but cold oozed up from the floor and through Priscilla's slippers.

They must have been among the last to arrive, because many of the chairs along the table were already filled. The only empty chairs were close to the head of the table.

"Just like in church," she whispered to Neville as he drew her hand onto his arm. "Everyone sits as far from the pulpit as possible."

"But that is because in church they don't wish to be reminded of their sins. I wonder what they fear they will hear this morning."

She put her finger to his lips and glanced at her younger children. Then she stiffened. Where was Daphne?

As if she had asked the question aloud, Leah said, "If you are looking for Daphne, Mama, she is over there with Lord Witherspoon and that high-and-mighty Miss Symmington."

"Come with me," Neville said to Leah and Isaac. "We will gather some food to break our fast while your mother gathers her wayward lamb."

Priscilla went to where Daphne was now seated on Lord Witherspoon's right while Miss Symmington had claimed the seat on his left. With a cool smile, she said, "Daphne, I would appreciate your help."

"With what?" Daphne looked both annoyed and curious.

"Oh, do go and help your mother," Miss Symmington fairly cooed, her voice so sweet Priscilla's teeth threatened to ache. "It will give me the chance to finish the amusing story I was telling dear Burke."

When Lord Witherspoon pushed back his chair and set himself on his feet, he said, "Allow me to assist you, my lady."

"Thank you," Priscilla said, meaning those two words with all her heart. Her opinion of the young marquess had been steadily rising, even though she was not yet ready to give him permission to court Daphne. "Even with Neville watching, Isaac has been known to clear a serving tray of every muffin." She smiled when he offered his arm. Putting her fingers on it, she added, "Coming, Daphne?"

Minutes later, Lord Witherspoon was entertaining Isaac with an outlandish tale while they sat side by side near the foot of the table. Priscilla was unsure how the marquess had

managed to get two free chairs next to each other, but she motioned for Daphne to follow her sister toward the table's other end.

"Mama, I wanted to sit with Burke," Daphne said softly.

"So I saw, as did everyone else at the table. What did you think you would gain by confronting Miss Symmington *this* morning? Not only are you a guest in her parents' house and owe the whole family a debt for their hospitality, but you would be wise to remember that few men wish to be forced to make a public decision on matters of the heart."

Daphne's face grew pale. "I did not think of that."

"You did not think of anything but the fact that he was speaking with Miss Symmington." Pulling out the chair beside where Neville sat, she said, "You wish to be treated like an adult, Daphne. You will be when you show an adult's restraint and good sense."

"I am sorry, Mama." She sniffed as tears filled her eyes.

"I know you are." Priscilla smiled and then gave her daughter a hug. "Don't worry. Nothing terrible happened, and you have made your brother very happy. He adores Lord Witherspoon."

Daphne drew in a breath to reply, then let it sift past her taut lips as the great room suddenly became as silent as if it had emptied.

When the guests' heads turned toward the door, Priscilla saw Lord Eastbridge hobbling into the room. His color looked high. Almost too high. If Miss Baldwin had not been helping him, Priscilla doubted he could have walked the length of the table to sit across from Neville. His late wife's companion sat beside him, and two footmen brought them food from the sideboard.

Another chair scraped against the stone floor, and Priscilla realized that the Symmingtons had come to the head of the table to take their own seats now that their guests were present. Alice Symmington wore a sick-ishly sweet smile as she sat between her father and Lord Eastbridge.

Any attempts at conversation quickly died, leaving only the sound of knives and forks against plates. Priscilla had never been so uncomfortable at a meal. She almost wished that Neville would ask Miss Baldwin where they might have met previously. The answer was sure to be interesting. She knew, however, he wanted to ask that question privately, so not to make the young woman fell ill at ease. Much of Neville's past had been spent at places where the *ton* and their servants did not go.

Lady Symmington stood and glanced around at her guests. "Thank you for joining us for breakfast this morning. I appreciate your understanding that fulfilling Lady Eastbridge's last wish is important. Even though I am sure your heart is no more into merriment than mine is, I have instructed the kitchen to bring the pudding in, so we might know the name of our Lord or Lady of Misrule for tonight's masquerade."

A sob came from where Lord Eastbridge and Miss Baldwin sat. When everyone stared at them, they quickly shifted away from each other. Priscilla wondered if anyone else noticed how the earl had been holding Miss Baldwin's hand. Then she chided herself for having such negative thoughts. If the earl and his late wife's companion wanted to mourn together, then no one should think badly of them. It was possible that Miss Baldwin was a distant relative, as many companions were, and that would lend countenance to such an action.

"You must be all about in your head," cried a tall, thin woman that Priscilla knew was Mrs. Wasserman. She and her husband attended the parish church where Lazarus had preached. "Christina, this is senseless. How can you expect us to enjoy ourselves when a woman died here such a short time ago?"

Lady Symmington could not hide her dismay. "But it was the lady's final wish—"

"How macabre!" Mrs. Wasserman stood. "I cannot continue being a part of this travesty any longer. We shall leave as soon as our bags are packed."

Several other people followed her as she left the dining room. Aunt Cordelia started to rise, too, but Duncan leaned toward her and whispered something. She sat again.

The door from the kitchen opened, and the grand Twelfth Night pudding was wheeled in on a cart. It was sliced with great ceremony, but again the room was hushed. As the pudding was put on a tray and carried around the table so each guest might select a piece, there was none of the usual teasing.

Priscilla wanted to leap to her feet and shout that Mrs. Wasserman had been correct. It was time for the Symmingtons to put an end to this mockery of Twelfth Night and to urge their guests to leave. She took a piece of the pudding, but did not taste it.

Lord Eastbridge was not hesitant. He took a hearty bite of his pudding. "Bother!" he muttered. Turning away, he spat in his hand. He wiped it on a napkin, then stared at the small metal crown.

Lady Symmington forced a smile as she said, "You have found the token, my lord. That means you are the lord of misrule."

Lord Eastbridge shoved back his chair, stood, and tossed the crown into the middle of the table. It bounced several times before landing on Neville's plate.

"If this is your idea of a jest, Lady Symmington—"

Neville got up and said calmly, "Eastbridge, there is no reason to accuse our hostess of such a heinous deed. We each chose the slice of pudding from the tray ourselves. There was no plot to guarantee that the crown ended up in your serving."

The earl snapped, "Come, Miss Baldwin." He grabbed her arm as soon as she stood and limped toward the door.

Every eye followed him, then looked at their hosts. Lady Symmington's eyes were filled with tears, and she had given up the attempt to smile. Her voice quavered as she said, "It would seem, Sir Neville, that you are now, quite by default, the Lord of Misrule for our Twelfth Night."

Chapter Eight

THE CORONER'S cottage would have been lovely in the spring when the roses climbing its stone walls were in bloom. Now, as snow fell on the rising wind, the vines looked spindly and as dead as the remains of the vegetable garden by the front gate. It was, Neville decided, the perfect setting for a coroner.

Drawing in a deep breath of the crisp air, Neville wished he did not have to return to Symmington Hall after this interview. What a ridiculous bumble-bath! Did Lady Symmington truly believe that her guests would be interested in music and dancing and pranks and games tonight? And did she think he would step up and play the role of the Lord of Misrule? While he usually would have accepted the honor with as much alacrity and exuberance as if he were Isaac's age, the whole masquerade should be canceled.

The cottage door opened as soon as Neville knocked, so he knew his approach had been seen. A gray-haired woman who wore a housekeeper's simple black gown beneath a pristine apron motioned for him to enter.

"I would like to speak with the coroner," he said.

"Mr. Grove receives in his book-room. If you will follow me . . ." Like the footman at Symmington Hall, she walked into the shadowed house without looking back to see if Neville obeyed.

He wondered idly if the *ton* had become so properly trained that its servants no longer needed to check that a housekeeper's or a footman's request was followed. What irony! The Polite World considered itself the elite, but it had been brought to heel by the very people who served them.

Neville shook the folderols from his head. Now was not the time to revel in the queer compromise that had evolved between the *ton* and their households. Answers had not been forthcoming from Eastbridge and Symmington, so mayhap Neville could obtain some from Grove, the coroner.

The housekeeper had an inner door open by the time Neville reached it. Stepping aside, she motioned for him to go in.

Neville took a single step into the room, then halted. No one had better been described as a book-room than this one. It was filled with books which had been stacked on every flat surface, including the two chairs facing the hearth. There might have been a table beneath other books, but he could not be sure.

"You wanted to see me?" asked a pleasant voice from behind Neville.

Turning, Neville had to look down to meet the eyes of a very short man. He was quite plump, but not obese. He had the appearance of a well-fed country squire, which was probably what he was because only men who owned land could be appointed as coroner. His most distinctive characteristic was a pair of bushy brows that looked as if two butterbur blossoms had been bleached and attached to his brow.

"Are you the coroner?" Neville asked.

"Yes. Jerold Grove. How may I help you . . .?"

"Hathaway. Neville Hathaway," he supplied as he shook the man's hand. "I was hoping you might grant me a few minutes of your time."

"Of course. Sit down." The coroner's mouth tightened, then altered almost instantly into a smile. Going to one chair, he lifted off the pile of books and put them, with care, on top of another mound leaning against the wall. "Please sit down, Hathaway."

Neville did as the coroner cleared books off the other chair. When Grove sat as well, Neville said, "I assume you know the reason for my call."

"No, I don't. Should I?"

"I am a guest at Symmington Hall."

Grove frowned. "Sad business there. 'Tis a right shame that Lady Eastbridge died just before Twelfth Night."

"Yes. I was hoping you might tell me your findings from your visit to Symmington Hall."

"Findings? There are none. I was not called to Symmington Hall." His bushy brows lowered. "Why should I have been called there? I was told the lady died quite peacefully in her sleep. There is no crime in that."

Neville sought into his memory. Who had first told him that the coroner had been called? Pris! He knew she would have told him the truth. So someone else must have lied to her. Who had mentioned to her that the coroner would be called to Symmington Hall? The Symmingtons themselves! Pris had learned of the coroner's impending visit when she tried to speak with them in the hours after the countess's death.

"Do you know something that I should?" asked the coroner.

"At this point, I feel I know less than nothing." Neville stood. "Thank you for receiving me, Mr. Grove. If you will excuse me, I shall endeavor to clear up some confusion at Symmington Hall."

"If you need my assistance, send for me."

Again he shook the coroner's hand. "You may be most certain I will. Thank you."

Neville walked out of the book-room and to the cottage's front door. Everywhere he turned, there were more questions. It was time to start getting some answers.

WHERE WAS ISAAC?

Priscilla had asked both her daughters, her aunt and Duncan, several of the servants and a few guests that same question. All of them had replied identically. They had no idea. Leah had revealed that she was supposed to meet her brother by the back garden door so they might explore some of the intricate gardens surrounding the house.

"But it is snowing hard," Leah had added, "and Daphne promised me to show me how she gets her hair into that twist."

"Which part of the garden were you going to investigate?" Priscilla asked, trying to hide her astonishment that her younger daughter might choose to sit in front of a glass and try a new hair style rather than sneaking out to frolic in the snow. It was another sign that Leah was maturing. To have two daughters eager to join the Polite World was a frightening thought.

Leah shrugged. "I am not sure. He mentioned something about a couple of follies, the dovecote, and the ice house."

"Which follies?"

"He has been talking about the Short Tower and the Bath House." Turning to look at Priscilla, Leah had grabbed a handful of her hair and twisted it up on top of her head. "What do you think, Mama?"

As she pulled a thick shawl over her head, Priscilla could not remember what she had answered. What a shock to get an image of her younger daughter as a miss who soon would be fired off in her own first Season!

But the problem at hand was Isaac. Over the past ten minutes, the snow had started falling harder. Priscilla opened the door and paused on the stone terrace beyond it. Mayhap she should bring a servant with her. The labyrinth of the gardens would be difficult on a sunny day.

She quickly found a gray-haired footman who was willing to act as her guide. He told her that his name was Whitelaw. He nodded when she explained why she needed his help.

"No boy could resist the lure of exploring those buildings," Whitelaw said. "We will start with the dovecote because it is the closest of the ones you listed."

Priscilla was glad she had listened to her own qualms as they went out into the storm. The footman had brought a lantern, and the light cut through the swirling snowflakes. It was not dark, for it was close to midday, but the color of the ground and the sky were almost identical. She could have gotten lost so easily.

The wind grew stronger, and the snow battered her bare face. She pulled the shawl up over her cheeks and mouth, leaving only her eyes visible. When the footman offered his arm, she took it gratefully. The snow was falling so fast that their footprints were being erased almost as quickly as they lifted their feet from the snow.

The dovecote was a large, shadowy box in the storm. Its top curved upward like a bonnet. Whitelaw led her directly to the door and swung it open. The coos of pigeons could be heard over the wind as she stepped inside. Hundreds of nest holes were set into the stone walls. Each

hole was big enough so a man could reach all the way to the back, and each had a chalk platform in front of it to allow the birds easier access to their nests. In the center, a thick stone column was edged by primitive steps so a servant could harvest eggs and birds.

Whitelaw held the lantern high, sweeping the light around the dovecote. He called, "Is anyone here?"

Priscilla heard her son shout, "Back here." Hurrying around the column, she saw Isaac on his knees and staring at the nest holes in front of him.

"Why are you hiding out here in this storm?" she asked.

"Storm?" Isaac looked up at her, his expression surprised.

"It is snowing, and we need to get back into the house."

"All right, but first. Look at this." Isaac pointed to the fabric sticking out from one of the nest holes.

"What is it?"

"I was trying to figure that out." He gave her a proud smile. "I remembered how you and Uncle Neville warned us never to disturb something that might be a clue to a crime."

"Crime?" Whitelaw made a strange, choked sound.

Priscilla ignored the footman as she said, "That is right, Isaac, but why would you think of that *here*?"

"May I show you?"

"Yes." She motioned to the footman to bring the lantern closer.

"Look here, Mama." His finger paused a hair's breadth from the cloth.

She bent to peer at the fabric. Dark stains ruined what appeared to be gray silk. From beneath it, a bit of lace was visible. The pattern of a Tudor rose glowed white against the stone. She had seen a similar lace recently, but where?

Her own gasp burst from her. "That must be Lady Eastbridge's." She reached past her son and tilted one corner of the fabric toward the light. The dark spots were unmistakable. "That is blood all over it."

"Really?" Isaac leaned forward. "Is that real blood?"

"It would appear so." Priscilla slowly withdrew the cloth from the nest hole. Her nose wrinkled as bird droppings fell to the floor that was littered with cast-off feathers. Glancing down, she called, "Whitelaw, bring that lantern closer."

The footman complied, but Priscilla saw that any signs of other footprints had vanished as surely as hers had outside in the snow. She saw her son's and her own, but nothing else.

She draped the silk over her arm. It was a woman's gown, and it looked identical to the one Lady Eastbridge had been wearing when she arrived at Symmington Hall. Yet it was covered with blood. How—and when—had that happened? There had been no sign of blood on the countess's deathbed, and the dress was intact. She examined it, front and back. There were no holes from a knife or a ball. That made no sense. Why was the dress bloodstained but not torn?

To her son, she asked, "Whatever gave you the idea to come out here?"

He shrugged. "I was talking to Leah about seeing what was inside some of the buildings, and a couple of servants mentioned the dovecote."

"Which ones?"

With another shrug, he said, "I don't know. Two women, one young and one older."

"Would you recognize them if you saw them again?"

"Mayhap. I am not sure." His brow furrowed. "But, Mama, if you think they *sent* me here apurpose, why would they? Only the person who stuffed that gown in the nest hole would know it is here, and why would that person direct me to where I could find it?"

Priscilla was impressed with his logical thinking, but she also reminded herself that he was just a boy. A boy who was excited about what he had discovered.

"Isaac, you must not tell anyone about this," she said.

"No one? Not even Leah? She will be envious that *I* was the one to find the gown."

She put her hands on his shoulders that seemed to be growing sturdier and broader with every passing day. "This is no jest. That is blood on the dress."

He grew serious and nodded. "Yes, Mama. I will tell no one else."

Turning, she affixed Whitelaw with her sternest stare. "I must ask the same of you."

"But, my lady, if my lord or lady were to ask—"

"Do you think they have any suspicions of foul play?"

The footman gulped and shook his head. His hand shook so much that light danced on the walls, flickering in and out of the nest holes.

"Then," Priscilla said in her most no-nonsense voice, "there should be no need for them to ask you anything about the dovecote. However, if they do have questions, ask them to send for me or Sir Neville before you answer them."

"Yes, my lady."

With that pledge from both of them, Priscilla gingerly wrapped the gown in one part of her shawl. None of them spoke as they went out into the storm. When Whitelaw grasped one of Isaac's hands, her son held his other one out to her. She took it, and they fought the strong wind to reach the house.

Priscilla thanked the footman and asked him to deliver her son to the room where his sisters would be waiting. "Then find Sir Neville and have him meet me. I am going to the Eastbridges' rooms, then I will return to ours."

Hurrying through the house, Priscilla did not allow anyone to halt her by drawing her into a conversation or ask what she carried beneath her shawl. She slowed only when she reached the door of the suite the Eastbridges had been given for their use.

A knock on the door brought muffled voices, the shocking sound of a giggle, then the rumble of another door closing inside the suite. When the door opened almost a full minute later, Priscilla was surprised that Jeannette did not stand on the other side. Instead it was Lady Eastbridge's companion, Miss Baldwin. She was patting her hair back into place, and one corner of her hem had been caught up in the top of her stocking.

"Yes?" Miss Baldwin asked. "How may I help you?"

Priscilla glanced at the hem, and Miss Baldwin looked down. Bright color flashed up her face as she tugged down her skirt.

"I would like to speak with Lord Eastbridge." Priscilla needed every bit of her composure to act as if she had not seen Miss Baldwin's blush. Truth be told, at that moment, Priscilla did not care that the young brunette was enjoying a secret lover's company.

"I don't know if he is available." Miss Baldwin kept staring at the floor.

"He is," said Jeannette as she appeared behind Miss Baldwin. The maid shot Miss Baldwin a superior look, then smiled at Priscilla. "If you will come in, my lady, I will let the earl know you wish to speak with him."

"Thank you," Priscilla said and stepped into the room. She noticed Jeannette held a dusting cloth. Now that her lady was dead, her position as abigail was no longer needed.

Again, Miss Baldwin's gaze followed Priscilla's. In a sharp tone, Miss Baldwin said, "Finish that later."

"But I just started," the maid protested.

"Later!"

Jeannette bowed her head and went through a door into one of the attached bedchambers. She closed it behind her, but Priscilla saw it come slightly ajar. Priscilla considered saying

something, then held her tongue. If the maid wished to eavesdrop, she would. As soon as Priscilla showed Lord Eastbridge what Isaac had found, word would spread through the hall anyhow.

A door opened and Lord Eastbridge emerged. His waistcoat was buttoned wrong. Had she disturbed him when he was sleeping? No, she realized with a pulse of shock, when his gaze met Miss Baldwin's and a smile pulled at his lips. He looked away, and so did the companion, but the one moment of connection told Priscilla more than she wished to know. If the widower was finding more than companionship with his late wife's companion, it was no bread-and-butter of Priscilla's.

"My dear lady," he said, as he crossed the room. "I was told you wish to see me."

"No," Priscilla replied. "I have something I wish *you* to see."

"What is it?"

"You may wish to see it alone." Her tone was clipped with the vexation she struggled to suppress.

He smiled, appearing cup-shot. "That is an enticing remark, Lady Priscilla."

He *was* drunk, Priscilla realized, and her anger eased. If he had been trying to find surcease for his grief by giving a bottle a black eye, she should not judge him. She could not help recalling her own grief at Lazarus's passing and her fear that she would never be able to climb out of the deep pit of sorrow.

He took a single step and collapsed to one knee. The door that had been ajar burst open and Jeannette rushed out.

"Jeannette, would you help the earl to a comfortable seat?" Priscilla asked, glad the maid had been watching.

Jeannette hurried forward to obey. The earl went with her compliantly, then turned to smile again at Priscilla and hold out his hand to her.

No, not at Priscilla, but at Miss Baldwin, who stood behind her.

Priscilla shrugged off her shawl and carried it to a settee in the middle of the room. Turning to face the trio, she said, "What I am about to reveal will be disturbing because it is covered with blood."

"Blood?" The single word seemed to sober the earl instantly. He stopped staring at Miss Baldwin, turning his full attention on Priscilla.

"Blood?" repeated a deeper voice from the doorway to the corridor.

Priscilla wanted to run to Neville and throw her arms around him. That was impossible while the bloodstained gown was hidden in her shawl. Neville's face was chafed red with the cold wind, and she guessed Whitelaw had gotten her message to him as soon as Neville returned to Symmington Hall.

Quickly, Priscilla explained how she had gone to find Isaac and discovered him in the dovecote. "He had noticed fabric sticking out of one of the nest holes. When he went to investigate, he found one of Lady Eastbridge's gowns. It was soaked with blood."

"Impossible!" The earl jumped to his feet, then gripped the chair before he tumbled off them.

"You must be mistaken." Miss Baldwin's face was as gray as a corpse's. "Lady Eastbridge died of heart pains. There was no bleeding." Priscilla draped the bloodstained garment over the back of a chair. "Didn't this belong to the countess?"

The earl and Miss Baldwin edged closer. Jeannette held back, her mouth working as if she fought not to be ill. She put her hand over her stomach and turned to face the wall.

Neville strode across the room. He clasped his hands behind his back as he leaned in to examine the gown. "What makes you believe it belonged to the late lady, Pris?"

"The lace. It has a Tudor rose design. This gown looks exactly like the one Lady Eastbridge was wearing when she arrived here." She pointed to the hem. "Look. There are the mud stains that were on it when she arrived. Is it the same gown, Miss Baldwin?"

"Yes," the companion said uneasily, "it looks like one of my lady's gowns, but I swear to you, Lady Priscilla, that the countess had not lost any blood."

"How do you explain this then?"

"I cannot." Her lower lip wobbled and tears flooded into her eyes. "You must believe me, Lady Priscilla. I have no idea how her gown came to be covered with blood. When I found her already dead, she showed no signs of any wounds."

"How long was she alone?"

Miss Baldwin shuddered. "Are you suggesting that someone came into her room after Lady Symmington left and did my lady harm?"

"I am not suggesting anything, but there must be some explanation for the state of this gown."

"I know none."

"Mayhap a servant should be dispatched to intercept the hearse. If the late lady's corpse was examined to determine how she lost so much blood when there is no tear in her gown, we would have the answer to this mystery."

Lord Eastbridge stepped forward and frowned. "Lady Priscilla, I believe this is a matter for the coroner to consider, not you."

She recoiled from his venomous tone. Halting Neville before he could fire back a retort, she gathered up the gown. "I will have it sent to him posthaste."

"No, she was my wife. *I* shall have it delivered to him." He snatched it from her, and she heard lace rip.

"Take care!"

"I do not need you two sticking your noses into this, trying to stir up trouble."

Neville stepped forward. His hands were clenched by his side. Priscilla knew he was furious at the earl, but remained determined to find the truth.

"Do you have any idea," Neville asked in a low and tightly controlled voice, "how the gown could have gotten bloody? Did you see any wounds on Lady Eastbridge when her body was wrapped in shrouds for the trip to your home?"

"Don't be absurd!" Lord Eastbridge said, rolling the gown into a ball.

"You did not see anything?"

"I left that task to the servants."

Neville asked coolly, "Which ones?"

Shoving the gown into Miss Baldwin's hands, Lord Eastbridge seemed unaware of her horror. He pointed toward the door. "I have answered enough of your questions. How do I know that you did not arrange for this dress as a Twelfth Night prank, Hathaway?"

"Have you lost your mind, Eastbridge?" asked Neville with the calm iciness that Priscilla knew was a thin cover for his most heated fury. "What sort of man do you think I am?"

"Good day, Hathaway, my lady." Lord Eastbridge turned his back on them.

"Lord East—" Priscilla began.

"I said good day." The earl walked into one of the attached rooms and slammed the door.

Miss Baldwin stared at the bloodstained dress, then dropped it to the floor. Putting her hand over her mouth, she ran into another room.

Jeannette picked up the dress. Without looking at Priscilla or Neville, she left, too.

Priscilla put her hand on Neville's proffered arm. With what dignity she had left and fighting to keep her anger at Lord Eastbridge's pigheadedness from exploding, she walked out with him.

Neville led her to the far end of the half-circle gallery that overlooked the foyer below. Standing in front of the great Palladian window, they could see if anyone came toward them on either floor.

"I see you were entertaining yourself in fine style while I was riding through snow and wind to get no answers," Neville said. He looked out at the swirling snow. "Actually I did get one answer. No one sent for the coroner."

"Then why were we told that he had been called in and we must stay in case he wished to speak with us?"

"Someone is lying, Pris. Someone wants to cloud the truth about Lady Eastbridge's death, betwattling us until we throw up our hands in defeat."

Priscilla arched a single brow, as he often did. "Then they invited the wrong guests to this Twelfth Night gala. You and I do not give up when there is a puzzle to be solved."

"That bloody gown complicates everything."

"Yes." She sighed as she sat on the windowsill. "I am realizing only now that I did not do more than glance in the direction of the countess's body. She may have been injured horrifically, but the wounds were hidden by the covers on her bed."

"A difficult thing to hide."

"I agree, but . . ." She rubbed her palms together. "I wish I had looked more closely."

"There is only one thing to do."

"What is that?"

He looked past her out into the storm. "We need to send the coroner in pursuit of Lady Eastbridge's corpse."

Chapter Nine

PRISCILLA AND NEVILLE sat at one side of their sitting room. Daphne, Leah and Isaac were playing cards on the floor closer to the hearth. The children were focused on their game, so they paid no heed of their elders' quiet conversation. Neville had suggested he and Priscilla speak in their private chamber, but Priscilla suspected a glass would be pressed against the door as the children tried to eavesdrop. She had learned long ago that holding a conversation where they could choose to listen usually meant that they paid no attention. There was no amusement in not getting the upper hand on their parents.

And there was nothing funny about the topic she discussed with Neville. "That much blood," she said, "suggests that the violence against Lady Eastbridge was devastating."

"And probably personal."

Priscilla wrapped her arms around herself and leaned against Neville's strong body. "I have been trying not to think of that, but after seeing that gown, I have to agree."

"If she was attacked while wearing that dress, we must assume it was someone she knew well. Someone she would allow close to her."

"That suggests her family and her servants."

"Yes. Which one of those apparently decent people would have slain her?"

He slipped his arm around her. "Pris, you always see the best in everyone. One of those people is wearing a mask as surely as if they were at the Twelfth Night masquerade. Also spreading lies, although I have no idea why anyone who may have played a part in her death would *want* the coroner to come here."

"Those small idiosyncracies are unsettling, Neville." She sat straighter and met his eyes. "I would swear that the grief I have seen on Lady Eastbridge's family's and retainers' faces is real. Even though I believe there might be an intimate connection between Miss Baldwin and the earl."

"All the more reason for them to put out the countess's lights." He arched a brow, giving him a devilish demeanor. "But we need facts, Pris."

"I know, and I hope neither the earl nor that young woman had anything to do with Lady Eastbridge's death. I—"

A frantic knock was placed on the door, and Pris stiffened.

"I will get it." Neville stood. "Mayhap it is Grove, wanting further information about what you discovered, Pris, before he sets out after the corpse."

"And what I found, too!" piped up Isaac.

"And most definitely you, you hawk-eyed lad." Neville winked at the boy, then went to the door. Opening it, he said, "Duncan!"

The spry Scotsman bounced into the room. "I must ask you a great boon. Come to my rooms."

"When?"

"Now!"

Priscilla came to her feet. "Is something amiss, Duncan?"

"No! Just come now." He smiled at the children. "All of you!"

"Why?" asked Neville. "Duncan, old chap, you are welcome to join us here while we have a comfortable coze."

He shook his head. "No. Come with me. Now! You will understand when you get there."

Priscilla hooked her arm through her husband's. "Neville, if you don't tell him that we will go with him, I believe he will burst."

The children pelted Duncan with questions, and, for once, Priscilla did not chide them for being too curious. She was, too, and she could not imagine why Duncan insisted they come to his rooms in another wing of the house.

Neville motioned for her to drop back so he could talk to his friend alone. If Neville had hoped that Duncan would be more forthcoming when it was only the two friends in the conversation, he was sorely disappointed. Or so it appeared from the taut line of Neville's jaw.

Priscilla almost stepped forward to tell Duncan that this was not the time for one of his hoaxes. She did not, because she and Neville had agreed to speak to no one else about what Isaac had found and the message Whitelaw had been sent to deliver to the coroner.

When Duncan opened a door and bowed them in, Priscilla was unsure to what to expect. She stepped into the room and stared. The chairs had been arranged in a half-circle, leaving the center of the room empty. Otherwise, the sitting room looked much like the one they had left.

"Do sit down," Duncan urged. "I am glad that you are here to witness this." For once, his eyes did not twinkle with mischief. In fact, his face had taken on a decidedly feverish appearance.

"Are you feeling unwell?" Priscilla asked.

He gulped, then motioned toward the chairs in the sitting room. "If you please . . ."

Steering her children to the chairs, Priscilla hushed their questions. She had no answers to give them.

She watched as Duncan stood in the very center of the space between the curved row of chairs. He glanced at a clock on the mantel, then at the door. He clearly was expecting someone to arrive in the next few minutes.

"It seems we are a bit early," Duncan said.

"Early for what?" asked Leah before Priscilla could speak.

"For what is to happen." His face became gray again. "Or what I *hope* will happen."

This time, Daphne asked, "And what is that?"

Either Duncan failed to hear her, or he pretended not to.

Priscilla put her finger to her lips and looked at each of her children in turn. They nodded, but she saw the curiosity burning in their eyes.

As five minutes became ten, then fifteen, then twenty, Isaac began to shift on his chair. Leah started rocking her feet back and forth. Even Daphne was finding it impossible to sit still. As for Duncan, he kept glancing at the clock, then going to the door. He opened it and looked out before closing it again. He kept repeating the same motions over and over.

Priscilla turned to Neville. "How much longer do you think he intends us to wait?"

"I have no idea," Neville whispered.

"Did he give you any clue as to why he wanted us to come here?"

"He said only that there is a great pronouncement he wishes to make."

Priscilla's eyes widened as she glanced from him to Duncan who paced back and forth like a fox trying to find its way through a hedge. "You don't think . . .?"

Before Neville could answer, the door opened.

Aunt Cordelia swept in, as always making an entrance worthy of a diva commanding the stage. She would be deeply offended at the comparison, but it was the only one that came into Priscilla's mind. Her gown of a deep purple was worthy of a Shakespearian queen.

"I trust this is vital," she said in her most vexed tone. "I was busy with overseeing the packing of my bags. As soon as we can leave this dreary place, I wish to be on my way."

Duncan walked over to her. His usual jolliness had vanished, and his hands shook. He clasped them behind him until he reached where Aunt Cordelia stood. Then he held one hand out to her.

"I am—" His voice cracked, and he began again. "I am pleased that you could join us, my dear Cordelia."

"Us?" She frowned as her gaze swept over Priscilla and her family. "What is this flummery, Duncan? I—" She gasped as Duncan dropped to one knee in front of her.

Beside Priscilla, her daughters drew in sharp breaths of anticipation. Priscilla looked at Neville who arched a single brow and began to grin.

"My dearest lady," Duncan began, his accent once more deepening into a Scottish burr, "'tis a fortunate man who chances to find the woman of his dreams. 'Tis an even more fortunate man who chances to find the woman of his dreams when she can return his favor."

"By all that's blue," murmured Neville, "the man is utterly addled."

Priscilla slapped him on the arm and hushed him. She did the same to Daphne when her oldest began to giggle with excitement.

"I know," Duncan went on, "that a fair lass like yeself could do far better than an ole gloach like me, but I ask ye, fair Cornelia, will ye do me the honor of being my wife?"

Priscilla could do no more than stare at her aunt and Duncan. She half-expected Aunt Cordelia to chide him for speaking of matters of the heart under the circumstances.

Instead Aunt Cordelia drew Duncan to his feet. She slipped her arm around his and cooed, "Isn't he absolutely the sweetest man? How could I say no?"

"So 'tis an aye?" asked Duncan.

"Of course it is, darling." She threw her arms around him and gave him a resounding kiss.

Neville murmured something that sounded like, "Now he will live beneath the cat's foot. Poor fool."

Priscilla could not argue with that. Duncan would be a henpecked husband, subject to regular curtain-lectures, but he clearly had a true *amour* for Aunt Cordelia, and theirs would be a love match. He was the only person Priscilla had ever known who could persuade her aunt to toss aside Society's expectations. Even a bit.

With her mind reeling at the very idea of actually hearing her aunt *cooing*, Priscilla gave Aunt Cordelia a hug. She was shocked when her aunt gave her a warm squeeze in return.

"I wish you every happiness, Aunt Cordelia," Priscilla said.

"Thank you, my dear. I knew if I waited another *good* man would come along." She scowled in Neville's direction.

Priscilla said something trite, then stepped back to let her children give their great-aunt a hug. One of these days, she would not be able to curb her tongue any longer and demand that her aunt stop insulting Neville. Knowing it would be a complete waste of her breath was not what halted her. It was the fact that Neville seemed to revel in discovering what new slur Aunt Cordelia had devised each time they met.

Giving Duncan a kiss on the cheek, Priscilla welcomed him to the family. He looked about ready to swoon, so she sent Neville to get him a generous serving of whisky. As soon as he tossed it back and went for a refill, Duncan's normally ruddy coloring had returned.

"And, my dearest Cordelia," Duncan said, "I cannot wait for you to see the gift I have had delivered to your country house."

"A gift?" Aunt Cordelia sounded as young and excited as Leah. "What is it?"

Before Duncan could tell her about the statue of the nude lovers, Neville decided this would be a good time for them to withdraw and leave the love birds alone. When neither Duncan nor Aunt Cordelia protested his suggestion that he and Pris take the children back to their rooms, Neville could not help smiling.

"Are you now my uncle?" he asked as he shook Duncan's hand before taking his leave. "Unc Dunc, mayhap?"

"Great name!" shouted Isaac. "Unc Dunc! Unc Dunc!" He began to dance around the room as he repeated the name in a singsong voice.

When Pris shook her head at him, Neville could only laugh. He had not realized the boy was close-by, but Duncan was chuckling at the joke, too. A storm was brewing on Aunt Cordelia's brow, however, so Neville decided they should make their escape straightaway.

The children chattered like a flock of magpies as they went out into the passage. When Daphne mentioned something about the wedding, her brother and sister teased her for being moony. Soon they were giggling together.

Walking behind them, Neville put his arm around Pris's shoulders and said, "Now *that* was quite the surprise, I must say!"

"I agree. Do you believe in fairies?"

He laughed. "Pris, if you are about to say that your real aunt has been spirited away by the fairies and replaced with a changeling, I must remind you that she is long out of her cradle. I have never heard of the fairyfolk stealing a grown woman." He winked as he leaned toward her. "And if they were want-witted enough to take her, you can be sure that they would have

returned her before any of us noticed she was gone. I cannot imagine Titania and Oberon welcoming her into their midsummer's night's dream."

"Maybe Puck. That trickster would enjoy switching my prickly aunt with this cooing copy." She shook her head in disbelief. "Did you hear her? Neville, she *cooed*."

"I believe we owe Duncan a tremendous debt, for he has tamed the she-dragon who is your aunt."

"Don't count on that." Priscilla smiled as she leaned her head once more on his shoulder. "My aunt may mellow when she is in his company, but Aunt Cordelia has never been changed by one of her husbands."

"I suspect Duncan is nothing like her previous husbands. I met only the most recent, and he seemed to be forever suffering from the dismals. Or was he simply regretting the decision he had made to offer for her?"

With a laugh that slid along his skin like a delicious caress, she said, "He was always a grim gentleman. I think he had high hopes for control-ling Aunt Cordelia's assets, but he quickly learned he was mistaken."

"Duncan is no fortune-hunter."

"Which may be why Aunt Cordelia was giddy at his offer of marriage. He . . ." As her voice faded, she raised her head.

Lady Symmington was walking toward them at a determined pace. She would have plowed right through the Flanders children if they had not skipped out of the way. They scowled at her back, but the baroness did not seem to sense their anger.

She halted right in front of Neville. "I have been looking for you every-where, Sir Neville."

"Your search was successful, it would appear."

"I need to speak with you immediately." Lady Symmington gave Pris a dismissive glance. "About matters of utmost importance."

Neville let a smile play across his lips when Pris did not take their hostess's less than subtle hint that Lady Symmington wished to speak with Neville alone. Putting his arm around Pris's waist, he asked, "What matters are these?"

"Sir Neville, I was wondering what you had planned for the evening's festivities."

"Planned?"

"You *are* our Lord of Misrule." She frowned. "I assumed you would understand that your title comes with obligations. Pranks, games, and other entertainments."

"In light of what has occurred, *I* assumed that such traditional farces would be set aside."

Lady Symmington shook her head. "You assumed incorrectly. Lady Eastbridge requested that we hold the masquerade as planned. Her hus-band has set aside his grief to make sure her last wish is carried out, and I intend to honor her request. Will you do less, Sir Neville?"

"Yes."

"What?" Lady Symmington asked, taken aback by his quiet answer.

"I thought my answer quite clear. I will do less. Much less. I will not be hopping about like a jester when a better way to honor the late countess would be to recall the grace and elegance she brought to her Twelfth Night entertainments."

"But *she* always had pranks and silly games. My guests expect the same."

"Then you, my lady, should have those arrangements already in place. Mayhap it would be better if you named someone else as Lord of Misrule. I fear my heart is not in the spirit of Twelfth Night tonight."

"Nonsense. You were chosen as tradition decrees."

"By having the crown bounce across the table and land on my plate? That is hardly traditional."

Lady Symmington threw her head back and jutted out her chin, a move that, if she had been a man, would offer an invitation for a facer. "*You* ended up with the crown, Sir Neville. The obligation is *yours*, and I would strongly suggest that you take it seriously."

"Why? This is nonsense."

"Is it?" Her voice cracked. "It is the only way I can think of to salvage the Twelfth Night assembly. Don't you hear it? Don't you feel it?"

"Hear what? Feel what?" he asked, wondering if the stress had unhinged the baroness's mind.

"The fear! There are over a hundred people in the hall, but it is so quiet you can hear the wind outside in the eaves. Why is it quiet? Because everyone is afraid! As soon as everyone heard that Lady Eastbridge's death might not be a natural one—"

"It did not take long for the rumors to spread, did it?" He glanced at Pris who listened with a blank expression. She was taking her cues from him.

"Not rumors, Sir Neville. We have heard what Lady Priscilla found. If it had not been snowing so hard, I doubt there would be more than a few guests remaining." Her mouth tightened. "I have spent months planning tonight's gathering, and I would have gladly set it aside, save for the countess's request that the party be held. But my guests are terrified that the murderer is still among us."

"That is possible," he said quietly.

Lady Symmington flinched. "I hope you are wrong. However, it does not matter. I will hold this Twelfth Night assembly, and, you, Sir Neville will provide entertainment as the Lord of Misrule." She turned on her heel and strode away.

"Do not heed her," Pris said. "She is so desperate to prove she is as good a hostess as Lady Eastbridge that she is acting half-insane."

"Desperate? Enough to do something appalling?"

Pris looked at him, astonishment on her face. "Do you think that Lady Symmington may have done something to the countess?"

"According to Jeannette and Miss Baldwin, our hostess was the last one seen with the countess before Lady Eastbridge's corpse was discovered." He put his hands on Pris's shoulders. "I am going to speak with Eastbridge. I want to know if he is the impetus behind Lady Symmington's fanatic declaration to act as if nothing has happened. If you will take the children back to our rooms, I will meet you there."

"That sounds like a good idea." She smiled. "I would like to go with you, but I understand that Lord Eastbridge might be more willing to speak with another man."

"Thank you, Pris." He ran the back of his fingers against her soft cheek. "I hate asking this of you because I know you want to follow every possible clue to the truth."

"We are a team." She put her hand over his, holding it close to her face. "In every possible way."

He bent forward to whisper against her ear's enticing whorls. "The Lord of Misrule is about to make his first and only decree."

"Yes?" Her breathless voice sent a pulse of craving through him.

"The Lord of Misrule and his lady shall not stay long at the masquerade. They shall enjoy a very private unmasking in their chambers."

She quivered and whispered, "My lord, your wish is my command."

With a laugh, he tapped her nose. "Keep that thought, darling." He kissed her with unfettered longing, then released her while he still could.

He strode toward Eastbridge's rooms with new resolve. More than ever, he wanted answers because, even though Pris had said nothing, they both knew that until the mystery of the countess's death was unraveled, those questions stood between them and their night's pleasure.

Chapter Ten

NEVILLE KNOCKED on Lord Eastbridge's door. The maid Jeannette opened it.

"His lordship is in his private room," she said with a curtsy in answer to his question. "Third door. Go right in."

"Thank you." Neville crossed the room, rapped on the bedchamber door which was slightly ajar, then walked in. He halted in mid-step. "By Jove!"

Miss Baldwin straddled Lord Eastbridge's lap, her gown raised up to reveal an improper length of leg. The bodice was loose, and Neville turned away when his gaze settled on her firm breasts propped in the earl's hands.

She gave a soft cry of dismay, and Neville heard her jump off the earl's lap.

Lord Eastbridge cleared his throat and said, "That will be all for now, Miss Baldwin."

Neville put his hand over his mouth to silence his laugh. Did the old cuff think anyone would fall for his moonshine? Pris had been right when she said the earl had designs on his wife's attractive, young companion, but did Eastbridge want her enough to murder his own wife? Or did Miss Baldwin want the earl's prestige and money enough to slay the countess?

When Miss Baldwin slipped past Neville, she was still trying to get her dress to cover her properly. Her face was as crimson as the earl's waistcoat.

"You could have the decency to knock," the earl said, standing.

"I did."

"Then you walked right in without permission."

"The maid told me to—" He smiled coldly. "I would warn you, Eastbridge, that your household is troubled by your *affaire* with Miss Baldwin. Servants have their unique ways of making their opinions known."

Eastbridge swore an oath, then asked, "Which one was it?"

"Does it matter? Long ago, I learned that the sentiment below stairs is usually shared by most of the household staff." Neville was not going to give the earl a reason to give a servant who was loyal to his late wife her *conge*. "I would not attempt to suggest how you should live your life,

Eastbridge," he went on, not attempting to keep his disgust out of his voice, "but there already are questions about how your wife died. If others see you in such a passionate embrace with Miss Baldwin, there may be those who believe the two of you have a reason for wishing the countess out of the way."

"What you are suggesting is an insult I cannot endure. I should ask you to name your friends."

"You will endure that insult and more if you continue to act impetuously." Neville laughed without a hint of humor. "Will you challenge to a duel everyone who chances to see you and Miss Baldwin tangled up together?"

The earl lost his bluster and swore under his breath. "Dash it, man! Have some sympathy for a man who has just lost his wife."

"Conveniently, it would appear, for you and Miss Baldwin."

Eastbridge snorted a laugh. "Quite the opposite. Don't you see, Hathaway? The arrangement with Annalee has been quite convenient for me while my wife was alive. Her death was no boon to me. Very much the opposite. Now that dark-haired fortune-hunter will not stop pestering me to make her my wife."

Neville crossed his arms over his chest and met the earl's eyes steadily. As Eastbridge looked away, Neville said, "I saw how you were bothered by her attentions."

"As long as I can persuade her that there is a chance for her to become a countess, she is willing to do anything I want."

"Even murder your wife?"

The earl stamped his foot and scowled. "Have you heard nothing I have said? My life was well-ordered with my wife overseeing my needs in my household and Annalee overseeing my needs in my bed."

"But does Miss Baldwin want to be your countess enough to kill your wife?"

Again the earl seemed to deflate. "I don't know. I honestly don't know. The girl has changed since my wife's death. She once was compliant. Now she is endlessly demanding."

"How long has she been in your household?"

"A year, maybe less."

"Where was she before then?"

The earl shrugged. "My wife handled the hiring and dismissal of servants. I can only assume Annalee's references met her standards."

Neville cursed silently. That Eastbridge knew nothing of his lover's background could mean nothing or everything. Each time Neville saw the young woman, he was certain he had seen her before, but not in a fine house. That meant he must have seen her in the lower sections

of London. Could Miss Baldwin actually be some sort of trading dame who had decided to find a better bed and better pay for her favors?

"Do you know where she was when the countess died?" Neville asked, hoping he could get at least one answer.

He walked toward the table where a bottle waited. "No, Hathaway. I don't know where she was at the time my wife died. I do know that Annalee was the one who discovered my wife was dead." He opened the bottle and poured out some of the amber liquid. Tilting it back, he swallowed it in a single gulp. "A week ago, I would have never guessed she could do anything horrible. Now . . ." He refilled his glass and drank it down again. "I don't know what else I can tell you, Hathaway."

Neville went out of the room. In the outer chamber, Jeannette worked dusting the lower shelf of a table. He nodded to her and continued to the door. As he reached it, he half-turned as he opened it. He caught, out of the corner of his eye, a satisfied smile on the maid's face. She had sent him in to intrude on the earl and his particular, and she was quite pleased with herself.

The maid, Neville decided, was up to something more than embarrassing her employer. Silently he added Jeannette's name to his list of suspects, but Annalee Baldwin's was now at the top.

NOW IT WAS Daphne who had gone missing!

Priscilla wished there was a way she could train a foxhound to chase after her children when they went off on their own without informing anyone where they were bound. Usually she trusted their good common sense, but with the possibility of a murderer in the house, she wanted to know where her family was at all times. She had assumed Daphne was in the room she shared

with Leah, preparing for tonight's events. Daphne had promised to help her sister with her hair, and that was why Leah had come to Priscilla, upset that Daphne apparently had forgotten.

There truly was only one other place where Daphne could be. She was so excited about being a part of the festivities, even though she was not officially out, that she might have sneaked into the ballroom to see what had been prepared.

Priscilla walked along the elegant corridor that led to the ballroom which was in a wing of its own. The space seemed oddly deserted, and even though she knew the remaining guests were preparing themselves for the bizarre assembly, she could not keep herself from looking around on every step. A creak as the house settled in the cold was unnerving.

The ballroom had doors on both the ground floor and the first floor. The lower doors led to the main floor of the grand chamber while the upper ones would open onto galleries or private boxes. She headed for the doors on the first floor. With servants busy with last minute details, Daphne would peek into the ballroom from above. The only question was which door.

Luck was with Priscilla when she opened the first door and realized the gallery around the Symmingtons' ballroom was continuous. It connected the various boxes and allowed guests to stroll around the ballroom and enjoy its beauty from every angle.

And the ballroom was stunning. The pale green walls between the tall arched windows were decorated with plaster flowers and vines amidst the paneling. The ceiling was painted with an *al fresco* scene of young people seated two by two in a meadow with butterflies and birds and cherubs flying around them. A trio of chandeliers were set equidistant from each other. Crystal prisms threw rainbows across the walls because the candles had already been lit.

That surprised Priscilla, but she appreciated the light that reached through the gallery's railing. She stood still and listened. From below, she could hear the hushed voices of the servants as they made sure everything was perfect for the Symmingtons' guests.

Then she heard a different sound. A soft, throaty laugh. It came from her right, and she recognized it as Daphne's. Her first reaction was relief. Her daughter would not be laughing if she were in danger. Almost immediately, Priscilla wondered what mischief her daughter was up to now.

Priscilla got her answer when she took two steps along the gallery and saw two forms entwined in the shadows. The pose was similar to the statue Duncan had purchased for Aunt Cordelia, but fortunately these two people were fully clad.

Very fortunately because the two in the embrace were her daughter and Lord Witherspoon.

Clearing her throat served when Priscilla had no idea what to say to break the two apart. They leaped away from each other as if someone had lit a fire between them.

Daphne had the decency to look abashed at being discovered in Lord Witherspoon's arms. He released her, stepping forward as if to defend her.

Priscilla focused her glare on him, and the young marquess almost crumbled in front of her eyes. A part of her was tempted to laugh because Neville had warned her that her "I am disappointed in your behavior" look could slice through the hardest armor. But she submerged her amusement. There was nothing funny about finding her oldest daughter wrapped in a man's embrace.

"Good afternoon, Lord Witherspoon." Her voice was as icy as her eyes.

The marquess wisely gave Daphne's hand a squeeze and took his leave.

Priscilla walked in the other direction with her daughter. Neither of them spoke as they went out of the ballroom. The silence continued as they returned to their rooms. Priscilla broke it only to ask her younger children to give her and Daphne some privacy. Closing the main door behind them, Priscilla pointed to the closest chair.

Her daughter did not hesitate, hurrying to perch on the very edge of the seat. Tears rolled down her cheeks, and she made no effort to wipe them away.

With a sigh, Priscilla asked, "Do you have any idea how I have had to fight your great-aunt to keep you children?"

Daphne looked up in disbelief.

"Yes, it is true. Aunt Cordelia believed that I could not raise you to take your proper place in the Polite World because I had turned my own back on it when I married your father."

"I had no idea, Mama."

"I had hoped that it was a truth I could keep to myself, because I did not want you to think poorly of me or your great-aunt."

Daphne cried, "I would never think poorly of you, Mama."

"That is good to hear." Sitting near her daughter, she said, "But you must understand, Daphne, that the *ton* will be eager to look askance at you because you are my daughter and Neville's stepdaughter."

"Mama, you always do the civil. Nobody would decry your manners and your grasp of the canons of Society."

"Save for one error, for the daughter of an earl should never consider an offer from a vicar. What they considered a *mesalliance* stained my name, and it made me suspect among Society." She smiled sadly. "Not that I became an outcast because I *am* the daughter of an earl. You, on the other hand, are the granddaughter of a deceased earl. Everything you do and say must be above reproach because the *Beau Monde* will be waiting for you to do the wrong thing and prove that you are unworthy of their company. They would gleefully send you to Coventry."

"But Uncle Neville—"

"He does not care a rap about the *ton*, and he is a man. Those two factors make him somewhat immune from being ostracized. Also he is rich, and the *ton* will overlook many social solecisms in the case of those who are plump in the pocket."

"It is not fair!"

"That is the truth, but it is the way of the Polite World. You can choose to accept its rules, or you can choose banishment." Her voice became stern. "And if anyone else but your mother had found you in Lord Witherspoon's embrace, you would be finding that out firsthand. Daphne, you are usually the one I can depend on for being sensible. What were you thinking?"

"When Mr. McAndrews asked Aunt Cordelia for her hand, it was so romantic." She leaned back in the chair and stared up at the ceiling. A wistful sigh slipped past her lips. "I simply wanted to enjoy something romantic myself."

"Kiss me. Kiss me. Kiss me," came her brother's and sister's voices.

Priscilla tried to frown at them, because she had asked them to remain in their rooms until she finished her conversation with Daphne. Even so, she could not keep from laughing when Leah bent Isaac back over her arm and made smacking sounds.

"Enough, you two!" she said as she held out her arms to them.

Laughing, they rushed over to be hugged. Daphne relaxed, glad that the scold was over. Soon she was teasing her brother and sister, and they were giggling together.

"I thought," Isaac said, his voice rising above the girls', "that Aunt Cordelia would give him a dressing-down about the *proper* way to propose."

"Mayhap," Leah said, "she thought she would save the lectures for after they are wed."

"I think they are cute," Daphne added, "even if they are old."

Priscilla wagged a finger at her children. "Listen to yourselves! Love does not solely belong to the young and the foolish."

"No," Neville said as he came into the room, "sometimes it belongs to the old and the foolish." He winked at Leah. "And don't say what you are thinking, young lady. Your mother is neither old nor foolish. Nor am I, for I was wise enough to fall in love with her."

Daphne dropped back onto the settee and draped her forearm across her brow. "Oh, how I wish Burke would say such lovely things to me."

"He would rather do the pretty with you," Leah said, grinning.

"Mama!" cried Daphne. "Tell her not to say such things about Burke and me."

"Next time you should not let Mama catch you kissing him."

"Mama!"

Priscilla waved them both to silence when she noticed the tension along Neville's jaw. Urging them to go and get ready for the masquerade, because the younger children would be able to attend the beginning of the ball, she took Neville's hand and sat with him on the settee.

As soon as the children were out of earshot, she asked, "What is wrong?"

Neville explained what he had intruded upon in the Eastbridge suite, then said, "You do not look surprised, Pris."

"I interrupted them myself. Or so I believe, because I did not see, only heard. Do you think Miss Baldwin is capable of such violence against the countess?"

"Eastbridge says she is eager to take the countess's place. He suggested she wanted that enough to be willing to do whatever she must to get it."

Priscilla shook her head.

"You don't believe him, Pris?"

"He would not be the first man to try to shift blame on his mistress."

Neville began to smile. "For a woman who used to be married to a parson, you have a decidedly wicked turn of mind."

"As I have said before, when one is a vicar's wife, one learns many aspects of what people will do to get what they want or avoid what they do not want."

"Then there is the countess's abigail Jeannette. She must have known that Eastbridge was with his paramour."

"With her lady dead, she has been demoted to a general maid again. That could make her resentful." She got up. "I must get ready for the masquerade. Mayhap you can present a prank, my Lord of Misrule, that will get us the truth."

Neville slapped his hand against his forehead as he stood. "Dash it, Pris! I never did ask Eastbridge if he agreed with Lady Symmington's plans for tonight."

"Then I guess there's no choice. You will have to preside as the Lord of Misrule while I use the distractions you create to see if I can find out some answers."

He hooked an arm around her waist and spun her up against him. "How will I ever be more distracting than you, sweetheart?"

She walked her fingers up his chest. "I know you, Neville Hathaway. You can be extremely distracting when you wish." She brushed her lips against his. With a sigh as she drew back, she added, "I hope both of us can do what we must tonight to find out what is really going on here. It may be our final chance because the guests will be leaving on the morrow."

"Then let's make the best of it." He sealed that vow with a heated kiss which made her remember her other one that they would leave the ball-room early tonight.

She wondered if that would be possible.

Chapter Eleven

AN HOUR AFTER the masquerade ball had begun, few of the guests had arrived. Those who had were clustered close to where the footmen were serving glasses of chilled wine. Priscilla noticed only a handful of guests, other than the youngsters, wore masks. The children seemed to be the sole ones enjoying the spirit of the evening. They kept daring each other to go and stand beneath the kissing bough. The space was empty, because even mistletoe and a stolen kiss could not tempt any of the adults.

Priscilla felt odd to be at the gala without Neville. As Lord of Misrule, he would be making his entrance later. Neither Aunt Cordelia nor Duncan had arrived yet either. She wondered if they would attend the ball. Aunt Cordelia would not want to miss the opportunity to show off her new betrothed. Or was her aunt planning to stay out of sight until she could announce her tidings at an assembly of her own?

Lord Eastbridge had been in the ballroom when Priscilla and her children walked in. He had been sitting in a corner, and he remained there with a glass that was never empty. Each time he took a sip, a footman appeared like a djinn to refill it. Lord Eastbridge had glanced in her direction once, then quickly away.

Miss Baldwin was not present either. At least, she was not on the main floor of the ballroom. Priscilla had noticed a woman who might have been the late countess's companion lurking in the gallery above. Mayhap the earl had decided to accede to proper appearances in the wake of his wife's death.

Daphne appeared at Priscilla's side. The smile she had been wearing in anticipation of the gathering was gone.

"I wish Burke was not so nice," Daphne muttered.

Startled, Priscilla asked, "What do you mean?"

"That." Daphne hooked a thumb toward the center of the ballroom as the orchestra struck a loud note.

Lord Symmington and his wife stepped out onto the floor, acting as if nothing out of the ordinary had happened in the days leading up to Twelfth Night. Trailing them came Miss Symmington with her hand firmly on Lord Witherspoon's arm. The young woman flashed a triumphant smile in Daphne's direction.

Instead of flaring up as Priscilla had expected, Daphne said, "She is deluding herself if she thinks Burke means to be anything more than gracious."

"People do enjoy creating their own perceptions." Priscilla chose her words with care, because she did not want her daughter to discern her astonishment at Daphne's maturity that had seemed impossible only the day before.

"I understand what you have been trying to tell me, Mama. If I want more than calf-love with Burke, I need to know when to trust him. I have watched you with Uncle Neville, and you

have dared to trust him when the rest of the world has warned you not to. And because you trust him, he trusts you."

"Of course, Neville trusts me. We have been friends for many years."

Daphne smiled. "But he trusts you with his heart. He never has trusted anyone else with that. I want Burke to trust me the same way."

Slowly some other couples went out to join the Symmingtons and Lord Witherspoon. Even so there were not enough to complete the line needed for the country reel, so several of the younger children partnered. The dance fell into chaos after a few steps, and Lady Symmington looked ready to dissolve into tears.

Taking sympathy on her, Priscilla took her children out onto the floor. She stepped into the pattern among the children. She motioned for them to copy her and Isaac who was her partner. Daphne and Leah faced each other and began to follow the simple pattern. With their help, the other children quickly learned the steps, and the dancers were able to move along with the music.

"Thank you," Lady Symmington said as she passed Priscilla in the dance.

Priscilla smiled and nodded before she linked her arm with Isaac's and twirled. Mayhap the night could be salvaged.

Her hopes dimmed when Priscilla noticed Miss Baldwin coming into the ballroom. She was dressed as a young shepherdess, her ruffled hem rising too high along her legs. The young woman made a beeline for the earl. As Priscilla stepped through the pattern of the dance, she kept her gaze on Lord Eastbridge and Miss Baldwin who sat on the chair next to his. When the companion boldly picked up his glass and took a sip from it, Miss Baldwin scanned the room to see if anyone had noticed. Her gaze locked with Priscilla's for only the length of a single heartbeat, then slid away.

Was that look a challenge, or was Miss Baldwin less confident than she tried to appear? Priscilla drew in a quick breath when Miss Baldwin spoke to Lord Eastbridge and pointed at the kissing bough. He began to smile.

And Priscilla's stomach sank. Had they taken a knock in the cradle? There was no other explanation for them even to consider such a fool-hardy idea. If one of them stood beneath the kissing bough, and the other took advantage of the tradition, would tongues wag? Or would the *ton* accept as inevitable that the lord would marry his mistress as soon as the proper amount of mourning had passed for his obviously unmourned wife?

She got her answer when the earl asked Miss Baldwin to stand up with him. That he was dancing when his wife was so recently deceased was outrageous; that he danced with her companion was even worse.

Priscilla groaned when she saw Lord Witherspoon lead Daphne out close to the earl and his paramour. Both of them should know better. She tried to signal to her daughter, but Daphne's gaze was focused on the marquess's face.

Finding her son by the buffet table, she sighed when she saw his face was covered with icing from the cake at the far end. The cake should not have been touched until the Symmingtons invited their guests to dine. She snatched a cloth from one of the footmen's arm and cleaned Isaac's face.

"Go and tell Daphne I wish to talk with her," Priscilla said.

"She is dancing with that moonling marquess." He grimaced. "She will not heed me."

"Tell I wish to see her *now,* and do not take no for an answer."

His eyes widened, and he sped out onto the dance floor. Priscilla walked to where she could watch while he spoke to his sister. If necessary, she could emphasize her request with a stern expression.

Lady Symmington stepped between her and Daphne. The baroness's smile was brittle and her eyes glittered with annoyance. When Priscilla tried to peer past her, she shifted so she blocked Priscilla's view of anything but her.

"Where is Sir Neville?" Lady Symmington asked, all hint of her gratitude to Priscilla gone. "He should have made his entrance as Lord of Misrule by now."

"Neville follows his own rules."

That fact only vexed the baroness further. "Is this his way of showing that he does not intend to fulfill the role?"

"Neville told you that, no matter how reluctant he was, he will serve as your Lord of Misrule. He is a man of his word."

"Then where is he? My guests expect him to entertain them."

"I believe they are entertained enough right now." She looked past the baroness.

Lady Symmington looked over her shoulder and saw the earl and Miss Baldwin in the middle of her dance floor. Alone now, Priscilla noticed, grateful to her son for persuading his sister of the social danger of seeming to give countenance to the earl's actions, when the baroness stormed out and motioned for the orchestra to stop playing.

Priscilla scanned the ballroom and saw Daphne and the marquess talking with her other children. Aunt Cordelia stood there, too, and Priscilla breathed a sigh of relief. Her aunt would not allow Daphne to chance making another enormous mistake. Priscilla hoped the guests had assumed that Daphne and Lord Witherspoon had simply cut across the dance floor to greet her great-aunt.

Then everyone's attention riveted on the middle of the ballroom. Lady Symmington's voice rose enough to reach the edges of the room.

"Mayhap you would like something to eat, my lord," she was saying to Lord Eastbridge. "You look hungry."

"I am neither hungry," fired back the earl, his words slurring, "nor am I drunk, as you seem ready to accuse me of being. I wish to dance with Annalee."

A gasp rushed around the room as he spoke Miss Baldwin's given name.

"My lord," Lady Symmington tried again, "I know you are deeply saddened by your wife's passing. Why don't you come with me, and we can—"

"I wish to dance." He called to the orchestra. "Play! Annalee wishes to dance."

"My lord—"

"Either get a partner or get out of our way." He took a single step and wobbled.

Priscilla had seen enough. Going out onto the dance floor, she linked her arm around Miss Baldwin's. With a gentle pull, then a stronger one, she tugged the young woman toward the nearby chamber where ladies could repair any damage done to their appearance during the country dances. Behind them, Lady Symmington still was trying to convince Lord Eastbridge to see sense.

"Where are we going?" asked Miss Baldwin.

"Where I may speak with you without every ear in the house listening in."

"About what?"

"I will explain when we get there." Priscilla added nothing more until she opened the door, motioned for Miss Baldwin to lead the way into the room, and then closed the door behind them.

The room had two chairs and a looking glass. A tufted bench was pushed against the wall beneath the room's only window. A washstand with a ewer and a bowl was set next to a second door, one Priscilla knew was used by the servants.

"Please sit, Miss Baldwin," Priscilla said.

Miss Baldwin did, rearranging her ruffled skirt around her. "Say what you believe is important, my lady. I wish to return to dance with Hora—with my lord."

"I hope that what I have observed means Lady Symmington is correct. That both you and the earl are half-mad with grief at Lady Eastbridge's passing. I prefer that explanation to any other when I see him flirting with you while his wife's body is on its way to be buried in the family's churchyard."

"If you have concerns about Hora—Lord Eastbridge's actions, you should speak to him."

"But my concerns are not only with his actions, but yours. That is the second time in as many seconds that you have almost spoken his given name. Are you addled to flaunt your *affaire d'amour* in everyone's faces? Where do you think it will lead?"

Miss Baldwin raised her chin. "To the altar."

Priscilla restrained herself to keep from laughing in the young woman's face. Miss Baldwin was, Priscilla reminded herself, not much older than Daphne. Without someone to remind her of proper behavior, Miss Baldwin had allowed her heart to steer her into these dangerous waters. Or was the companion the calculating woman that the earl had named her?

"Do you truly believe that an earl will marry his late wife's companion, especially when he has paraded his paramour openly before these people? Is that the way a gentleman treats a lady he loves and respects?"

Miss Baldwin stood. "I have listened to as many of your comments as I wish to, Lady Priscilla. I had never imagined that a vicar's wife would speak so."

"Just as you never imagined that your lover has suggested you played a part in his wife's death."

"He would not do that!"

"No? Listen to what he told Sir Neville."

The young woman's face grew pale, then a sickish gray, as Priscilla repeated what Neville had told her. She pushed past Priscilla and threw open the door.

"Wait!" called Priscilla.

Miss Baldwin did not heed her. She stormed into the ballroom and right to where Lord Eastbridge still argued with Lady Symmington.

"How dare you!" Miss Baldwin slapped the earl's face so hard that the sound echoed throughout the room. "How dare you accuse me of killing your wife! You know I was with you when she died!"

Lord Eastbridge's scowl matched the anger in his voice when he snarled an oath before saying, "Remember your place, chit!"

"Don't call me that!"

"Would you rather I called you what you truly are? A pug-nasty doxy!"

"That is not exactly true." Neville's voice from a doorway halted Miss Baldwin's retort.

Uncertain applause met Neville's entrance into the hall over which he was supposed to rule. He was dressed in a bright red cape and silver breeches that caught the glow from the candles overhead. A crown that was painted gold and glittering with paste gems was perched on his black hair.

Looking neither left nor right, he walked directly to where Priscilla stood. He offered his hand, and she put hers on top of it as if he truly were a great king.

He led her to where the earl, the baroness, and Miss Baldwin were staring in silent shock. He bowed his head toward the baroness. "Lady Symmington, I stand before you as your Lord of Misrule."

"Y-y-yes, I can see that," Lady Symmington replied.

"Eastbridge," Neville said with the slightest nod, then he turned to Miss Baldwin. "And you, fair shepherdess, shall be in great trouble once Mimi discovers you have stolen that costume. It was her favorite amongst all her performances in Covent Garden. Were you her dresser before you decided to seek a change in your fortunes?"

"I don't know what you are talking about," Miss Baldwin said primly.

Priscilla caught the young woman's gaze. "It might be easier later if you tell the truth now. It is simple enough to check with Mimi about your costume."

Sweat beaded on Miss Baldwin's forehead, then she said, "All right. I did take it from the theater, but what choice did I have? If I wanted to get a role on stage, I would have to sleep with the theater manager. If I had to sell myself, why not to a man who could offer me more than a tumble behind discarded sets in a dirty theater?" She raised her chin with pride. "And I have proven that I am a great actress, because no one else doubted me. Not this old lusty goat, and not his wife."

Lord Eastbridge began to bluster at her insult, but Neville cut him off by saying, "Now that you have been honest about that, Miss Baldwin, or whatever your true name is . . ."

"My true name is Annalee Baldwin. Why change it when nobody knew it?"

"Now that she has been honest about that," Neville said with a cool smile, "I can be honest as well. Miss Baldwin did not kill Lady Eastbridge." Neville turned, his flamboyant cape swirling around him, to look at the guests who were watching in disbelief.

"Then who did?" demanded Lord Eastbridge.

"That *is* the question, is it not?" His gaze caught and held each person's in the ballroom. Lastly, he looked at Priscilla. He smiled, but his expression grew grim as he continued, "When clues began to point to Lady Eastbridge's death not being a natural one, everyone assumed that the clues would point to the murderer."

"What else?" asked Duncan, as he walked toward the center of the ballroom.

"What else indeed?" Neville's smile grew as cold as the wind battering the windows. "That is what I asked myself. Who had the best motive and an opportunity to kill Lady Eastbridge?" He looked at the Symmingtons. "It was quickly established that Lady Symmington and the countess were in the midst of a brangle when the countess's abigail last saw Lady Eastbridge alive. Lady Symmington usurped the countess by claiming Twelfth Night for her own ball. Was the countess threatening to spirit Lady Symmington's guests away and take them to her own house for her traditional celebration? Was that reason enough for Lady Symmington to strike the fatal blow?"

The baroness shook her head vehemently. "No! I did not do any injury to the countess! She was alive when I left her rooms." Raising her hand, she pointed a quivering finger at Miss Baldwin. "You should talk to *that* woman! If Lord Eastbridge suspects her, then there must be a reason."

"Yes, there is a reason, and it already is quite public knowledge. And, my lady, I know you did not slay Lady Eastbridge. Not you or Miss Baldwin." He glanced up at the gallery. "Come forward."

Priscilla watched as two forms draped in heavy capes walked out of the shadows and close to the railing that circled the room. The shorter one threw back his hood, she heard Lady Symmington gasp in shock. But Priscilla did not recognize the man. He had his hand on the arm of the other caped figure. Was he trying to keep the other person from fleeing?

"Allow me," Neville said, "to introduce you to Mr. Grove, the parish's coroner. Mr. Grove, would you like to introduce your companion? Mayhap then they will understand why I say neither of these ladies—nor anyone else in this house or Lord Eastbridge's—killed the countess."

The coroner nodded. He drew back the other person's hood to reveal a familiar face.

It was Lady Eastbridge!

"Aha!" she called in a shrill voice. "I am still the premier lady of Twelfth Night. The *Lady* of Misrule! Who else would have faked her own death to pop out during the celebrations? My pranks are still the very best, whether the party is at my house or at this upstart baroness's house."

As the countess kept lauding herself, Priscilla heard one thud, then a second, and a third. She whirled to see the earl and his former lover sprawled on the floor, senseless in a swoon. Beside them, Lady Symmington lay.

"Your idea?" Priscilla asked as she stepped over the baroness's prone form to reach Neville.

"Partly. When I encountered Grove on my way to the ballroom, he suggested a public exposure of the lies. I am sorry to be delayed." He grinned and took her hands. "I will explain later. For now, I want to keep that promise I made to you, sweetheart. Let us retire from these Twelfth Night celebrations."

She started to agree, but halted when a wild shriek came from the gallery. Looking up, she saw Lady Eastbridge's face was taut with fury. The countess's eyes were focused beyond Priscilla.

Glancing over her shoulder, Priscilla saw that Lord Eastbridge had regained consciousness. But, apparently, not his senses, because he was kneeling over Miss Baldwin and chafing her wrists while he cried, "My dear Annalee! My dear Annalee! I forgive you. Come back to me. Please come back to me."

Another scream came from the gallery, and the countess fell to her knees, sobbing.

THE CHILDREN WERE tucked into their beds and asleep while Priscilla stretched out on the settee. She leaned back across Neville's lap, his arm cradling her. That allowed her to watch the flames on the hearth, the snow drifting past the windows, and Neville's face. She paid little attention to the fire or the storm.

"Is it a crime to fake one's death?" Priscilla asked.

"Not that I know of, but in the wake of what happened in the ballroom, I suspect she will be deemed insane, driven there by her husband's infidelities."

"But it was obvious she had no idea that her husband was having an *affaire* with her companion. I wish Jeannette had let me in to speak with the countess."

"Jeannette is not without blame, for she clearly helped the countess from the beginning."

Priscilla nodded. "I asked her about the bloody dress, and she avoided giving me a direct answer. I have a feeling that she arranged for Isaac to go into the dovecote to find it. She will not own to that, of course."

"Of course, because she knows that her punishment would be more severe than the countess's." He ran a finger along his chin. "Pris, I think she has an *amour* for the earl—or at least the earl's prestige—as well. Too often she 'arranged' for Eastbridge and Miss Baldwin to be interrupted at a most inopportune time."

"That is for them to work out. What do you think will happen to Lady Eastbridge?"

"As a woman of her rank, she will not be sent to Bedlam. I would guess, rather, a mad nurse will be secured for her, and she will be imprisoned in a wing of her own home."

Priscilla sighed as she sat up and clasped her hands around her knee. "To think this all was caused by her desire to be the hostess of a Twelfth Night masquerade."

"If she had spoken calmly with Lady Symmington—"

"No, Neville, do not excuse the Symmingtons. They knew what they were doing when they usurped Lady Eastbridge's traditional claim to the Twelfth Night ball. I fear there are more villains than victims in this muddle."

He tilted her face closer to his. "Enough of this, Pris. I have not had the chance to give you your Twelfth Night gift."

"Nor I to give you the one I have for you."

He stood and held out his hand. "Shall we find some place far less public to exchange the sweetest gift of all?"

"No tricks?"

"Maybe a few." His eyes twinkled rakishly as he drew her closer. His lips lowered toward hers, and in the moment before they melded in the heat of their yearning, he whispered, "But I can promise you that you will enjoy them."

The End

Dedication

For *The Lord of Misrule*

To Bill—let's always celebrate each day together like it was Christmas

A Delicate Footing

by

Karen Frisch

Chapter One

SOPHRONIA TEMPLETON shivered despite being bundled in her warmest pelisse. In the thin light of waning afternoon, her clothing failed to keep the chill of winter at bay. Sophy contemplated her skates doubtfully. Had it really been three years since she last skated?

"Come join us, Aunt Sophy!" Sensing her hesitation, eleven-year-old Susannah executed a graceful twirl as if it were as natural as breathing. "It isn't cold once you're moving."

The sight of her nieces and nephews gliding across the glistening ice and the enchanting lilt of their laughter proved irresistible. Sophy lowered herself onto the log positioned beside her family's pond, certain her feet had grown. She squeezed the toes of her shoes between the skate's wide leather straps and thick rosewood soles, careful to avoid the high, curled wrought iron prow blades that protruded from underneath.

"I was once quite adept at figure eights," she assured Susannah and young Emily as she inched tentatively onto the ice, "but you're all so skilled I daresay you've surpassed me in my absence."

Taking care to avoid Teddy as he grabbed the tail of Jonathan's coat and held on for the ride, Sophy struggled to find her footing. She laughed, along with the children, at her own awkward stiffness, their encouragement restoring her confidence until she was able to skate nearly as well as she remembered from childhood winters. She felt so lighthearted she began to spin in tandem with Susannah, easing herself into the routine and closing her eyes for the briefest of moments.

When she opened them she was startled to see a newcomer's familiar face flash before her. Suddenly self-conscious, she knew the spell was broken as she realized she and the children were no longer alone. A visitor stood casually on the banks of the pond, watching with a smile. For a second she forgot where she was, as if the years had fallen away and returned her to her youth.

Sophy failed to comprehend words in the jumble of exclamations that issued from the children, but the alarm in their voices was unmistakable. She glanced forward in time to see a jagged fallen branch looming before her at the pond's edge. She was not in time to avoid tripping over it, or to keep Teddy, the youngest who followed at her heels, from toppling over her.

The severe pain stunned her momentarily, making events immediately afterward a blur, yet she knew at once the thin ice at the edge of the pond had not cracked with as much force as her ankle had when she landed upon it and heard it crunch beneath her. As Teddy jumped to his feet and the children gathered about her, she quickly reassured them she was fine, despite her doubts. It was when she struggled to sit upright and regain her balance in spite of the shooting pain that she noticed the visitor approaching her. He bent slowly beside her, taking her hand.

"Might I offer some assistance, my dear Sophy?"

The agonizing pain was forgotten as the words penetrated her consciousness. She knew the smooth cadence of his voice even though she hadn't heard it in years. Turning, she found her face inches from the gentleman's whose countenance displayed deep concern as his woolen greatcoat brushed her cheek.

His presence here startled her, dissolving the distance between them and melting the years away. Emotions struggled within her before her composure won out. He must not see her looking such a complete romp after taking such an awkward spill.

"Jeremy," she managed, fighting to keep her emotions at bay while shifting her weight. "I didn't expect to see you here, and certainly not from this position. Children, this is Captain St. Laurent."

"I'd advise you not to move more than necessary until the doctor sees you," he urged in a gentle tone. "Are you able to rise? You fell so hard I shouldn't be surprised if the pain is excruciating."

Focused more on embarrassment than pain, Sophy attempted to slide her ankles under her as pain sliced through one leg and took her breath away. Jeremy laid a gloved hand on her calf, instructing her to remain still. Even through her thick cloak she felt his powerful grip steadying her.

Childish, gasping sobs startled her back to the present. "It's my fault," cried her nephew Teddy, tears streaming down his cheek. "If I hadn't fallen on you you'd be up by now."

"Nonsense, Teddy," she said gently, trying to numb the hurt so as not to frighten him more. "Soon enough I'll be back on the ice trying to keep up with you. You shall see."

"Perhaps not this season, however," Jeremy cautioned quietly. "I saw enough of this type of injury in Spain to suspect you won't be skating for some time."

Ignoring his unwelcome diagnosis, Sophy declined to be carried, fearing it would be altogether too awkward considering Jeremy's arms were the only means of transportation available to her. She was relieved when he agreed he also felt it unwise. Instead she waited by the pond, shivering, until a pair of strong and trusted servants lifted her onto a litter and carried her to her room while the doctor was summoned.

The results of Doctor Evans's examination two hours later dismayed her, for he concurred with Jeremy's assessment of her condition. By that time Jeremy St. Laurent had disappeared. Standing anxiously by in her room were her mother, her brother Barclay and, of course, Teddy.

"Barely home a week," Barclay exclaimed, laying his hand on her shoulder, "and look what you've done to yourself."

"She certainly has done some damage," Doctor Evans agreed. "This ankle has suffered a severe sprain."

Leaning against the headboard of the bed, Sophy relaxed with relief. "That is fortunate indeed, for if it is only a sprain, I should be well enough to travel again after Christmas."

"I wouldn't expect to go anywhere for some time," the doctor cautioned. "I've seen some disastrous sprains in my day that have resulted in excruciating and prolonged pain. Mind, I'm not saying that is the case in these circumstances, but I would judge your present pain to be quite severe if you can barely stand. Am I correct?"

Under the covers her ankle throbbed so that Sophy had to grit her teeth before she was able to grunt in answer.

"I thought so." The doctor sighed. "This will probably leave you at a severe disadvantage for much of the holiday season, I'm afraid. But as you have family and servants here to help, your recovery should be relatively comfortable. Under the circumstances, I don't think travel is advisable. I doubt very much this ankle will be completely healed for some time."

Sophy felt the color drain from her face. His words made her feel much worse than when she'd first fallen. "But I have plans to sail to America toward the end of January. I've been engaged in missionary work there for the past two years. I teach with Reverend Bixby's team, and they are anticipating my return."

Doctor Evans smiled thinly. "I'm afraid they must make do until you are well enough to walk."

Sophy sat still, scarcely able to believe her ears. "How soon do you think that will be?"

The doctor shrugged as he packed his bag. "I don't believe the ankle is broken. It is entirely dependent upon how the ankle feels. Judging from the pain you're experiencing, however, I would expect your recuperation period to require a minimum of two months."

The shock took Sophy's breath away. "Two months! I couldn't

possibly consider remaining in bed all that time. I'll simply have to limp along using a walking stick."

"You won't be in bed the entire time, but I'm afraid you'll have to wait until you're completely healed before traveling. Walking on this ankle before it's ready might result in a setback that could cost you dearly." Doctor Evans paused as he watched her reaction, concern in his eyes. "Instead of complaining, Miss Templeton, I would suggest you count your blessings. When I see the condition in which some of our soldiers return to us—"

He shook his head, unwilling to continue. Sophy stared at him, challenging him to explain.

Finally, he relented and said, "Let me just say you could have faced dangers far worse. Had you shattered your ankle rather than twisting it and infection set in, you might have lost the foot were we forced to amputate." He stared at her over his glasses. "With a bit of rest and time, you shall be ice skating with your nieces and nephews again before we've seen the last of winter this year."

Trying to absorb the disastrous news, Sophy was too upset to speak as Doctor Evans discussed her care with her mother. She heard him recommend that she stay off the ankle for at least a week or two, depending on her progress, before testing it for strength. Fighting back tears at her misfortune, she could hardly believe such a thing had happened, until she remembered seeing Jeremy St. Laurent standing at the pond's edge. Her thoughts darkened at the memory.

"Don't let this put you in the dismals, Soph," Barclay advised, sitting beside her. "Once this heals you'll still have your leg, unlike Harry. Maybe crutches will get you back on your feet sooner. Harry's become skilled at using them."

Sophy sat back, brooding in silence. She chided herself for behaving so selfishly when her older brother had lost his lower leg below the knee. Hers would heal, but it would require time. Time she did not have, she worried.

"Be glad, my young woman, that you did not break your femur," Doctor Evans advised, closing his bag. "In time, when your ankle starts to feel better, you might find you need to use a cane or walking stick for a time."

Standing beside the bed, Teddy reached for her hand with a quivering sob. Sophy pulled the child closer, inviting him to huddle together in the bed with her in order to comfort herself as much as to ease his guilt.

"I would encourage you," the doctor warned, his tone more ominous than she liked, "to stay off that foot as much as possible so the ankle can heal properly. And I warn you, even if you do stay off it, walking might not be the same for quite some time."

Alarm surged through her. "Are you saying I might never walk again?"

"You'll likely walk again, but there is a strong possibility that it will be with great difficulty and might involve some pain for awhile. Remember, none of these are certainties. You can hasten your recovery better than anyone by heeding my advice."

"But it is only a sprain," Sophy objected faintly.

"Severe sprains can be quite debilitating. It takes surprisingly little to leave one incapacitated for long periods." Doctor Evans's serious tone silenced Sophy. His sternness warmed to affection as he reached for Teddy, tousling his hair. "You watch yourself on that ice so you can take care of your aunt. Don't you slip, too."

Even as her alarm subsided a sense of dread lingered. Her return to America was a mere month away. What if she were unable to resume her duties by then? She thought of the children on the edge of the Missouri frontier. Without her, they would have no one to teach them.

Worse, Sophy had promised the ministry she would return for another session. She had been raised to keep her word. She felt not only a deep commitment to the Mission Society but an obligation to fulfill her obligations to them.

She swallowed, forcing a smile as she glanced down at Teddy curled up beside her. She tried to put her fears aside so he would not notice her worry and blame it on himself.

"That's good advice, Teddy," she said quietly, hugging him close to her. "Don't follow Aunt Sophy's example."

Even if she took the doctor's advice and stayed off her feet, it might not be possible for her to return to teaching, as she had planned. Her mission work meant she often had to walk miles between pioneer settlements where she taught the children of traders and fur trappers, whose families generally traveled westward into areas where no churches or schools had been built.

Her heart sank as she contemplated what they would do without her. The British Mission Society depended upon her not only for her teaching skills but for her courage and physical strength. Reverend Bixby and his team would find it difficult without her.

She was aware of Teddy gazing up at her with solemn eyes, as if his world were about to collapse without her forgiveness. "I'm sorry, Aunt Sophy," he lisped, his childlike guilt breaking her heart. "I didn't mean to make you fall. I feel bad."

"It isn't your fault, my pet," she assured him softly, slipping her arm about his small shoulders and drawing him closer.

It's that man's, she thought irritably. The image of Jeremy St. Laurent standing beside the pond remained stubbornly in her thoughts, refusing to leave.

Her throat constricted with acceptance of her plight, but she managed to bid Doctor Evans farewell as her mother promised to ensure her daughter heeded his advice. Her mother and Teddy remained after he departed with Barclay leading the way. Tears pricked behind her eyes, but she held them at bay until her mother offered a sweet from her pocket in exchange for Teddy's agreement to play with his sister. Tears fell openly as her mother seated herself on the edge of the bed after Teddy left.

"Why? How could this happen?" Sophy burst out between sobs. "For a mere moment of pleasure the payment is weeks of recuperation."

"It does indeed seem a rather steep price," her mother commiserated softly, "but most likely it won't be months. Rather than running back to your responsibilities, mayhap this is a sign that it is time for you to pause and savor your blessings."

Sophy reached for the lace handkerchief on her nightstand and blew her nose noisily, comforted by her mother's presence. She had forgotten how uplifting Mama could be under the worst of circumstances and wished she could be more like her. Sylvan, the family's spaniel, made his way toward the bed, wagging his tail at her sniffling in an effort to comfort her. She reached down to pat his head absently.

"What do you mean?" Sophy took a deep breath as her mother's steady hand stroked her back and smoothed her long dark curls.

"I know how much your work means to you," her mother said, "and Reverend Bixby will miss you sorely, I am sure. But your family has missed you as well, especially the children. This is the time you belong here with us. 'Tis Christmas after all."

"And I am here." Irritated by her mother's obvious remark, she prepared to defend herself against the expected criticism.

"Yes, you are here for a matter of weeks before you are off again to a foreign land far from your family. Jonathan and Susannah recognized you, but Teddy and Emily were little when you left. They knew you only because you were the one they didn't recognize. You are the aunt they barely remember."

Her mother's tone was patient, but Sophy heard a weariness in it that gave her a twinge of guilt. Before she could voice her objections, her mother startled her by guessing her thoughts.

"I understand you are grown now, and I know how you love to travel and share your excitement at discovering new places," her mother continued, a smile wavering on her lips. "Yet you are my one and only daughter and my youngest. You and your brothers were always competitive as children. You are still competing with them. They finished their travels years ago, yet you want to travel more than they ever did."

Sophy did not resist when her mother took her hand firmly. Her mother's grip was still strong.

"But you know my travels have purpose and meaning to them," Sophy protested.

"A most important purpose. But so much travel for a proper young lady is unseemly, even in the name of religion. And now that Mrs. Amesbury has passed on, it is hardly appropriate for you to return without a chaperone," her mother reminded her gently. "I daresay the American wilderness is no place for a young woman like yourself who has reached her childbearing years. Your letters worried me so with their descriptions of the Indian wars."

Sophy grimaced but refrained from criticizing her brother. She had written Barclay in confidence about the Indian raids upon the villages where she had stayed, a confidence not intended for her mother's ears.

"Poor Mrs. Amesbury," her mother continued with a polite shudder. "I suppose she was lucky it was her heart and not Indians that killed her."

"The raids are done, Mama," Sophy protested. "Missouri signed a treaty to put an end to them. It's a much more civilized place now, one that's growing. There is a great need for someone to teach the children. You always told us charity was important."

"And it is, child," her mother agreed, laying a tender but firm hand on hers. "But you have done your share, and the children of countless families have benefited from your efforts."

Persistent twinges of pain in Sophy's ankle reminded her that the doctor had not exaggerated the need for rest. "Then you see how important it is that I return so I may continue."

"Perhaps the Lord has decided it is time you learn a lesson. Try to look upon this as a sign from above, to listen rather than speak. Maybe you are meant to stay home for a change."

Suggesting her daughter get some sleep, she squeezed Sophy's hand a final time before she extinguished the lamp and let herself from the room quietly.

Sophy was saved the struggle of having to quiet her fears long enough to nod off. Sleep lost its chance to overtake her with the return of her brother Barclay, who slipped into her room while looking furtively over his shoulder to make sure their mother was not listening. When he was satisfied they would be alone, he closed the door behind him, lit the lamp by the door, and came to sit beside her. He perched at the foot of her bed like a pesky crow they used to chase from the moors where they played as children.

"I know you feel as Mother does, but don't sit near my foot," Sophy warned crossly, turning over and sitting up in bed.

"You'll have plenty of time to rest the foot. It's not as if you're going anywhere. I'll keep you home any way I can, Soph." Barclay gave her a smile as he moved to a chair. "It's so deuced good to have you back at Deervale Hall where you belong. It's about time you got over this wander-lust and stayed put for awhile."

"It isn't by choice, Bark." Trying to keep her voice steady, Sophy changed the subject. "I didn't expect to see Viscount Cobleigh at the pond. 'Twas the sight of him that made me fall. You might have told me you were planning a house party."

Had he told her he'd invited Jeremy for the holidays, she thought darkly, she might have departed early.

"I intended to, you know. I didn't get to tell you St. Laurent was com-ing until it was too late," he lamented. "I'd no idea he would go directly to the pond. He'll be joining the other fellows I've invited that I told you about. Two arrived this afternoon, one with his sister, and the last comes this evening."

The awkward apology hung in the air between them. It made perfect sense to Sophy that Jeremy St. Laurent would return to the pond. It had been the setting of many of their most precious childhood memories.

Her initial reaction was anger toward Barclay for inviting him. It was no wonder he had not asked her opinion. He knew she would reject the idea of including Jeremy in their holiday plans. The pain in her ankle being more than enough to contend with, Sophy decided not to discuss her resentment toward the viscount with her brother. Jeremy had made his choices years before and would have to abide by them.

"It might have been better had I known," she said simply. "With an impediment such as this, it's difficult to have callers."

"St. Laurent called here briefly on his way home to Cheshire for a short visit with his father," Barclay explained, "though he shall return to us for the holidays. He only waited to hear the doctor's assessment of your condition before setting off."

Her dismay at the idea of Jeremy's presence with them this holiday must have shown on her face, for he spoke up at once.

"Anyway, there's no need to have a fit of the sullens over this," Barclay said. "Jeremy knows a bit about medicine. You can get his opinion about your foot. Among other things, I understand he delivered babies during the war."

Sophy kept her disappointment to herself until Barclay filled the ensuing silence with attempts at consolation.

"You needn't feel as if you must entertain our guests," he hastened to assure her. "They're tolerable sorts of fellows who will understand. You can simply retire to your room if you don't feel like facing everyone."

"Harry and Jane will think it graceless of me."

"As the oldest brother the weight of responsibility for our family is on his shoulders," Barclay reminded her. "He worries about Mum, who I can tell you is relieved more than you know to have you safely home. She was afraid you'd never come back."

Sophy needed no reminder of her mother's fear of Indian attacks during her American stay. Safe in the Derbyshire hills, her mother often overlooked the importance of her mission work.

"Had I foreseen your accident I wouldn't have invited so many," Barclay admitted. "It's a bit of a crowd, I know."

"We already have a house full of children," Sophy pointed out. "What made you decide we needed anyone else?"

Apparently seeking an answer that would satisfy her, he settled himself comfortably in the chair and put his feet up on the bed, until a warning glance from her made him remove them.

"It's your first time home in six months. You're only here for a few weeks." He shrugged. "I thought it was time you might wish to become acquainted with some gentlemen."

"To what purpose? It isn't as if I intend to remain here. As soon as I am able, I shall be on the next ship back to America."

"If you stayed we'd get to see you more often," he said with a resigned look. "But we all understand you love to travel and see the world."

"Should I not? Harry and Eddie had a chance to go to war, after all. You had your Grand Tour of Europe."

"The war is over," Barclay reminded her, his tone so sharp it surprised her, "and don't tell me it's still going on in America. Their problems are their own now, Soph, not yours. Charity is the same the world over."

She tightened her lips, checking her annoyance. "What are you saying, Bark?"

"I'm saying charitable concerns are fine, admirable even," he conceded, "but you mustn't overlook family. I know how competitive you are. You're used to having brothers rather than sisters. Perhaps that's where the difficulty lies."

Sophy refrained from asking what difficulty he referred to. Her brothers were all accomplished. Rather than emphasize the delicacy of her gender and class, she had attempted to keep pace with Harry, Eddie, and Barclay, even as a child. He rushed on, no doubt expecting her silence might produce an outburst.

"At any rate you've no idea how pleased Mum is to have you home. She's glad I'll finally have a chance to introduce you to a few of my acquaintances over the holidays before you rush off again. This time, of course, you might not," he added awkwardly, "with your recovery in question."

Sophy disregarded his concern. She would find a way to return to America as soon as was physically possible. "Are you saying you've invited them here as potential suitors for me?"

"Where's the harm? You might find one of them to your liking. Isn't it worth a try? We miss you, Soph. It's like old times having you back. And Prindle's brought his sister Arabella with him." He winked. "She's an early present for me. I think you'll like her. Anyway, do your best to get to know them a bit so you'll see what I had in mind, and we shall see what happens."

Chapter Two

BARCLAY'S ADMONITION, combined with the pain in her throbbing ankle, left Sophy unable to sleep. Desperate to believe she would one day walk again as well as she used to, she felt suddenly anxious to be surrounded by her family as if nothing were wrong.

Impulsively, she summoned a pair of servants to bring her downstairs. When they could find no comfortable way to transport her, she demanded they send Barclay back up. Her favorite brother would find a way to allow her to enjoy the conversation.

"Too bad you didn't arrive sooner," he puffed, as he gently carried her step by step down the daunting flight of stairs. "Herbert, Sampson, and Humphrey just retired for the night along with Arabella. Mother knows them fairly well, and Harry and Jane and Eddie and Emma were getting better acquainted with them."

"Just as well," Sophy murmured, feeling sorry for herself all of a sudden. "I want it to be just our family tonight."

As Barclay approached the drawing room with her in his arms conversation ceased abruptly. Sophy suspected she had been the subject of debate. Her mother was perched on the sofa, her smile brittle but her face troubled. Seated before the fire with his stump of a leg stretched out before him, a remnant of the Peninsular War, her oldest brother Harry, flanked by his wife Jane, greeted her with his usual solemnity, a seriousness their children Jonathan and Susannah happily had not inherited. Her middle brother Edward and his wife Emma, parents of Teddy and Emily, the younger pair, greeted her with smiles of encouragement.

"What an absolutely appalling return, and after only a few days," Jane sympathized, shaking her head. "Such a shame to have this happen before the holidays. It will likely ruin your chances of making a suitable match. This would have been an opportune time."

While Sophy gritted her teeth Emma spoke up quickly. "It's most unfortunate, but if I know Sophy she'll make the most of circumstances as she always does. Thank you for being so gracious with Teddy this afternoon," Emma confided to Sophy. "If not for your kindness and understanding he would have been distraught. He's upstairs making a posy for you now."

"Teddy's such a thoughtful child." Sophy smiled. "Whatever will he find to make a posy?"

"Bits of greenery from Cook's quarters, one would imagine." Emma laughed. "Where else could he find them under so much snow?"

One of the reasons she regretted her fall, Sophy reflected, was that she could no longer skate with the children as she wished but instead would be forced to spend time indoors. As familiar and comforting as she found her mother's drawing room, it seemed bare at this time of year without the trimmings of Christmas. Disappointment filled her as she realized she might not be able to help decorate. Her brothers completed the more challenging tasks like hanging the kissing bunch, placing the small presents on it, and arranging the dolls in the manger scene that perched within its boughs. She could hardly do her share if she were hobbling about or, worse, unable to walk at all.

The very idea brought tears to her eyes. While she was happy to be home with all her family assembled under one beloved roof, she had begun to realize this year would be different from the others, for there was less she would be able to do. The thought made her feel like an outsider, a guest who needed to be waited upon hand and foot. It was a thought that was unbearable as her limitations became more real.

"The difficulty with this injury," Sophy said meekly, conscious of the fact that Harry had suffered far more than she, "is that I have no idea how I shall occupy my time. I can no longer skate or walk in the snow or climb the Pennines as we used to. Truth to tell, it's among the things I had hoped to do while I am home."

"Why don't you knit something for the poor?" Jane suggested. "At least it would occupy your hands."

"I don't knit." Sophy felt inadequate and unprepared suddenly, wishing she'd spent less time at play with her brothers as a child and more in learning the domestic arts.

"Never mind," Emma consoled her. "I shall teach you."

"Never worry about Sophy," their mother finished pleasantly, "for we know that mind of hers is always occupied. It is one of the reasons she is so self-sufficient. Besides, the suitors Barclay has invited for the holidays will keep her occupied."

Her mother's words, she discovered, were an early warning as to what she might expect. The next morning she learned precisely what Barclay had in mind. He startled her by arriving in her room soon after she awoke. As soon as she was properly attired, he lifted her in his arms and carried her to the hallway outside her room where he deposited her in a chair against the wall.

"On my way here I was waylaid by our nephews seeking ideas for the day's activities," Barclay told her. "While I tend to that, I shall send you up a surprise."

The words filled Sophy with dread. The surprises she'd had to date hadn't been the kind she wanted. "What kind of surprise?"

"The fellows have rigged up a sedan chair to carry you downstairs so you might enjoy their company. Wait here."

As if she could do anything else, Sophy thought dismally, her ankle throbbing and now the foot as well. Moments later male grunts and exclamations preceded the strains of an awkward struggle on the staircase.

A trio of gentlemen eventually appeared, setting down a creation of fabric and wood before they approached and bowed to her. Having learned of her accident, the suitors Barclay had assembled were most solicitous, expressing sympathy and offering support all at once. She was happy to see they were accompanied by a woman. This must be the Arabella Barclay had mentioned.

"We've brought you a gift," announced the most imposing of the three. "A homemade one, but one that should please you."

Peeking over their shoulders, she was startled to see they had combined their efforts at courtship to create what appeared to be a homemade sedan chair. The contraption alternately dismayed and intrigued her as she eyed it with uncertainty.

"Allow me to introduce myself, my lady." With a sweep of his arm, a thin gentleman before her bowed low and gallantly, revealing an unfortunate bald spot on his pate. "Sampson Hodge, at your service."

"Your brother told us of your most unhappy mishap," another chimed in, pushing the first aside in his eagerness to present himself. "I am Herbert Prindle, a close friend of Barclay's. And this is my sister Arabella."

Sophy offered him a smile, recalling the name from Barclay's forays into London society. Traveling in America had denied her the opportunity to immerse herself in the *ton* as her brothers had done. Clearly Barclay had solved that problem by bringing the *ton* to her.

"I'm charmed to meet you, Miss Templeton," Arabella said in a soft voice that had a charming lilt.

Herbert Prindle took her hand in his briefly before the third stranger, the first of the three who had spoken to her, edged his way in front of the others.

"Allow me to offer my condolences on your most ill-timed accident, Miss Templeton," he sympathized, taking charge of the situation as he lifted her hand in his. "I am Humphrey Fotherington. We decided to arrange for your comfort during your recuperation by providing you transportation so you shan't feel quite so housebound."

"Indeed. What conveyance have we here?" she inquired, forcing pleasantry as she saw the makeshift vehicle for the first time, relieved to hear her brother's footsteps on the stairs.

"It is a unique sedan chair, a one-of-a-kind carriage," Fotherington explained, standing beside the chair and gesturing to it with pride. "We prevailed upon your tenant, Mr. Riggs, to find us a board and the two wooden poles you see here on the outside. As you can see, we padded the board for your comfort and added sides and drapery to your chariot to give you privacy."

"How very thoughtful." Sophy studied the chair with an uneasy smile, trying to imagine how she would gain anything but embarrassment from riding in it. She struggled to find a diplomatic expression of thanks for her potential suitors. "In America where I spent the last two years, the pioneers are exceptionally mobile, walking miles when necessary. Though I appreciate your efforts, and while the chair might be fashionable in Bath or Tunbridge Wells, I fear it might not be entirely suitable for Derbyshire's hills."

"What my sister means to say," Barclay cut in on his return, forcing a smile as he gave her a warning glance, "is that since she is most concerned about her ankle healing properly she would be happy to accept your kind offer of transportation."

"We guarantee a comfortable ride," Sampson Hodge hastened to assure her. "We've taken pains to see to your comfort."

"Someone as light as yourself would be a pleasure to transport," Herbert Prindle concurred, gesturing to the seat. "Would you care to try it?"

"We promise not to drop you," Sampson Hodge said, giving her a mischievous wink.

Sophy glanced up at Barclay in alarm. "Dare I?" she whispered, trying to keep the doubt from her voice.

"Give it a try," he encouraged. "Doctor Evans says it will be awhile before you'll even be able to use crutches. Why not try this as a substitute means of transportation in the meantime?"

"I take it you had a hand in this and shall take charge of directing this arrangement," she said darkly.

Barclay slipped his arm about her waist, supporting her so she was able to keep her weight on the right foot while easing herself into her conveyance. The softness of the cushioning surprised her. The gentlemen had left space enough so her legs could extend outward and lie flat, allowing her to sit in a position that would keep her as comfortable as possible.

Impressed with their efforts, she settled in for a ride that promised to keep her free from pain. Together the men lifted the chair and set off for the staircase. Rather than drag her, she realized with surprise, they appeared intent on carrying her downstairs.

Their strength held up admirably until they angled the sedan chair around the corner. They moved toward the stairs, navigating their way uncertainly, bumping first one wall before striking the other. Enclosed within the surrounding draperies that blocked her view, Sophy felt herself jolted left, then right. The bouncing caused a sudden sharp pain in her ankle before the men paused to discuss various approaches to maneuvering the staircase which was apparently narrower than they expected. Apparently, Sophy reflected crossly, they had not considered the effect of her added weight, slight as she was, when they carried the contrivance upstairs.

"Barclay, if there is a problem, perhaps you might carry me," she suggested from inside her box chamber, struggling to find the elusive opening in the fabric. "I fear this chariot might be less capable of transporting me safely to breakfast than your arms."

Heedless of her discomfort, they continued until an alarming stumbling sound met her ears followed by thumps. The men seemed to have lost their grip as the chair tipped first one way, then the other. It bounced its way down each stair tread, sending her off-kilter and wracking her leg with pain as it went. The ride came to a sudden halt as she felt the conveyance gripped awkwardly by what she assumed were human hands.

"Release me at once!" Sophy fumed, shaking with fear and humiliation. "Let me out!"

She managed to pull the curtains aside to see the gentlemen had set her down on the landing. She was loath to allow them the opportunity to drop her again. Slipping her strong leg from the box, she seized the sleeve of Barclay's coat.

"Would you please carry me downstairs," she instructed, "else I land on my head so that it is more scrambled than the eggs on our breakfast table? I fear before we are done I shall have more limbs severely damaged."

If she had been worried about disappointing her suitors, Barclay informed her, with some irritation, later that day, her callous dismissal of their invention had failed to discourage them. She might, he suggested, be more open to receiving their ministrations since they promised to offer other helpful suggestions.

The gentlemen he had gathered to woo her remained so solicitous of her welfare they took it upon themselves to position themselves at her beck and call throughout the day. There they remained against her wishes.

Tired of finding at least two out of the three waiting to serve her whenever she showed the least interest in becoming mobile, she retreated to the company of her mother that afternoon.

"Haven't we a pair of crutches somewhere that I might try?" she begged. "I would feel more secure if I could ambulate under my own power."

"I believe we have a set you might use, but I think you might appreciate the efforts of our guests a bit more," her mother remonstrated gently. Closing her book, she gave Sophy a tender smile. "Before you returned from America, Barclay gave a great deal of thought as to whom to invite to share the holidays this year. He was only thinking of your future happiness."

"But I am happy now," Sophy insisted, "or I was until this accident."

Her mother gave her a bemused half-smile. "I am glad to know it," she replied, a look of serenity returning to her face, "for it is sometimes difficult to judge from your behavior whether you are truly happy. Your injury will heal in time and you shall be restored to full health, but in the meantime you must learn to be patient. Shall I find you something to read to help pass the time?"

Sophy puzzled over her remark as her mother set her book aside and rose to peruse the shelves, searching for a selection that would please her. For the moment, Sophy decided, she was content to remain with her mother in the library, away from the helpful ministrations of her suitors.

It was in the library where Barclay found her the following evening, reading a book with her leg stretched out on the chaise. Since he was alone she decided his gentlemen friends must be occupied in pursuits other than her.

"I wondered where you'd disappeared to." Barclay closed the door quietly behind him. "Hiding from everyone, are you?"

"Not especially. Just trying to fill the time until my ankle heals and I can leave for America once again."

"It's not so bad." Barclay shrugged. "If you'd been at war you'd have been sent home anyway. And defending our nation is far more important than teaching Indians."

"But I wasn't in the war," she retorted. "I was simply skating. The only war I'm fighting is against this army of unsuitable suitors you've assembled."

Barclay studied her dress critically. "You aren't wearing that in their presence, are you? You're supposed to impress them, not convince them you're a country dowd."

"Would it matter? It's obvious none of them goes to Beau Brummel's tailor. Mr. Hodge is so skinny he doesn't look like any Sampson I know. And while Mr. Prindle barely says a word, Mr. Fotherington says far too much. When will you admit we aren't well matched?"

Sophy shook her head, amused in spite of herself, as she continued, "I felt like hiding after I spilled juice down the front of my dress this morning while trying to manage a crutch. Mr. Hodge didn't seem to mind. He came to breakfast prepared to tell me how beautiful I looked, and he fulfilled his mission despite the juice." She pulled a face. "And later, when I dropped the book I was reading, all three men rushed to retrieve it for me."

"You have to admit they're helpful sorts. I hope you don't read so much you scare them away," Barclay cautioned, glancing at the book in her hand. "They'll think you're a bluestocking."

"Sometimes you try too hard to make me happy. Oh, I do miss our talks." Sophy closed her book, happy for the company after reading for the last hour. "Come, sit and join me. The tea is still warm if you wish to have some."

Barclay shook his head. "Thanks, but I prefer something a bit stronger. I'll join you, though, if I might."

"By all means." Sophy watched him make his way to the sideboard. "Were you searching for me or the brandy?"

He dropped into the chair opposite, brandy in hand, his shoulders slumping. "I hope I'm not the only one searching for you. I don't want your obvious indifference to discourage Herbert or Sampson. I doubt it will scare off Fotherington."

Sophy opened her book again, seeking refuge in its pages. "They're grown men, Bark, probably experienced with women if not terribly worldly. I'm sure they've dealt with rejection."

She was startled when he ripped the book from her hands and tossed it aside where she was unable to reach it without hobbling to the spot where it landed. She looked at him in annoyance.

"In case through some complete lack of perception on your part you don't already know, our mother is most desperate to see you wed, and soon. Harry is as well because Mother wants it." Barclay slouched lower in the chair, looking more tired than annoyed. "I've done my best, Soph. I've given you three good men to choose from, and you've all but rejected them outright."

"You've given me three graceless buffoons," she returned. "One dropped me on the stairs in an accident that could have injured me again. Another is either half-witted or blind if he thinks I look lovely with juice all down my dress. And the last is full of himself."

"Herbert is a bit clumsy, but he had your comfort at heart. Sampson was simply being polite, which is more than you've been to him. And if Humphrey is full of himself, he has reason to be. He never has pockets to let. He's a marquess, and you would do dashed well to consider him." Barclay turned away, his face set as if he were unable to think more about the subject. "It's the best I can do at present. All the snow is keeping people away."

To shake off his reprimand Sophy gazed out the bay window at the softly falling snow beyond. She had always found snowfall quite magical and regretted not being able to walk in it, preferably alone.

"Don't discount them so easily, Sophy. They want to prove themselves worthy of you. Give them a chance." When she didn't reply Barclay sighed. "If nothing else, Jeremy St. Laurent arrives back later tomorrow. I know that probably is no consolation to you."

She felt her insides tighten. "I suppose he's bringing his family," she said, trying to sound casual rather than sarcastic.

Barclay gave her a puzzled look. "He has only his father, and as he's quite infirm now, it's doubtful he'll come."

"I meant his wife and child."

Sophy stared as his expression turned solemn.

"His wife and child died during the war. His son expired days after his birth, and his wife was killed by enemy fire."

Sophy's heart skipped a beat before guilt and remorse flooded over her. She felt the heat rise in her cheeks. She cringed to think she harbored such resentment while Jeremy had suffered. The realization shamed her into silence.

"I thought you knew." Seeing the expression on her face, Barclay muttered, "But then how could you? You've been in America so long you're out of touch."

"When did it happen?" Her heart still pounded uncontrollably as her shock began to subside. Sorrow mixed with a curious relief that filled her with guilt.

"Three years, perhaps. He never speaks of it." He shrugged. "It was common enough for soldiers abroad to partner the ladies. I imagine that's how their union came about."

"Oh." Trying to absorb conflicting emotions, she closed the subject. How terrible to lose a child under any circumstances, but especially those Jeremy had endured.

That was the cost of war, she told herself, trying to dismiss him from her thoughts. One could not expect otherwise. It was far better to devote oneself to charitable and philosophical causes, where one was not vulnerable to the pain of such loss but instead open to inspiration and true devotion.

"I'm going up to bed," she announced. "Wait—no, I can't."

With dismay she realized she would have to summon the servants to carry her upstairs on the stretcher they had made.

"Come," Barclay offered, "I'll carry you in my arms."

He set his brandy aside with a thud, the effects of his indulgence throughout the evening obvious in his tired eyes and in a slight slurring of his speech.

"C'mon, I'll carry you up over the threshold to your room. Someone might as well put you to bed." Her brow darkened as he muttered, "I might be the only man who ever has the chance."

It was fortunate Sophy stayed long abed the following day, for she was not the only family member forced to spend the day indoors. Upon waking she realized from the bright crystal coating on her window that snow had fallen steadily overnight. She passed the remainder of the morning in the playroom with her nieces and nephews, turning it into a makeshift classroom as she shared her experiences in the New World. She found an opportunity to relive her experiences abroad as she explained to them that the natives were not as savage as those on the Continent believed.

Her lesson was interrupted by the arrival of her sister-in-law. Jane stood frowning in the doorway, having overheard part of her discussion with the children.

"Really, Sophy," Jane remonstrated, "can't you try to enjoy our company a bit more in the short time you're here? I know you haven't felt up to snuff lately, but we've hardly seen you. This isn't the time for such talk. The children are on holiday."

"I was giving them a bit of a geography lesson." Sophy smiled, knowing Harry's wife was likely to disapprove. "And I'm happier than you know to be home again, even if I'm not as demonstrative as you might wish."

"The children have a governess," Jane reminded her. "We'd rather not fill their heads with dreams of going abroad as soon as they are able. I need to borrow them so they might help select the ribbons the men will use to pull in the yule log Christmas Eve before we set it alight. What do you think, children?"

Sophy shared in their exclamations of joy as the children ran from the room ahead of Jane. She remembered reacting just as they had when it came to honoring the same holiday traditions.

Warm thoughts of Christmases past lifted her spirits. While reluctant to give Barclay the satisfaction, she decided it would be more respectful in this season of generosity to open her mind as well as her heart. Remembering how much she valued being able to spend time with Barclay, Eddie, and Harry, she vowed, as she engaged in conversation with the gentlemen throughout the day, to keep an open mind and get to know them better. She would give each his chance, as Barclay wished.

Since she was limited physically and had little choice of outdoor activity, she devoted time to each in turn. She listened politely to their prattle as they sat by the drawing room hearth, expressing curiosity about their collective pursuits. She feigned interest as Herbert Prindle described the thrill of fox-hunting, unable to keep her mind from wandering to the natives in America who took an animal's life only for sustenance and would find the idea of fox-hunting repulsive and wasteful.

She managed to smile as Sampson Hodge, small and skinny with a horse face and uneven teeth, spoke of his favorite amusements. While he bragged of his winnings from wagering at Watier's, she thought of the colonists' skill at bartering with the natives for provisions they needed.

She pretended admiration when Humphrey Fotherington described his pride and talent for selecting a crack team and carriage at Tattersall's, her thoughts returning to the Missouri frontier where horses had a more critical purpose than satisfying the whims of the wealthy.

At least Sophy had the consolation of Arabella's company. She never felt the need to impress Herbert's sweet and charming sister, for her intentions seemed honorable and her motives innocent. The only inconvenience was that Barclay continually stole Arabella away for conversation, leaving Sophy with the pair whose company she admittedly did not find as stimulating.

By the end of the day their behavior had not changed Sophy's mind. The men Barclay deemed appropriate seemed pompous and full of conceit, with breeding the only common thread they shared with her. Nor would she fit their version of the ideal female, she suspected, once they got to know her. She felt guilty avoiding conversation with the very men whose attention she should be seeking, for it would disappoint her family and sabotage her future if she ultimately rejected them.

"I'm sorry, Barclay," she told him earnestly at day's end. "I am certain these men are wonderful friends. But they do not appeal to me as potential husbands. Please don't misinterpret my words, but I suppose it's because they are all like you. And there is only one of you. At any rate, you know it has always been my intention to return abroad once my ankle has healed. Last month I wrote and asked the British Mission Society to find me a suitable chaperone now that Mrs. Amesbury is no longer with us."

"You have a deuced admirable way of looking at death. Well," Barclay sighed, "if that's how you truly feel I shan't stop you. I hoped having my friends here might convince you to assume the lady's life you were born for rather than live out a lingering childhood. I don't mean to be cruel. There's no one I adore as much as you, Soph, but I'd prefer to see you with an easier life."

"Thank you, Bark, but I'm happy with my choice," she insisted, leaning back against the drawing room sofa pillows.

"Still, it's a shame we shan't see you more often. If that's how it is with you then, I'm off to court Arabella. Perhaps I might make a match with Prindle's sister. I'll be dashed if I have to deal with competition from Hodge and Fotherington. You aren't the only female here, you know."

Sophy had hardly recovered from Barclay's words when Harry, their oldest brother, appeared in the doorway, his eyes burning.

"How dare you spoil our celebration with such talk?" he demanded. "How can you think of crossing the ocean with the holidays so close? I would advise you to keep such words from our mother."

"Harry, be reasonable," Sophy pleaded. "Mother understands how important my mission work is to me."

"Have you so little consideration for her when she has only your welfare at heart? You've no idea how sorely she has missed you or how deeply she fears for your safety. I strongly urge you to consider Barclay's suggestion and choose one of the men who so graciously joined us this year specifically to court you."

Sophy was stung by his blunt speech. Even Barclay had no reply. Embarrassed into silence, she had no choice but to listen.

"Mother won't say it, but I will," Harry continued boldly. "You owe it to your family to assume a more traditional role and fulfill your familial duties. At twenty-four, Sophy, you're already on the shelf. Who knows what damage you might already have done to your reputation? You should consider yourself fortunate, by God, that Barclay has been able to find men who would consider marriage with you."

Sophy flushed at the harsh words. With Harry the head of the household since their father's death, she could not disregard his wishes. Her ankle injury had upset her so deeply she had thought of no one but herself and the children this holiday season. Harry's disappointment sobered her, adding another layer to what already promised to be a darker season than usual.

And yet, she reminded herself, brighter times waited across the ocean, if only her ankle would heal before her ship sailed.

Chapter Three

THE SUBDUED MOOD of the residents in the house had little effect on Jeremy St. Laurent, Viscount Cobleigh, when he arrived late the following day. If life at Deervale Hall were more somber than usual, he would not have noticed. His life was quiet and well-ordered from one day to the next now that the war had ended, with little variation in his routine even around the holidays.

Business affairs and social concerns had kept him in London until very recently. Yet he could not accept Harry's invitation without first returning home to Cobleton to see to his father's comfort and ensure his well-being. Having accomplished that, he set off for Derbyshire with high hopes of enjoying Christmas and New Year's Eve in the company of his oldest and dearest friends.

As his luggage was unloaded and taken upstairs, he surveyed the great hall, familiar joys called back from memory. He remembered playing hide-and-seek with the Templeton brothers on the broad staircase with its carved balusters and mullioned windows. Its many steps somehow encouraged a chase. He wondered if children today did the same. In their younger days, Sophy had always wanted to be part of their games. Concern filled him as he recalled the fragile state of her ankle when he'd left and the anxiety in the depths of her cornflower blue eyes.

Her sorrowful face was pushed to the back of his mind as the merry salutations of Barclay and Eddie reached his ears.

"Jeremy," Barclay greeted him, embracing him heartily. "Just like old times, with a few more bumps and bruises along the way."

"Good to see you, old fellow," Eddie said warmly. "How's dad these days?"

"Dad never seems to change," Jeremy admitted. "He's stayed the same since his Revolutionary days. He doesn't speak of it, but I suspect he relives battles in his imagination, wondering what he might have done to bring about a different outcome."

"Even your father's brilliant military maneuvers couldn't have done it alone," Barclay scoffed. "No doubt he's pleased this one ended differently, as we all are, thanks in part to your efforts. Wouldn't surprise me if he feels your reputation outshines his."

"It's enough to have the men home again. For those who made it, this holiday will be better than the last." As Jeremy's memories stretched back three years, he tried to repress the painful images from Ciudad Rodrigo and Badajoz that haunted him. The only relief was to change the subject. He glanced from one to the other. "How's Harry coping?"

Their hesitation answered his question. "He hasn't been the same since," Eddie confessed. "Some view amputation as a badge of honor. While his service to the Crown was commendable, I fear he was injured before he could fulfill his own expectations."

"He proved himself but never had a chance to follow through with his command," Jeremy asserted. "He experienced the worst of war without being there at its conclusion. It's unjust. At least he has Jane and the children to see him through the future."

Gripping their shoulders in turn, he changed the subject. "Lady Fairfax greeted me when my carriage arrived. She looks as well as ever. Your mother's a lovely woman, so lovely I might court her myself if she were a few years younger or I older," he admitted. "I look forward to spending the holidays here. I doubt we'll still fit on those sleds, but it might be fun to challenge the Pennines and see who can hike the furthest once I settle in."

"Let's plan on it," Barclay agreed, "though with the gales of late, we'll need to be properly clad or we'll freeze."

"I'll check on your bags," Eddie offered. "Good to see you."

"How's that sister of yours?" Jeremy inquired casually after Eddie had left. "Is she up and ready for a quadrille yet?"

"It'll be awhile before she'll dance." Barclay grimaced. "Doctor isn't sure the leg will ever heal properly. Her greatest worry is being unable to return to America a month from now."

Jeremy attempted to hide his surprise. "It's a wonder she wants to after that spill on the ice. One would think she'd take advantage of the time to recover. She's home with family and has a chance to see her nieces and nephews."

"First time in a long time." Barclay shrugged. "But that's Sophy for you. Always ready to be off to win over the savages. Let's take a walk tomorrow to check out those hills, shall we?"

Jeremy followed his old friend, trying to thrust Sophronia Templeton from his mind. Despite his attempts, being back in Deervale Hall where a new generation of children skated and played brought back a vision of Sophy as a youth, the long brown hair that fell about her shoulders tickling the nose of a sickly calf she cradled in the barn. The innocent faith he remembered seeing on her face that day matched the look he saw recently as she expected her leg to heal fully despite the doctor's warning. He had seen her only briefly after the doctor's visit, but her face reflected a mixture of desperation and determination. Smiling involuntarily, Jeremy suspected he knew which would win out.

He thought back to that night so many years ago. The tender calf had survived worries about its demise, he recalled, and come through its early ordeal to thrive. As had Sophy Templeton.

She had survived the intervening years quite nicely indeed.

SOPHY HERSELF WAS not sure how she would endure the days until Christmas and New Year's were past and their guests would go home. She not only had to contend with the attentions of Herbert Prindle, Sampson Hodge, and Humphrey Fotherington, but now Jeremy St. Laurent as well.

Perhaps she might make good use of the ridiculous sedan chair after all, she decided. Word had reached her of Jeremy's arrival before she retired that night. When he did not appear at breakfast the following morning, she decided to solicit the three other able-bodied gentlemen visitors for assistance with a ride outdoors. In addition to taking advantage of the sunshine and brisk air, she would be away from the house and the risk of seeing Jeremy. She suggested Miss Prindle accompany them.

"It will be an invigorating walk," she warned them, "but that is one of the best things about the Pennines."

While she could not expect to climb while riding in the sedan chair, as she would if she were healthy, a walk through the fields around Deervale Hall might be pleasant, she told them. While the makeshift chariot made her feel too much like an invalid, she tried to feel grateful. Her only consolation was that the curtains made it impossible to identify her from a distance.

As seemed to be customary, Herbert Prindle and Sampson Hodge carried the conveyance while Humphrey Fotherington walked alongside with Arabella Prindle on the other. Fotherington took advantage of the opportunity to become better acquainted with her while Prindle and Hodge spent their strength transporting her. Miss Prindle gasped for breath while trying to keep up as they trudged through snowbanks that deepened the farther they walked.

"When you are well again," Fotherington told Sophy, "you must come to London and enjoy Hyde Park with me. Less strenuous than this walk, but even more lovely in spring and summer when the blossoms emerge. We might take in one of Mr. Kean's performances in Drury Lane.

Perhaps you might prefer to spend an evening in the grove at Vauxhall Gardens."

"While they all sound entertaining," Sophy demurred, "I fear I shall be abroad by then."

She made certain her return to America became a familiar theme for all three men, for whenever one suggested a future activity they might share, it served as a satisfactory excuse to keep her from attending. When her suitors took turns walking beside her and wielding the chair poles, she took turns varying her excuses for dismissing them all from consideration.

The tactic succeeded until the sight of Jeremy St. Laurent, Viscount Cobleigh, approaching from a distance caused her spirits to fall. He knew where to find her, having spent nearly as much time at Deervale Hall as a child as she had. He exchanged pleasantries with the men before turning to her.

"You appear to be feeling quite well this morning, Miss Templeton," he observed, his eyes meeting and holding hers, "seeing as how you've ventured out for a morning excursion. Lady Fairfax told me I would find you here."

"How fortunate my mother was able to help you." Sophy turned to avoid the intense gaze of his brown eyes.

"I am pleased to see her looking so well. And you also, despite your ankle." Jeremy appeared to attempt to probe her mood before glancing away. "You have given your chair bearers more exercise carrying your throne than they would have received on horseback, yet they still cannot keep pace with the children who are so actively entertaining themselves on your lawn."

"Are they?" Sophy inquired.

Her ears perked up along with her spirits. Her trio of unsuitable suitors had begun to rub their gloves together, muttering about chilled fingers and awkward footing on slippery hills. The slight irritation she heard in their voices made it clear they were ready to return to the warmth of the house, where they could relieve their discomfort by putting their feet in a basin of hot mustard-and-water.

"Shall we return to join the children, gentlemen?" Sophy suggested. "Their joy is infectious, and I feel somewhat in need of joy at present. Plus we shall be that much closer to returning indoors, if you so wish."

She turned her head slightly and bestowed a smile of kindness upon her companions, just enough, she hoped, to make Jeremy St. Laurent feel a bit slighted. Yet if she had succeeded he did not show it, for she saw a hint of humor crease his face that annoyed her.

Jeremy walked alongside as her suitors struggled to turn the cumbersome sedan chair toward home and return its passenger to the lawn where he had left her nieces and nephews. The bulk of the weight that left her chairmen so out of breath must have come from the chair itself, for Sophy Templeton was as slim today as when he had last seen her. Slimmer, perhaps.

The reason, according to Barclay, it was the exercise in which she claimed to have partaken while in America. She had proven herself to be quite the adventuress in his absence. Jeremy wondered if she had changed in other ways or if she remained the same sweet, thoughtful young woman she was when he last saw her. Certainly the desire to return to America proved she possessed the same curiosity and courage she had as a child. She did not appear to have changed as much as he had, he mused.

By the time they reached the gates of Deervale Hall they were met by not one but a family of snowmen. Jeremy noted with amusement that the children had shown great consideration for their snow family by tying plaid scarves about their throats so tightly they would have choked had they been human. Built in graduated sizes, the snow father, mother, and children stood like sentinels along the drive leading to the front door.

The boys had now engaged the girls in a snowball fight, with Sylvan the spaniel too excited to take sides, running between enemy camps. Their strategic decision to hide behind a stand of evergreens and fire volleys from between the thick trunks seemed to be leading to victory, until the sedan chair came into view and Teddy defected to his aunt's side, forcing Jonathan to be a one-man army.

Jeremy abandoned the team of sedan chair bearers and hurried to Jonathan's side behind a pine tree.

"I see your sister and your cousin have moved from behind the parent snowmen," Jeremy said in a low voice.

The eldest at thirteen, Jonathan frowned, turning his head toward the snowman family. "Where'd they go?"

"Look there." Jeremy pointed them out. "They've ducked behind the stone wall. You can see Sylvan's tail wagging from here. What an utter lack of loyalty. He's taken their side."

Jonathan hurled a snowball in their direction. "They've less protection there," he observed as a cry came from Emily before Susannah jumped to her feet.

"Yes, but they've one advantage over us," Jeremy said.

The warning came too late as Susannah's high snowball found its mark in the branches above their heads and clumps of snow fell in a shower, sticking to their hats and shoulders as delighted laughter issued from the girls.

"Is the advantage that they've blown up our cover?" Jonathan laughed, wiping snow from his hat with his mitten.

"Precisely."

Jeremy brushed snow from Jonathan's sleeves, then his own, as Sophy's chairmen pulled up alongside the lane, depositing their lovely load. He tried to hide a smile as he saw the reason for their labored breathing. Young Teddy had climbed inside the box and was seated comfortably beside his Aunt Sophy.

Jeremy turned away to hide a look of amusement combined with disdain. Clearly, the three men who so obviously sought Sophy's favor had not been soldiers in Wellington's army. Their clumsiness had frustrated him when he'd watched from a distance as they attempted to maneuver their way even across the lower parts of the snow-covered Pennines. The small hills had proven to be a challenge.

They had not, after all, led a troop of cavalry on horseback through the Spanish hills, as he had. They had not carried wounded men to safety over their shoulders, or faced and beaten an onslaught of French soldiers who outnumbered them. Their weariness at carrying a slender female and her young nephew did not surprise him.

What did surprise him was that Sophronia Templeton allowed any of them to court her.

He was no less surprised, nor was he pleased, that evening when Sophy deliberately snubbed him, choosing the attentions of Humphrey Fotherington as they matched wits at a game of chess in the drawing room. Fotherington had pressed his suit rather strenuously throughout the day, and Sophy had finally succumbed to his insistent requests for her company.

Two things became clear to Jeremy as he watched them together. The first was that she was every bit as skilled as any of her brothers at winning at chess.

The second was that it was not Fotherington she wanted to be with so much as she seemed to want to avoid St. Laurent.

To Jeremy, Fotherington seemed a colossal and arrogant bore hardly worth wasting time on. While the man hadn't the reputation for chasing ladies, as did so many who passed their days in London, Jeremy wondered how long Sophy could hold Fotherington's attention with her stories of life on the American frontier.

Jeremy seized the chance to accentuate his familiarity with her the next morning, when he was fortunate enough to arrive for breakfast just as she did. As he poured chocolate for Sophy, he addressed her in the presence of the trio of men who hastily rose to greet her, noting with satisfaction that they were still forced to address her formally.

"It's so lovely to see you again, Sophy," he ventured, "just like old times. I thought perhaps you and I might take a ride through the countryside to visit some of the places you loved so as a child. You must find it tiresome being confined to the house much of the day with that ankle."

"Thank you, Captain St. Laurent, but no," she declined, her tone polite but cool. "Since Barclay has been so thoughtful as to invite his friends for the holiday, and they have provided me with their kind companionship during my recuperation, I feel I must divide my time evenly among our guests. I do appreciate your offer, my lord, and I am confident there shall be a day during your visit when we shall have the opportunity to pass an afternoon together."

Jeremy divided his time that day in separate conversations with Harry and Eddie, the older Templeton brothers, fighting a lingering irritation at Sophy's cold indifference to his presence. He had been put in his place by a mere slip of a girl who, as a child, had done everything from pulling his hair when she was angry to pushing him off her first pony when he attempted to ride it. This slight was far worse than anything she'd done in their youth. He found himself feeling far too disgruntled as he mulled over her behavior.

Yet despite her attitude, he was forced to admit the sister of his oldest and dearest friends had grown into a lovely and most desirable young woman. She had managed to retain the warmth and outspokenness she'd displayed in childhood while developing a grace and charm over time. Her obvious sincerity prompted those who knew her to overlook her occasional lapses in tact.

Unlike other women he had met in society, he conceded with some surprise, she appeared to be a prize worth the risk. Her attitude troubled him until it occurred to him that he must fight fire with fire. Appealing as she was, Sophy Templeton was not the only available young woman at the house party. While Barclay appeared rather smitten with the lovely Arabella Prindle, Jeremy considered her rather young for himself. He suspected Bark would recognize and understand a light flirtation, as he intended it, as another way to Sophy's heart.

That settled, Jeremy vowed to try every way possible until he discovered the path that led to winning Sophy's hand.

The leisurely pace of the holidays was shattered the next morning when the hall doors burst open. Emily, Eddie and Emma's daughter, ran sobbing into the drawing room, alarming the adults. Jeremy was among those present, as were the adults in the family, Arabella, and the other suitors. He had been watching Sophy chat with Humphrey Fotherington on the far side of the room.

"Emily, whatever is wrong?" Emma asked at once, hurrying to her daughter's side. "Why aren't you with Teddy and Uncle Bark?"

"They're outside," Emily cried, dropping the wooden pail she carried. "We were pretending to be Jack and Jill. We carried our pails all the way up the hill. Then Teddy tumbled and rolled all the way down until he struck his leg on a rock, and now he can't walk. And then I came tumbling after."

With that Emily burst into tears again. Her mother had no sooner gathered her in her arms than Barclay appeared, holding Teddy. The boy's small round face was streaked with tears.

"It appears someone felt such sympathy for his Aunt Sophy," Barclay said, "that he decided to copy her by twisting his own ankle."

"Ow, my knee hurts," Teddy cried as Barclay handed him over to his father.

"What have you done to yourself, little one?" Eddie demanded gently, drawing his son close with a sigh. "At least you didn't break your crown like Jack did. Perhaps just your leg. Never mind, we shall summon the doctor so he can have a look. In the meantime, young Master Edward, it's up to bed with you."

"Dear Teddy, poor sweet," the Dowager Lady Fairfax murmured, rising to stroke her grandson's cheek. "We simply don't do well with legs. It would appear all three generations of our family are prone to leg injuries."

Jeremy saw her glance furtively at Harry's leg, shortened in battle, flushing as she realized how insensitive she must sound to her eldest son. Barclay rushed to relieve her with humor.

"That's why we must get Sophy leg-shackled as soon as possible," he teased, glancing at his sister, "before she does so much damage to herself she is unable to walk down the aisle."

"And it is quite a fine leg to be shackled to," Sampson Hodge added quietly from his corner of the room.

Jeremy wondered darkly how Hodge could have any idea how fine Sophy's leg was, though he did not doubt it was true. He could not repress a grin as Sophy, her cheeks coloring, adjusted her skirts discreetly about her ankles before she responded in kind.

"For that, Barclay," she retorted, "you shall carry me upstairs. Take me to Teddy's room, for it is there I shall await the arrival of Doctor Evans."

Staying until they were certain Teddy had suffered no serious harm, Prindle, Hodge, and Fotherington excused themselves discreetly. Jeremy noticed Arabella Prindle hesitated but lingered at Barclay's urging. Jeremy lingered as well, anxious to be of help. He seized the opportunity to insinuate himself into the conversation politely but poignantly.

"Miss Prindle, might I escort you outdoors while the family is otherwise occupied?" he asked, offering his arm to Arabella who accepted it dutifully. "It's a lovely day, if a bit cool, but I've no doubt we shall manage to find ways to keep warm."

Giving her an attentive smile, he gazed at Arabella until she blushed and returned his smile. Jeremy nodded to Sophy, noting with satisfaction the concern that darkened her brow as he left arm in arm with Arabella.

Sophy watched the pair depart, indefinable emotions tugging at her. They seemed a most unlikely pair. Jeremy St. Laurent was a man of substance, serious and introspective by nature, while Arabella, though pleasant enough, lacked the depth of one even of Sophy's own twenty-four years.

Before they went upstairs to wait for the doctor, her thoughts still on Jeremy and Arabella, she requested, in a voice sterner than she intended, that Emily set aside the pair of wooden pails she had dropped on the drawing room carpet. It was hardly fair to blame Riggs for delivering them, she knew. While she did not question the honorable intentions of her mother's tenant farmer who lived with his wife in a cottage a half-mile from Deervale Hall, she was not sure she could say the same of Captain St. Laurent, who had looked rather pleased with himself when he left with Miss Prindle.

She set aside what was surely a silly resentment to focus on Teddy's troubles. While Eddie carried his son upstairs, Sophy allowed Barclay to carry her to Teddy's room as well.

"What was that about?" she demanded.

"What was what about?" Barclay sounded slightly out of breath as he struggled to balance her on the staircase.

"Captain St. Laurent and Miss Prindle."

Barclay shrugged as best he could under her weight. "Dunno. Being discreet, I suppose, so the doctor might see Teddy in private."

Or so they might see each other in private, Sophy suspected.

"They'll be cold very shortly, if they remain outdoors too long," she declared, "for the doctor won't arrive for some time."

Then she remembered an earlier conversation with Barclay. Fearing competition from Hodge and Fotherington, he had reminded her she wasn't the only available female at the house party.

Her heart turned over as she wondered if that was how Jeremy St. Laurent suddenly viewed the situation.

"He'll do the gentlemanly thing, I s'pose, and use his cloak to keep her warm. Or he might put his arm around her. She's a young woman of marriageable age. St. Laurent can do as he pleases," Barclay muttered, irritation creeping into his voice, "but he'd damn well better not if he knows what's good for him."

Sophy was glad when he deposited her in Teddy's room at last. Since this unexpected call would give him a chance to evaluate her ankle and report on its progress, Doctor Evans's visit held as much suspense for her as it did for Teddy.

But first they must tend to Teddy's knee and determine the severity of his injury. She tried to thrust Jeremy and Arabella from her mind until Doctor Evans arrived over an hour later. He was as prompt as possible considering the amount of snow through which his barouche had to travel, though it seemed an eternity.

Her nerves on edge, Sophy waited silently, her impatience showing only in the steady rocking of her chair. With her mother sitting opposite her, Emma and Eddie stood on opposite sides of Teddy's bed as Doctor Evans pulled down the covers to inspect their son's knee.

"It appears your son has a bad sprain," he announced after a painstaking and lengthy examination, "It should cause no permanent damage in a lad as young as this." At this he ruffled Teddy's already tousled brown locks.

"Oh, thank you, Doctor," Emma said with relief.

"At most it will hamper him for a week or two," the doctor continued. "But this sprain is nowhere as severe as his aunt's."

Sophy's throat went dry as Doctor Evans turned to her. "Perhaps I should look at your ankle while I'm here. It's been about a week since your accident. Let's check your progress, shall we?"

Sophy tried to read his expectations in his voice but could not. She lifted her skirts at his approach, as Eddie moved an upholstered footstool close enough for her to rest her ankle.

"You have not put pressure on this foot yet, I trust?"

The doubt in Doctor Evans's voice insulted her, but Sophy remained humble for her mother's sake. Perhaps it would earn her some sympathy from the doctor. Teddy saved her from answering.

"She hasn't, Doctor," he said earnestly. "Aunt Sophy has been the bestest patient. The visiting gentlemen have rigged up a fancy chair for her. They carry her wherever she wants to go."

"A bestest patient? That's something I have yet to see." Doctor Evans grinned at both of his patients as Teddy giggled. "I'm delighted to hear it. It sounds as if your aunt is in most capable hands as she gives her ankle the time it needs to heal."

Of course her ankle would heal properly, Sophy told herself. There wasn't the remotest possibility it wouldn't, for she could not face the possibility of having to abandon her mission work.

She tried to steady her nerves as the doctor examined the ankle. He was silent for an agonizingly long time, pressing on the tender bones, squeezing her ankle and lower leg, turning her foot over in his hand. It could practically have healed, she thought in exasperation, in the time he spent examining it.

"Well," Doctor Evans said slowly as he replaced her foot on the stool, "these things work out in their own time, of course, but that ankle still has a fair amount of tenderness."

"It really feels much better," Sophy objected weakly.

"Not well enough that I'd recommend putting pressure on it yet. You reacted with pain when I examined it. You'll get better. It just takes time and patience."

And time, she thought miserably, is the one thing I don't have. She saw sympathy in his face as he gazed down at her.

"Keep up your spirits, Miss Templeton," he encouraged with a gentleness that surprised her. "The holidays are nearly upon us. Be grateful for the love of your family. It will go far to cheer you."

Sophy managed a smile. He was so kind it was difficult to keep the tears from her eyes. She wanted healing, not sympathy. She needed to know she would be aboard the ship that would set sail for America at the end of January.

But she was not to hear those words today.

By late afternoon the stress of his visit had done her in, and she could not face the strain of trying to be pleasant with gentlemen callers who would be strangers after their visit ended.

To avoid having to make the attempt she retired to the library for a quiet moment. Sylvan must have had the same idea, for as she opened the library door, assisted into the room with the help of a servant, the dog merely lifted his head and gave her a thump of his tail before returning to sleep in his favorite spot. The bottom shelf of the bookcase nearest the fire had been his chosen spot ever since he was a pup.

She was irritated when a knock on the door disturbed her peace after only a few minutes. She hoped Barclay's friends had not discovered her hiding spot.

"Come in," she invited, somewhat crossly.

She was startled to see Jeremy St. Laurent in the doorway, closing the heavy oak door softly behind him.

Chapter Four

"GOOD AFTERNOON," he said in a formal tone. "Might I join you? I had hoped to keep you company, even though you seem to prefer solitude these days."

Sophy kept her eyes on the fire before her, setting aside the book she had not yet opened. "You may suit yourself as you wish, Captain. Guests are always welcome in our library."

That included other visitors as well, she reflected. If Jeremy intended to remain, she hoped one of them might interrupt so she was not forced to deal with the viscount alone.

"Thank you." Jeremy seated himself opposite her, close to the fire, smiling with a familiarity that did not put her at ease. "I believe your suitors prefer the comfort of the drawing room after their forays outdoors this week. Perhaps they had enough snow during the children's snowball fight."

She remained silent as he gazed at her, studying her so long it made her uncomfortable. When she didn't reply he continued.

"Did you hope to discourage them by keeping them in the cold?" he asked lightly. "Hodge is from Cornwall, not used to this weather. I believe Prindle's from the south coast also. Not a bad sort, but not accustomed to cold. Fotherington, now he's a Londoner. Used to snow, but also used to more society."

"And your point, my lord?" Sitting back in her seat, Sophy absently began to fold her legs under her as she might have done when they were children. Suddenly self-conscious, she kept her feet on the floor, remembering her place.

"My point, my dear Sophy," he said boldly, "is that we have much to discuss, and it has nothing to do with Prindle, Hodge, or Fotherington."

"Has it anything to do with Miss Prindle?" she shot back.

"Why would it?" He stared quizzically until recognition hit, and his face softened. "Can we not pick up where we left off?"

She tightened her lips in annoyance. If he were willing to venture into the past, she would join him. "Very well, my lord."

"It's Jeremy," he cut her off. "It has not been that many years that you can have forgotten."

"Very well, Jeremy," she resumed stiffly. "Be warned, however, that my memory is as good as yours. It seems to me we left off with Charles Ferris."

"Ah, yes, Charles," Jeremy said, "the notorious Earl of Dunstreet. I knew he had a *tendre* for you."

He laughed softly, a laugh she knew so well it was etched in her heart. At this moment his laugh had an awkward ring to it.

"You know," he admitted, "after I entered the war I assumed some other lucky man had married you. It was only upon my return six months ago I learned that was not the case."

"And once you assumed I was married you never asked again," she said, her tone sarcastic. "You stopped caring."

His shoulders were hunched with tension. "Why would I after I'd learned you'd returned to Charles?"

"You seemed to find the Earl of Dunstreet notorious, though I found nothing notorious about him," she retorted.

"Since the noble among us strive to protect those of the delicate gender, perhaps you know little of his private life." Rising, Jeremy walked to the sideboard and poured himself a glass of brandy before returning to his seat. "If you'd spent time in London, as your brothers did, you would have been well aware—shocked even—by Dunstreet's exploits. He was what those in our class refer to as a bounder. A womanizer. Surely you experienced some of that firsthand. Am I correct?"

He turned to stare at her, his eyes challenging her and filling her with uncomfortable warmth. This feeling, one she'd never experienced, had nothing to do with the fireplace before them that made her jump with its crackling.

"I had every right to be angry with you for disrupting our relationship." She attempted to explain rather than accuse. "I lost my chance with Charles because of you. Had you not suggested he court Isabella Wallingford, I might have married him."

"You might have," Jeremy conceded, "and it's fortunate you didn't even if you can't see it. I was acquainted with both and considered them a perfect match."

"Clearly they were not," Sophy continued recklessly. "After you and I argued and you went to war, Charles left Isabella to return to me. We became better acquainted in your absence."

If Jeremy was troubled by her words, he did not show it. His chin set, he did not move a muscle as he sat listening. "And is there is a reason you and he never married? Pray, tell me."

Sophy swallowed. She remained silent, having backed herself into a corner. She had realized Charles was a rotter when he left her for another. Soon afterward she learned Jeremy had married a Spanish girl, and her plans to go to America began to develop.

"If you were as well acquainted with Charles as you believe, you would know he takes advantage of women. Isabella is not the only one, but she plays her role perfectly. That's why he married her. They were meant for each other."

Sophy started, unable to hide her shock. She assumed Charles would marry eventually, but she had no idea he had returned to Isabella. She felt her haughtiness falling away.

Jeremy sounded as if he struggled to keep the spite from his tone. "So you did not know."

"I thought you and Charles were friends," she confessed. "I never understood why you introduced him to such a mean woman."

"Charles was just as mean. His courtship of you was intended to make Isabella jealous." He shrugged. "There's little to envy in her, believe me. She is beautiful but heartless. He had plenty of women besides her. Still does. Do you think she is as happy as you? She isn't. I receive news from London. You do not, having been in America, where you are obviously happier without anyone."

Sophy was shocked into silence, absorbing his words as much as their harsh tone. She was surprised to see bitterness tighten his features as his posture tensed.

"Charles and I were acquaintances, never friends. Rivals, in fact, when it came to you. Perhaps you never knew." Jeremy rose from his chair, giving her a look of disdain. "You've misinterpreted several things, Sophy. It was because I cared that I chose to separate you from Charles. I never stopped caring."

Sophy was not prepared to hear the words.

Setting down his half-finished brandy, Jeremy turned and headed for the door, saying, "I think it best that we not continue this conversation, at least not at present. Since you are still fairly immobile and unable to depart under your own power, I shall do so and allow you to return to your reading. I will see you tomorrow."

Left alone with Sylvan, still snoring in his bookcase shelf, Sophy was uncertain what to do next. Her thoughts swirled with confusion from the new revelations. Concentrating on a book was impossible. Her night ruined by the encounter, she might as well retire to bed and request that a tray be brought to her room. After the unpleasant encounter that had just ended, she certainly had no intention of dining with their guests this evening.

She would use Barclay's excuse and claim weariness. Having decided the matter, her annoyance with Jeremy lingered. She refused to believe the Earl of Dunstreet was as shallow as he claimed. Had Jeremy not interfered, she might still be in England, married to Charles Ferris with children of her own.

She had to concede that was not what she'd wanted, certainly not with Charles. Yet the thought of a home with children and dogs running across the lawn was appealing. The concept was new to her, and it startled and confused her.

As she pulled herself back to the present, ready to retire, she realized she had no way to get upstairs without assistance. She disliked being left alone with her past. She much preferred being first to leave an unpleasant conversation.

There would be no more relying on others, she vowed, or waiting for servants. She would show them she didn't need either Barclay or Jeremy or even the servants. First thing tomorrow she would find a pair of crutches to give her more mobility.

The next day she located her mother's old pair. While the ankle still pained her enough that she wasn't tempted to try putting weight on her foot just yet, the crutches allowed her a degree of independence. She had managed to maneuver the stairs with them, slowly but carefully, just as Thomas Riggs called. He carried a child-sized pair of crutches.

"I heard about the lad. Shame, that." The tenant farmer shook his head sympathetically as he addressed Sophy and her mother. "Poor li'l tyke. Hope to have one of me own just like him one day soon."

He winked at them, his cheeks flushed pink from the cold, as a broad toothless smile spread across his face.

"Mrs. Riggs must be nearing that time." Mrs. Templeton returned his smile. "How proud and excited you must be, Thomas."

"Real proud, ma'am. Won't be long now. Maybe we'll have a Christmas baby."

"Wouldn't that be lovely." Sophy's mother looked up as Eddie came downstairs slowly, Teddy in his arms. "Teddy dear, look what Mr. Riggs brought for you."

The boy's face brightened at once. "Aunt Sophy and I will be twins!"

By the time the laughter subsided, Barclay approached, amused to see both his sister and his nephew on matching crutches.

"Soph, I was thinking," Barclay announced. "Bath isn't known only for its sedan chairs. If I'd thought sooner I'd have gotten you one of John

Dawson's Bath chairs. It has two large wheels in back and a smaller one in front, with a handle for steering. It even has footrests and a reclining back if you tire of riding."

"That's kind of you, Bark," she said gratefully, "but by the time it arrives I'll be back on my feet. With crutches, I needn't rely on anyone. Besides, this way Teddy and I match."

"Your injury might have your suitors competing among themselves," Barclay said when they were alone. "I'll bet they'll trip over each other trying to assist you with those crutches."

She gave him a secretive smile, pleased to think how annoyed Jeremy would be if she gave Humphrey the nod. When she encountered her admirers in the drawing room later that morning, she was less inclined to dismiss them now that they might prove useful. She permitted them to consume the remainder of her morning before she invited them to join her outdoors to watch the children play in the snow.

While each had been quite agreeable to slipping his arm about her waist to help her adjust to using crutches, they all declined to step outside, just as she expected. She set off by herself, enjoying the freedom her crutches afforded her. She was delighted to see Barclay heading toward her, until she saw he was with Jeremy who paused to watch the fun the children were having.

"Any closer to making a decision, Soph?" Barclay asked her privately.

"You mean regarding the unsuitable suitors?" She smiled uneasily, reluctant to resume the issue of her leaving. "It can't be about America. You know I plan to return when I'm well."

Barclay hesitated. "Mum isn't getting any younger, you know. I'm not sure you know how much it means to her to have you home again. It would break her heart if you left."

Sophy hesitated before replying, trying to ignore the nagging guilt that tugged at her heart. She had promised the ministry that she would return. While she did not take her obligations lightly, her sense of responsibility to her family weighed heavily upon her conscience. "I've already written the Mission Society to see if they have a suitable chaperone for me," she said in dismay. "That should put Mother's mind at ease. She doesn't want me to travel without one."

"Mum doesn't want you to travel at all, but you must suit yourself. You've scared the other men off, I see," Barclay observed dryly. "You spend so much time with the children the adults are beginning to treat you like one. Apparently Jeremy is braver than the rest."

Her spirits fell somewhat when Barclay walked on and Jeremy stepped up beside her, watching the children at play.

"I see Jonathan's made a snow fort," Jeremy said casually. "It's almost as impressive as some I saw in Spain, except they weren't built of snow."

"Two weeks ago I barely knew my nieces and nephews." Sophy sighed wistfully. "Now I can't imagine life without them once they go home."

"Perhaps they'll stay if you will. I suspect they're more entertaining than your suitors," Jeremy added slyly. "I overheard you telling Barclay they're all too much like him. Is that why you've done so well on crutches, so you can avoid them?"

Sophy smiled. She knew her behavior warranted teasing, and she was grateful he had smoothed the rough waters between them so graciously.

"I thought it rather decent of Riggs to make those pint-sized crutches for Teddy," Jeremy continued. "Why don't we call at the cottage? We could bring the couple something from the kitchen as thanks. And no more sedan chair. This time we'll go by sleigh so you can travel as you should."

"Are you certain you wouldn't rather have Miss Prindle accompany you?" she challenged.

"Quite certain," he said in a tone that left no doubt in her mind.

Within minutes Jeremy had the sleigh brought round and had harnessed the horses. He eased Sophy into the sleigh by offering a supportive hand while holding her crutches.

"It must feel good to be home again," she said, as they rode. The gleaming white snow crunched beneath the sleigh's runners and blew a fine spray past them, and it was so bright it was almost blinding. "I understand your cavalry unit distinguished itself at Villagarcia, and you as well."

"Is that what they say? It was certainly a victory for our side," Jeremy conceded, "and better than Ciudad Rodrigo and Badajoz where misconduct overshadowed bravery. But anywhere there is death isn't a place where one wants to be distinguished as much as absent. By God's grace I was spared. There were others, too many, who weren't so fortunate. I was indeed happy to return to my family."

Jeremy focused his gaze on the path ahead, and Sophy let his memories recede in silence. As they passed a barn alongside the road, happier memories filtered back to her.

"Barclay suggested I ask your opinion about my ankle. He said you knew a bit about medicine, having delivered babies while abroad."

Although he continued to stare straight ahead, she saw his eyes cloud over briefly. "I delivered one. I happened to be in the right place at the right time."

"Remember the baby lambs in springtime? One year when we were little, you carried out the first born." She smiled at the memory. "You stood in the doorway of the barn holding the sweetest, tiniest lamb. As I recall, you helped deliver it."

"I'd no idea it would be such good practice." A grin spread across his face as the childhood memory displaced more recent ones. He gave her a teasing glance. "As I recall, you said you were going to have a whole flock of lambs when you grew up. Where are they?"

"I suppose my flock are the Indians in the New World," she said. "The settlers refer to them as heathens, but I find them enchanting. I like to watch the mothers carry their babies on their backs."

There was nothing savage about it, she reflected. Yet she hadn't been able to attract a very large flock of followers in America, among either the settlers or the Indians.

They were pleased to find Thomas Riggs chopping wood outside his cottage. Since Dolly was preparing their noonday dinner, Sophy expressed hesitation about lingering, but the mistress of the house insisted they remain for a warm drink. As she readied the mugs they delivered the pheasant they had brought from the larder at the main house as thanks for the child-sized crutches Thomas had made.

"Our own wee one's due any day now." Dolly's face beamed over the bulge beneath her skirts, her cheeks pink from the heat of the stove. "Just in time for Christmas."

"What better present could we have?" her husband added with an affectionate laugh. "We've waited a long time for this child."

As Sophy sat beside Jeremy and enjoyed hot cider with the couple, she felt herself relax in the cozy comfort of the cottage. Sophy watched Dolly's pleasing awkwardness as she moved about, collecting cheese, bread, and apples as offerings of their hospitality. Despite the extra weight she carried Dolly did not seem the least encumbered. For the first time Sophy found herself wondering what it must feel like to be with child.

She sensed it was the faith and joy the couple exuded rather than the spiced cider or the fire in the hearth that filled their surroundings with bliss. She felt so warmed by their company that she felt a stab of disappointment when it was time to leave.

"I'm glad we decided to reacquaint you with things you once enjoyed, like riding in the snow in a sleigh," Jeremy said on their ride home. "The only activities you can't do yet are going for country rambles or having a good skate. At any rate, sleigh rides will help you pass the time until you're well enough to skate again. That might be sooner than you think."

Sophy settled back contentedly with the rug wrapped about her, a warmth coursing through her that defied the freezing temperatures. Apparently, Jeremy understood how much it mattered to her to walk again so she might return to America and fulfill her destiny as a teacher. If only her family could see it.

Upon her return she found Barclay waiting impatiently not for her but for the sleigh. Within minutes he had set off in the company of Arabella and his gentlemen friends. When the party returned that night she was not surprised to see Herbert Prindle and Sampson Hodge rather inebriated.

"In their cups." Jeremy shook his head with disdain. "Foxed. Had a bit more brandy than is good for them. Not used to country ways, apparently. They've found nothing better to do than drink."

Sophy hoped it was a sign the men were giving up, though she suspected Humphrey Fotherington would persist in his courtship. She found the following evening more to her liking, when a round of teasing regarding newly purchased Christmas presents lifted the children's spirits.

Moods brightened and hearts lightened as the Christmas holidays moved a day closer. Maggie, the Scottish cook who had presided over Deervale Hall's kitchen for as long as Sophy could remember, insisted on keeping everyone away despite the tempting scents permeating each room that seemed to come from the pantry.

The infectious mood began with Teddy and Emily and spread to their older cousins. Susannah and Jonathan could not disguise their excitement, and even their stern parents seemed to relax at the thought of the merriment in store this year.

"Sophy was absent last year at this time," Harry explained to Herbert, Sampson, and Humphrey Fotherington.

"And we're happy she is with us this year, even if her spirits are a bit downtrodden from her fall," Jane said glibly.

Even her sister-in-law's outspokenness did not dim Sophy's spirits. True, it was the first time they had all been together in nearly two years, she reflected, but there was something special about this year. It was especially noticeable one evening after the ladies had retired to the drawing room for needlework and gossip and then returned to the gentlemen who were enjoying their port. As they gathered around the fire, she had never seen her family so happy, despite their assorted injuries.

Reminiscing about a masquerade he'd attended at Covent Garden years earlier, even Harry was in a jovial mood, appearing to forget his devastating leg injury as he engaged in conversation with Humphrey Fotherington. Arabella Prindle attempted, without much success, to play a piece on the piano she remembered from a London soiree, with Barclay leaning over her shoulder playfully. Eddie and Emma regaled Herbert

Prindle and Sampson Hodge with memories of a summer visit to the Royal Academy with the children in tow.

Sophy looked around for Jeremy, a feeling of contentment filling her as she spied him chatting with her mother, who smiled repeatedly. She wondered if they were remembering the halcyon days of childhood. How remarkable, she mused, that they had grown close in their youth when they met in London and discovered they lived in neighboring counties. When her mother's face grew serious, Sophy suspected Jeremy was updating her on his father's health. Concern welled within her as she hoped Jeremy's aging father had not suffered any setback.

Later that evening, as Humphrey Fotherington's attentions became a bit too intense, Sophy managed to excuse herself. She noticed Jeremy had disappeared. Perhaps he'd decided to retire early. She chose to escape to the library for peace and quiet.

She opened the closed door and slipped inside, startled to see Jeremy St. Laurent had beaten her there. He smiled and lifted his brandy in welcome.

"Join me, won't you?" he invited. "Please."

Sophy hesitated. "I've no wish to disturb you."

"I admit the turn of the doorknob disappointed me, but only until I saw your mischievous smile behind it. I suspected you might require a respite and seek refuge here." Leaning forward, Jeremy glanced past her. "I see Sylvan behind you. Bring him in as well." He paused a moment, then asked, "Are you disappointed to be in the company of another?"

"I confess I was surprised to find you here." She closed the door quietly behind Sylvan. "But I thank you for sharing your privacy."

She was more surprised to see a grin crease his thoughtful features, and he said softly, "That's what I like about you, Sophy. Your honesty outshines your tact. Why don't you sit for a spell before facing them again, if you feel obligated to do so at all? I've always found this library intriguing. It has much more than mere military tomes. You must feel at ease here, surrounded by books and with your dog, though perhaps less so with me here."

She felt the curiosity in his brown eyes penetrate her soul. "At least you understand and respect my wishes," she said, seating herself. "Even about my desire to return to America. For that, I thank you."

"I cannot say I understand your desire to return to America," he admitted, "but I do understand the attraction."

"If only my family could. There is no question I must return and do what I was meant to," she said earnestly. "It wasn't until I went to America that I discovered I had a talent for teaching."

"You read so much as a child that it's not surprising you would enjoy teaching. Just as I knew I must fight for my country," Jeremy mused, "as my father did. I thought of you often while I was abroad. Sometimes I hoped you were thinking of me."

Sophy felt her cheeks flame, and he smiled in amusement.

"I did not know whether I should think of you," she confessed. "I heard you had married and had a child. Forgive me for raising what must be a painful subject. I—I was reluctant to speak of it for fear you are still not over their deaths."

He hesitated. "I shall tell you the truth, but you must keep it to yourself. I don't often tell it—never, in fact—but I did not father the child of the woman I married. I'll try to explain, and I hope the truth does not horrify you."

Sophy's heart thudded as he took a deep breath and said, "Her name was Rosalita. Her father, a diplomat, came from an influential family. I married her only to give her child a name. The baby's father was one of my superior officers. He wasn't wedded to another but considered her inferior to the women had had left behind in London." Jeremy shook his head, an expression of disgust spreading across his aristocratic features. "Hardly the pride of the Crown. I married her to pacify her family, and to keep peace between our countries. We were supposed to be their allies, by God."

"Were you under orders?" Sophy asked, horrified by his story.

"No, it was my choice. She was a sweet girl, but I had no romantic interest in her. The fighting forced us to live in unimaginably difficult conditions. I had no time to think about courtship—especially when my mind was here at home with you."

Sophy's heart filled with unexpected joy as he continued. "At any rate, since I feared my opportunity with you was gone, the noble thing to do was to marry Rosalita and take care of her child." He paused to take a gulp of his brandy. "Barclay wasn't quite accurate when he told you I delivered babies during the war. Rosalita's was the only child I ever delivered, and that was out of desperation. He was weak from the start and died two days after birth. She was devastated, and her joy turned to bitterness."

"How horrible for you."

Jeremy shook his head slowly, his voice husky when he finally spoke again. "Rosalita only lived a short time after that. She was wounded at Badajoz and never recovered." He took another drink. "My consolation was that the senior officer also died in battle."

"I'm terribly sorry, Jeremy," she whispered. "I knew none of this."

"Life sometimes turns in ways we don't expect. I won't forget Rosalita, though it isn't a part of my past I care to dwell upon. While we were able to support one another through a difficult time, I don't believe Rosalita and I were intended for each other." Jeremy set aside his brandy. "I ask only that you refrain from speaking of it to anyone. As I said, I've told no one but you."

"I am honored by your confidence," Sophy said meekly, "and I assure you it will go no further. I'm glad you are at peace with it."

"Then we shall leave it in the unhappy past where it belongs. Truly, upon my return I had no idea you remained unwed," he admitted. "While I was away, Harry wrote me that Charles Ferris was courting you, and it appeared to him a wedding was in the offing."

Harry, Sophy reflected, never did understand her heart as well as Barclay and Eddie. "Eventually I recognized Charles for the boor he is. That is when I broke it off between us. I am afraid I behaved as I did to make you jealous. You had gone off to war—"

Jeremy resumed the conversation when she stopped, too embarrassed by her own actions to continue. "Sometimes I fear you view the experience of war as mere traveling. I did not go to war simply because we argued. It was expected of me, my father having been a hero in the Revolution."

It was Sophy's turn to feel discomfited. "I very much regret that my words make you think I view your contribution as anything less than heroic."

"It is my fault as well," Jeremy hurried on, stammering. "I-I assumed you were spoken for. Clearly I was mistaken."

"And so you married Rosalita."

He shrugged. "Someone had to protect her honor."

"I should have known you'd do the honorable thing." She felt her heart soften not only at his heroism but his chivalry, as well. "I owe you an apology for behaving so foolishly."

"No apology is necessary, my dear Sophy." He smiled. "We have grown into different people. People who know their hearts and minds and are able to make them up with true sincerity."

"As I have done with my plan to return to America," she reflected aloud.

Jeremy sat back in his chair. "Did you have the luxury of enjoying the companionship of dogs while you were in America?"

"I did, but their lives aren't as easy as Sylvan's. Some were forced to sleep outside. Each time I return home, Sylvan is older," she observed wistfully, bending to pet the dog.

"It's always worrisome to see one's beloved dog age," he agreed, his tone kind. "I know the feeling well. I imagine you have many worries these days, as we all do. We worry about different things nowadays than we did when we were younger."

Sophy studied him, fascinated. "What do you worry about?"

As he paused to consider the question, she admired the strength the firelight revealed in his rugged features.

Finally, he said, "I worry about my father's health. About the future of England. I worry about what the years ahead will bring now that my military career has ended." Jeremy gazed at her intently. "No doubt you and I worry about some of the same things. How do you feel about traveling abroad despite your mother's wishes?"

Sophy tensed with irritation. She needed no reminder of her responsibilities. "She knows I love my mission work deeply. As soon as I begin to recover, I shall make plans to travel again."

"My mother found it difficult when I left to go to war. She had passed by the time I came home again. It is probably just as hard on your mother to see you leave." He smiled wearily. "What else do you worry about?"

Sophy tried to repress the resentment that welled within her. The reproach she sensed in his words left her brooding, but she said, "I worry one of the men Bark has invited for the holidays will come up to scratch and delay my return further, if I feel compelled to accept merely to please my mother."

To her chagrin, he chuckled. "That's possible. Our families are the only ones we must please ultimately." He grew serious again. "I've no doubt your work is exceptionally fulfilling, but do you not find life here changed on your return? I imagine your friends have all but abandoned you to the New World."

"We do have so little in common now that I suppose I might as well be on the other side of the world to our circle of acquaintances," Sophy reflected.

While his tone was kind, his words made her see how friends must view her. They could not possibly understand the fulfillment she felt. Jeremy had opened her eyes to the truth, but his manner was blunter than she was prepared to hear. The thought lowered her spirits right at the time of year they should be highest. However, tonight she refused to concern herself with new worries.

"There are times I wish I were in America simply because it is where my heart lies." She rose abruptly, giving him a curt nod. "On that note, my lord, I shall retire for the evening."

Chapter Five

THE FOLLOWING DAY Sophy ruminated over their conversation even as she brooded about it. She would use Jeremy's words to prepare her to face her conflicts, for she was determined to win the upper hand. Emma and Jane were helping her improve her embroidery skills in the drawing room that afternoon when Barclay rescued her, taking her outdoors despite her crutches, where they could talk privately.

"I applaud St. Laurent's idea to travel by sleigh," Barclay said. "You needn't use that silly sedan chair again, I promise."

She smiled broadly. "Your friends were thoughtful to consider my comfort. If only they talked about something other than the Season. It isn't part of my life now."

"I had hope for Herbert, but I know none of them are right for you. It isn't a waste, for I plan to take advantage of the holidays to chat up Bella." Barclay's cheerfully mischievous wink was replaced by a more serious expression. "Don't avoid the real subject, Soph. What if you can't get around well enough in time to sail? You said you depend upon walking in America."

"I know." She had no answer. She tried to keep her annoyance from sliding into despair, understanding that he had her interests at heart. Her America dream was not a goal she could relinquish easily.

"I don't wish to pressure you, but remember how civilized it is here. And think of Mother." Barclay shook his head. "I guess I don't understand your desire to leave us. It would be different if we were mean and demanding, but we aren't that terrible. We might have been as children—"

"Of course you aren't," she hastened to assure him with a gentle laugh. "You are still my favorite brother. You were always my champion when we were growing up."

"And I always shall be. But with Mother getting older, you have to give me a reason to argue for you other than defiance."

Their conversation left Sophy filled with uncertainty. Even if her family did not understand her motive in leaving, she loved them deeply. Yet their village was quiet and secure. Her life at home was missing a significant way to help those in need.

The passing days brought Sophy little relief from a dilemma that became more poignant with each conversation. Her mother expressed support and understanding of her daughter's obligation to her responsibilities abroad, words Sophy knew were intended to ease the separation. Yet her agony grew with her indecision as the days passed.

In the meantime she continued to struggle and pray. Now that she had crutches, this would be the first Sunday she could attend church. It was a start, she told herself, one that might help her make a decision that would satisfy her family as well as herself.

In the privacy of her room one evening, she decided the time had come to test her ankle. The only way to ascertain whether there had been any improvement was to stand on it.

Sitting on the edge of her bed, she put gentle but steady pressure on her foot. As she did sharp pain shot through her ankle. Too alarmed to continue, she sat down abruptly.

She tried to retain hope. Her ankle had not collapsed completely. Yet her determination to defeat her own doubt about returning to America was crumbling faster than the ankle was healing.

AS JEREMY HEADED downstairs for breakfast, he doubted that he would see Sophy, for she had managed to avoid him for two days. If he saw her at all today, he expected she might wish to be on the other side of the world from him. Her dubious mood when they parted in the library disappointed him, yet the physical distance America placed between Sophy and her family were issues he felt he must address. Since he found Barclay's concerns legitimate, he wanted to offer as much support to those concerns as he could during his visit.

Approaching the breakfast room with hesitation, he paused before entering, wondering whether he would find an attitude of childish insistence or mature compromise regarding the difficult decision she faced. He was surprised to find himself Sophy's company of choice at breakfast. For some reason he could not fathom she gave him the victory over his competitors, granting him the honor of accompanying her first that day even though Humphrey Fotherington continued to press his suit faithfully. Her encouragement allowed Jeremy to walk away with Sophy hobbling along on crutches beside him and a smug expression on his face.

Upon retiring the night they had last spoken in the library, he hadn't been surprised to find himself focused on Sophy Templeton. Since Rosalita's death he had given no thought to women. He'd loved Rosalita in the way a gentleman cared for a lady's welfare. He was her protector in a marriage built on social and political necessity, motivated not by choice or passion but by diplomacy. Although she was a lovely girl, the arrangement had been more strategic than heartfelt. While he'd done the honorable thing, romance had not played a part.

They may have grown to a deeper love for one another, he determined, but they had spent little time together before battle summoned him and ended her life.

But even if they'd spent a lifetime together, he knew he would have never felt toward Rosalita as he did toward Sophy. And he had competition. While the men Barclay had assembled for his sister's consideration weren't a good match for her, he particularly disliked Fotherington. Hodge was too foolish, Prindle too foppish, but Fotherington was a genuine threat. If he truly wanted her hand, Fotherington might be the only one strong enough to withstand Sophy's determination to leave England.

Another day passed before Jeremy decided to test her commitment to returning to her mission work. Restless from being indoors, Sophy told him she longed to go out to pick greens for decorating. Confident that the warmer temperatures of the past few days would pose no danger to someone on crutches, he offered to take her by sleigh to the woods beyond the west lawn.

As she watched him harness the horses at the stable, he was tempted to ask where she had slept and how she lived while abroad, but he suspected she would think it none of his affair. Or worse, have those memories make her more determined to leave. He remained silent on the matter as they rode across fields that sparkled with white instead of their usual verdant green.

"That ankle is taking time to heal," he said, his tone gentle but direct. "What will you do if you're unable to return to America when you wanted?"

Her blue eyes clouded over, reflecting both courage and fear, as if she were considering the possibility for the first time. "It would be the most devastating news I could hear. It would mean I could no longer help the children who need it most."

"America isn't the only place in need of charity." He smiled encouragingly, hoping she might relent. "You haven't been to London in some time, have you?"

"No, and I hope not to be there anytime soon."

"I'm sure you don't." Jeremy suppressed a grin of amusement. "You talk of educating Indians and frontier children, but there are children in orphanages, almshouses, and workhouses here. They need someone to teach them, someone to care. London is not so different from the wilderness you are used to. Rosalita's son entered the world in the middle of war. I was horrified to come home and find babies here at risk as well—and we aren't at war."

Her eyes were averted, but he sensed he had struck a chord. They disembarked in the woods, following a footpath someone had cleared that meandered along a brook no longer frozen but instead one that allowed water to flow gently. He had been correct in assuming the unusual warmth of the day would melt the ice, making it safe to maneuver the path on crutches, especially since he remained vigilant enough to catch her if she slipped.

"There is suffering everywhere," she admitted, averting her face as she snapped some evergreen boughs from a branch. "That is why I don't want my own physical weakness to be the reason I cannot return to America. I've seen missionaries sidelined by illness and some who died of tropical fevers, but I never thought an ankle sprain would end my days abroad. While my health was delicate when I was young, it is no longer an issue today. Besides, I'm fairly headstrong now, which is to my benefit."

Jeremy smiled but remained tactfully silent as she went on, "I don't want to see my involvement curtailed because of a simple skating accident. It's impossible to believe I won't return. I refuse to think it even possible."

"What drove you to America in the first place?" Jeremy asked, suspecting he knew the answer.

A smile, awkward yet humorous, curved her mouth. "Mostly to avoid places you and I had gone together. Patriotism was a valid reason for you to leave. I'm afraid I left for the wrong reasons, initially at least. Perhaps, though, when you thought of me—" She colored at her own words. "If you did—"

"I most definitely did," he prompted softly.

"Perhaps then you felt the same."

"I went to war not only to please my father but to do my part for the Crown. But I missed you and thought of you often." Jeremy felt not only his concentration but his fingers slipping from the boughs of greenery he was carrying for Sophy. "Now, of course, I follow my heart."

He looked away, reaching for a falling branch he might focus on while Sophy digested his words. When he felt she'd had enough time, he turned back to her, trying not to appear as if he were issuing a direct challenge. They were not at war after all.

When Sophy changed her expression only minutely, making it, if anything, yet more stubborn, he pursued the matter. "One of the things my father taught me about war, you see," he continued, "is that it always comes to an end. War never lasts, though its political crises cannot be put off. They won't wait."

She held a fragrant evergreen branch beneath her nose before extending it to his so he might do the same. "They are rather like women then," she countered. "They cannot wait either."

"Some do," he retaliated, albeit gently.

She withdrew the evergreen, turning away. "Everyone expected I would move on," she said in a cool tone. "You left for war without a commitment. You didn't ask for my hand before leaving."

She turned and stared at him directly, waiting for a reply.

"I have no good excuse, Sophy. It would have been unfair of me to ask you to wait." He gave a helpless shrug that offered an apology while he stood his ground. "I had already lost one brother to this war. My father was a commander in the Revolution, and I saw how difficult that was on my mother. She did not approve of my father's decision. He was loyal to the Crown first, as I was."

There, he had said it. He'd spoken the truth as he knew it, although he was certain it would not please her.

"I missed you," Sophy replied with a catch in her throat, "rather terribly. I wanted to see the world as you did."

"You make it sound as if I were traveling for pleasure." What on earth had she meant by such a remark? He made no attempt to hide his resentment. "That was most certainly not the case. I thought I had made that quite clear."

She shook her head, frustration evident in the tightness of her lips. Jeremy suspected she was struggling with tears that were too close to the surface, and she had chosen to hide them with a stubbornness he found most unappealing. He tried to control his impatience with her but failed when her petulance became increasingly annoying.

"That is not what I meant. Why did you return?" she demanded.

"I returned because I knew you would be here," he retorted, finding himself rather breathless. "It was only upon my return to London several months ago that I learned Charles Ferris had wed Isabella. It was then I discovered no one had claimed you."

"You would have discovered it if you had tried a bit harder," she snapped as she returned to the sleigh, laying down her crutches and thrusting aside the greens he had just piled near the spot where her feet would go.

The woman was a puzzle, he decided as he assisted her into the sleigh in silence. Perhaps she did not know her own heart as well as she thought she did. A glance at her face told him her emotions were too close to the surface for her to carry on a civil conversation. He opted for discretion and remained silent rather than offer conciliatory remarks that might fuel her fire further.

Jeremy drove them back to the house in stony silence. The fragile joy they had shared while collecting greenery for the holiday had shattered over a matter of words.

Her anger toward him made him realize his mistake. He believed he'd found the words to touch her heart and change her mind. Now he was forced to admit he'd been wrong. Very wrong.

Hard as he might try to make her see the value of staying in England, it was a struggle—and he was beginning to think it was a battle as difficult as any he'd fought in Spain.

THAT AFTERNOON Sophy gave serious thought to Jeremy's question as to why she had left for America. It was true she had gone for the wrong reasons, but the mission work had been so worthwhile she had never thought of returning to England to stay. Now she was not so sure. It was pointless for her suitors to continue to press the wonders of London upon her, for her time in the wilderness had stolen her desire to see the city again. Nor was it for the wishes of any of her suitors that she would choose to remain in England. She had begun to realize that her mother's and Barclay's opinions were the only two that mattered to her, for they most influenced her own. Now she was forced to add Jeremy to that group. It made her feel ill at ease to be at odds with the men and worse when she thought she might fail to please Mama.

Had she indeed been as self-centered as Jeremy seemed to imply she had? It was obvious he saw her mother's side more clearly than her own. A lump formed in Sophy's throat at the thought that she might be disappointing her mother, despite her parental encouragement to follow her heart. Her mother had always taught her to abide by her convictions. Yet the idea of leaving when her mother needed her most made her heart ache.

Her fear that she was letting down her family was not her only source of remorse. She had treated Jeremy harshly during what should have been a pleasant afternoon selecting holiday greens. He could not possibly know she needed to discuss her dilemma about returning to America with someone but resisted because she doubted his objectivity. Whatever insights others might share, she knew the decision rested squarely in her hands.

Her worst fears were realized when Barclay and Eddie sought her out the next day. She anticipated grim news from their troubled expressions even before they spoke.

"Mother's taken a spill on the stairs," Barclay said soberly, "and we've summoned Doctor Evans. He's been here three times in a matter of days. Might as well give him a room."

Sophy found her mother more jovial than any of her children.

"We have all inherited bad bones," she said philosophically. "It appears I have injured my knee. We know none of us will be First Footing this year. Only Barclay or Eddie could, and Eddie is already taken."

Sophy ignored the reference to the medieval tradition. Not only was the custom ludicrously old-fashioned, but it was utter nonsense to think the first man to cross the threshold of the home in which a young unmarried woman resided would be her betrothed. As they waited for Doctor Evans to arrive, Fotherington, Prindle, and Hodge volunteered to craft splints for her mother's knee by using a pair of small wooden planks from the barn.

"We shall have Riggs clean them," Prindle prompted.

"Then we shall tie them about the fracture if there is one with ropes and cloth," Hodge added.

Sophy smiled appreciatively at their efforts, thinking if she were on the frontier they would use rawhide if someone broke a leg that was able to be saved. She told her mother of their good intentions while her sisters-in-law advised Maggie on Christmas preparations.

"I suggested timber and padding if it comes to that," Sophy said, "but perhaps the hip is not broken after all."

"I am glad your unsuitable suitors are making themselves so helpful to me." Her mother smiled gratefully. "We haven't enough crutches to go around, I fear."

Doctor Evans brought happier news than anticipated, for as with Sophy and Teddy, the Dowager Lady Fairfax had suffered a sprain rather than a break. He examined their mother in the privacy of her room with only Sophy, Teddy, and Emily present. Sophy feared his next words, though his offer was not long in coming. He examined her ankle as thoroughly as before.

"You must have taken my advice, for I'm pleased to tell you your ankle is much improved," he said with some surprise. "It's not completely healed yet, but this is quite encouraging. Your footing is so secure I think you can stop using your crutches now. You just might be able to make that trip after all."

Sophy realized she had become far more hesitant about traveling over the last few days.

"Oh, thank you, Doctor," her mother spoke up, a resigned smile pasted on her face. "I know how much Sophy wants to return to America. It's what she's been waiting to hear, isn't it, Sophy?"

"Yes. Thank you." Sophy managed a smile.

Her mother embraced the grandchildren who reacted to the news with cautious enthusiasm as she explained to them how Sophy's commitment to the ministry in America meant that their aunt might be leaving. Sophy was relieved when Doctor Evans motioned her aside, for it prevented her from seeing the children's reaction.

"Of course your mother's heart condition is still a concern, as is her frailty," the doctor told Sophy quietly. "Those might be factors in your decision to travel in addition to the weakness in your ankle."

His unexpected words about her mother's health hit Sophy with such force she swayed on her feet. This was the first she had heard of a heart condition. Her mother had never mentioned such a thing to her. The doctor continued as he packed his instruments.

"As I've told your brothers, these are critical days in your mother's life. It would be most unfortunate if you were to be absent during this time. And you're young enough yet, Miss Templeton, to travel again after your mother is gone."

Still reeling from the news, and too embarrassed to admit no one had confided her mother's health problems to her, Sophy saw the doctor out. Then she confronted Barclay and Eddie directly, an ache in the pit of her stomach as she confronted them in the entry hall far from their mother's hearing.

"Why did you not tell me about Mama's heart?" she demanded. "This is the first I knew of this."

"I knew she'd worry, Eddie, if she found out," Barclay said.

"*If?* Did you mean not to tell me?" She was astounded as they seemed to struggle for words, their awkward silence confirming the worst.

Eddie hesitated before making a reluctant admission. "It's not the way we'd have chosen to tell you, but I'm relieved that you finally know the truth. It was difficult keeping it from you."

"I wish you had not." Sophy glared at her brothers in turn. "How could you not share such a thing? When was this discovered?"

"Eight months ago," Barclay explained. "She's had some minor but worrisome episodes."

"For which you were not here," Eddie said in a cutting tone.

Sophy's anger softened. Barclay was the only other family member who resided with her the year round. No doubt it had been an excruciatingly difficult time for her entire family. "I'm upset with you for not telling me the truth at once."

"We didn't want to alarm you with the news straightaway upon your return," Barclay explained, his apologetic tone edged with frustration.

"Within a week of your being home, you seemed more concerned with staying in America than with matters here. At the time the diagnosis was made, Mother didn't want us to summon you home. Doctor Evans couldn't say with any certainty how much time she has. It might be as much as a year or more, and there's a good chance she could live much longer than that. Once you'd arrived, she thought it best that we say nothing."

Gentle as they were, her brother's words stung Sophy into silence. To think her mother preferred to suffer in silence rather than tell her the truth humbled and humiliated her. No one other than Mama would do such a thing. It was a display of genuine love only a parent could show, and one that left her devastated.

Chapter Six

HER MOTHER'S HEALTH concerns were utmost in Sophy's mind when she retired to bed early that night, too despondent to engage in the festivities downstairs. While she strongly doubted she would spend her life in America, perhaps she might return if only for a few months, just until a replacement could be found for her. She knew her unmarried state was among her mother's greatest concerns. Perhaps she could convince Jeremy to return with her.

He might not be the most suitable of chaperones, she conceded, but in her confusion she was desperate to find a solution. She debated raising the subject the following day when she had a chance to be alone with him at the breakfast table.

"Since no one has arrived yet but you and me," Jeremy said in a confidential tone, "I want to show you what I found in my Bible. Remember when we exchanged written goals? We were about ten. We wrote what we expected to be doing twenty-five years in the future." He gave her a reminiscent smile. "When we're old, we said then. We're almost those ages now. It doesn't feel quite so old today, does it?"

"We were playing school," Sophy recalled, smiling fondly at the reminiscence.

"I thought us rather old for it at the time. Even then you wanted to teach, though your mother disliked the idea." Jeremy grinned. "Some things never change. This was the assignment you gave us. I kept it."

She watched, fascinated. The years fell away as he handed her a yellowed paper, looking at her meaningfully.

"You wrote that you wanted to travel to faraway places and have your own flock," he reminded her with a chuckle. "At the time, you were referring to sheep. You achieved part of your goal."

"You, of course, wanted to be a war hero like your father." Sophy smiled at the memory, adding with happy surprise, "You still have your childhood Bible?"

She realized with a guilty flush that she was not sure where hers was. She decided it must be upstairs in her bedroom. The Bible she carried with her now was one the Mission Society had issued her.

"Took it to war with me." Jeremy shrugged. "Even if I hadn't, it didn't need to be there in physical form, Sophy. We carry our lives with us, all we've learned and love."

She felt her heart stir as it had not in years.

"I never wanted you to go to war," she admitted. "We never even had a proper farewell."

"I wanted to be a soldier like my father," he conceded. "Of course Henry died when we were children, leaving Robert and me. And then we lost Robert in battle." Jeremy turned to her with a tentative smile. "But there is no running anymore for you, my dear. You always wished you could see into the future to know what awaited us. Do you think you can see it now?"

"I wish I could," she said with a catch in her voice. Her vision seemed cloudier than ever.

"Where's that flock of yours?" he teased gently. "You were Susannah's age when you wrote this. Maybe it's time to consider new goals. You never knew it was my secret wish to have a family like yours. Since I don't, I might have to join yours. You were part of that dream of the future for me. Now that I've returned from war, I don't ever want to leave England again. Nor do I want to leave you."

Sophy caught her breath as she absorbed Jeremy's statement. That he did not wish to leave England concerned her. The latter part, about not wanting to leave her, thrilled her. If the second part were true, she told herself fervently, surely it must triumph over the first.

Her worries vanished and her heart fluttered as Jeremy reached for her hand, covering her trembling fingers with his strong ones. Self-conscious suddenly, she turned away to avoid looking in his eyes. There was so much she wanted to say, but she could not be certain he was ready to hear them given his feelings about being home. Her fear of speaking and losing the moment turned her shy.

Before she could speak, the warning thud of footsteps beyond the breakfast room announced the presence of another. Sophy saw Jeremy's face darken, and he drew his hand away abruptly. Sophy turned and saw Humphrey Fotherington had joined them.

"Good morning, Miss Templeton," he greeted her jovially. "I was considering how I might spend my day. I've decided I'd like to call at the nearest village to make some purchases for Christmas. I hoped you might accompany me. It would allow you to exercise your ankle while doing some shopping of your own."

"Actually," Jeremy cut in pleasantly, "Miss Templeton and I have just made plans to go walking this afternoon."

He sipped his coffee, giving Fotherington a moment to react.

Fotherington's face fell. "How disappointing, though not for you, St. Laurent. Are you certain, Miss Templeton, you are up to that much exercise?"

"Thank you for your consideration," Sophy said sweetly. "I intend to take the utmost care with the ankle. I shall see you this afternoon, Captain St. Laurent."

She let herself be guided by the belief that his desire to be with her was stronger than his desire to remain in England as they walked to the pond that afternoon. Jeremy had suggested the path because the walk was long enough to test her ankle without straining it. She hoped he had also suggested the path because it would allow them to talk privately.

"Are you finding the steps difficult?" he asked with concern. "Let me offer you my arm, Sophy."

She accepted his offer happily, linking her arm through his as they strolled, using one crutch for the other arm to allow her to extend the walk a bit longer.

"I was about to tell you at breakfast," he continued, "how happy I am the war is over. I hope you and I might resume that part of the past before we parted, when we were truly content with ourselves and each other, and pursue it into the future. Tell me, Miss Templeton," he inquired teasingly, "do you think it possible? And do you still wish to have your own flock one day? This time, of course, I'm not talking about sheep."

The warmth of his companionship coursed through Sophy. She could feel it not only in his touch but in his words.

"Yes, one day," she ventured, bold yet shy. "For now I have nieces and nephews that I love. But my ankle is healing, and America is also in my future. Would you consider coming with me?"

The hesitation in his voice alarmed her as he said, "The past three years have given me excitement enough for a very long time. I might travel in the future. At present, however, I look forward to the peace and certainty of the familiar. I find that here."

Jeremy must have seen the sorrow in her face, for he reached for her hand at once. Sophy found herself wishing he were not quite so honest until she heard the sincerity in his voice as he added, "At the moment I would not be sorry to never leave England again, but even should I wish to do so, I couldn't. My father's health is questionable. He hangs on, but I could not think to abandon him in his final years."

Sophy felt the heat rise in her neck at his heartfelt explanation. Each of his words increased her sense of guilt, reminding her of her mother's tenuous health and the effect her departure might have upon her.

"For diplomacy's sake, can we not negotiate a treaty?" she asked, appealing to his military days for help.

"I know it is difficult for you to understand," he said softly, the tenderness in his voice twisting her heart, "but I have just returned from fighting a war—a horribly cruel and agonizingly long war—and I am relieved to be among civilized society again. Here there is no killing or maiming, no innocent citizens dying at the hands of soldiers drunk with victory and vengeance. Perhaps one day I will be ready to leave England again, but not now. I beg you to accept my life as it is."

A deeper frustration than she had ever known filled Sophy. Except for her injured knee, her mother appeared so healthy now that the doctor was aware of her heart problem and monitoring her care. Jeremy's presence abroad seemed ideal, for it would calm her mother's fears of Sophy being abroad without a family friend nearby. A part of her wanted to remain in America as long as her mother's health would allow. If only he would agree, Jeremy's companionship might provide an acceptable compromise to everyone in her family.

"Would you not consider going to America for a matter of months until a suitable replacement can be found? I understand your loyalty to our homeland, but you cannot put the Crown first any longer. You must be loyal to your family—your future family." She faltered at the words, feeling her heart breaking within.

"It seems odd to hear this from you, when you have failed to heed your own advice. And what will happen if your mother fails in your absence?" His voice was tight with irritation. "Your mother needs you, Sophy. Mine died while I was away, and I was not able to say goodbye. Do not lose the chance to spend time with yours."

Sophy fell silent, stung by Jeremy's rebuke. She resented his comparison of their mothers' situations. Her brothers had indicated the doctor was hopeful her mother might have a year if not more of good health ahead of her. His dismissal of her suggestion made her fear his love was not as deep as he had proclaimed earlier. While he probably felt she was behaving unreasonably, she was not prepared to dismiss her sense of duty to the ministry. She had not yet convinced herself that her resignation was entirely necessary.

She had promised the Mission Society her help. Her commitment to their cause was strong, an attribute that Jeremy St. Laurent obviously failed to appreciate, she told herself bitterly.

An hour later, in the throes of frustration over Jeremy's refusal to consider her suggestion, she found herself responding to Humphrey Fotherington's attention. The children's growing excitement as the holidays approached, and their challenges to see whose sled could go farthest, provided entertainment as well as conversation free from tension. She might at least make someone happy, she decided, knowing her brothers would be pleased to see her keeping company with Humphrey.

"I understand you spent more than a year abroad in the wilderness. I should very much like to see America one day," Humphrey surprised her by admitting one afternoon.

Sophy's ears perked up at the welcome words. "I think you would enjoy it very much," she told him. Wistful at the idea of giving up her dream of staying in America longer, she wished her time abroad could stretch longer than the next few months, even though she knew it was probably inevitable. Instead she pointed out the practical advantages. "It's a growing country, and opportunities abound for anyone with the desire and ambition to create a new life."

"And money, of course," Humphrey reminded her. "There is little one can accomplish without money to support new endeavors. That would not be an issue were I to go abroad."

The idea of having a companion abroad appealed so to Sophy that she spent considerable time with Humphrey over the next few days. She'd begun to fear no one would find the idea of traveling to America agreeable, even if only for a short time. When Humphrey expressed an interest in the New World she did not press for more.

Instead she challenged him to a game of chess one evening and even refrained from showing excessive jubilation when she defeated him handily. He in turn was a most gracious loser. Spending time with him removed the pressure of making a decision from her shoulders. While she wished Jeremy might change his mind about accompanying her abroad if only for a few months, the distance he placed between them, both physical and emotional, told her otherwise.

Sophy found herself getting on surprisingly well with Humphrey. His presence troubled her only when he focused their conversations on the social opportunities London afforded. He did not hesitate to boast of its many glorious distractions.

"America has its wildlife, yet buffalo cannot surpass the variety of animals in London's Menagerie," he said. "One cannot find exotics like the elephant, tiger, and lion in America."

"No," she was forced to concede, "yet they do not run wild in the countryside here as do America's buffalo."

Instead of arguing as Jeremy would do, Sophy found Humphrey equal to her intellectual challenges without the disapproval she'd come to expect from Jeremy. She enjoyed the banter she exchanged with Humphrey and thought his nature less disagreeable than Jeremy's. The time they spent together allowed her to put her marital prospects in perspective. Humphrey had made London sound somewhat appealing while at the same time expressing an interest in at least visiting America, unlike Jeremy.

Her intention to distance herself from Jeremy seemed to be succeeding until one evening at dinner. She had found her fan effective at keeping Jeremy at bay. A single wave of it drew Humphrey to her side and called attention to her feminine attributes.

She began carrying her fan regularly, waving it absently at dinner one evening, until Jeremy abruptly reached out and stopped its movement.

"I think that is sufficient," he said with a polite smile. "The fan creates rather a strong breeze for such a cool evening, don't you think? I fear you're creating a draft Arabella finds unsuitable."

Sophy flushed and glanced across the table where Arabella seemed too deeply engaged in conversation with Barclay to have noticed, but she acquiesced and set her fan aside.

The following day she noticed Jeremy seemed to spend less time in pursuit of her, even for casual conversation, preferring instead the company of Harry or Eddie. The strain in their relationship became obvious enough for Humphrey to notice, who responded by pursuing her vigorously in Jeremy's absence.

To Sophy's dismay she found the more constant a companion Humphrey became the less appealing she found his attentions. He struck her as a vulture that saw his chance, resuming his true nature as he scavenged the refuse left by Jeremy.

The realization angered her, for she did not intend to allow someone for whom she cared deeply to ignore her. They had resolved their differences about relationships that were now in the past, yet their lives were now headed in opposite directions.

She attempted a new approach with Jeremy that afternoon. "You would have the opportunity to deliver babies if you traveled to the New World with me," she said plaintively. "Surely it must have been a highlight of the time you spent at war."

"My efforts might suffice in an emergency," he said, frustratingly reluctant. "Childbirth is probably still better left to the skill of an experienced midwife. It is not what I would desire to do with my life."

"I have no wish to be petulant, but I believe a man who cares for a woman would sacrifice for her—as he has done for his country." Bitterness rose within Sophy. "If I do not choose my future course soon the next ship will leave without me, and you will be glad of it."

"A man who truly cares for a woman would not stand in the way of something she wishes to do as deeply as you wish this." Jeremy's brown eyes searched hers. "Would you have me deny it? Where is the strategy in lying? We are not at war, are we?"

Sophy found it difficult to disguise her exasperation with him. "You would know better than I, would you not? I would never receive such treatment from Mr. Fotherington."

Jeremy's scornful laugh infuriated her. "If you think Fotherington will accept your traveling, you are mistaken. Are you pleased that he acts as if he is willing to try the New World to set up a business? He says it to please you. Fotherington's interests are here. His words are merely the lies one tells when attempting to win the woman of his heart. Fotherington's no better than Charles Ferris."

The idea sent a rush of doubt through Sophy, but she dismissed it at once. She'd begun to believe Mr. Fotherington might prove a more agreeable companion, and Jeremy's infuriating decision to remain objective rather than loyal to her only strengthened her belief.

"At least he entertains the idea of accompanying me at some point," she concluded. "He has always wanted to visit America, unlike yourself."

Jeremy reflected on her puzzling attitude after they parted, wondering if she had heard a word he'd said. Despite his outspokenness about his reluctance to travel to America, Sophy continued to press the issue. Spitfire that she was, she intended to promote her cause until he consented. While he loved her and admired her determination, he decided that the best way to win her heart was not to point out a solution he considered evident. Rather it was to find a diplomatic way to help her view situations in a different way while tempering her fear of rejection, for that was what he believed her resistance to be. His love for her told him that in some ways he knew her better than she knew herself.

Her generous heart, strength of character, and innocent belief in her mission made her the most desirable woman he could possibly imagine for himself. Her love of children was evident in her commitment to her missionary work.

Yet that passion made him wonder if she truly wanted to be a wife and mother now that she'd had a taste of America. How could domestic life compete in her plans after her adventures? But he also saw the pain she forced her mother to undergo by insisting on returning to America, and he was concerned that Sophy failed to recognize it. Having lost his own mother while he was away had drained him emotionally. He knew the guilt grown children felt when a parent died in their absence. He did not want Sophy to have to endure the pain and regret that accompanied such guilt. He had to spare her that suffering despite her inability to recognize the risk if she chose to travel abroad now.

Lady Fairfax had been gracious in not insisting that Sophy, her only daughter, remain at home to care for her in her waning years. His concern lingered as he wondered why Sophy could not comprehend the seriousness of her mother's frailty and react as he'd expect.

WHEN, SOPHY wondered, had she faced a decision more painful than the one that faced her now? She had never felt more conflicted. Now that she was home she recognized how much she loved England, her home, her nieces and nephews. The world she saw today was different from the one she'd left. The words in the note she'd written predicting how she would be spending her life twenty-five years later came back to her. She wished desperately that she could predict the future, even as far as next month. Unfortunately, she could not.

To her chagrin, the men attempted to settle the decision for her the next day. A discussion of holiday traditions had arisen, along with the concept of First Footing, the holiday tradition she feared most. The subject arose casually but soon took shape as a challenge as they gathered in the drawing room that night. Snow fell softly beyond the window as Sophy listened, patience mixing with frustration, while Arabella attempted to teach her the difference between two embroidery stitches.

"We have had so many injuries this month," their mother remarked, stitching on her own embroidery hoop, "we must hope our First Foot is a tall, dark-haired gentleman. According to tradition, that is who will bring our house and all who are in it good luck for the twelve coming months."

"We can't let it be Herbert then," Barclay joked, seated by the fire with a glass of brandy, "for with that blond hair he looks far too much like a Viking. Sorry, Herbert, but that coloring suits Bella far more than you."

Arabella Prindle blushed a becoming shade of rose, Sophy thought. She turned toward Barclay in as subtle a fashion as possible and saw the change had not gone unnoticed by her brother.

Barclay threw his leg over the arm of the chair. "In ancient times, it was believed that, after the New Year, the first single man who entered a home inhabited by a young unmarried woman was the man she would marry. Perhaps the only way to determine who shall have Sophy's hand is to see who the First Foot is."

Humphrey Fotherington exchanged a meaningful glance with Sampson Hodge, their faces thoughtful, as if they were considering such an outrageous challenge. Sophy held her breath. Surely Barclay could not be serious.

"Let us not jest about this," Fotherington said cautiously. "Is it truly appropriate to vie for the hand of such a desirable creature as Miss Templeton using such a haphazard method?"

The discussion left Sophy's nerves on edge. She imagined such a challenge resulting in a race to the front door, with Jeremy the winner, settling the matter once and for all—but only if he were willing to accept her decision, she thought.

"I believe there are far more sensible ways to choose a mate," she declared, rising and excusing herself as gales of laughter followed her departure.

Sophy listened in disbelief when the subject arose again the following evening at dinner, as Harry carved a joint of mutton.

"We must all know and understand the rules of First Foot," Lady Fairfax cautioned. "There is no stepping outside right before midnight, with the first bell that rings in the New Year, and returning indoors just as quickly."

"Let's make it fair, then, to give everyone a sporting chance," Humphrey Fotherington proposed. "If we—and Miss Templeton, of course—are to abide by First Foot rules, the first gentleman across the threshold is the one she will marry."

The conversation continued along the same lines. By the time the sweetmeats were served Sophy agreed at last to consider the ridiculous tradition, desperate to end the discussion. By New Year's Eve her plans to sail to America for her temporary stay would be finalized, and any betrothal that came that night would be put on hold. Her future husband, she decided, must either agree to the arrangement or forfeit the First Foot victory. All was silent until Barclay chuckled, drawing everyone's attention.

"What kind of bumblebroth have we gotten ourselves into with this?" he said, shaking his head. "Perhaps a better question is why Sophy is so accepting of the idea."

Smiling sweetly, Sophy returned to her dessert in smug silence, satisfied that everyone was pleased with her decision.

As Christmas drew closer she made it clear to the trio of suitors that presents were unnecessary, unless they cared to give gifts to her nieces and nephews. That her injury made her unable to reciprocate made a most appropriate excuse. The truth was that she had no desire to encourage any of them.

Finally, two days before Christmas, while the others in the household were outdoors at a skating party, the snows had melted sufficiently to allow the mail coach to pass through Sheffield and for deliveries to be retrieved. The improvement in the weather brought the answer Sophy had waited for. She would remember it as the day she was able to discard her crutches for good.

She accepted the letter from the British Mission Society with trembling fingers, so impatient to read the long-awaited answer that she tore it open in the hall as it was handed to her. She scanned the missive until she found the words she so desperately sought, her heart leaping as she learned they had found a chaperone. While no one could replace Mrs. Amesbury, the director noted, the minister bound for America would be accompanied by his wife who was unquestionably suitable.

As she let out a sigh of relief and her heart began to beat again, Sophy felt her spirits plummet. Having waited so long for the reply, more events had transpired in the past fortnight than she had ever expected. She was startled to find herself hesitant to accept the Society's offer.

Three issues held her back. She had become uncommonly attached to her nieces and nephews in the time she had been home. Her mother, frail now, had injured herself in what could have been a disastrous fall.

And Jeremy had returned to her life.

The combination left Sophy unsure whether she wanted to return to America. How would she feel leaving behind those she loved most? Her mother, Teddy and Emily, and Jonathan and Susannah were here—as was Jeremy.

Her faith was shaken as she realized she must reconsider her decision. She need not respond to the letter just yet. If she were to change her mind, she would need time to adjust emotionally. For the time being she would say nothing.

Her emotions were buried so deeply that making the right decision would require time and patience. And privacy. It would be, she knew, the biggest decision of her life.

But she had no time to dwell on it, for the Christmas whirlwind kept her mind occupied, leaving her no time to fret over her undecided future. The aromas wafting throughout the house distracted the guests from their card party as fragrant pine mixed with cinnamon, nutmeg, and savory meats and cheeses from the larder. The merry mood indoors kept everyone from grumbling and fretting about the weather and turned their hearts toward laughter and sharing.

Guilt flowed through Sophy as she realized too late that she had forgotten to make a present for Jeremy. She had spent all her time making gifts for her nieces and nephews, creating games from ideas that had occurred to her while she lay abed letting her ankle heal. In the bookshelves she discovered cherished books from her childhood that she knew would appeal to the children. Their gifts had been a joy to consider and to make.

Then she'd put her newly gained knitting skills to work on presents for the adults, but she had forgotten Jeremy's because his posed the most difficult decision for her. No matter what gift she contemplated giving, no matter how common, none seemed devoid of emotion.

With Christmas Eve on their doorstep, she had nothing to give him and no ideas. She could not get to a shop in such deep snow, and she hadn't time to knit anything, for her presence was needed for holiday activities. Given their emotional stalemate, she could think of no suitable present.

Then she remembered their childhood days and the objects that delighted them most. On a whim she decided to look inside the old toy box in what had been their playroom in childhood.

And there she found just what she'd hoped to find.

Chapter Seven

ON CHRISTMAS EVE morning Deervale Hall bustled with such activity that the day went by almost in a blur.

"Sophy claims she needs no presents," Barclay joked with his companions that morning over breakfast, "but perhaps someone might give her proper skating lessons before the season is over."

By late morning, after making decisions for Maggie in the kitchen, Sophy removed herself from the activity downstairs and made her way to her mother's bedchamber. Lady Fairfax sat by the window, blanketed in sunlight that warmed the room as it patterned the carpet and bathed Sylvan's wagging tail in a golden glow. On the table before her mother sat a tray with a cup of chocolate. A flowered plate held assorted rolls with raspberry preserves and bacon.

Removed from the holiday bustle, her mother looked completely at peace and appeared well on her way to recovery from her fall. The atmosphere was so inviting Sophy pulled up a chair beside her, wishing she might take refuge there for the rest of the day.

"Good morning, Sophy," her mother greeted her with a wistful gaze, turning back to the view of the gardens beyond her window. "There is something in the magic of morning that makes me wish it might last the entire day, especially a day such as this. If only your father were alive to see it." She smiled sadly, turning back to Sophy. "But, of course, the afternoon has its charms as well, and Christmas Eve day particularly. But never mind that. I'm sure the letter you received from the mission is on your mind."

Sophy felt so guilty raising the subject that she tried to think of another to bring up, but there was no avoiding the matter. Before she could speak her mother continued, "I'm so glad the society has found a suitable chaperone for you. It seems everything has turned out as you wanted."

The finality in her voice tugged at Sophy's heart. Mama's willingness to sacrifice her own care so Sophy could follow her heart to America was almost more than she could bear.

"Mama, that's why I've come. It's turned out as I'd hoped, but many things have changed since I wrote that letter to the ministry."

Her mother gazed at her in surprise. "But your plans are all set. You no longer need crutches. The slight limp you still have will go away in time. All that's left to do is send your letter of acceptance."

Sophy searched for the words she had not yet been able to articulate even to herself. "But it has been so wonderful to see the children again, and I worry about leaving you, and—"

Her mother cut in at once. "You must not worry about my health, Sophy," she said adamantly, "and I mean it. I have a house full of servants who have nothing better to do than wait on me. Isn't that enough to convince you to follow your heart? It's obvious you were meant to teach."

"My deepest devotion is to you and our family." Sophy's voice quavered as she managed a smile. While she agreed with her mother's assessment of her talents, she recognized the truth of her own words.

"You have my blessing on this, darling. Don't let me be the reason you sacrifice your dream." Her mother hesitated before releasing a sigh. "I never told you this, or anyone for that matter, but before I married your father I was a fairly accomplished artist."

Sophy began to recall the few occasions from childhood when she had watched her mother make use of the light in the drawing room to sketch the landscape beyond their window. Her mother had been able to capture the scene vividly. She was so talented Sophy wondered why she had not spent more time in artistic pursuits.

"I remember some of your drawings," Sophy said. "They were very good. It always surprised me that none of them were hanging on the walls here at home."

Her mother's face held the shadow of a smile. "Your father considered it unseemly for me to waste my time sketching. He thought it improper that women should do anything other than care for their children. Not that I minded, of course. Spending time with all of you was my greatest joy." She shrugged. "Looking back, I cannot see why I could not have managed both."

"You would have done both splendidly," Sophy concurred feelingly.

She was silent for a moment, dismayed by her father's reluctance to allow her mother the artistic freedom she craved. Her mother's next words stunned her even more.

"That is why you must travel to America as planned," her mother insisted, taking hold of Sophy's hands and gripping them tightly. "Doctor Evans expects no change in my condition in the few months in which you will be gone. His concerns are for the future. I was not allowed to pursue my dreams. I will not let you make the same mistake. The time to follow your heart is now while you are young, before you have a family of your own." She released Sophy's hands. "I want you to write that letter today."

Sophy felt herself shaking within. Despite her own confusion, the best advice she received was always her mother's. Even if she doubted herself, she had no reason to doubt Mama now.

"Thank you, Mama," she murmured, humbled into acceptance as she gave her mother a quick embrace. "I promise I won't let you down."

Her mother's smile was laced with humor and affection as she squeezed her hand. "You never have, child. You won't now."

Sophy rose and hugged her mother before leaving her to her breakfast, her heart still unsettled. She might not be letting her mother down, but there were others who did not understand her as well as Mama did and would not see things the same.

The announcement of her decision became progressively more difficult as the day progressed. Sophy broke the news to Barclay in passing on the staircase, telling him the long-awaited letter had come and she planned to accept.

Her heart tightened as she watched his face fall before he pulled himself together, no doubt putting her welfare first. She berated herself for not being a more loyal sister. She wished she had been home when her brothers had received Mama's diagnosis.

"I'm glad, Soph," he said with a lopsided smile. "It's what you hoped for. You're a dedicated teacher. They're lucky to have you."

As difficult as breaking the news to Barclay had been, the moment seemed less poignant that afternoon when she carried Christmas decorations downstairs and saw Jeremy talking in low tones with Barclay in the great hall. Their sudden hesitation to speak as they glanced awkwardly in her direction pricked her conscience. Guilt mixed with regret flooded through her as she hurried past them, relieved at the jocularity that filled the drawing room where her sisters-in-law and their guests had gathered.

She remained in the farthest corner of the drawing room, refraining from partaking in refreshments or sharing in the merriment. It was enough to hear their laughter in this season of comfort and joy as she placed the Christmas greens in the windows and about the room. Comfort and joy was what she needed most now, and she would find both in the American routine to which she had grown accustomed and to which she would return.

Ready for another task to help her pass the hours in this emotionally draining day, she was startled to come face to face with Jeremy as she left the drawing room and stepped into the entry hall. He closed the doors behind her.

"I understand you've decided to return abroad after the holidays," he said in a soft voice. "I'm disappointed, Sophy."

"I decided some time ago," she said firmly, "and I see no reason to change my mind. I'm sorry if that doesn't meet with your approval, but it is only for a matter of months until the Mission Society can find someone to take my place. Would you have me do otherwise? It is where my heart lies."

"And apparently your destiny as well." Jeremy's next words were crisp and his voice challenging, as if he expected her to answer to charges. "I know you've given adequate consideration to your future, but you've forgotten your past. Your mission includes no provision for your mother. It's unfortunate your sense of charity doesn't extend to those who love you most."

Sophy felt her neck burn with anger. She could not begin to fathom the cause of Jeremy's irritation. While his mother had passed away during his absence in the war, it could not be compared to her situation. Was it anger that she had chosen to leave him for America? If he loved her that deeply, she mused, he should make an effort to express his emotions more directly.

"My mother shall remain here in the joint care of Barclay and Doctor Evans while I am away," she returned. "She has given me her blessing. That's more than I can say for you."

"What would you expect her to say? Spending your days on another continent seems rather unfair, especially when your family has been most generous." His tone turned icy as Sophy continue to burn. "Your time abroad has given you confidence, but it appears to have robbed you of the kindness you possessed as a child. I did not know you could be so heartless."

"If anyone has been heartless," she whispered, "it is you."

Her frustration overflowing, Sophy lacked the ability to control her speech or emotions. She stormed upstairs, beyond words in the face of Jeremy's criticism.

Did he not understand she needed time to adjust to her decision to return to England within a few short months and perhaps seek companionship in marriage upon her return? Her mother had at least been kind enough to remember her calling. Despite her advice, doubt lingered. The thought of not returning to America was somehow not as disappointing as it had been.

Although Jeremy could not know it, she still debated her decision. His method of discussion was selfish and insulting. She had attempted to make him understand her point of view, and although he had been kind to her, she had obviously failed to convey adequately the disappointment she felt upon having to change her goals. After hearing his low opinion of her she was forced to face a realization of her own.

Jeremy St. Laurent was, once again, the one who should be left in the past.

Sophy filled the late afternoon hours by putting decorative touches in the drawing room. While setting candles about the room and edging the sideboard with strands of ivy added to the festive appearance, it failed to improve her mood. Her sisters-in-law moved about, discussing tomorrow's dinner in low tones and contemplating a seating arrangement that would please everyone. Glad they were preoccupied, Sophy gazed out the window, trying to bring the turmoil she felt under control.

She was standing in the oriel window when she realized the twilight of another Christmas Eve had fallen over the landscape. In the lantern light she watched the sparkling snow fall gently, as if time were of no consequence, blanketing the gardens and covering the flagstone paths in pristine white, making everything new. Briefly, she wished she could live the past few days over again, if only to find a way to spend them better.

Her solitude was broken by the boisterous exclamations of Barclay, the three suitors, and Arabella as they burst into the room, their presence heralding the start of Christmas Eve. Soon afterward, the children joined them to prepare for the family's favorite tradition of celebrating the coming year by bringing in the yule log.

The anticipation Sophy saw in the eyes of Teddy and Emily lifted her spirits. At the same time, she felt a pang of regret at having been away last Christmas Eve. How much she had missed. The excitement the children felt shone clearly in their animated faces and their giggles. Sophy found her own heart reverting back to childhood as the evening wore on.

Soon all had gathered to await the arrival of the yule log. The children waited as patiently as possible in the drawing room, the women listening to the laughter of the men as they struggled to drag in the thick tree trunk they had cut in the forest to fulfill the tradition.

"We've outdone ourselves this year," Barclay gasped, as he helped haul the massive log to the fireplace.

Teddy and Emily clapped at the sight of the log, ribbons attached, as the men deposited their find in the hearth. The group admired the trunk as the men paused to catch their breath.

The log must have been especially heavy, Sophy mused, for it had taken the efforts of two of her brothers as well as Barclay's three friends and Jeremy to drag it indoors. Amused, she wondered if they were all needed or if they had chosen to participate for the sake of tradition. With a pang of regret, she noticed that Jeremy, while included in the ritual, remained on the far side of the room where he and she could not antagonize each other.

"I trust Mother had the foresight to save pieces from last year's log," Eddie said, "so we might light this one properly."

Watching as the new yule log was lit with the remains from last year, Sophy put aside her troubles and found herself swept up in the sentiment of the moment. She was glad she had chosen to wear her favorite winter dress of green velvet with narrow satin ribbons down the front that were decorated with tiny mauve silk roses. Christmas Eve was meant for festivities like these, she reminded herself, meant to be spent with family. She watched as Harry said a blessing over the yule log, welcoming it by dousing it with wine.

Those gathered for the ceremony fell silent, lost in reverent reflection as the log caught and crackled with the promise of another holiday together. Soon the sparks would become a fire hearty enough to warm the coldest winter night. Teddy and Emily had found it difficult to stay out of the kitchen all week and allow the staff to perform their tasks without interruption. Now they had insisted Maggie join them for the lighting of the yule log. They cuddled in the cook's ample lap, watching the hypnotic flames.

"Do you know why this night is special?" Maggie asked them.

"Because it's the night Jesus was born," Emily replied.

"That's right. And at midnight," Maggie said softly, "all the sheep in the fields turn and bow toward the East."

"Shouldn't they be in the barn keeping warm?" Teddy asked with concern.

When the laughter and exclamations of affection had subsided Susannah piped up. "That's what you told us last year, Maggie," she said, curled up beside the cook. "I like hearing your stories."

"I'd best return to the kitchen and leave you wee bairns to your holiday," Maggie announced. "It's said bread baked tonight never turns moldy, so I must get to work."

"Isn't that just a superstition?" Jonathan asked, skepticism in his voice.

"If you'll be wanting some fresh bread tomorrow you'd better not say such a thing," Maggie warned with a wink before she left.

"And here we all are," Harry said meditatively, as quiet fell over the room, "for another Christmastide together."

"I hope Thomas and Dolly are managing in all this snow," their mother said in a worried voice. "Dolly must be nearly ready to give birth."

"They're fine. I rode to Riggs's cottage to see if they needed anything when the snow began falling this afternoon," Jeremy said, his deep resonant voice startling Sophy. She felt so relaxed she had momentarily forgotten his presence. She kept her back to him, retaining a distance on the far side of the room.

Now that she had made the commitment, at least emotionally, to return to her mission work for the next few months, she was content to stand apart from the others. It was time to take in the sights and scents of Christmas so that she might have the memories to hold close once she was absent from her loved ones.

She was saved from further reflection when the steaming punch was carried in from the kitchen and set by the hearth where the women bustled about, readying some for the children. It was followed by the lamb's wool, reserved for the adults. The aroma of the hot ale with its roasted apples, sugar, and spiced pieces of toast floating on top was another sign that Christmas had truly arrived. The fragrance of bay, rosemary, and laurel filled the house, adding the magical touch so familiar from years past.

As Jane ladled out punch, whistling winds from outside penetrated a lull in the conversation, making the group gather closer to the hearth.

"It's fortunate we are all safe and sound indoors," Harry said, "for no one shall reach us on a night such as this."

They were all surprised soon after when their closest neighbors, a couple who lived a half-mile down the lane, knocked on the door. Next a family from further away in the village called, having arrived by sleigh. Despite the servants' efforts to keep the children inside at the festivities where they belonged, the children bundled up and ran outdoors to greet the horses and see to their comfort in the stable before returning indoors to play with their guests.

Almost before they knew it, a cluster of friends and neighbors that included their minister had gathered in the drawing room to exchange holiday wishes. When Sophy looked about the room she saw familiar faces she had known all her life, many grayer now and infirm but smiling heartily as they embraced one another. Old friends expressed such delight at seeing Sophy again and were so eager to hear her stories of the New World that after telling her tales she was enthusiastic to hear theirs.

Looking about, she realized family, servants, and neighbors had gathered, regardless of class. It was rather like America, she thought. The Peninsular War had ended, and everyone was happy and shared the spirit of good will toward men.

Her mother, delighted at being surrounded by villagers, clergy, and family, took her seat at the spinet and played the carols so familiar to those gathered. Voices, both melodically high and sonorously low, in tune and out, joined in a harmonious union to celebrate the season with verses from the traditional hymns.

Afterward, the guests departed contentedly, having sung the songs they had sung every Christmas Eve for as long as Sophy could remember. Their visitors wished everyone Happy Christmas and a prosperous New Year, bidding each other farewell until tomorrow when they would greet each other in church. Sophy was sorry to see them go, for it meant she would have to wait until tomorrow to talk with them again.

Having seen them off at the door, she returned to the warmth of the enormous hearth. As she walked into the drawing room, her eyes fell upon the painting over the fireplace that her father had commissioned so many years ago. While arranging holly and ivy about the frame earlier she had remembered how much its subject once meant to her. The oil painting featured trees in a sunlit glade on the property where she and her brothers used to ride when they were young.

Tears sprang to her eyes at the memory. She had been so full of anger when she hung the greenery that she had not taken time to appreciate those who were still part of their lives.

Pulling herself together, she told herself such maudlin thoughts were natural at holiday time when she might be gone from home for many months. She must take in all the sights and smells and memories to sustain herself while she was away, she reminded herself fiercely. Although the country's war had ended it still waged at Deervale Hall, she realized as she glanced toward the circle of gentlemen in the room. Humphrey Fotherington appeared to have the advantage over his enemies.

But was it what she truly wanted? Sophy remembered Jeremy's warning that Humphrey would say what she wanted most to hear simply to win her hand. The gentlemen present were about ready to put her to the test, she realized, as Barclay called everyone's attention to the kissing bough.

"Here in Derbyshire," Barclay explained, "we call it the kissing bunch. Whatever name it goes by, we make the most of it. One mistletoe berry, of course, entitles you to one kiss. When the berries are gone, so is the opportunity. Bear that in mind, gentlemen."

"That's an impressive collection of holly and ivy," Humphrey said, studying the greenery hung about the sphere.

"In Derbyshire," Barclay said, "you need both for luck."

"Then may this be a lucky year for us." Humphrey flashed Sophy a smile that made her blush.

Sophy felt her insides tighten with trepidation as Sampson Hodge gazed first at the plant with its white berries attached to the bough's center, then raised an eyebrow to give her a surreptitious glance. She glanced quickly toward Jeremy, looking for his reaction. It irritated her to see he was too engrossed in conversation with Arabella to have heard the conversation.

"We haven't much mistletoe in Derbyshire," Barclay chuckled, "but Riggs manages to get us some every year."

They waited for the annual tradition to begin, as the butler was called upon to bring the long taper to light the candles set among the greens for the first time this season. Sophy looked forward to the ritual that would be performed tomorrow and every night during the twelve days of the Christmas season.

Her suitors took turns requesting her hand so they might bestow a proper kiss. Humphrey Fotherington waited until Herbert Prindle and Sampson Hodge had taken their turns to lift her hand lightly and peck the back side with a kiss. Sophy suspected he'd gone last for dramatic effect.

She waited impatiently for Jeremy to rise and offer the same, but he remained on the far side of the room, engaged in conversation first with Harry and then with Arabella, who at least had the grace to show interest in the festivities.

She had waited through the others' attempts for nothing, she realized angrily, for Jeremy had barely watched the proceedings. Harry and Eddie appropriately kissed only the hands of their wives in their turn. The men then took turns politely kissing Arabella's hand.

Sophy's heart leaped as she watched Jeremy at last pick a berry for the right to take his turn at the kissing bunch. Her relief was short-lived. Instead of approaching her it was Arabella's hand he sought, bestowing upon it a kiss Sophy felt was destined for her. It was also a kiss she considered longer than was customary.

She fumed. Whether his display of affection was intended merely to be polite or for her benefit alone, it was uncalled for.

By the time the last mistletoe berry was about to be pulled, she realized Humphrey Fotherington had refrained from kissing Arabella's hand, no doubt leaving it to Barclay. Yet her brother had taken his turn earlier, seizing the opportunity rather than leaving it to chance. Sophy was horrified to see Fotherington pick the final berry from the bunch.

"The last kiss of the evening, I fear," he said with a smile. The act was deliberate, Sophy thought with irritation, giving Jeremy no opportunity to kiss her hand. The privilege disappeared with the berry Humphrey had just picked. She watched as Humphrey lifted Arabella's hand idly, raising it to his lips for a meaningless light kiss.

The only meaning it had, Sophy reflected, was to deny Jeremy the opportunity to kiss her hand through this mean-spirited triumph. Humphrey had stolen his rival's chance. Trying to keep tears of frustration from her eyes, Sophy looked away as applause heralded the conclusion of the night's romantic ritual.

It was not until everyone had turned to other activities that she glanced back at the kissing bunch to remind herself of the season's real meaning. Her mother and Maggie had done an admirable job decorating it, combining hoops to form the frame that was then covered with garlands of holly, ivy, and other greens. Apples and oranges were suspended from the center ribbons, while roses crafted from paper, snippets of colored ribbon, and bright streamers and ornaments the children had made children brightened the green globe.

But the highlight of a kissing bunch in Derbyshire, the part unique to her home province, was the three small dolls painstakingly crafted and detailed to resemble Mary, Joseph, and the baby Jesus. They hung from the top to form a simple manger scene. This year, especially, they reminded Sophy of her mission work.

With so much of her future in question, the sight made her wistful. She had no idea what might await her after America. She had no idea whether Jeremy might still come up to snuff or whether Fotherington would try to claim her hand as part of the First Footing tradition. Worse, if she were asked at that very moment, she had no idea what she herself wanted.

And that, she realized dismally, was her greatest worry. Of all those gathered at Deervale Hall, the person she had become was the biggest stranger of all.

Chapter Eight

IF HE FOUND Christmas Eve difficult, Jeremy realized with sobering clarity, then Christmas Day would likely prove even more challenging. The wandering musicians from the village had reached Deervale Hall surprisingly early considering the deep snows that lay beyond the window. As they stood caroling beneath the breakfast windows to welcome in the holy day, Jeremy's head ached from the glare of the snow. It would be worse for the others, he thought, for only he and Harry had not imbibed any liquor other than the lamb's wool the night before.

The high point of the morning was the delight on the faces of the children as they opened their presents. Even the family's spaniel was enjoying his present. Teddy and Emily had tied a bright ribbon around a piece of meat so tasty that Sylvan made sure to get every last bit of grease from the drawing room rug.

Accustomed to the discordant noises of war for so long, Jeremy found the children's squeals of laughter and surprise as enchanting as music. He wished he might experience the sound more frequently, but Fate did not appear cooperative in that regard.

He had not helped his cause last evening by foolishly displaying his resentment. Having used a mistletoe berry to kiss Arabella's hand, he'd found none left to kiss Sophy's. No doubt she suspected his action had been deliberate rather than the mistake it was. He hadn't expected Fotherington to seize the last berry.

Kissing Arabella's hand had been a waste. Perhaps Sophy had not noticed, distracted as she was by Fotherington, Hodge, and Prindle.

Jeremy sat quietly to one side, returning his attention to the children until Barclay startled him by handing him a very small box from a branch amidst the kissing bunch.

"A gift from my sister," Barclay told him with a grin.

Jeremy glanced across the room to the spinet, where Humphrey sat on the bench beside Sophy, who ran her fingers slowly across the instrument to produce a gloomy sound.

He held the box for a moment, looking up briefly to see others opening small gifts as well. He was relieved, for he felt more comfortable knowing he was not the center of attention. He proceeded to remove the wrapping from his gift.

Inside he discovered the familiar figure of a toy soldier on horseback. The paint had worn away from the small wooden figure in spots, but the musket with the bayonet was still intact, and the horse looked as majestic as ever. The sight of it stunned him, the memories even more so.

How well he remembered playing with the soldier as a child, but seeing it again as a battle-scarred cavalry officer stirred him deeply. He vividly recalled thinking of the toy soldier as a battle hero when he was young.

Now, as he studied the small figure seated on a rearing horse with his sword raised in triumph, he alternated between pride and regret. War was not a matter for childhood, despite how strong an impression the figure had made on him.

He set the figure aside, glancing toward Jonathan and Teddy and hoping they need never fight as he had. He glanced across the room to see Sophy watching him with anxious eyes.

"Thank you," he murmured.

Realizing his words were lost in the crowd, he rose and walked across the room to her. Was it hope he saw in her eyes? At his approach, Fotherington stepped aside to greet Barclay.

"Being hindered by this ankle, I only ventured as far as the attic for a gift," she said awkwardly. "I found the soldier you played with as a child. You always chose that particular one. It was Barclay's, but I know it has more meaning for you."

"I remember this fellow well." Jeremy smiled, seeing the relief on her face. "Thank you. I trust Barclay won't miss him."

Sophy took a deep breath. "You've earned him with your service to the Crown. Perhaps you might keep him in case—in case you have a son one day."

"I shall keep him in a safe place." Obviously she intended to go ahead with her plan to leave. If he were ever to have a son, it appeared he must find a wife elsewhere. The thought made his holiday meaningless. He nodded to the kissing bunch, useless as it had been to him. "There is one there for you as well."

"Wait here," she instructed, rising. "I am well enough to walk independently. I shall find it."

He watched carefully as she discovered his present hanging among those left on the kissing bunch. Thinking he detected a slight spring in her step, he waited as she removed her gift and returned to sit beside him. She seemed more subdued this morning, careful to avoid his eyes as she unwrapped the package slowly.

"I hope you like it." He felt suddenly inadequate and shy, as if he were courting a girl for the first time. "It's just a trinket. I made it while I was in Spain."

He heard her draw a sudden breath. "It's a horsehair bracelet. Is it Sir Walter's hair?"

"Yes. In retrospect it was rather risky to take my horse to war. I'm extremely fortunate he survived and was able to return with me. This way we—you shall have something of his after he's gone."

She looked at him in confusion. "Was it—did you make it—for me?"

Jeremy spoke up to ease her mind. "I made it for you long before I knew Rosalita. I'd forgotten about it until I discovered it among my things recently."

"It's truly lovely," she said simply. "Thank you. I appreciate it."

"You're most welcome." He watched as she stared at the bracelet in her hand. Her fingers appeared to tremble. "Would you like to wear it? Allow me to fasten it for you."

As he fumbled to tie the knot his fingers were as useless as hers. They exchanged a smile, and the tension eased slightly. He set the bracelet aside, noticing Sophy's expression had sobered.

"I shall take it with me to America," she promised, "and keep it as a remembrance of my past."

Jeremy's spirits fell, but his smile remained. "Well then."

"What a marvelous pair you are," Barclay said dryly in passing. "You have even given each other matching presents."

The remark made Jeremy turn to his friend. The reservation in Bark's voice surprised him. It seemed unfounded after the merriment of the previous night, for he had been fairly giddy last evening with Miss Prindle.

At least Barclay had reason to be merry, Jeremy acknowledged. As for himself, he and Sophy might have exchanged matching presents, but he was not at all convinced their hearts matched.

THE MORNING'S church service was appropriately respectful, with the time of fellowship at the parting afterward uplifting and hearty. Sophy was glad to see again those with whom she had renewed her acquaintance last night. Conscious of the poor among them and the returned soldiers who were crippled and unable to work, everyone deposited as much as they could spare in the alms box for those less fortunate.

As she made her contribution, Sophy remembered Jeremy's admonition about England's needy. The reminder prompted her to give more than she had planned.

Beneath her long sleeves she felt the soft horsehair of the bracelet he had given her. His thoughtfulness had touched her beyond words. She was so overcome words were inadequate.

Yet words had not changed his mind about accompanying her into her future. The inevitability of their parting weighed heavily on her. If he were not willing to join her abroad for only a few months, what might it foretell about the years that lay before them? His reluctance did not bode well.

She was relieved that the bustle of Christmas dinner preparations prevented close contact with Jeremy when the family and their guests returned home to Deervale Hall. Conversation that was already merry and optimistic became more so when Barclay surprised everyone by providing more cause for celebration.

"I am delighted to inform you," he announced just before they went in to dinner, "that I have given Arabella my hand and my heart, and she has graciously agreed to give me hers."

There were exclamations of joy and congratulations all around on the engagement, as Arabella met the gazes of each of them in turn, blushing a flattering shade of rose.

"Now that I've done this," Barclay confided to Sophy, taking her aside, "you know everyone is hoping for a second betrothal today."

Sophy smiled shakily, trying to remain lighthearted to keep up her spirits. "I'm afraid it isn't likely. But there is still First Foot."

The family's jubilation continued over the sumptuous Christmas dinner Maggie had prepared. The enthusiastic chatter during the preliminary courses diminished once the main course was delivered on a gold platter arranged with greenery and the pungent aroma of roast goose filled the room. Those gathered turned serious as they tended to their dinner.

"Now that Christmastide has come, even the rabbits and birds outdoors can have extra food," Emily piped up, proud of the gifts she, Teddy and Susannah had offered nature's creatures.

Instead of feeling uplifted by the Christmas cheer and contentment, Sophy felt heartsick at the thought of leaving such kind and precious nieces and nephews and, of course, her loving mother. What would the holidays be without her? she wondered, gazing at her elderly parent who sat at the end of the table. She was too distracted to eat.

When Maggie appeared with the plum pudding, the jocularity returned among family and friends. The familiar frumenty filled with plump, mouth-watering raisins and currants was Maggie's specialty, the like of which Sophy would never find in America.

"And it's made proper," Maggie advised them, "right after church the

Sunday before Advent, and stirred east to west, as it should be, in honor of the Three Wise Men."

Maggie's words hit a strange chord inside Sophy. Three men had come to court her, but how wise were they? They had chosen to court a woman who was bound for another life in a foreign land. If even for a few short months, she thought indignantly, they might have expressed more interest about the cause to which she was deeply committed.

After its arrival, the steamed plum pudding was cut up and devoured quickly. The silver sixpence hidden inside that supposedly brought good fortune was discovered in Jonathan's slice, a happenstance all considered a good omen for the family.

"Why do we no longer pass the wassail bowl as in days of old? Let us drink to our health," Harry announced, summoning for the potent ale to be brought in, "for we have much to look forward to."

Afterward, they gathered in the drawing room again, quiet and reflective now, their energy dulled by the heavy dinner they had consumed. Playing cat's cradle with Emily in the window seat, Sophy watched from a distance as Barclay talked privately with Jeremy. She saw Jeremy's face drop and lose color as he turned toward her, an expression of profound regret on his features.

She turned away quickly. Barclay must have told Jeremy she still intended to travel. Glancing back furtively, she saw Jeremy nod his head slowly, decisively, before rising to leave the room. His departure went unnoticed because he had been so quiet over the last two days. Perhaps he hadn't been as quiet with others, she thought, as he had been with her.

The finality of his movements told her he had made up his mind about her, even if she was the one who had made the choice.

They were as cool and distant, she realized with a pang of dismay, as they were when they were first reunited. His leaving made it feel as if the intensity of the past few weeks had never happened.

In the absence of Jeremy's constant attention, Humphrey had been extremely attentive to her throughout the day, but she remained withdrawn, preferring the companionship of the children. Being in their presence saved her from conversing and helped her smile again.

The day passed quietly thereafter, with the tiny mince pies saved for a supper treat. Everyone ate theirs in customary silence as they would for all the twelve days of Christmas.

Later in private she had a chance to offer her future sister-in-law her best wishes.

"I am certain you and Barclay will be very happy together," she told Arabella after they exchanged an embrace. "You have the good sense not to allow misunderstandings to keep you apart."

"Do you not think you will join us?" Barclay encouraged kindly. "It would be so appropriate if you were to get leg-shackled on the same day as us. It is not too late."

Sophy shook her head, her throat tight. "The honor of being first to the altar is yours if you'd like it."

The following day, Boxing Day, meant the children would have a special visit to Thomas and Dolly Riggs's cottage, something they greatly anticipated. Boxing Day being the day they would give presents to the staff and to tenants, they had decided to bring their own handmade gifts for the tenants, in addition to those their grandmother had prepared.

With Harry and her mother, Sophy accompanied them on the visit, surprised to see how much Dolly's midsection had spread since she last saw her. Dolly practically radiated joy.

Upon her return, however, she was dismayed to discover Jeremy had already left.

"He's going home to his father," Barclay told her, "but he plans to return in time for the New Year."

"Why did he leave?" Sophy demanded. "What else did he say?"

"He said he had to leave regarding a business matter." Barclay shrugged. "He didn't elaborate."

Sophy fought a growing resentment as she walked upstairs to her bedchamber. What business was more important than she, especially at Christmas and with their future hanging in the balance? Jeremy had not even taken the time to say goodbye.

It was a short time later that day, after the group had enjoyed a light supper and tea, that the children called Sophy downstairs to give her their present.

"You already gave me lovely drawings," she reminded them, surprised.

"We gave you what we had ready," Susannah corrected her. "What we really want to give you is this. We're sorry it's late, but we had to wait for Riggs to finish it."

"We wanted something special for you," Emily explained proudly.

Together they turned and lifted a long narrow object from behind them.

"It's a walking stick," Teddy announced, "to help you walk when you go to the New World."

Hands extended before them, they presented the walking stick to Sophy as a group. She caught her breath as she accepted her gift, studying the animal figures carved into the chestnut. Riggs had done an admirable job with the design, carving the faces of wolf, deer, bear, and buffalo to represent the animals the British commonly associated with the American wilderness. He had obviously spent a great deal of time and effort on the gift.

"We'll let you go if we must," Jonathan said softly, "but you need something to help you with that limp—and something to remember us by."

Sophy looked at the children, their faces alight with hope before their expressions turned sad. Sophy was at such a loss for words that her mother thanked them for their thoughtfulness.

"What an ideal present for Aunt Sophy," she praised them. "You put a great deal of thought into giving her something that would make her happy. And now," she said to Sophy with a smile, "you are all set, despite the tenderness in your ankle."

Choking back tears, Sophy thanked the children, hugging each in turn. Her feelings overcame her again when she was alone in her room. She could not stop thinking of the kindness and devotion the gift represented. The children were willing to let her go because it was what she wanted. Yet how could she leave the nieces and nephews who loved her and whom she loved so? The gift left her feeling as burdened as she was grateful.

She sat at her desk and reread the letter from the mission society. Beside it lay the acceptance letter she had delayed posting because of the holidays. The walking stick was propped beside the door, ready to see her off. Now, with Jeremy gone and that part of her life behind her, the truth struck her.

She knew for certain she could not go. She would remain in her country with her family where she belonged. The wave of relief that swept over her nearly crushed her in its intensity.

But it was too late, she realized, forlorn again, to salvage the other part of her life. Jeremy had left. And what she might have had with him was gone as well.

"AND SO," SOPHY concluded the next morning, glancing from her mother to Barclay, "now that I am staying here rather than going to America, it seems only appropriate that I keep an open mind as I turn my attention to my future. No doubt my decision will please you both. I am happy with it as well."

Having described the change of heart that had brought about her decision, she sat back in her chair at the breakfast table where she had asked the pair to remain with her after the others had finished and departed. She did not have to wait long for their reaction, for exclamations of joy and enthusiasm burst forth from both almost before she had finished speaking.

"It really is time you seriously considered marriage," her mother said gently. "You have made a great sacrifice in giving up your plans and staying here instead, but now we must see to your happiness."

"But I am happy," Sophy insisted. "Being here with you is all I need."

"Perhaps for now," her mother said as she smoothed Sophy's hair from her face tenderly. "I appreciate your loyalty to me, but I have already discussed it with your brothers, and we feel it is time for you to find some-one you can love as well."

Sophy groaned inwardly at her mother's words. If the subject had been discussed among her mother and brothers, her fate was already de-cided.

"Now it's Sophy's turn," Barclay declared, as if reading her mind. "Since she hasn't decided, perhaps we should allow Fate to find her a mate and leave it to First Foot."

The reference to the ancient custom sent a shiver through her. "We have discussed this already. Surely you can't be serious."

"You know," Barclay continued, his enthusiasm growing, "it might be the best way to find a husband for you. Not to take it lightly, but whoever makes the first appearance at our door will be a man who is putting his best foot forward with you in mind."

Sophy had to admit she had given unfair regard to the attentions of her potential suitors. They at least had been willing to get to know the part of her life they had observed on this side of the ocean. Realizing her mother and Barclay knew her better than anyone and had her interests at heart, she reluctantly agreed to consider the plan. It hardly mattered who she married after all, she thought wearily, for the one who probably would have made the best match was now out of consideration.

The men who were left had all been in a frenzy when the First Foot tradition was brought up. Sophy knew Barclay must have told them of the plan.

"I haven't known any of these men long enough," she complained to her brother. "How long have you known Arabella?"

"We met in town toward the end of last Season. She can be stubborn, but I'm used to that." Barclay gave her a teasing glance that made her hope she too could become as flexible when the dreaded time came. "Do you think I haven't known her long enough?"

"No," she admitted. "Even when you've known someone for a long time, you sometimes don't know them as well as you think. Or they believed in you and supported you once, but no longer do so."

She had no time to wallow in regret, for the First Foot discussions reached a feverish pitch over the next few days.

"The game is on for Miss Templeton's affections!" Sampson Hodge said one evening with such relish it alarmed Sophy. "Who shall be her First Foot? With Viscount Cobleigh having left early, the odds have improved considerably."

With the pressure on, Sophy found herself unable to avoid Humphrey's attentions. He courted her furiously during the week following Christmas, suggesting activities they might enjoy in London from the horsemanship at Astley's Amphitheatre to the latest exhibition at the Royal Academy.

"Let us set the First Foot rules," Eddie reminded them one evening, when their ministrations had all but worn out Sophy.

"The First Footer must not arrive empty-handed," Herbert Prindle spoke up. "Tell us, would you prefer coal or salt?"

"I like the idea of staying warm," Harry said with a smile, "so I find coal the ideal gift. In rural areas such as ours, some residents leave a lump of coal outside the door so they can serve as their own First Footer."

"But there are some rules as well," Sophy's mother cautioned. "It is not permissible to wait beyond the gate until after the New Year and then rush the door at the stroke of midnight."

"Anyone else?" Humphry Fotherington continued lightly. "Bread? Money? Perhaps whiskey would suit better."

"Whatever you bring," Emma said, "you shall be offered food and drink in return."

Only after he was invited inside, Sophy thought. Maybe she would not invite any of them in, and the silly tradition would come to an abrupt end. She smiled, attempting to find joy in the realization that these men were willing to compete for her hand.

"Of course, it's best," Jane spoke up with what Sophy considered ridiculous solemnity, "if the First Footer is a tall, dark-haired man. No one who resembles a Viking. Sorry, Eddie," she added, flashing a smile at her brother-in-law amid laughter.

"I am neither tall nor dark-haired," Herbert Prindle said, crestfallen, "so perhaps I am eliminated by virtue of my build."

"You might not be tall," Sampson Hodge joked, "but you'll appear that way if we have Teddy answer the door."

With the competition mounting, Sophy was not surprised to find Herbert Prindle talking with Barclay late one afternoon. The pair were smoking cigars, while the others in the household had paired off to engage in rounds of piquet.

Barclay blew a puff of smoke, grinning at Sophy. "One less for you to worry about," he announced. "Herbert's dropped out of the race."

"I am sorry to hear this, Mr. Prindle," Sophy said gravely. "Pray do not do so on my account. Having come to the realization it is time for me to wed, I will make the best choice possible."

"Lovely as you are, Miss Templeton," Herbert replied, "I believe I am destined to be a bachelor."

Sophy smiled. "Then we have more in common than I thought. Perhaps I am destined to be a spinster."

"Never," Herbert said. "I don't believe it's in the cards. I suspect great things are in store for you, with many happy surprises along the way."

"Then it is down to two gentlemen," Sophy surmised, intrigued with the concept suddenly.

"Two that we know of," Herbert reminded her with a wink.

"Whatever you do, Soph," Barclay warned sharply, "at least act as if you intend to go through with it, else the fellows at the clubs will start taking odds that you'll cry off."

She suspected he had consumed too much brandy to see the depth of her pain. "Perhaps as Herbert suggests, spinsterhood is not in my future after all. Ah, well, I shall simply have to be patient to see who begs my hand at the door after midnight."

No matter who it is, she thought with a pang of dread.

AS THE DAYS passed, her family made Sophy well aware she must consciously choose one man over another. Yet how was she to do so when the one her heart yearned to see, the one who mattered most, was in the next county? He was not far when it came to counting miles, though he might as well have been, for he felt impossibly far beyond her reach. Worse, it was all her fault—again.

Once, as she tiptoed throughout the house, avoiding places the men gathered, she overheard them when they thought her out of earshot. As they competed in the race for her hand, they discussed which amusements might please her and what they would show her in London. She was both amused and exasperated to hear their thoughts, with grumbling and excitement part of everyone's journey to the New Year, just as they had been in the old.

Satisfied to see his sister happily betrothed, Herbert Prindle remained impassive while Sampson Hodge continued to press his suit. Humphrey Fotherington treated her as if he had already won her hand.

"You do have a choice here," Barclay reminded her, "though Fotherington seems to feel he is in the lead."

This time Sophy remembered to think before she spoke. "It is not precisely the solution I might have chosen, but if he asks for my hand, I suppose I shall accept."

Having consented to the idea, she could find little else to say on the matter. Some days her future felt as bleak as the winter landscape, for she had no realistic hope of a relationship with Jeremy. Meanwhile, as speculation continued as to what would make the most appropriate First Foot gift, two men waited here for her to decide among them. She saw no reason to look further.

SHE WAS PARTICULARLY vigilant the day before New Year's Eve as she watched for some sign of hope. Fate responded with a snowstorm that whitewashed the countryside, bringing a bitter wind that whipped about and blinding snow that seemed to fall endlessly. The view from the window reminded her of an old rhyme about wind that came out of the northeast. Flee it, man and brute, the rhyme advised. Jeremy had certainly fled it as best he could.

Even if he changed his mind, she realized with growing dismay as snow continued to fall the next morning, he would never make it in time because of the deep snows. Fate, she was forced to admit, had apparently decreed that they should not be together.

Tonight her family would ring in the New Year with the customary toast of "Waes haeil," Be well, with the clink of glasses. The custom was medieval, but Sophy's dilemma was modern, one that brought quiet despair.

She wondered if it were even possible for her to be happy without Jeremy. In his absence she saw the truth. If she had felt devastated thinking she might not return to America, it was nothing compared to knowing someone else would be first through the door on New Year's Day. Her future was one day closer, and the truth hung heavy over her.

It was customary that all quarrels were put aside on New Year's Day, but Jeremy was too far away to know of her change in heart. While no one was required to pay any debt for the first week of the New Year, Sophy owed him a debt she could never repay.

"Well, this is it," Barclay said to her when they met in passing on the staircase that afternoon.

"This is it." She managed a strained smile. She would be brave for her family, for they mattered more than anything. "Bark, I must ask. Did you talk to Jeremy before he left?"

"We talked, but not about you." He must have seen her face fall, for he added, "He only said it was a business matter he had to attend to. Whatever it was, it seemed very important to him."

Sophy accepted Barclay's words and tried to dismiss Jeremy from her thoughts. At midnight, she promised herself, just as she had promised her mother, that the first man through the door would be the man she would wed.

The evening hours passed with gay revelry. Barclay and Arabella looked forward to their nuptials in the year to come, while Harry and Jane and Eddie and Emma looked forward to watching their children continue to blossom. Their mother, Sophy knew, looked forward to seeing her only daughter settled at last, living closer to home where they could resume the intimate bond they'd shared before Sophy went away.

For Sophy, the hours ticked by painfully slowly as the stakes were raised. The merriment of the holidays and the humor that accompanied their First Foot dares had faded for her, with tension left in its wake. With two hours left until midnight, raucous laughter dwindled to casual conversation, then quiet reflection, and, finally, to silence.

Stick-skinny Sampson Hodge broke a wine glass when he accidentally dropped it in front of the fire, while Herbert Prindle, exasperatingly calm, paced repeatedly from one end of the drawing room to the other, increasing his pace, then slowing it, until Sophy feared the carpet would be in tatters before midnight.

Only Humphrey Fotherington managed to maintain his confident demeanor, a realization that frightened Sophy more as the minutes ticked by.

At one point, Teddy and Emily grew so sleepy that Emma and Eddie carried them upstairs to bed, with her mother volunteering to stay with the children. Jonathan and Susannah sat quietly by the fire, playing cards and enjoying staying up late in the company of adults.

At one point, Barclay passed close to where Sophy sat, leaning over to whisper in her ear, "Perhaps Jeremy will come yet."

"What makes you say that?" she returned, hoping she did not sound as frantic as she felt. "Did he give you reason to believe he might?"

"I can't put it into words," Barclay confessed. "It's just a feeling. I don't suppose it means much, but I hope he comes." He rested his hand on her shoulder briefly. "If this is a contest," he whispered fiercely, "it's one he ought to win."

Then he walked away, returning to the silent group.

As the grandfather clock chimed eleven, Herbert Prindle expressed a desire to go out for some air. Fifteen minutes later, Sampson Hodge gave Sophy his wide smile and promised to return by morning. Looking around, she saw no sign of Humphrey. Her heart pounded so hard she found herself sweating.

"What do they plan to do?" she asked Barclay in desperation.

"I don't know," he replied, the curiosity in his eyes so evident she did not doubt him. "No one shared his plans with me."

Her mother returned downstairs several moments later, taking a seat beside Sophy as she attempted to offer support. "You made this decision with the courage I've come to expect from you," she said softly. "I'm proud of you, Sophy. I am certain this New Year promises great happiness for you."

Sophy returned her smile, unconvinced. She tried but failed to steady her nerves as midnight approached. Over the past week this moment appeared to be coming too quickly. Now time seemed to have stopped, as if it, too, were unable to make headway in the storm that raged beyond their windows.

Midnight ushered in a silent New Year. While the clock pounded out twelve beats, Sophy's heart pounded equally hard, but no knock followed. Eventually her family resumed casual conversation in the drawing room.

The great hall remained silent for so long she decided it was not worth the wait. She was prepared to retire for the evening when a pounding on the door made her heart nearly stop.

Her family drew a collective breath and stepped aside, leaving the way to the door clear for her. Sophy glanced at each face in turn and demanded in consternation, "Must I answer it?"

"It appears to be that time," Barclay said. He glanced at their mother. "There's no tradition that says the unmarried young woman must open the door, is there? Here, I shall lead the way."

As he and Sophy walked alongside each other into the great hall, he turned to her and whispered, "Let us hope."

Let it be Jeremy, Sophy prayed, closing her eyes briefly as she stopped in the hall. When she opened them Barclay had reached the doors. She drew confidence from his presence. It would be as it had been in childhood, the trio together again—herself, her favorite brother, and his closest friend. After a second's hesitation Barclay threw open the doors.

Sophy stepped forward, imagining she would see Jeremy there. Before her stood Humphrey Fotherington, a bunch of greens in one hand and a lump of coal in the other.

Disappointment overwhelmed her. She could barely stifle the cry of agony that formed in her throat upon realizing the First Footer was not the one she had hoped to see. It took her several moments to regain her breath in the face of such extreme dismay.

Before she could utter a word, the family who had gathered behind her began to cheer and clap. Barclay invited Fotherington inside, accepting the coal in exchange for the ale Eddie proffered along with a tray of meats and cheeses from Emma.

Once their First Footer had delivered his wish for luck to last the coming year, the excitement died down as the family returned to the drawing room. They stopped as Fotherington set aside his refreshments and cleared his throat. Before Sophy could react, he bowed before her on one knee, taking her hand in his.

"My dearest Miss Templeton—Sophronia," Humphrey began, his voice humble, "I wish to request your hand in marriage. I would ask you to be my wife and to accept me as your husband."

Sophy was horrified to be in such a position with onlookers waiting for her reply. She'd so desperately hoped Jeremy would be first through the door that she had nearly convinced herself it would be him. When she saw it was Humphrey, she was heartsick. She realized in a flash that Jeremy was the only man she could ever truly love and want to marry.

She stood ready to cry as Humphrey awaited her answer.

"Oh, look," she heard Arabella murmur to Barclay. "Sophy is so happy she's ready to weep."

Opening her mouth, Sophy was on the brink of declining when the second visitor of the New Year in as many minutes pounded on the door. Before Barclay could open them, the doors burst open. Jeremy St. Laurent entered the great hall swiftly, in his arms the tiniest baby Sophy had ever seen bundled in blankets.

"A Happy New Year to one and all," he exulted. "I apologize for the delay, but here's one arrival who was not held up by the storm."

The baby began to wail as he held out the child for all to see. As the family gathered round, pulling the blankets away to view the world's newest arrival, Thomas and Dolly Riggs stepped into the great hall, smiling effusively, unnoticed at first by all but Sophy.

"We were fortunate Viscount Cobleigh passed through when he did," Thomas exclaimed. "He brought our son into the world. Says it's only the second delivery of his life. You'd never know it. He handled it like a regular surgeon."

The family congratulated the couple on the baby's birth by offering blessings and wishes for health, happiness, and prosperity.

"Does this make the baby the Second or Third Footer?" Barclay exclaimed.

"He ain't a footer at all," Herbert Prindle laughed, "since he didn't come by foot."

"We don't refer to him that way now that he has a name," Thomas said proudly. "His name is Jeremy Thomas Riggs."

What an appropriate time to be born, Sophy thought. The baby's birth promised a happy future filled with hope and possibility. Jeremy returned the child to his mother's waiting arms in the drawing room where Dolly had been made comfortable on the sofa. As the others gathered about her, Jeremy took Sophy's arm and drew her toward the hall.

She was startled when Humphrey Fotherington blocked their path, bowing to Jeremy with a gracious smile before he turned to her. She was stunned to hear a gentle humor in his voice she had not thought him capable of.

"I have not received an answer to my question," he reminded her with a tentative smile, "but I believe Captain St. Laurent has traveled further than I this evening for the very same purpose. Under the circumstances, I feel it only fair to allow him to ask you his question also."

Fotherington paused, glancing from Sophy to Jeremy, a hint of expectation in his face.

"I suspect I know the question he wishes to ask you," he continued, turning back to Sophy, "and your reply as well. Before another celebration is announced, I want to wish both of you in private the very best in the coming year. And now, if you will excuse me, I shall wish Mr. and Mrs. Riggs the congratulations due them."

With a deep bow Fotherington turned and walked back to the drawing room.

"Now that," Jeremy said under his breath, "was more than sporting of him."

Sophy watched Humphrey depart with tears in her eyes, realizing how she had underestimated his character. Before she could reply, Jeremy took her hands in his and turned her toward him.

"It's rather difficult to find lambs this time of year," he told her, gazing into her eyes with an intensity that made her heart flutter, "but I found a shepherd who sheltered me during the storm, and we have three men here. I believe they are wise enough to know there is no longer any need to vie for your hand."

Sophy's spirit soared as she smiled back at him playfully. "Then they are wise indeed," she said softly, "for they have read my mind. They have, however, given gifts in the form of a sedan chair and splints for Mother."

"Might I consider myself as wise?" he teased. "I have brought a gift also. On my journey I found a jewel for which I request permission to place on your finger."

Sophy felt herself grow faint. She could find no voice to speak.

"Sophy, my love," Jeremy said tenderly, taking her hands and squeezing them in his, "you have never been afraid to do away with tradition for a more suitable arrangement. I would ask that you disregard our First Foot custom and accept instead the proposal of the Second Foot. It is a rather delicate matter, but then, you come from a family that has the most delicate of limbs."

Sophy felt her heart pound. "I would be most willing to accept the hand of a Second Foot," she whispered, smiling at how silly it sounded.

Jeremy removed a simple gold band from a small velvet-lined box, slipping it onto the third finger of her left hand where it fit as comfortably as if it were made for her.

"As for this ring," he explained, "it was my mother's, and I am quite certain she would want you to have it, having known you as well as she did."

"I would be most honored," Sophy said, fighting back tears of joy and disbelief.

"There is another matter as well," he reminded her, again holding her hands. "The matter of your mission."

"Oh," she assured him meekly, "I know now I could not leave those I love again. It was a hard lesson for this former teacher, but I am grateful I learned it in time."

"Do not think for one moment that all is lost. There are children here who have no parents to teach them right from wrong or to teach them the gospel." Lovingly he cupped her chin in his fingers. "I left here to go home and confirm that I would serve on the board of a new children's charity in London. The charity will address issues concerning children in the workhouses and in orphanages. Children who have no home; children who need teachers and someone who will love them. Someone like you. Am I correct in thinking you might enjoy that work very much?"

Sophy's heart skipped a beat. Such fortune could not be happening to her. "I would indeed, my lord," she said disbelievingly.

"One day, of course, you might be too busy for that," he said, linking arms with her and patting her hand, "if we have our own little ones. In the meantime, I can think of no one better than you, dear Sophy, to help with such a project."

For the third time in the year a knock on the door announced a new arrival. Jeremy opened the door to find Sampson Hodge shivering in the cold. Hodge hurried indoors away from the cold, his thin form nearly bending in two as he tripped over the threshold.

"Am I too late?" he demanded, eyes bulging when he saw Jeremy.

"Only if you do not mind being Third Foot," Jeremy said.

As she sauntered into the drawing room on Jeremy's arm, Sophy saw that Barclay had observed their approach. He made his way toward them.

"Since no one took me up on my suggestion of skating lessons as a Christmas present for Sophy," he teased, "might I suggest them as a wedding present?"

"I already have all the presents I need." Sophy laughed, taking her brother's arm on one side with Jeremy's on the other. "Including the presence of mind to know where I belong."

Barclay gave her hand a tender squeeze as he led them to a private corner and asked, "When do you plan to marry?"

"As soon as possible, I should think," Jeremy said, "though I have not yet discussed it with my future wife. I shall soon turn thirty. At my advanced age, I see no reason to wait for happiness."

"Nor I," agreed Sophy.

"It is no wonder there is so much you want to achieve, Sophy. When we were little we played together, you, Eddie, Harry, and I," Barclay told her reminiscently, "and we always won our races while you struggled to keep up. We were bigger and older, but that didn't stop you. You sailed to America before we did. You touched our nieces' and nephews' hearts in a way none of us could. As adults I think none of us has experienced joy as fully as you have. And now, it appears, you shall beat me to the altar."

After Sophy and Jeremy announced their engagement to the rest of the family and their guests, Barclay remained in the corner, watching as his sister and his best friend walked arm in arm, not doubting for a moment that she had outdone them all.

The End

Dedication

For *A Delicate Footing*

To Carolyn Sullivan, Jeanne Paglio, Paula Scully, and Janet Jones.

For the blessing of your friendship, a cozy Christmas story to enjoy over a cup of tea, with a little love stirred in.

On the Twelfth Day of Christmas, My True Love

by

Sharon Sobel

Chapter One

"I'VE NEVER KNOWN a man to ignore a call to claim his inheritance, even if he has to crawl on his hands and knees through rain and snow to do so," said Lord Peter Milton as he selected a handful of dainty tea cakes from a silver tray. "Though I suppose having to crawl all the way to Penzance would try the fortitude of any man."

"I have experienced a good deal worse than that," Nathaniel Evander pointed out, his hand hovering over the tray. But he did not have much of an appetite for sweet things, and he settled on his dark, rich tea, which was the specialty of the club. "And I have no intention of crawling, or even riding, for that matter. My leg is still not strong enough for a ride from London through Cornwall, and I shall be perfectly content to stretch out in a warm coach and do nothing more than admire the passing scenery."

Peter raised his eyebrows and said nothing. Perhaps realizing the tray of delectables was all his, he pushed several more pastries onto his own plate and devoured them as if he had not eaten in a week. Nathaniel watched, reminded of Peter's conquests through all the years of their friendship, and considered how much stock Peter put in the very art of winning. Then, with a start, he realized what his friend had just said.

"Are you suggesting I must suddenly assert a claim to my inheritance? Whatever gives you that idea? I assure you, my relationship with my Uncle Michael is as strong as ever and I remain his only heir. He has called me home to celebrate the Christmas holiday at Pencliff with him and a few guests." Nathaniel raised his cup and studied his friend through the steaming mist of the hot tea. Peter looked a little self-satisfied, if a trifle ridiculous with a smear of pink icing on his chin.

"Do you know who else is of the party?"

Nathaniel shrugged. "I suppose Lady Westbrook will be there, as they are the oldest of friends. My uncle enjoys hunting with the local squire, so I am sure he will be of the number. And there will be others, as it is a family tradition to welcome all who are alone for the Christmas season. To what do your questions portend? Are you fishing for an invitation?"

Peter laughed. "Not at all. I am following a certain Mrs. Rolande to

Danbury House for Christmas, and shall pack an ample supply of mistletoe in my bag. I will not be very far, as Danbury House is in Helston, but undoubtedly will be far more comfortable. I will not envy you in your ancient and drafty fortress."

"Pencliff has a vast library, where I intend to spend a good deal of my time. The house has not been tested against invaders for hundreds of years, so hardly qualifies as a fortress."

"It only has to hold off one invader this season."

"Surely you do not mean Lady Westbrook. She and Uncle Michael have known each other since the beginning of time. He reads Latin poetry to her. She bakes him cakes, little decorated things that look better than they taste."

Peter leaned closer and whispered, "She has a niece."

"She has one niece," said Nathaniel. He had not thought of the girl in years, but recalled her in an instant. She was a bit of a pest, always following him around and wanting him to teach her to swim, or climb trees, or heal small animals she found along the road. Her hair was very dark and hung in a long braid down her back. He once dipped the tip of her braid in ink and wrote out her name in bold print on a piece of wood. But what was her name? Emily? And what had he heard about her? He thought about it for a moment. "I believe she married many years ago."

"She did not marry," Peter said, emphasizing each word. "Not once, not twice, not thrice. She was betrothed three times and each man died before the wedding. Lady Westbrook's niece has a fine reputation indeed. She is known as The Black Widow, and now, it is generally understood she has designs on your uncle."

Nathaniel snorted. "Impossible! She's a girl!"

Peter slapped his hand down on the table, as if he held the winning hand at cards. "Very possible! She's nearly the same age as you and I, old man! And we both know that men of sixty, like your uncle, think nothing of marrying women half their age."

Could such a thing be possible? While Nathaniel was canoeing down unchartered rivers in America and digging through ancient ruins in Italy, could Lady Westbrook's little bit of a niece have become a woman capable of luring men to their death? He laughed out loud. It was lucky he managed to avoid her all these years, for he proved himself perfectly capable of nearly killing himself without any help from a girl. As it was, his most recent fall in the largest Greek temple in Paestum and the indifferent skills of the Italian surgeon were likely to leave him crippled for the rest of his life.

"I do not understand what you find so amusing, my man," said Peter.

"A woman of thirty is very likely to produce an heir, if your uncle is up to the task."

"But you have just given me some degree of reassurance, for you tell me the wedding is not likely to happen at all. I do love my uncle, however, and he has always treated me like a son. Therefore, you have also given me a motive to travel through the ice and snow that is even more compelling than my inheritance or a Christmas party—it appears I must save my uncle's life." Nathaniel pushed away from the table. "I will leave at once."

Unfortunately, his resolution was stronger than his broken and ill healed leg, and he required the assistance of his friend to rise to his feet. To the other men in the club, it must have seemed an embarrassing business to witness, but to Nathaniel it was only another bitter reminder of the end of his adventurous life.

Peter handed him his cane, looking overly pleased to be of service. Perhaps the man had bets down on Nathaniel's likelihood of success; though if success was measured by saving his uncle's life or losing him, Nathaniel could not say. For his part, there was no paradox. He loved the old man dearly and was content to wait for many years before inheriting the Earl of Bristol's title or fortune.

"Have a safe journey, my friend," Peter said. "Even more important, have a safe Christmas party. I think you and your uncle should avoid slippery stairs, archaic weaponry, rabid dogs, and roaring fires."

"Have you forgotten anything?"

"Do you have something specific in mind?" Peter asked.

"You tell me Lady Westbrook bakes fine cakes. Should I not be concerned that she or her designing little niece might include a heavy dose of arsenic among the ingredients?"

Peter looked down at the few remaining pastries on their table and pushed the tray away.

"If there is sufficient chocolate, it might be a very excellent death," he mused.

"If there is chocolate in abundance, it would be better not to die at all," said Nathaniel, as they walked through the dining room and into the snowy night.

MISS EMMA PARTRICK paused in the process of folding her favorite evening dress and glanced out the window of her Aunt Daisy's townhouse. The snowfall had quickened in the last hour and it was now impossible to see the houses across the Square. A few hardy pedestrians moved like dark shadows against the white backdrop, huddled against the onslaught.

"The roads will be very poor," Emma said. "Should we not wait until we are certain the conditions will be better?"

Aunt Daisy looked up from where she knelt on the floor, carefully folding her garments into her travel trunk. Their maid, who ordinarily would do the folding and packing for them, was already on her way to Scotland, where she would spend Christmas with her own family.

"I fear we can never be certain the conditions are entirely suitable, my dear," said Aunt Daisy. "When they are beastly in Mayfair, they may be lovely in Cornwall. And I am convinced that when we wake on the morrow, all this snow will be gone."

Emma smiled, already too familiar with her aunt's wretched skills in the art of prophesy.

"I know what you are thinking, you ungrateful child, but this will be no ordinary house party, and I promised Lord Michael that we will supervise the house decorations and the preparations for the feast."

"And bake for the feast, as well. Should I set aside my gown and bring a few old muslin dresses instead? We may spend all our hours belowstairs, in the kitchen."

"We will not, my dear. But you know how much he has always loved my Twelfth Cake," Aunt Daisy said, and ducked back down into the trunk.

I know how much he has always loved you, Emma thought. And wondered if her dear aunt had reason to believe this was not to be the usual Christmas affair. After all, they had been guests of Lord Michael since she was a little girl, joining him for holidays at Pencliff and for occasional dinners at Pomfrey House in London. In the old days, she looked forward to playing with his nephew Nate. As she grew older, she realized she more likely tormented the boy, bullying him around as only a young girl could do. And so he escaped, not only her, but the confines of home and society. Lord Michael must have missed him terribly, but he seemed to rejoice in the frequent letters from foreign ports, recounting adventures that seemed both exciting and exceedingly foolhardy. When last Emma and her aunt visited with Lord Michael, he told them of a dreadful accident in Italy. Or perhaps it was Greece. Certainly there were Greek temples and crumbling pediments involved. And the news that Nate Evander would probably never walk again.

"Well, you needn't look so unhappy about it all, Emma," said Aunt Daisy. "I enjoy baking it, and he enjoys eating it. I am packing silver tinsel and green paper, so we can decorate it to perfection."

"I am not unhappy about your cake or our appreciative host," Emma said, still thinking about her old friend. She remembered him fondly, and wished that in all the intervening years, their paths had crossed again so she could have also known him as a man full of health and vigor. Now, if they ever met, he would be crippled, and perhaps bitter about what had befallen him. "In fact, I look forward to helping with all the projects Lord Michael has given you."

"There will be other guests who might occupy your time," Aunt Daisy said thoughtfully.

"I am sure there will be," said Emma, thinking about the circle of her aunt and Lord Michael's elderly friends. "But I would rather spend my time with you and the flora."

"Yes, of course! I am envisioning ivy entwined along the banister and holly in large vases in the center hall. The gardeners will bring in small trees from the orangery, and I asked Lord Michael to acquire a nice, plump partridge."

"Will one be enough to feed all his guests?"

"I do not intend to eat the poor thing, my dear, but to display him in one of the trees. I never saw a pear tree in his collection, so quince will have to do." Aunt Daisy rubbed her hands together, clearly delighted with the prospect. "In fact, it will do very nicely."

Emma looked around at their simple but elegant surroundings. "Do you think we should put up some greenery here, as well? This will be the first time we will not be home for any part of Christmas and I feel the house will be very sad without some festive wreaths or sprays of holly in the foyer."

"There will be no one here to see it. Even the staff will be gone to their own families," said Aunt Daisy, clearly reluctant to take on another task.

"Let me do it, Aunt. I will be packed and ready soon enough, and I will send Annie out to Covent Garden to buy what is needed."

"No, my dear. I will not have it." Aunt Daisy folded her arms across her breast and looked quite insistent. "We will not return to London by Twelfth Night, and it is unlucky if the greenery is still on display. The tree sprites in the wood, who have been given a respite from the coldest days of winter, will remain in this house and do their mischief here."

Emma put down a fur muffler and leaned back in her seat. "Surely you do not believe that nonsense, and you did not raise me to be a superstitious, silly girl. Tree sprites? They will be perfectly content to spend a few extra days in the relative warmth of our home I daresay, and be grateful we have not tossed them out onto the London streets. And besides, I doubt they know how to read a calendar, and would not know the Twelfth Night from the thirteenth."

"You find this very amusing, I see," said Aunt Daisy glumly. "But I do not wish to take any chances. You have been most unlucky in love, Emma, and I have exhausted all my prayers. Now, I do not wish to tempt the fates, pagan or not."

Emma's good spirits melted like the snow on their windowpane. Was her situation so desperate, her history so tragic, her aunt would deny her the simple pleasure of a few sprigs of holly or ivy in their own home?

"I know what I am called by members of society, but surely no one thinks I am responsible for the deaths of three charming and amiable young men. Beaconstone contracted influenza from his own mother, and poor Dennis was delivering a sermon in his church when the ceiling fell down upon him. And we know Bart was drinking heavily and carousing with other officers when he fell into the Thames. Does anyone think I dressed up in regimentals and pushed him into the water? It is absurd." Emma knew she sounded a little desperate, but before this moment, she had no idea her aunt was so concerned about her prospects. She had already accepted the very real possibility she would never marry, and live out her days as Aunt Daisy's devoted companion.

"And yet the absurd or impossible is often true. I do not think you pushed Bart Fitzhugh into the river, but you have lost three suitors in eight years. Some bit of evil is working against you and the men you choose. I do not want to give it the opportunity to work its spell again."

Such words coming from her practical aunt were nearly incomprehensible. When Emma's own parents decided to defect to the wilderness of America, they abandoned her to the care of the one relation who was sensible and clever, and Aunt Daisy had ever proved true to their expectations. And yet now she spoke of tree sprites and pagan mischief and encroaching evil. Emma scarcely knew how to respond.

"I will not choose another man, so all of their sex will be safe from harm," she said, solemnly. It was an awful pronouncement, and yet she knew not what else to say. And then, something else occurred to her, and she smiled, if somewhat weakly. "And perhaps you can put me out on the doorstep after Twelfth Night, instead of the greenery, since I am more likely to wreak havoc than the innocent tree sprites!"

Aunt Daisy hesitated, which was almost as upsetting as anything she already said. But then she raised her hand with her pointer finger extended, in a gesture Emma had not seen in years. Of course, Emma had not spilled her milk, or torn her petticoat, or muddied her shoes in many years either.

"I am not amused, Missy!" Aunt Daisy admonished her. "There are many eligible gentlemen out there who will not be able to resist your charms."

"But more to the point, will they be able to resist my ill-favored luck?"

"I daresay there is at least one. Yes, certainly there is."

Emma felt suddenly weary of the pointless argument and the series of disappointments in her life. Aunt Daisy was the only one who had never abandoned her, and yet she now seemed overly eager to push Emma out the door.

"And only one?" Emma asked. "And what makes this poor man unique among Englishmen?"

Aunt Daisy waved her hand casually, as if they again spoke about the weather. "He has already had uncommonly bad luck and will suffer for it all his life. I suspect he is already immune to anything your company will have in store."

AUNT DAISY'S PROPHETIC words hummed like a chorus in Emma's mind during all the long journey to Pencliff. She refused to ask the identity of the last suitor, for she knew her aunt would produce him in good time, if such a man even existed. And to know his name would surely result in rejecting the man, which would make her aunt very unhappy. It was not in the spirit of Christmas to do such a thing.

Unfortunately, the weather spirits were not as benevolent. The journey to Penzance was punctuated with delays due to ice and mud, and one evening of blinding snow. The inns along the way were adequate and comfortable only in contrast to the cramped carriage. And yet, Aunt Daisy's spirits remained high, and she seemed to be unable to sit back in her seat once they crossed into Cornwall.

The sun broke through the gray clouds as they finally passed through the gates of Pencliff and Aunt Daisy clasped her hands in joy.

"I knew it would be like this! Did I not tell you that all would be fine? The castle is best seen in such a light, with the sun glinting off the white stone and reflecting off the snow cover."

Emma massaged her shoulder, which was rather sore from all the bumping of the carriage, and looked out the window. From her side, there was only a view of the treacherous cliff, the natural fortress that had rebuffed invaders for centuries. Suddenly, a tall man came into view, and as they came closer, she recognized Lord Michael himself. He cut across the snow covered lawn and when the carriage turned sharply, he appeared at the entrance to his home. A few servants stood attentively behind him.

Aunt Daisy was first from the carriage and both she and their host seemed to exercise considerable restraint by not embracing in front of their audience. Emma, alighting from the carriage, sensed it at once, and looked away to give them some privacy. She knew they loved each other;

she'd recognized it so many years ago when she first reveled in a love of her own. But Aunt Daisy and Lord Michael either didn't admit it to themselves or decided to maintain the illusion of nothing more than a congenial companionship. Now, something had changed. Did it happen in the letters that had passed between them in the autumn? Or was something promised during one of the frequent visits to Manchester Square?

Is this why Aunt Daisy renewed her interests in matchmaking for Emma? So that she might see Emma settled before marrying again?

Wavering on her feet as she reacquainted herself with solid ground, Emma suddenly realized they may wish nothing more than her approval, for she was the only other person affected by such a happy change in circumstances. *Not true, Emma. There was Nate to be considered as well. In his crippled state, he might be more dependent on his uncle than ever.*

"Welcome to Cornwall, Emma!" said Lord Michael, now beside her. She shielded her eyes from the glare of the reflected sunshine and smiled at him. "We shall enjoy a wonderful Christmas together."

"Thank you so much for inviting us, Lord Michael. Penzance is a wonderful change from London, and I'm so glad we came."

"So am I," echoed Aunt Daisy.

"Are you truly, Marguerite? I am glad as well," said Lord Michael.

"I am glad," said Aunt Daisy. "So glad."

Emma blinked at the overly glad couple as Lord Michael took her aunt's hand and led her into the house. *Dear God, they were not merely in love, but deliriously so.* They were as children, experiencing the first blush of passion. And who else dared to call her aunt Marguerite? Was Emma hardy enough to withstand two weeks of cooing and flirting?

"It appears Lord Michael has left his baggage behind," said a voice behind her.

Emma turned into the sun, but could only discern a tall and lean form, leaning on a cane. As he came forward, she came into his shadow and was able to look up into his face.

She knew him, and yet she did not. His hair was the color of mahogany, streaked with several lines of gray. His eyes were as dark as his hair, and hooded by half closed lids. He had lines wrought of pain and care on his brow and around his mouth, and she realized they made him look older than he surely was. In fact, he might not be so many years older than herself.

"Nate?" she whispered. "Can it be possible?"

He took her gloved hand and bowed deeply over it. There was a spot of snow on his dark hair.

"Is it so very difficult to believe, Miss Partrick? Surely my uncle did not tell you I was departed from this world?" he asked as he released her hand. "If so, I am sorry to disappoint you."

"I am not disappointed, only surprised."

He grimaced. "That I am not dead?"

"That you are here at Pencliff and . . . standing before me. I expected you, that is to say, I thought you to be . . ."

"Crippled? Well, so I am."

Emma glanced down at his cane and realized his hand was clenched very tightly over its crook. "You are not as I expected, Nate. And it has been an age."

"So it must be, as there is no one who still calls me Nate. Even my uncle has finally acceded to my advanced old age and allows me to be Nathaniel."

"Nathaniel," Emma said, allowing the syllables to roll over her tongue. "I did not even realize it was your name."

"And I am not even sure of yours, though you did not correct me when I called you Miss Partrick. Are you not married after all this time?"

Emma shivered, though the day was warming nicely. "I wonder that you are so ill informed, as my affairs seem to have become everyone else's business of the past eight years. Indeed, I might have been married to either the Duke of Beaconstone, Mr. St. John, or Mr. Fitzhugh but circumstances conspired against me. I remain Miss Partrick."

"And is the condition permanent, or do you have new prospects?"

As quickly as she had grown cold a moment before, Emma now burned with embarrassment. Of what concern were her marital prospects to Nathaniel Evander? Did he think she was in Penzance to pursue him? Perhaps she ought to punish him for his impertinence by worrying him a bit.

"I am not sure it is any business of yours, but I do have prospects, and my aunt is actively pursuing them. Will that satisfy you?"

He looked over her head to the house and frowned. "It is as I expected. And yet my uncle has abandoned you on the doorstep, perhaps so he can scheme with your aunt."

He really was a rude man and nothing like the boy she remembered. Nate Evander was cheerful and easy to know, and allowed a little girl to follow him all about. He scowled at her, and pulled on her braids and teased her about her fear of horses, but she always trusted him. Perhaps this is what illness and pain did to one.

"I have never heard 'scheming' used to describe what I suspect they are doing, but I will leave them to it without my interference," said Emma, and blushed again.

He studied her and she knew he read the years on her face as easily as she did his. "Yes, I am sure they will arrange matters to your satisfaction."

"And to yours, Nate? Do you have any reason to object to their arrangements?"

He opened his mouth and closed it again, his lips so taut they nearly disappeared. Was he so close minded that he could not sanction love and marriage between two older people? Or did he fear the loss of his uncle's attention? Certainly, it could not be concern for his inheritance, as Aunt Daisy was no longer of an age to produce an heir. But perhaps Nate did not know that.

"You are a fool, Nate Evander," Emma said with unexpected—and perhaps unjustified—conviction. She turned away from him and started towards the house, as her toes were too cold to endure much more of his cryptic argument.

"My name is Nathaniel," he called to her retreating back.

HE WAS AN IDIOT. If nothing else was certain in his miserable life, it was that he was an idiot. Nathaniel had a whole week to dissuade the conniving Back Widow from marrying his elderly uncle, and yet he pounced on her at the very minute of her arrival, when she was worn and weary from her journey.

And yet she looked quite splendid. Her hair was just as he remembered, for the jostling in the carriage had loosened strands about her face, and she looked very much as she had as a child. Perhaps not quite. But her eyes were still overly large in her face, as if she lived in a constant state of wonder, and her lips were very pink and well formed. He remembered watching them pucker as she ate a very sour lemon he once picked for her from his uncle's orangery. Now, fool that he was, he wondered what it would be like to taste those lips.

Until this day, he'd thought of her as a girl. But she was a woman, nearly his own age, and truly the most beautiful one he ever beheld. No wonder Uncle Michael desired her, for there was no more brilliant jewel in an old man's crown than an elegant lady. He could not fault Uncle Michael his choice.

But then, she was not simply any young lady; she was one with a very bad history. Could his uncle be unaware of that? Or does love make fools of us all, and allow one to imagine that the rules change at our own selfish desire?

At the moment, he had his own selfish desire and his uncle had nothing to do with it.

Where was she?

After he returned from his afternoon walk about the estate, he escaped to his room which was well situated above the great foyer of Pencliff. When he arrived a few days ago, he discovered there was much greater strain on his leg when the ground was covered with ice and snow than when the path was clear and dry. Therefore, every outing was an exercise in agony, though he was certain his surgeon would attest that it was to his benefit.

But he believed the only thing to his benefit was pulling off his boots and sitting with his leg propped on a low chair, warmed by the heat of the fire in the grate and a Scottish blanket. A good book had the additional advantage of hastening the passage of time, and allowing him to briefly forget the disaster of his expedition to the south of Italy and the likelihood his adventurous days were over. Today, however, he utterly lacked all powers of concentration, for he was diverted by something of greater immediacy than the events of a year before.

Where was she?

He heard voices on the veranda below, and edged closer to the window so that he could spy more effectively from his eyrie. His book, the estimable *Guy Mannering*, fell off his lap and the rough wool blanket slipped to the floor.

His uncle, Lord Michael Pomfrey, Earl of Bristol, had gathered up a handful of snow and tossed it at Lady Marguerite Westbrook before running towards the woods. It hit the lady on the shoulder, and she responded by trailing after him, with some sort of weapon in hand. Dear God, had the two of them been drinking? Were they about to murder each other?

Nathaniel braced his hands against the arms of his chair and tried to rise. His leg was too painful, and the process too difficult, for him to act quickly and thus save them from whatever nonsense was about. By the time he arrived on the scene the damage would be irreparably done. However, the lady had a niece and a rather aggressive one at that; for all her disarming demeanor, she must be capable of interceding.

But where was she?

Was this her plan, about which Peter was so confident? Was his uncle destined to fall, for no reason other than expressing an interest in the lady?

Miss Emma Partrick suddenly appeared on the stairs beneath Nathaniel's window, with an overlarge basket in hand. She still wore a woolen plaid cape, but her dark hair was now covered with a shawl that was knotted beneath her chin and tossed over her shoulders. She called out to the others, who beckoned her to join them. Nathaniel had a better look at their faces and realized they were laughing. Yes, they must have gotten into that limoncello he had shipped to his uncle from Naples. It clearly made them ridiculous, if not necessarily dangerous.

What was even more ridiculous was that his uncle, who had a household of servants at his bidding, apparently decided that he wished to do a spot of gardening. He took the knife from Lady Westbrook and studied the trees at the edge of his wood. Once Emma joined them, they seemed to have nothing more compelling to do than prune branches off bushes that still were green, and gather the whole mess in a bundle into Emma's large basket and on the snow. A few more snowballs were thrown and Emma slipped and would have fallen if his uncle had not caught her. And the three of them laughed about everything, which irritated Nathaniel more than anything else.

Finally, undoubtedly after the effects of the limoncello had worn off, they stood in a small, tight circle facing each other. More laughter. And then, on cue, they lifted their arms around each other and joined in an intimate embrace.

Nathaniel was too late. It was all settled. Uncle Michael was doomed to marry the Black Widow.

Chapter Two

EMMA SUPPOSED SHE deserved a few moments of leisure after her long journey from London, but somehow everything was happening without a moment left to spare. The Christmas decorations had been left for Aunt Daisy to orchestrate, cakes remained without icing in the kitchen, and Emma needed to inform Lord Michael's maids as to which of their gowns needed to be pressed for immediate wear. And then, there was the wonderful news, delivered to her in such a fashion as to warm her to her very toes while she stood in the snow.

She sighed, as she braided a sprig of ivy through the handrail in the grand foyer. How wonderful a conclusion to the years of building a loving, trusting relationship. Perhaps marriage was not for the very young, who often rushed into marriage without truly knowing their mate. After all, how well had she known the Duke of Beaconstone when she agreed to marry him at age eighteen? He was very handsome, and surely wealthy, and he was very polite. She could not know he had weak lungs. She also would never know how she and he might have fared together at thirty or forty years.

But her aunt and Lord Michael knew just what to expect, as far as anyone could predict the future. And they loved each other, which was more than many married couples had any reason to expect.

"Something is different here, is it not?" said a voice above her.

Emma heard the irregular footsteps at the very moment Nate spoke, and prepared herself for another confrontation.

"I should think everything is now different in this house," she said, "but I suspect you mean the greenery."

He paused on a step to give him even more of an advantage in height, and looked casually about the hall. Emma wondered if he might also need a respite from the awkward business of managing a long staircase, for he seemed somewhat breathless.

"Ah, yes. Now I see it. It is remindful of Burnam Wood coming to Dunsinane, is it not?" he asked, demanding that she recall her reading of *Macbeth*.

He was testing her, as always. But she knew her plays of Mr.

Shakespeare and had been to a performance of Macbeth not many weeks before.

"I suppose one could apply some poetic power to the image. But there are no Scottish warriors hiding beneath the boughs, and no one is about to be killed," she said.

He looked startled, and she wondered if she ought not refer to attacks or death in his company. She knew not how he came to be injured, nor if there were other men who fared worse.

"Everyone is quite safe, you say." He did not sound convinced.

Now that she recognized his heel of Achilles, she would not stab him there again.

Emma held up one hand. "Indeed. Unless you consider the damage done to my favorite gloves by the sap on the pine branches. And, of course, the tree sprites that live within the wood."

He rubbed his forehead, though she couldn't tell if it was due to his exertion or the tediousness of her conversation. As he did so, he came down the rest of the stairs and stood beside her, which still gave him the benefit of height. He reached for her hand and lifted it so he might examine her sticky glove.

Here was the Nate she best remembered, and she knew the part she must play for him.

"It is very sweet, you know. I understand the sap is made into a sort of molasses substance in the Americas and is used to sweeten tea."

Nate rubbed a finger over the dark stain, which sent a shot of heat down her arm. And then, quite unexpectedly, he brought her hand to his lips and licked her glove. She stopped breathing.

"It is sweet, but not particularly tasty. I will stay loyal to my cane sugar, unless I find myself in the American wilderness with a chest of bitter tea." He still held her hand.

"Nate . . ." Emma began.

"Are you about to tell me that you have poisoned me, beautiful Emma?" Nate asked.

She changed her opinion. This was most definitely not the Nate she remembered or the part she'd expected to play.

"I would never poison you, old friend," she said softly. "I rely too much on your good sense, and the things you might yet teach me. I lost you for too many years, but we will now have the excuse of family to bring us together more often."

He released her hand and frowned. Perhaps he tasted something else in the sap that was neither as sweet nor as compelling.

"And yet all you have done thus far is teach me," he said. "What is it about the tree sprites?"

Emma laughed, breaking the rather serious mood. "Your uncle and his guests are awaiting our arrival in the parlour so that we may all go in to dinner. My Aunt Daisy is better versed in the old customs than am I, so she could tell you about it herself. Come, will you join me?"

She warily accepted his proffered elbow, now that she began to understand what effect contact with his body, no matter how impersonal, had on her senses. But as soon as they started to walk towards the parlour, Emma was concerned with other things, such as slowing her gait to accommodate his.

"Are you in much pain?" she asked.

He hesitated just long enough so that she guessed his answer was a lie. "No," he said. "But is that not a very personal question?"

She glanced up at him in surprise and realized his eyes were on her, and on not their steps.

"That seems an odd question from someone who has just licked a lady's glove," she pointed out. "But I ask not to satisfy any idle curiosity. I wish to know what happened to you, and what you might expect."

"It is a very foolish business and one that does not get any better in the retelling. My companions and I were in the south of Italy, not far from Naples. Though most adventurers in the area are digging at the base of the treacherous volcano, I have always been more intrigued by the abandoned Greek settlement at Paestum. One gentleman of the party climbed to the top of a hill of rubble and set off an avalanche of stones. I was partially buried and might have gotten off relatively unharmed, but that a startled horse dashed over the stones and crushed my leg. It is not a very heroic story."

Emma heard the delicate tinkle of wine glasses and soft voices as they approached the parlour. "But most men do not suffer fortune in a heroic way or in a manner befitting their importance." She thought of her own Dennis St. John, felled by the ceiling of the church in which he was delivering a sermon. "And you did not die," she added.

She felt him stiffen.

"Though at times I wish I had," he said, just as they entered the room.

"Well, it is about time you children arrived!" Lord Michael said cheerfully. "We are not nearly as hardy as you, and hope to enjoy a fine dinner before we fall asleep in our chairs."

Emma quickly pulled her hand away from Nate's arm and managed her brightest smile. "We are no longer children, my lord."

Of course, her glib answer might bring on even more suspicion as to what detained them in the hallway, but everyone in the audience seemed to take it in good spirit. As she glanced at the assorted guests, she realized that in such company Lord Michael and Aunt Daisy themselves might well be considered children. She recognized an ancient aunt of Nate's, two of Lord Michael's hunting partners, and the local vicar and his sister. There was also a lady in a bright orange wig, a man in uniform already asleep by the fire, and another gentleman with the unlikely name of Lord Lesser Biggs.

"No, you most definitely are not," the latter said. "I do remember you when you were a little mite, always running around after Nathaniel here." Before he could pinch her cheek, Emma ducked back, right up against Nate's chest. His hand came around her waist, though he otherwise let her face this ogre alone.

"Shall we go in to dinner?" Aunt Daisy said sweetly. She gently woke their uniformed guest and partnered him into the formal dining room. There, she led him to his chair at one end of the table, and took her place at Lord Michael's side at the other end. Nate was seated to the left of his uncle, and from her seat next to her aunt, Emma watched the considerable difficulty he experienced in the simple act of sitting. There was more to the story he'd told her, she realized.

But soon they all were settled, and drinks were poured all around. Aunt Daisy's ivy and juniper creation graced a silver salver at the center of the table, and everyone was overly enthusiastic in their compliments.

"Do you not think it a fine idea to allow Lady Westbrook to grace my table at all events?" Lord Michael said.

"Yes," said the orange-bewigged lady, wagging her finger. "But Lady Westbrook is not your servant, Michael, and will not be at your call whenever you plan a dinner party."

"Ah, you misunderstand me, Lady Tregaris. I do not intend that she must twist about leaves and twigs to my every whim. The lady, herself, must grace my table."

"Please explain what you mean, uncle," said Nate. Emma realized they were the first words he'd uttered since they walked into the parlour together.

"I mean—" Here Lord Michael paused for effect and raised his glass. "I mean that Lady Westbrook has this very day agreed to marry me. This, on the night before Christmas Eve, is our betrothal dinner."

"It is about time," muttered Lady Tregaris.

"What did he say?" asked Nate's elderly aunt, cupping her ear.

But everyone one else raised a toast and cheered very loudly.

Emma thought she was the happiest of all, until she caught Nate's speculative gaze across the wide table.

PETER MILTON HAD gotten the whole business wrong, and Nathaniel was a fool to have believed him. His own inheritance was secure, his uncle's happiness was complete, and no one suggested Miss Emma Partrick's misfortunes extended to anyone other than her own cursed lovers. To be sure, no one had tested the full range of her reach, but it was difficult to anticipate any ill tidings whilst Pencliff was a veritable crucible of joy.

The whole house hummed with excitement. He heard the maids singing carols as they polished the silver, the aging guests now wanted a New Year's ball, Lady Westbrook looked about ten years younger than she had when she and her niece arrived at Pencliff, and Uncle Michael whistled as he went about his business. Nathaniel had never heard such a thing in his life.

Which is why he found comfort with familiar things in his uncle's library. Here is where he first discovered the civilizations of Greece and Rome, and traced the old military routes of the ancient soldiers as they pushed their way northwards through Europe all the way to Hadrian's Wall. Early on, Uncle Michael recognized his passion and respected his curiosity, and took him to Chester to see what remained of the Wall. They also examined old mosaic floors in Fishbourne, and found treasures in Bath that had nothing to do with the Assembly Rooms or the Paragon.

And now, Nathaniel only wished to escape into his old geographic atlas, but could not find it anywhere. Instead, he settled for a volume describing the antiquities in the Ashmolean Museum. It certainly was more satisfying than listening to Uncle Michael whistling *Greensleeves* off key. After all, what did the man know about unrequited love?

He heard the door open behind him, and asked the servant to put the bottle of limoncello and wine glass on the desk.

"I am not Hiller," said Emma. "And I have something better than lemonade."

"I am not expecting lemonade," Nathaniel said, "and there is nothing better than limoncello."

But as he turned in his seat, he knew there were many things better than the potent liqueur of Southern Italy. Miss Emma Partrick in a close fitting blue dress was one. And Miss Emma Partrick carrying his atlas was another.

"I expect I am interrupting something terribly important, Nate, but I wish to find Paestum on a map. I have searched all over for it, and cannot locate it," she said, and opened the book on his desk.

"Are you looking in Italy, Poppet?" he asked. Why had he thought of that name now? Surely he had not used it in at least twenty years.

"Oh, that must be the problem. I was searching for it in London," she said sarcastically, and pulled up a chair next to his. "Do you think me a complete idiot?"

"Are you not the girl who thought Coriolanus was our neighbor in Manchester Square?"

"I believe I was ten years old at the time. And the Earl was rather terrifying." She leaned forward and he had a very tempting view of the back of her neck, where little tendrils of hair curled. "Please do not call me Poppet. It is not very dignified."

He blew very gently and watched the tendrils dance. "Please do not call me Nate. It puts me in mind of a little insect."

"Very well, Nathaniel," she said sweetly, with the air of one who has not yet given up the argument. "If you will only show me Paestum."

"The problem is that it is not on the map," he said. "Though it is situated just here."

His arm brushed against her breast as he pointed out a green spot.

She did not notice his unintended intimacy in her agitation about the apparent misunderstanding.

"But you have told me it is an ancient place! Is that another joke?"

Nathaniel shifted position and felt the grinding pain in his knee. "If only it were. Paestum is real enough, and it is the site of some of the grandest Greek temples ever discovered. But the settlement was abandoned when the surrounding marshes became malarial, and over the centuries Paestum was lost to memory. That is an excellent example of your Aunt Daisy's tree sprites at work, for they quite overran everything."

"How did you find it, then?" Emma asked.

"The locals knew it was there. One could hardly ignore three massive temples in the neighborhood. Builders had been looting the place for centuries. Before the accident, I managed to find a few interesting pieces that had been overlooked."

"Will you ever be able to return, Nate—Nathaniel?"

"Right now, I should be happy to manage a stroll from Mayfair to Hyde Park. No, I doubt I will be able to return."

"But what if you had someone to help you? To ease your way?"

Nathaniel wondered whom she might have in mind when Hiller came into the library, with the limoncello.

"Thank you, Hiller. No, we will not need another glass."

"But I should like some lemonade," Emma said when the man left the library.

"This stuff is not for you, little girl," Nathaniel said, and reached for the glass.

Emma's hand, soft and warm, closed over his. "I am not a little girl, and I have shared a glass with you before."

She was not, and indeed, they had.

"Take it easy. Try just a taste of it," he said as they raised the glass to her lips. She seemed to do no more than wet her lips, when she started to cough and fan her face with a frantic hand. The potent liquid splashed onto both their hands and he gently set the glass down. Then, with some effort, he stood and patted her on her back until she regained her breath.

"I take it you somehow managed to get to the advanced age of twenty nine without experiencing the ambrosia of the Roman gods?" he asked her, after several moments had passed.

"Thank you for reminding me of my encroaching infirmity. But this drink does a great deal to explain some of the more naughty behavior in their pantheon. It must be pure alcohol?"

Nathaniel answered by downing half of what remained in the glass. "In Southern Italy, babies sip this with their porridge."

Whether consciously or not, Emma put her damp finger in her mouth and gently sucked on it. She was definitely not a little girl if she had any idea what effect this had on him. He cleared his throat.

"Ah, so perhaps it doesn't quite agree with you either," she said.

He was still standing above her, and reached down to take her hand. "No, I believe it is too bitter," he said, and kissed her finger. "Now, that is an improvement."

Emma pulled her hand away, and stood to face him.

"What are you doing, Nathaniel?" she asked softly.

"For once, I am acting on my instincts. And it is not such a big deal. After all, you have already reminded me that we used to share a drinking glass."

She waved her fingers at him. "This is not a drinking glass. And even were it so, one does not kiss a glass."

"You are quite right. I suppose there are some things you can teach me after all," he said, and then pulled her into his arms and kissed her most improperly on her lips.

Why had he sought comfort in limoncello when Emma Partrick was a guest under the same roof? The taste of her lips, the scent of her hair, the way she clung to him, was pure intoxication. She had been only a little thing when he last knew her, but now she seemed the perfect height to fit along the lines of his body. With what little sense was left to him in these moments, he hoped his leg would not betray him and cause him to stumble as she pressed against him.

Emma retained at least as much sense. She suddenly leaned back, though she still clung to his arms, and asked, "Should you be standing like this?"

"Do you prefer to lie down on the chaise? I think we'll both find it infinitely preferable," he said.

She released him. "I daresay we would under ordinary circumstances, but that is hardly the case now."

"No, it is not. In fact, everything feels rather extraordinary at the moment."

He caught just a glimmer of a smile before it was replaced by something that was either concern or even sadness.

"Then let us savor this moment, dear friend, for it shall be something to hold in memory," Emma said, as she straightened the lace at her breast and patted down her wrinkled sleeves.

"Why are you so anxious to break this off, Emma? We would hardly embarrass ourselves if someone walked in, for we are of an age to do as we like. We are no longer children experimenting with the science of kissing behind the stable."

"I do not recall we ever did such a thing."

"Then either my memory, or my fondest fantasies, are more active than yours. But no matter; what of the here and now?"

"It is only hours before Christmas Eve, and there is much to prepare. Uncle Michael—for I feel I may call him so under the circumstances—already gave over much responsibility to my aunt, and now I understand why that is so. I need to help her in this, as in all things," she said.

There was the cause of her concern.

"And there is something greater, and less likely to end happily." She looked away, unable to meet his eyes. "You are somewhat removed from London gossips, so you may not be aware of my dreadful reputation. I am known to some as the Black Widow."

There was the cause of her sadness.

Impossibly, he laughed. Truly, it was more at himself than her words, for had he not been prompted to make haste for Pencliff by Peter's warning? It seemed so absurd now, for whatever he remembered of Emma Partrick was very much improved by what they just shared. Emma, however, did not think so. She turned on her heel, and would have made a hasty departure, but that her lovely gown caught on the outstretched finger of a china sea nymph.

"Wait, please," he said through his laughter. "My uncle is quite fond of this statue, though goodness knows why." For good measure, he held Emma at her waist while he unhooked her. And then drew her closer when she was released.

"What is this about?" he asked against her hair. "Have you been betrothed so many times the gossips cannot resist you? Are you secretly married?"

"I have never been married, Nathaniel, as you know perfectly well. I have never even . . ." Her voice dropped off when he moved his lips down her forehead to her nose.

"Never even what?" he asked.

She broke apart from him, and looked as if she were about to admit to some confession before changing her mind.

"It will not do. I love your Uncle Michael as if he is already my own, and you are soon to be my cousin."

"I believe the relationship can bear some degree of closeness between us," he said, suddenly realizing he wished to be a great deal more to her than cousin.

"I am not sure it can and I will not risk harming you. I have never believed that I was anything but the victim of very bad luck, but it turns out my aunt is somewhat more cautious about my prospects. I must respect her. And I do know if something happened to you, your uncle will be inconsolable. My aunt will take to her room and cry out her despair for weeks and weeks. And besides," she said as she pulled out of his embrace and backed away from him, "I could not endure the thought of you in any more pain and knowing I caused it."

He could not laugh off something that so clearly plagued her. Though the tongues of the gossips wagged for malicious pleasure and a source of amusement, they somehow convinced the object of their whispering that they had the right of it. It had been many months since Nathaniel Evander thought of anyone but himself with any degree of pity, but now he recognized something as startling as the fact he desired her.

Emma Partrick was as damaged, in her own way, as was he.

AS EMMA DASHED up the grand staircase of Pencliff she nearly bumped into her aunt coming down.

"Oh! I am so glad to find you," her aunt said. "No one knew where you had gone. I hoped to have your help to add some greenery to the library, to liven things up."

Emma thought things in the library were already quite lively, but this was not the moment to say so. "Why bother with the library, Aunt Daisy, when there are so few people who would use it? I am sure it does not matter to Nathaniel if he ruminates over his John Donne beneath a bower of holly."

Aunt Daisy narrowed her eyes. "Nathaniel, is it? I suppose one cannot go on calling him Nate forever, as he is no longer a boy. I doubt your Nathaniel would notice, but as Lord Michael intends to serve coffee in the library this evening, the room deserves our attention. It is one of the few rooms in this great cave of a house that holds the heat well, and Lord Michael is concerned for the comfort of all his guests." She put a cool hand on Emma's cheek. "Dear girl, you are burning up! Do you feel feverish?"

Emma was glad she could tell her aunt the truth in this. "I have come from the library and it is, indeed, the warmest room in Pencliff."

"Just the same, you ought to rest before the festivities this evening. Do not worry about my projects, as I am sure I have it all in hand."

"I am sure you do, Aunt Daisy," Emma said, and waved her off. Aunt Daisy always had everything in hand and must already contemplate a future that involved renovating Lord Michael's great cave into compliance with her vision of perfection. The man must have offered it as an additional nugget in his courtship. "And I believe I shall rest for a few hours."

But even before she reached her room, Emma knew rest was impossible. How could she idle away the afternoon when such a burden was upon her? Where she'd expected a cripple, she found a man who was both bigger and stronger than she. When she would have resumed an old friendship, so long interrupted, she instead found a sudden attraction, capable of becoming so much more. And while she hoped to help a man heal, she now threatened to do him harm.

She had loved before, with disastrous results. She would not love Nathaniel Evander. Even more important, he could not love her.

As she kneeled before her trunk and opened it to retrieve the Christmas presents she'd already wrapped, she wryly considered how her gift to him could happily turn him away from her forever. She'd spent weeks crocheting a cheerful lap robe for him, expecting him to find it very useful as he sat confined to a chair. Now, she knew she'd miscalculated the extent of his injuries or Lord Michael's tale of his nephew's plight. For him, her new uncle, she'd crocheted a scarf in the same bright yarns, which took her less than half the time. In the rush and excitement to leave London, she'd yet managed to find time to paint little watercolor scenes on plain paper and to wrap her gifts with it. Foolishly, she'd imagined Nathaniel would never again walk through Hyde Park or along Jermyn Street, and she'd wished to entertain him with her city views.

She had no idea what he would make of them now, and could only hope he would tear open the wrapping, crumble it all into a ball, and toss the whole thing into the fire. When he realized what she'd made for him, he might toss that into the fire as well.

But she knew he would not, for that was not in his character, either then or now.

Emma placed her carefully wrapped offerings on a table near the door, and loosened her gown as she walked towards the comfort the large bed promised. Outside, it had started to snow again, but here she was warm and protected. She lay down in the center of the bed, against the overstuffed pillows and on the beautifully brocaded counterpane, and attempted to think of anything but Nathaniel.

But that was impossible. She could think of nothing else but Nathaniel—the way his arms felt around her, the warm pressure of his lips on hers, and how close she came to being thoroughly compromised. And all that in a matter of moments. Where she thought to have a discussion with him as they perused an atlas together, instead he became her lover, the face to a passionate presence in her spinster's dreams. She had not asked for this and told herself she did not desire it. But she did not pull away from him when he embraced her and gave him nearly as much as he gave her.

The fire in the room nearly burned itself out, but Emma thought she might incinerate where she was.

Why had Nathaniel never married? Heir to an earl, adventurous, intelligent, and wonderfully handsome, he surely was the object of a good many matchmaker's plans, and young women's fancy. She liked him well enough when they were children and tossed together by their aunt and uncle.

No, she did not merely like him then. If she was honest with herself, she must admit that she loved him then, as only a small girl could love, adore, and idolize an older boy who had the dubious good sense to merely tolerate her. Even then, he spoke of travels, and treasures to be discovered. And even then she wished to be drawn into his circle. As a ten-year-old, she was content to follow him about town, listening to his explanations about every tree and insect they discovered. Now, she just wanted to be drawn into his arms, and not talk about anything at all.

She must escape his company. But anything she might contrive, including feigning illness, would put a damper on Aunt Daisy's happiness, so long delayed. So instead she must be vigilant, and not allow her passions to rule over her good sense.

THE SNOW STARTED to fall heavily, and Lord Michael voiced concerns that several of his guests would not venture out on such a night. The vicar, however, had arrived early in the day and had been readying Pencliff's private chapel for hours.

Emma walked behind her aunt and Lord Michael as they made their way to the ancient sanctuary through a labyrinth of hallways. It was easier to arrive at the chapel directly from the outdoors, as most of the guests would do. But the advantage of a shorter walk was diminished by the deepness of the snow, and Lord Michael seemed to enjoy introducing her and Aunt Daisy to all his many dead relatives, whose portraits hung upon the walls.

To Emma, they were not all that interesting, unless she was able to discern an arched brow or Roman nose that reminded her of Nathaniel. But then, as they continued down the hall, she considered how many ancestors there were and how few of their descendents remained. There was the one very old aunt, the sister of Lord Michael's father. Lord Michael's younger brother died many years before, leaving one son. And that was Nathaniel, who was now like a son to his uncle, but who might have died ignominiously under a pile of rubble in Italy. There was no one else.

But where was Nathaniel tonight? Did he already regret their misdeeds of the afternoon? Or was he not a religious man and unwilling to attend services even on Christmas Eve? Was he avoiding her or a lengthy sermon?

He chose to avoid neither, apparently. When they arrived at the chapel, Emma saw Nathaniel's broad back and dark hair above the boxed pew reserved for the family. With sudden realization, she knew instinctively that he had come ahead of them to avoid being pitied, as he would should he have been seen slowly making his way on the long march to the chapel. And to give reason to his earlier arrival, he now seemed very interested in the preparations on the altar. He scarcely acknowledged her as she stepped over his cane to take a seat on the far end of the box so that she and Nathaniel framed her aunt and his uncle.

Behind them, and despite the snow, others silently joined them. And in the stillness of one of the longest nights of the year, the ancient chapel witnessed yet another celebration of life, and light, and love.

NATHANIEL, WHO knew no family other than Grand Aunt Cora and his uncle Michael, sat in Pencliff's massive dining hall and considered this Christmas Eve as extraordinary a discovery as any he'd ever made on distant shores. They'd often welcomed guests, and Lady Westbrook and her little niece were always among the numbers. But that was many years ago, and in the intervening years he did not always manage to join his uncle, nor did he ever remember so many celebrants gathered under Pencliff's roof.

And then he never remembered his uncle so happy. Why did he not ask the widow for her hand when they both were young? Then Nathaniel might have had cousins, including one already very devoted female. He glanced across the table at Emma's face, gently lit in the candlelight, and her delicate hand settled on her goblet. He gazed on her a moment longer than he intended and noticed the wine in her glass shifting, as if her hand was not quite as steady as the rest of her. Though she must have known he studied her, she refused to meet his eyes.

No, he would not want her as a cousin. But he very much wanted her.

"Will you dance at your uncle's ball, Mr. Evander?" asked the young lady at his side. She was the vicar's cousin and a lady of indeterminate age. He was somewhat unpracticed in the art of flirtation, but he suspected she was fishing for a partner.

"I would love nothing more than to join you for a reel, Miss Cartwell" he said gallantly, but regretted that with those careless words he raised the poor lady's hopes. "However, you may find me a very poor partner. I was never a very fine dancer, and recent circumstances have not improved my skills."

She blushed a fierce and unflattering red, which he supposed had to do with the indelicacy of referring to his injury. It was a sad fact of his life, however, and stumbling through country dances was the least of his new concessions.

"But I am sure you will find several excellent partners," he added, reassuringly. He forked a slice of lamb and it seemed unusually tender, making him wonder if Uncle Michael had imported his London cook for the season. After he sampled it he was convinced that this could not be the workmanship of Mrs. Corcoran, Pencliff's resident fire-starter. The meat was not at all charred. It was wonderful, in fact.

"This house has not seen a ball in decades," said Uncle Michael, as he raised his goblet. "Let us welcome in the New Year with our resolve to start the year fresh, with all our old pages torn from our books. A new chapter begins on January first!"

Nathaniel looked around the table and saw that some of the guests were confused by the metaphor. Undoubtedly he would have to barricade the library before Lady Tregaris started ripping apart the famed Leonardo codex. But tonight the room would have to endure the whole company, for coffee and hot chocolate was to be set under a spray of mistletoe. The thought did not make him happy, but Pencliff was not his. And for the first time in many years, it would soon have a mistress.

Therein was the difference in this great house, this dinner, this Christmas, he realized. A couple of bachelors could subsist very comfortably with hired cooks and servants and a library full of books. Uncle Michael and he enjoyed each other's company and managed very well. But now there were warm coals in every fireplace, a temperamental little partridge that would not stay near the quince tree that had been brought for him, the scent of fresh greenery in every room, and people laughing and talking throughout. Pencliff was a home, and the great difference was due to the elegant lady who sat at the foot of Uncle Michael's table.

"Shall we let the gentleman retire to the game room, ladies?" she asked, and actually winked at his uncle. Nathaniel looked around and realized everyone was quite finished with their dinner, while he had not yet touched his haricots vert. Across the table Emma watched him, and he guessed she understood his surprise.

But it was too late for regrets or the green beans. He stood along with the other gentlemen and helped the ladies to their feet. His knee was an agony, but he would not let the others see that. And still Emma watched him.

"Do not tarry too long with your cigars and sherry," Lady Westbrook said. "For I cannot promise anything will remain of my excellent orange cake."

The blessings of married domesticity extended even to the cavernous ovens of Pencliff, it seemed. Now Nathaniel could only wonder why it taken so long for this charming lady to bring Uncle Michael to his knees. Not only was she kind and lovely and capable of doing interesting things with leaves and twigs, but she was a baker. Could such an irresistible combination of talents run in the family?

EMMA WATCHED AS the ladies admired the decorous cake Aunt Daisy unveiled for them in the library, and as they each admitted they would like only the tiniest portion, then perhaps another—but very small—piece. And then it was all gone, save for a piece of orange rind shaped like a wreath curling on the platter.

But when the gentlemen entered the room, smelling like smoke and warm wool, Aunt Daisy was quick to reassure them.

"I promise to make a much larger cake for Twelfth Night, so there shall be enough for all," she said.

"I have seen your Twelfth Cakes, Lady Westbrook," said Lord Biggs, "And you know they are far too beautiful for anyone to eat. It seems a pity to tear through your gilded flowers and little sugar birds."

"Oh, you are very kind to say so, Lord Biggs. But the ornaments are only trifles. One must toss them away to get at the real treasures," said Aunt Daisy.

"I suppose you mean the cake itself," said the vicar, patting his stomach.

"I mean the bean and the pea hidden inside. Whoever finds the bean is king for the evening, and the finder of the pea is his queen."

"And luck will be with he or she who does not break a tooth on the discovery," said Lord Michael.

"It is a pagan custom," murmured the vicar.

"But this is a very large home, built in dark times," Lord Michael reminded him, "and there is room enough for all traditions to reside within."

The company, save the vicar and his niece, took the pronouncement in very good spirit. They continued in good spirits until, one by one, they left the library for either their own nearby homes or the guest rooms upstairs. Before long, the only people remaining were the host, his lady, Nathaniel and Emma. In a corner of the room, Lord Michael and Aunt Daisy stood by the window, as he attempted to clasp something large and sparkling onto her wrist.

"I have a gift for you, Emma," said Nathaniel. "It is not as impressive as the weighty thing that is now on your aunt's wrist, but I think you will like it."

"I did not expect anything from you, Nathaniel. Indeed, I was not even certain that we would see you. But I have a gift for you as well." Emma walked to the library shelves, where she'd earlier tucked her wrapped gift next to the atlas.

She handed it to him and he opened it carefully, folding the hand painted paper into a neat packet as he commented on its beauty.

Emma had not expected him to notice her artistry and now wondered what he would make of the actual gift. "I am not sure you will find this useful," she said, already certain he would not.

He contemplated the large crocheted lap blanket. "Why, it is a scarf, is it not? And a good size for our cold winter nights. Thank you very much, Emma."

"Yes, that is what it is, of course," she murmured. "I worked on it through the autumn."

"I wish I could claim to have worked as hard," he said as he reached for a package on the desk. "But I did spend several hours in the hot sun until this was mine. And now it is yours. Hold it carefully, as it is quite heavy."

It was. Emma guessed what it might be, for it had the shape and weight of a brick. Though it was wrapped in nothing finer than an old broadside, she unwrapped it slowly, savoring the moment. Finally, with as much delight as if she herself discovered it in the ancient ruins, she gazed upon a small relief sculpture of a woman.

"She is a goddess, perhaps Aphrodite," Nathaniel said. "It is just as well the vicar is not here to witness this Christmas Eve offering."

Emma glanced around and saw that Aunt Daisy and Lord Michael were not likely to witness anything either, as they were engaged only with each other.

"It is the most wonderful gift I have ever received, Nathaniel." She leaned forward and kissed him on the cheek, as she might have done when they were children. But he caught her arm and held her close. "Is it from Paestum?" she asked softly.

"I uncovered it hours before my accident. The excitement of the discovery likely distracted me and made me careless," he admitted.

It took but a moment for Emma to understand the import of those words, by which he told her that he understood the warning she had given him and the reasons why they must stay apart. And yet he teased her with this lovely gift and by holding her so close she could feel his warm breath on her ear. "And so, every time I look upon it, I shall be reminded of your laming? You need not fear me, Nathaniel. I have already said I will keep my distance." She pulled away, and his cane dropped between them.

Nathaniel looked like he had been slapped. He released her arm and stumbled backwards.

"I thought only of Aphrodite," he said, "and you."

But Emma already knew the goddess of love was a fickle enchantress. "And I am thinking only of you, dear friend," she said.

Chapter Three

"WELL, WE SHALL soon see some changes around here," said Aunt Daisy, looking around the Pencliff kitchen several days later.

Amused, Emma wondered if her aunt wanted Lord Michael or his ancient home, but preferred to give the man the benefit of the doubt. Still, she had rarely seen her aunt so excited about a project, although the diamond and ruby bracelet she wore undoubtedly did much to spur on her enthusiasm.

"Of course, it shall have to wait until after the New Year's ball. I daresay we cannot have the carpenters competing for table space with Mrs. Corcoran and our new staff of cooks. The lamb was quite excellent, as we managed to keep Mrs. Corcoran diverted with the potatoes." Aunt Daisy twirled around as if she were a girl at her first Assembly. "And you and I should manage just fine on our twelfth cake. I saved all the ribbons from the gifts opened on Christmas morning, to use as additional finery. And there are plenty of beans and peas stored in the dry pantry."

"Have a care, Aunt Daisy, or your lovely new bracelet might fall into the batter. Then the Queen of Twelfth Night will have something infinitely grander than a pea."

"Dear girl, you sound as fussy as Lady Tregaris. What did Nathaniel say to you to put you in such a mood?" Aunt Daisy paused in her dance and held a hand to her heart. "Is it because he gave you a rock?"

"It is a fragment of an ancient Greek sculpture. And, really, what Nathaniel says or does has nothing to do with me."

"It did not look that way on Christmas Eve."

"I suspect we had too much to drink. It makes one do things quite out of character or natural inclination."

Aunt Daisy considered this for a moment. "Or possibly it makes one do things that are entirely one's natural inclination. Is that not the point?"

"I would not know about that," Emma said stiffly.

"If so, it is because your inclinations have been stopped at every turn. You found three young men to love and care for and were not given the chance to do so."

"I count their loss of life more grievous than my own thwarted desire for a husband and children and a home of my own. To think otherwise is to be very selfish," said Emma, before she realized she had brought them to a moment of reckoning. "You have always been my example of generosity, Aunt Daisy. Uncle Westbrook died so many years ago and you must have had many suitors. Why did you wait until this new year to marry again?"

Aunt Daisy pulled a wooden stool to the scarred work table and sat. Her agile and capable fingers explored the cuts and indentations in the worn wood, pausing here and there.

"I had you, the most blessed gift I ever received. And I always had Lord Michael, my dearest friend. We suit each other to perfection, know what the other needs, and share more good memories than most marriages create. We have always been true to each other." Aunt Daisy lifted her hand, frowned, and started to pluck at a splinter in her finger. "My marriage to your uncle was not a happy one, for he did not treat me very well. And when he died, in the bed of another woman, I was suddenly set free. The estate in Kent went to his brother, but the house in Manchester Square was mine, as were sufficient finances to keep me comfortable for the rest of my life. Then, a year or so later, your parents left you on my doorstep before they went off to farm in America, or some such place. It was a temporary arrangement that somehow became a permanent one. But in any case, I am certain I would not have been willing to give you back to them."

Aunt Daily removed a tiny sliver of wood, and pressed her finger so any fragment could bleed out. Emma handed her a stiff linen dishcloth as she thought about her parents, whom she scarcely remembered, and who had dutifully sent a small gift to her on her birthday. This year, it either was misdirected or they forgot about it. In any case, she knew that if they ever had sent for her, she would not have been willing to go.

"And was Lord Michael satisfied with the arrangement? Did he not wish to marry?"

"He did not wish to dispossess his nephew of an inheritance he felt was rightfully his, which might have been the case had we married and had a son." Aunt Daisy wiped away the blood. "But, yes, I believe he was satisfied with the arrangement."

It was not what Aunt Daisy said, but the way in which she said it, that made Emma realize there were some things that would remain unspoken. And then the many pieces of a puzzle began to fit together: the mornings Lord Michael appeared at the breakfast table, Aunt Daisy's occasional visits to friends Emma never met, the hours during which she and Nathaniel were left to their own devices. And yet she had never heard a word against Aunt Daisy's pristine reputation, in a town where the slightest provocation could cause permanent injury to one's name.

"Then I am glad to know that you are not merely happy at last, but have been happy all these years," Emma said, wiping away sudden tears.

Aunt Daisy nodded and handed back the dishcloth. "Now what do we do about you?"

Emma put down the linen, startled. "I suppose I could live in a cottage here on the estate or find a small house in town."

"Yes, my dear," said Aunt Daisy, as if she spoke to a child, "but with whom?"

"Why, I might manage very well on my own. You have taught me so many things, I am sure I shall be quite comfortable."

"Then I daresay it is time for another lesson. Solitary pursuits are highly overrated." Aunt Daisy put her hands on her hips. "Perhaps a new companion can convince you that living alone in a small cottage is a very poor idea indeed."

"YOU SHALL HAVE to tell me more about my bit of sculpture," Emma said as she entered the library, "so many years hence I shall be able to speak creditably on the subject."

Nathaniel looked up from his book and removed his spectacles. There were furrows along his brow, as if he had to concentrate very carefully on the words he read.

Finally, he said, "After your accusation, I felt certain you would not hold onto the piece for ten minutes, let alone many years. I half expected to find it at my door, or set out with the refuse at the kitchen door. To what do I owe this change of heart?" Belatedly, he began to stand, but Emma prevented this by sitting down at once, though a little farther off than she would have preferred.

"It was not an accusation, but merely an acknowledgement that you and I have a perfect understanding about our relationship. I am a woman who must be avoided, who has already caused much grief to three families. If we stay as we always were, we will manage just fine," she said. And yet, she suddenly felt as if she was choking and took several deep breaths.

"There, now. It is all in the past," Nathaniel said, somewhat awkwardly.

"It is not," Emma protested. "It is the present and the future. You may have meant the gift with no such intent, but I feel it is a reminder of the misfortune that has already befallen you."

"What happened to me in Italy has nothing to do with you or the other men you have known. I was careless and shall pay for it for the rest of my life." He studied his leg, which seemed poised at an awkward angle. Using his hand, he shifted it to align with the other.

"And that is why we must never become closer than we are at the moment, for you shall also pay for it for the rest of your life," Emma insisted.

Amazingly, he smiled. So unaccustomed was she to this expression upon his countenance, she imagined she gazed upon a stranger. He looked younger, so much more like the boy she remembered, and the lines of wear on his face vanished.

"Are you the woman who insists your mind rules over your passions? Have you sought me out in my library to tell me of some superstitious nonsense that you must surely discount?"

"It is not nonsense if it follows me around like a dark shadow on a sunny day." Emma said, and resisted looking over her shoulder.

He studied her but didn't speak.

She shifted uncomfortably beneath his gaze and said, "You have lived out of the country for too long. You do not know what others say." Even to herself, her argument sounded increasingly absurd.

"I have not been so removed as to be completely unaware. It is one of the reasons I chose to spend this Christmas at Pencliff."

This was quite unexpected.

"To chance Fate?" she asked.

"To . . ." He stopped, his search for a plausible explanation as transparent as the melting snowdrops on the window. "To see you again."

"How very flattering, Nathaniel. And yet, have you not been in town these many months, recovering from your injuries? We might have saved ourselves a journey."

"But we would have missed the delights of the season," he pointed out, sounding more like his usual confident self. "The betrothal of my uncle and your aunt among them."

"Yes," she said, and smiled. He looked at her in surprise, as if it were a rare sight for him as well. "I am very happy for them. My only regret is that the event seems so long deferred."

"They did it for us, for you and me," Nathaniel said.

"Become betrothed?"

"No, Poppet. They deferred their happiness on our accord." He laughed, and she guessed if they stood next to each other, he might tousle her hair, as he used to.

Emma stood, feeling a great need to be close to him. This was a dangerous impulse indeed, but she could not help it. She waved aside his impulse to stand as well, and settled herself on the hassock next to his chair. Before he had time to protest, she raised herself just a little and removed his spectacles from beneath her bottom.

"Here you are," she said as she held them out to him. "They are as good as new."

"They have not been as good as new since the week after I purchased them and stepped on them, but thank you, just the same." He held them up to the light from the window and squinted. "Perhaps your words should guide us through this season, so we might anticipate a new year filled with good things."

"A marriage," she murmured. "And a new kitchen at Pencliff."

He raised his brow, but did not ask her about that.

"And a ball," he said.

"A ball?" she asked in disbelief. "Did I not hear you tell eager Miss Cartwell that you are an indifferent dancing partner?"

Nathaniel shrugged. "I am not so eager to dance with Miss Cartwell. Indeed, I am not eager to dance at all, but if I can find a lady to tolerate my awkwardness, I shall be happy to please Uncle Michael. Do you suppose there is such a lady?"

Emma said nothing.

Nathaniel cleared his throat and rephrased his request. "She would have to be a sensible lady, able to shrug off silly superstitions and gossip. And she must have some adventurous inclinations, for every step one takes comes with some risk."

He knew her better than anyone, perhaps even better than she knew herself. She felt herself relenting ever so slightly, even as she recognized his very unique attempt at seduction. She knew he wanted her, which was bad enough. But she also wanted him, which was worse. And quite wonderful.

She leaned forward, fully realizing she presented him with a rather advantageous view. "There is such a tolerant lady, and her aunt might be pleased as well. And the awkward gentleman already understands how much he risks by his headstrong decision, no matter how logically it has been presented."

He leaned closer to her, so that she saw her reflection in his fine, light eyes.

"For some things, the gentleman is prepared to risk a good deal."

THE SOUND OF music reached Nathaniel in the library hours before the start of the ball. The musicians, accustomed to small assembly rooms in town, surely needed to acquaint themselves with Pencliff's vast spaces and decide where to play for the best advantage. As he walked past the ballroom in the late afternoon, he noticed a frustrated fellow with a violin in one hand, fighting off the partridge with a large spray of ivy held in his other hand. Perhaps the tree sprites were already hard at work, doing their mischief.

Certainly, the outdoors seemed to be safe from their influence. Though a fine layer of snow covered the estate, the last day of the year dawned splendid and bright. Icicles broke off the window ledges and a great avalanche of ice tumbled off the roof and into the kitchen garden. Uncle Michael, fearing for the safety of his glass orangery and his guests, spent much of the day outdoors, calling out orders to his gardeners and anyone else who offered help. One man slipped on the ice and hurt his wrist. Another was struck by an icicle, which missed doing any serious harm by lodging in the collar of his coat. Nathaniel, not wanting to add any credence to Emma's reputation, stayed safely within doors.

And yet, had he not heard that one of her suitors was killed in the very church of which he was vicar? She would likely tell him that he was not safe anywhere and he might as well be with his uncle, barking directions as to the disposition of fallen branches and cleared snow.

But he had other reasons for staying within and not overly exerting himself this day. He was not truly confident about his ability to deport himself with any degree of grace at a ball. In fact, if Miss Cartwell had not pressed the point, he would not have agreed to dance at all this night.

But then, when Emma returned to his side and spoke to him of appropriate behavior, and seduced him with nothing more than a few words and a glimpse of her lovely breasts, he was incapable of speaking anything but nonsense. He could recall nothing of what he had said, but he was fairly certain he uttered something about a new year and a promise to dance with her this eve.

It was a bad business. But, in truth, he did not know how else she might be delivered into his embrace without excuses or arguments.

EMMA HAD BEEN kept in seclusion on this last day of the year, as if she were a bride and ought not allow her groom to catch a glimpse of her. Now she sat patiently on her low chair as a maid managed to work each hair on her head into an artfully arranged crown of curls, but her hands revealed how nervous she actually felt. There was no groom, and most likely would never be one, but tonight she would be with her own Nathaniel. Surely she had every right to claim him—as her oldest friend, her dearest friend. And tonight they would dance.

She hoped they would dance. She did not misunderstood his words to

Miss Cartwell, nor was she blind to the silent struggle he endured each time he walked too rigorously or went up or down the stairs. He was not the helpless cripple she feared he might be, but neither was he in full health. He might very well falter on the twists and turns of a reel, though he might do fine with her support in a waltz.

She would very much enjoy a waltz with him.

"You need not worry yourself about the ball, Miss Partrick," said the maid. "His lordship and ladyship have not rested all day, and the great hall is a piece of perfection."

"Whyever do you suppose I am worried, Jane? My aunt is in her element, planning all sorts of things and ordering people about. I believe Lord Michael is very much the same."

"Then perhaps you doubt my ability to dress you hair, Miss Partrick?" She met Emma's eyes in the small mirror of the dressing table. "You have nearly shredded your handkerchief to bits."

Emma looked down into her lap, feeling the pull of Jane's fingers on her hair, and seeing the bit of lace that she had worried into a damp rag. Really, it was just a ball, and Nathaniel was just an old friend.

But it was not, and he was not. He risked everything by dancing with her tonight, and she could not bear the thought of causing him pain. He already suffered too much.

And she loved him too much.

"Will you allow me to braid a sprig of greenery in with the pearls? It will suit your green gown to perfection." Jane held up a feathery twig of pine, crushing the needles to release the sweet aromatic oils.

"I hope I will not attract small birds and squirrels."

"I think you will attract many dance partners, Miss Partrick," Jane said sagely.

"I only wish to attract one," Emma murmured to herself.

But Jane heard, and nodded. "And he has been roaming the house all day, waiting for you."

Emma would have liked to hear who "he" was, hoping it was not the vicar's homely nephew, but knew better than to ask.

"And the musicians have already started to play, so we ought not keep him waiting," said Jane, as she tucked up the last stray hairs. She went to the bed, where Emma's lovely velvet gown was laid out, and arranged it on the rug so that Emma might step into its soft folds.

No, she was certainly not a bride this night, she thought as the gown was pulled up the length of her body, and fastened along the back. There was nothing demure about green velvet shot through with threads of gold.

And there was nothing virginal about the way in which the fabric clung to her curves.

She pulled at the lace-edged bodice. "I have changed my mind, for this will not do. I chose to wear velvet to keep myself warm on this winter night. I fear too much skin is revealed here."

Jane pulled her hand away and smoothed down the lace. "You will be warm enough, particularly under the gaze of every man in the ballroom. It is not too much with a complexion such as yours."

Emma flushed right down to her toes and knew Jane was correct; just now she thought she would incinerate.

The journey through the cool corridors did little to soothe her nerves or her flesh, as she walked unaccompanied down the stairs and into the main foyer, where the guests were assembling. Though the master's betrothal was to be announced to the company this night, she doubted there would be any surprise, as Aunt Daisy stood at Lord Michael's side, welcoming everyone in out of the cold. The music had already begun, but the foyer remained a crush, as well-wishers greeted each other and introduced family and friends who had joined them for the holidays. Everyone seemed connected to another, but for Emma, who stood like an island in this sea of congeniality.

Suddenly, the sea parted, and there was Nathaniel. He saw her at once—indeed, he might have been watching her all the while—and then he pushed himself off the column against which he leaned and started towards her. He stood tall and straight, and moved easily through the crowd, though he did not have his cane. On the lapel of his black wool jacket, he wore a sprig of pine.

"Emma," was all he said, but it was enough to make her feel there was no one else in the crowded hall.

"Nathaniel."

She accepted his arm as she turned to walk wordlessly with him to the ballroom, moving into the brighter light and musical harmonies.

"In a gown such as this, you will put the tree sprites to shame," he said. "They will be utterly disarmed, as am I."

She looked up at him. "That is a very odd choice of words, Nathaniel. Certainly, you are not planning any mischief this night."

And yet, judging by his expression, he did indeed intend mischief. She was not so naïve as to be unaware of what he was thinking. Nor was she so missish to not think it might be mischief of a most pleasurable sort.

"Ah, here are our aunt and uncle," he said evasively. "I believe the ball is about to formally begin."

Lord Michael found his place in the center of the ballroom and beckoned the servants to deliver glasses of champagne to all the guests. Aunt Daisy stood close, her bright eyes glistening and her smile radiant. If there was anyone present who doubted what Lord Michael was about to announce, the expression on her aunt's face would reveal all.

"Welcome, friends, to Pencliff. It has been many years . . ."

It had been many years. She had known Nathaniel nearly all her life, and the recent years of separation did little to make them strangers to each other. She knew what pleased him, what bored him, what he might be thinking to be on display at his uncle's ball. But there were parts of him yet to discover, the changes inflicted by nature and happenstance that made him the man he now was. Though the room was crowded and quite warm, she shivered.

". . . and the new year shall be additionally blessed because a most excellent lady has consented . . ."

Nathaniel's arm tightened as he drew Emma closer.

". . . we wish you to join us at our marriage . . ."

Nathaniel was the first to raise the cheer, though possibly the last to drink the toast. Instead, he turned Emma in his arms and kissed her.

She pulled away, though very gently. "Nathaniel! What will people think?"

"They will think we are to be cousins, just as they will when we take our places next to Uncle Michael and Aunt Daisy on the dance floor. Drink your sherry, my dear, for the music has already begun." He started to draw her through the crowd.

"Are you quite sure?" she asked, thinking only of his knee.

"That we are to be cousins? No. I actually do not know what will be the formal state of our relations, but I doubt anyone else cares overmuch." He took Emma's untouched glass from her hand and delivered it and his own to a servant. "They did not seem concerned about it when we swam together in the river, or looked for fossils on the cliffs."

Emma laughed, wondering how she had forgotten those things.

"But we are not children anymore and ought not do those things," she reminded him, after greeting a few of the guests who opened a path for them. They stood at the edge of the floor, watching their aunt and uncle dance until Lord Michael beckoned they join them.

"It is just as well," Nathaniel said, putting his large hand on her waist and marking the very moment in the melody when it was time to join in. "Because I have learned about other things in the years since I saw you last, and would enjoy teaching them to you."

HE WAS A FOOL to allow himself to believe his damned knee would follow his inclinations, simply because he willed it to be so. He was scarcely into the third dance when he felt himself falter, though he managed to remain upright and not disgrace himself. Miss Eveline Porter, the very young granddaughter of the local squire, seemed oblivious or indifferent, or just too pleased with herself for snagging the heir to Pencliff to partner her in a contra dance. She was a pretty little thing, just the sort of lady someone like Peter Milton would finally decide to marry.

But she had nothing to say to him, either before the dance or as they now departed the dance floor, and a woman who lacked conversation was not for him.

"Dear Miss Porter," said Emma, who suddenly appeared at their side. "It is so good to see you. Is your brother returned from India?"

Miss Porter murmured something as she patted down her hair.

"And Mr. Evander. I hope you have not forgotten your promise to dance this reel with me," Emma said and smiled so broadly that for the first time he noticed a small twist in one of her lower teeth. He wondered if he was responsible, for he remembered something about a ball thrown too hard and smashing into her jaw, and much blood and tears. Emma turned her gaze on Miss Porter, who looked like a child next to her.

But she was clearly a child with some attractions, for a young man quickly asked to partner her for the reel. She did not hesitate to accept, and seemed happy to escape.

"Did I indeed promise such a thing?" Nathaniel asked Emma when they were alone.

"Of course you did not. We already shared two dances, and to do more would invite speculation, despite your insistence that we are happily related as cousins." Her smile vanished. "You looked positively green out there, and I thought I should rescue you."

He needed rescuing, to be sure, but he hated the fact it was so obvious to her.

"Perhaps it is because of this bit of greenery on my jacket. My man seemed quite insistent about it, but I am sure it does not suit me."

Emma put up her hand to her dark curls and he saw she wore a similar sprig. "It does suit you," she said. "It suits you a good deal more than dancing for a full hour without rest."

"My dear, you are being overly solicitous. Are you perhaps concerned that the rumors about your deadly powers will be renewed if something should happen to me tonight?"

It was a stupid thing to say; he saw that at once. Emma turned very pale before turning away from him altogether.

"Emma," he began, but she was through the crowd, ignoring those who greeted her on her way. "Emma."

He did not, could not, catch up with her, until she was out of the ballroom and leaning against one of the carved columns in the foyer. Her breast rose and fell, and she seemed to be gasping for air.

"Emma," he said, fairly breathless as well. "I thought we already settled this business between us. I only teased you. Do we not know each other well enough for that? Can we not put it to rest?"

"But I cannot think of it with any good humor, nor could I ever. It is not my reputation, for I had little enough to lose, but what of the lives of three men? Beaconstone was healthy and hardy before he met me, and then died of influenza. Sir Dennis perished under the fallen ceiling of his own church."

"And Fitzhugh drank himself into a stupor and fell into the Thames," Nathaniel said impatiently. "Did Beaconstone catch his illness from you?"

"I do not see what it has to do with anything, but his mother was ill the week before him." Emma sniffed and used the handkerchief he handed her.

"Then I fail to see how you can be accused of anything other than the coincidence of bad luck."

She looked up at him, her face lovely even with a red nose and teary eyes. "And what about you?"

"Surely you don't think a two thousand year old Greek temple collapsed on me just because we knew each other once. I can scarcely claim to have been thinking about you before the accident, since we had not seen each other for years."

"And what now? Do you really think people will not notice every time you cough, or limp, or put your hand to your head?"

"I rather think they will instead notice you at my side, instead of my normal human frailties."

He saw the slightest glimmer of a smile. "I cannot be at your side all the while, Nate."

"I do not see why not, Poppet."

The foyer was nearly empty, but there was no privacy while his uncle's ball surged just footsteps away. Dinner would soon be served, and it was possible they would not be missed in the crush. It was also possible they would be missed. But nothing mattered except Emma and this moment and making her believe that what had befallen those other men had nothing to do with him and her.

He took her hand and led her along the shadowed perimeter of the foyer, beyond the wooden columns, to the library. She followed him in silence, her hand trembling with either fear or excitement.

The room was theirs, as it always was. The boughs of greenery looked a bit weary, but otherwise the library welcomed them with the scents of leather and smoke and the comfort of being surrounded by the wisdom of every generation that came before them. Nathaniel turned the key in the lock, and brought her to the ancient chaise, now covered with the oversized scarf she had made for him. It was large enough to use as a blanket and kept him warm when he read late into the night.

He sat down upon it, and pulled off his dancing slippers.

"What on earth are you doing, Nathaniel?" Emma asked.

"You have bared your injuries to me. In fairness, I believe I should do the same."

"Nathaniel, please. It is not necessary." She held her hands out to him. "I do not need to see them to know they are there. I believe you."

"Why, what is this? Surely you have seen me undressed before?"

"You were ten years old. It is quite a different thing."

He studied her face and knew another moment of reckoning was upon them. "And you have been betrothed to three men. Surely you saw one or all of them undressed?"

A log cracked in the fireplace, sending out a spray of sparks. Emma's face appeared half in darkness, half in light, but her reluctance was plainly visible.

"Then we will stop right now. I do not wish to do anything you will regret for the new year."

Something changed in her expression just then. "You said you would teach me things this night," she insisted, sounding like the little girl he remembered.

"I thought to build on what you already knew,' he said, feeling his resolution faltering.

She kneeled on the chaise beside him. "But that is just the point, Nathaniel. I only know what I read in books. I look at the statues you have sent home from Greece and Italy. But I want more than that, and I live with regret that I will never know the real thing. Now I do not know what I fear more—hurting you by loving you, or never knowing what it is to love you."

He pulled her down onto his lap and caressed the smooth skin of her throat. She raised her hand, making him think she would do the same to him, but instead she started to tug on the complicated series of knots that made up his necktie. His heart leaped in his chest and he knew this night would prove the answer to all his Christmas prayers.

Chapter Four

A COLLECTIVE shout and the chiming of the church bell awakened Emma from her sleep, but it was several moments before she realized where she was and with whom. She opened her eyes to see row after row of books, and she wondered if she might be in heaven. But then something sweet and pungent scratched her cheek and she reached beneath her face to pluck a sprig of pine needles. She remembered everything; indeed, she was in heaven, and it was Cornwall, and she was with Nathaniel. And after the things they did last night, she believed there could be no finer world than this one.

Her lover, the man she knew all her life, faced her, his eyes shuttered closed, his breathing steady and strong. His bare chest was tanned, though she could see the V at his neck where his shirt was probably open in the hot Mediterranean sun. A jagged scar near one shoulder attested to acts of recklessness in his past. It had not healed cleanly but did not seem to threaten his health. Unless he was bothered by ladies who wished to follow its path with an inquisitive finger. She tried this and, indeed, it did not seem to bother him at all.

In fact, his sleep was so deep she doubted he would be bothered by anything she did just now. But to be sure, she decided to experiment. Her hand moved along the lines of his chest, smoothing the light hair near his nipple, and then dipping lower, to his waist.

"I would not go there this morning, if you wish to make an appearance at this day's luncheon," Nathaniel said softly.

She smiled as she looked up at his face, but her hand stayed where it was. "What if I say I do not have an appetite for eggs and kippers this morning?"

Nathaniel turned onto his back, pulling her onto him so that her head rested on his shoulder. One of her legs fell between his, and he shifted his body.

"Is it your leg that troubles you?" she asked.

She heard the rumble of his gentle laughter in his chest.

"Nothing troubles me in this new year, save the thought that your Aunt Daisy might send out a rescue party to Scotland, thinking we are in

Gretna. Or even worse, that she and Uncle Michael will come bursting in here, suddenly desperate to read Fordyce's *Sermons* or something of that sort."

Emma lifted her head but could not see his eyes. Instead, she studied the start of the new day's beard on his chin, and the delicate line of his lower lip.

"They never seemed overly concerned about our whereabouts before. I recall you spent nearly a week building a flying machine before anyone wondered for what purpose those large paper wings were intended. I shudder to think about it now, for if you had managed to get out of the tower window, you would have dropped like a stone."

"But I did not die that day in the pursuit of science, and for no other reason than that you were not yet finished painting feathers on the wings." He laughed again. "So, you see, you bring me luck when we are together. I would not have been buried at Paestum if you were with me then. And now you will be with me for the rest of our lives, which may be for many, many years."

"Please, Nate, there is no need to change anything between us."

He brought his arms around her, pulling her along his body until their noses touched.

"Everything has changed, my love. We will be lucky if our absence at dinner last night was noted only by half the people in attendance. But surely our aunt and uncle noticed and will likely rejoice in the prospect of a double wedding. They might not have bothered us overmuch years ago, but we are no longer children."

Emma rubbed her cheek against his rough one. "So we keep saying, and yet it is all wonderment. I feel as if I know everything about you, and yet hardly know you at all. I suppose you must shave everyday?"

He laughed. "I do." They lay together several minutes in silence. The household stirred outside their locked door, and carriage wheels splashed in the puddles in the drive outside the window when he said, "And I suppose we might have made a baby last night."

Her body reacted in a startled movement, and she accidentally kicked his leg. He responded with a sharp intake of breath, and then settled back against the cushions.

"Would it be so very terrible, Poppet? he asked.

"But it was only once . . ."

"Three times," he pointed out.

"But only one night." She sighed. "And I am no longer young."

"Oh, indeed. I reckoned you among the antiquities in ancient Greece. Though now that I think of it, you are not yet thirty, young enough to still have many children." He shifted his position, and started to raise himself up with her still clinging to him. "Emma, did your several lovers leave you completely untouched?"

She blushed, though why she should be embarrassed to speak of these things while she lay naked with a man, her legs between his, was beyond her understanding this morning.

"Beaconstone did kiss me once. And Mr. Fitzhugh took me to Vauxhall, but he drank overmuch and passed out on a bench."

"It seemed to have been a habit of his. I pity the man, but you must admit you will do much better by marrying me." Now that they were sitting upright on the chaise, Nathaniel pulled the wool shawl over their shoulders for either warmth or her modesty. "It is not possible that anyone could ever have loved you more than I do."

Emma knew everything he said was true. He was her best friend, he was clever and caring, and their lovemaking was both passionate and all she ever dared to imagine. More, in fact, than she had ever dare imagine. But she had already weathered so many storms that it remained difficult to imagine arriving at a safe harbor, even with Nathaniel.

"Is it because we know each other so long and so well?" she asked.

"I have known Rutherford, the stablemaster, longer than I have known you, and I do not feel I must ask him to marry me." Nathaniel pulled the strand of pearls from the nest of curls on her head and seemed to be weighing them in his hand. "Do you not trust me?"

"I do trust you. I always have," she said gently. "I know what you are feeling because I have adored you for all my life."

"Then it is settled. What say you to a wedding on the morn after Twelfth Night?"

Still, it was impossible for Emma to simply say, "Yes."

"It is only six days hence. Do we not require a special license?"

"My beloved Emma. I have managed to obtain permission to dig beneath a man's house in the agora in Athens and sailed on a pirate ship while claiming to be one of their brethren. Surely I can manage this small bit in good time."

Finally, it did seem quite settled. "Perhaps I do not know you so well, after all. You have never told me about pirates."

But before he could, there came the sound of loud footsteps from the hall.

"What do you mean they are locked in the library?" Lord Michael shouted. "They are probably doing some damned experiment with wings or feathers or whatnot!"

"Well, he certainly is right about the whatnot," murmured Nathaniel, and kissed Emma's racing pulse at the base of her neck. "And I believe we should get dressed so we can tell him about the 'what now.'"

NATHANIEL WAS NOT the very last to appear for breakfast on the first morning of the New Year, nor did he seem to be the one worst for the festivities of the night before. In fact, he felt like celebrating all over again.

His valet managed to get him bathed and shaved in record time and refrained from commenting on the wrinkled state of his clothing or on the scent of lavender that lingered on his skin. It seemed a sacrilege to wash it off, but he guessed he could return to the source for more.

Emma was already in the dining room when he arrived, and he did not recall ever thinking her as beautiful as she was this moment. Her hair was simply set into a coronet braid, and her plaid gown was both modest and fitted well enough to set his body on fire. Her hand hovered over a plate of sliced bread and cheese, but it looked untouched. Her eyes caught his as he entered the room and held.

Nathaniel strolled over to the buffet table with as graceful an air as possible for a man whose damaged leg had supported him above a woman the night before, and filled a plate with sliced meats. He turned towards Emma, but another gentleman slid into the seat next to hers. He found a place at the foot of the table, closer to his uncle.

"A good morning and year to you, sir," Nathaniel said to Uncle Michael as he sat. Emma still watched him and the rogue next to her watched her. "I believe last night's ball was most successful."

Uncle Michael stirred his coffee, as if the act required all his attention. "Indeed," he said at last. "Those who attended thought it an excellent evening."

"I thought the same," said Nathaniel. "Though I cannot comment on the ham or oysters. In fact, I have an announcement to make this day."

"It had better be what I hope or, in my new role as protector of Lady Westbrook's family, I shall have to meet you at dawn in the meadow. And it's damned cold out there."

"A duel is not necessary, as it appears I shall share the role of protector with you. In any case, Miss Partrick is mine."

"Congratulations, my boy. I prayed you would have the good sense to grab her in between her other ill-fated betrothals and make her see the right of it." Uncle Michael paused to take a gulp of his coffee and coughed. Nathaniel gently tapped him on his back. "Fancy that, though. I always thought it would be the other way around."

"Whatever do you mean?"

"Lady Westbrook and I decided to postpone our own nuptials until we thought the two of you were quite settled, though not necessarily with each other. Only recently did we finally give up, convinced the two of you were old enough to blunder along your own paths."

"That is not a very kind way of putting it."

"You are quite right. Let me instead say that we were convinced the two of you could find something to do in the library other than peruse the collection of fossils."

"Uncle . . ."

"The chaise near the fireplace is quite comfortable for two people who are willing to share extremely close accommodations."

"Uncle, please."

"You need not look so horrified. Lady Westbrook and I do not yet count ourselves among the fossils."

"What about the fossils?" asked Lady Westbrook, suddenly standing between them. "I should like to have a glass case made so they can be displayed without the necessity of the maids dusting them every day."

Uncle Michael patted her on the hand and smiled. "You see how well she will manage my household? Am I not getting a good bargain?"

"My dear love, when you see my first dressmaker's bill, you may wish yourself and Nathaniel back in a bachelor's household."

"It is too late for that, Lady Westbrook," said Nathaniel. "In fact, I hope I will not steal your thunder when I make an announcement this day."

Emma's Aunt Daisy was already looking down the length of the table to her niece, who smiled a little too brightly for one who was doing no more than nibbling on her cheese.

"It is about time," she murmured as Nathaniel rose a little awkwardly to his feet.

Suddenly, the door opened, ushering in a blast of cold air and the scent of damp wool.

"Peter Milton," Nathaniel said, even as he wondered if it could be so. "What are you doing in Pencliff?"

"Did you not invite me several weeks ago? I have decided to accept."

PETER ATE LIKE a starving man at Lord Michael's table, earning the amused looks of the other guests. At one point he studied the hollybush centerpiece on the buffet, and Lady Westbrook warned him that not only was it inedible, but also poisonous. His eyes turned to Emma, but she was studiously avoiding him, as she had from the moment they were introduced.

Nathaniel guessed Emma already knew his friend, but wondered how well Peter knew Emma. For all his friend's warning about her reputation and the deeds he attributed to her, Nathaniel could not help feeling Peter was oddly taken by her. He complimented her on her appearance and excellent taste, offered to escort her back to town, and tried to engage her in conversation. Emma's responses were terse, though polite. She seemed vastly more interested in a discussion of trout fishing at the other end of the table.

"For someone of your censorious nature, you seem rather complimentary to Miss Partrick," Nathaniel said to Peter when they were finally alone. Emma had vanished along with her aunt, and the rest of the company went off to bore each other with a game of charades. "Do you fear she might curse your existence unless you flatter her into good humor?"

"I suppose her beaux tried that, to no avail," Peter mused. "One has to pity the poor sots, though. To be seduced by such beauty, and then betrayed by Fate. It is a very bad thing."

"Why, my friend, you sound very tempted to try your own luck with her."

Peter looked startled. "Oh, not at all. The pater believes it a miracle I have not already killed myself in some misdeed, and I do not need anyone's help in that regard. But I have come to Pencliff to save you, my friend. You have been out of society for so long, I thought you might be overly susceptible to her charms."

Nathaniel rubbed his hand along his chin, thinking if such were the vagaries of society, he had done well to keep out of it. For what little he had witnessed spoke of foolishness and gossip, and the slandering of reputation. He could only wonder how his uncle managed to carry on an affair for so many years without damaging his or Lady Westbrook's good names. And why Emma chose not to find refuge, far from society, with her unconventional and undoubtedly wise parents.

"You came to save me? This is a new turn of events. I would not have been here at all, if you had not given me the dire prediction about Miss Partrick and my uncle. In fact, I might have broken my neck on that treacherous carriage ride, and it would have been entirely on your account. And all for nothing, by the way. Your informants gave you a false report, as Lord Michael announced his betrothal to Lady Westbrook at last night's ball."

"So I heard, in the early hours of this morning. One of your uncle's guests was carrying on a bit of business with a certain lady, and rode through the night to return to his wife in Danbury House before dawn. Luckily, I had already removed my weary body from her bed chamber and happened to meet him in the hall. We chatted a bit, and so I heard the truth about the upcoming nuptials. I am sorry I got that story wrong, old man."

"Mrs. Rolande's husband was here at Pencliff?"

"He might not have been using his real name." Peter shrugged as if it really did not matter, and Nathaniel knew his own assessment of society was perhaps too generous. "But then I wondered if Miss Partrick, disappointed, might transfer her affections to suit the circumstances. She seems rather adaptable. After all, how many women can claim to have been in love with three men in the span of just a few years? I came here, just in case."

Nathaniel was startled. "Do you mean, that she might come to fancy you?"

Now Peter looked surprised. "Not at all. I feared she might make a play for you. You are your uncle's heir, after all."

Nathaniel sat back in his chair. "It is far too early in the day for a drink, but you are sorely tempting me. Emma Partrick never had any designs on my uncle, whom she loves like her own. And she did not, as you say, make a play for me, because I stole a march on her."

Peter leaned forward. "You held her off?"

"Quite the opposite. I held her close. And did everything else in my power to seduce her. In fact, she has agreed to be my wife." Nathaniel allowed this bit of news to settle in, as he doubted Peter would have received a report of this turn of events as he came out of another lady's bed chamber. "And I believe I may have to challenge you, for you have certainly impugned her honor."

Nathaniel could not imagine another circumstance in which he might twice be discussing the prospect of a duel in the space of a half hour.

Luckily, Peter ignored the last comment. "I am too late, then. It is as I feared."

"You are at least twenty years too late, for I now believe I may have loved her since the day we met."

"And look what has happened." Peter sighed heavily and rested his head on the table.

Nathaniel waited for several moments, believing his friend's gesture was all for dramatic effect. But when he parted Peter's hair so he could see his eyes, he realized Peter was sound asleep. Delivering bad news was surely a job better done on a full night's sleep.

"I AM GOING TO marry Nathaniel," said Emma. She sat at a small table, helping her aunt curl little bits of ribbons into rosebuds. Aunt Daisy had decided to have the Twelfth Night Cake represent the four seasons, and having finished sugaring tiny pine cones and holly leaves, their attention was on the pleasures of spring.

"I know, my dear. Surely you don't think his uncle and I were grinning like fools over the quality of the eggs this morning? I shall have to discuss the most effective cooking times with Mrs. Corcoran." Aunt Daisy reached for her sewing scissors. "Nothing could make us happier."

"Are you quite sure? If something happens . . ."

"The only thing that will happen is you will make us grandparents at last. I did not particularly envy my friends who had babies with startling regularity, but I should very much like to have many grandchildren."

"Thank you very much," Emma said somewhat sarcastically. But in truth, ever since Nathaniel startled her with his logical speculation about the events of the night before, she had been thinking a lot about babies and how lovely it would be if they looked like Nathaniel. Her own mother and father had proven themselves unworthy of parenthood, but Emma thought she and Nathaniel might manage it all very well.

"You will be a wonderful grandmother, Aunt Daisy," Emma said more generously. "As you have been a wonderful mother to me."

"Oh, my darling girl," Aunt Daisy said, and reached a pink-stained hand across the table. "I have only wished for your happiness."

Emma took her hand, finding comfort and warmth in her aunt's grasp, as she always did. "I dare hope it is now mine."

"If I may disturb this cozy moment, I await your commands," said Mrs. Corcoran. She glared at Aunt Daisy, who grasped Emma's hand more firmly, steadying herself against an attack by the beast of the Pencliff kitchens.

"How lovely to see you, Mrs. Corcoran. I quite forgot you were there, undoubtedly listening to all my niece and I had to say to one another. Do you have a question about the length of time required to boil an egg? I believe they were a bit watery at lunch." Aunt Daisy's quiet, ironic tones were customarily the signal for Emma to escape from the conversation, but her aunt held her fast.

"I have never heard a complaint about my eggs, your ladyship, and Lord Michael and the young master have always eaten heartily." The cook might have said more, but she appeared to suddenly recall she spoke to the future mistress of Pencliff. "I wish to discuss the Twelfth Cake, your ladyship," she said politely.

Aunt Daisy released her hold on Emma, for she required both hands to explain what was required. "It shall have to be very grand, even larger than those in the past. There will be many more people, for one, and it will celebrate the two weddings that will come in the morning. I should like four layers, with a five inch step between each. And it shall be round, of course."

"Of course, your ladyship," said Mrs. Corcoran, though Emma thought she might have gotten stuck on the first step. "Are you certain you would not wish to prepare the batter yourself, as you are such a proficient baker?"

Emma winced, knowing her aunt would come up with a retort. And that she did, though it was subtle enough to seem a compliment.

"Oh, no, Mrs. Corcoran. I am certain you will do an excellent cake for us. And in this case, appearance is more important than taste."

The cook hesitated, clearing mulling the words. "And what of the icing?"

"You shall leave the decoration of the cake to Miss Partrick and me, for it is there we are indeed proficient," Aunt Daisy said most convincingly.

Mrs. Corcoran wiped her hands on her clean apron. "And is this the way it will be, your ladyship?"

Emma understood, as Aunt Daisy perhaps did not, that the cook questioned the future of her preeminence in the Pencliff kitchen.

"Not quite," said Aunt Daisy, with a warning finger raised. "There is also the matter of the pea and the bean, and another little object to be added into the batter. Please see me before the cakes go into the ovens."

"As you wish, your ladyship." Mrs. Corcoran bowed and retired to the pantry where the stores of limoncello were kept. Emma could not fault the woman for needing a potent drink.

"You will not be her favorite in this household, I fear," said Emma.

"Cooks enjoy the company of other cooks. When everything is quiet in a few weeks, and you are safely married, I shall visit her here and share recipes. She shall be quite happy. As will you, my dear."

"When I am safely married? Dare I even contemplate such a thing?" Emma sighed, feeling a thrill of expectation. After all these years of loneliness and abiding sadness, she finally allowed herself to believe she would have a beloved partner for the rest of her life. "And dare I hope that Nathaniel will be safe with me?"

"Oh, yes," said Aunt Daisy, speaking with all the authority of a countess, soon twice-over. "The two of you had best be safe and happy with each other, because I assure you, his uncle and I do not want you back."

"Thank you, dear Aunt Daisy," Emma laughed. "You always manage to say the right thing."

NATHANIEL HAPPILY delivered his friend Peter into the eager care of Miss Eveline Porter, knowing a man already an earl and with two sturdy legs beneath him was worth far more than a cripple with nothing more than expectations. Peter was a rake of the first order, of course, but Nathaniel supposed there was a time in every man's life when he had to admit his adventuring days were over, be it amongst the ruined temples of Italy or amongst the bedchambers of the ton.

It was a hard thing to admit, of course.

"You cannot convince me of your happiness when you look so dour," said Emma.

Nathaniel paused and leaned on his cane, wondering where she was. He looked around the parlor and saw her white slippers before he saw the rest of her. She stood on a table with both arms above her head and a length of ribbon dangling from her lips.

"Are you posing for a bit of statuary?" he asked.

"Is that why you look so concerned?" she countered with another question. "That I would be recognizable as someone's lawn ornament? I am only refreshing the greenery and am happy to report there are no tree sprites loose in Pencliff yet."

She dropped to her knees, and in a light fluid motion that Nathaniel could only envy, slipped off the table. As she came towards him, fingering the ribbon, he recognized a playful, teasing expression on her face that he had not seen in many years. Perhaps she intended to tie him up.

And if she did, he would allow her to do so. In fact, he would happily hold out his wrists in complete surrender.

"What made you think of statuary?" she asked, in what he perceived as an innocent tone. She stopped inches away from him and slipped the ribbon around his neck. "I wonder, because when I awoke on New Year's Day I thought you looked like nothing so much as one of the statues in the hallway. Of course, that chap is wearing a toga and you certainly were not."

She most certainly was no longer an innocent, and he was delighted to admit he was entirely responsible for her new awareness.

"I can be persuaded to wear a toga," he said cheerfully.

Emma tugged on both ends of the ribbon, bringing his lips very close to hers. "And yet I prefer it if you do not."

In the next few moments, she managed to convince him that he would be much happier without yards of fabric between them. He was responsible for this as well, and was very satisfied with himself.

After some time, he managed to speak of sensible things. "I thought of statuary because I recalled my days among the ruins, in the heat and the dust."

She looked up at him, her eyes half closed and her lips rosy and moist. No sculptor ever beheld such a model.

"You will miss that. No library of books can replace the journeys you have taken. And I confess I have had some doubts that domesticity will truly suit you."

"I have little choice in the matter and have spent months in bed with nothing to do but contemplate my future." Somehow those days, not all that long ago, seemed a lifetime away. "But I am completely reconciled to my new life. Domesticity suits you, dear Emma, and you suit me. We shall manage very well."

He knew the new adult Emma well enough to recognize that something he said displeased her. He saw it by the way her eyelids lowered and she chewed on her lower lip. What now? he wondered. Did she again intend to trot out the argument about her bad luck and the three unfortunate beaux and how he ought to avoid her at all costs? If so, he was now prepared; he knew her in the most intimate way, intended to marry her in a few days' time, and the worst that had befallen him was finding a bit of eggshell in this morning's custard. True, some men might have choked to death on eggshell, but he was already immune to the dangers of Mrs. Corcoran's cooking.

Nathaniel leaned on his cane, readying himself for the familiar nonsense.

"Domesticity does not altogether suit me, Nathaniel. I am quite proficient at it all. How could I be otherwise with Aunt Daisy's mothering? But it is not what I dream about, what I have always longed for."

Nathaniel leaned so heavily on his cane it almost cracked. "What exactly are you saying?"

Emma sighed. "I am saying that for years I listened to your uncle's tales about your adventures and looked at the things you sent home to him. I wanted to be you. I wanted to stow away in one of your trunks and be with you."

"And now that you have finally convinced yourself that you are not a bad bargain, you realize that it is I who is damaged goods?" Nathaniel had dismissed this possibility days ago because Emma, of all women, knew the extent of his limitations. But his bride—if ever he managed to get her before the vicar—was determined to examine every facet of every gemstone.

Incredibly, she smiled and placed both her hands over his on the cane, as she leaned closer to him.

"Oh, no, Nathaniel. You are just perfect," she said, and he was happy to believe her. "It is just that I hoped you might continue your adventures, but take me with you. I know some things will be difficult, and you may not yet be ready for a long journey. But let me be your partner in this, as in all other things."

"What of our children?" If she imagined they were going to leave their babies behind with Uncle Michael and Aunt Daisy, as her own parents had, she had vastly misread his priorities.

She blushed. "I am sure our children will do well wherever they are, as long as we are with them. That is what matters most, is it not? At the very least, they may become articulate in other languages and speak about us behind our backs."

"And probably complain to each other about why they are not spending the winter in a drafty old fortress in Cornwall."

"Precisely," she said, smiling.

"*Mi piace moltissimo*," Nathaniel said.

"*Wie heissen Sie*," she answered promptly.

"I believe, dear lady, you just asked me my name. At this point in our relationship, it should be fairly familiar. All the more so because it will be yours in a few days' time."

"Ah, I should have guessed your friend Lord Peter did not really know German. *Entschuldigung*. I still have to practice my verbs," she said.

Nathaniel nodded, thinking of all the ways he knew how to say "I love you," both by word and by deed.

"You will find Lord Peter improves upon acquaintance. There are many things about which he is wrong, but somehow it all works out in the end."

"For Miss Porter's sake, I do hope that is the case. The poor girl seems quite smitten with him," said Emma.

"From experience, I believe we can say that could be the start of a very fine affair," said Nathaniel, sagely.

Chapter Five

TWELFTH NIGHT Day seemed a harbinger of good things to come. The morning was sunny and bright, and the sounds of preparations for a dinner party and two weddings were punctuated by occasional crashes of ice and snow sliding off the roof and hitting the ground below. Old blankets lined the entrance foyer, absorbing the water that melted off boots and clothing. But there was no hope for the mud, tracked throughout the house and causing much consternation among the staff.

Nothing, however, could dampen Lady Marguerite Westbrook's excitement. She waved off everyone's concerns, including her niece's fears about the safety of her betrothed on a slippery floor, and applied all her attention to the massive Twelfth Night cake being assembled in the kitchen. Pots of colored sugar and bits of ribbon and greenery spilled onto the floor, but Lady Westbrook, with a true artist's temperament, saw only the masterpiece and her own vision of the seasons. Mrs. Corcoran did her part by hiding in the pantry.

Somewhere in this mountain of sugar and flour, there were a bean and a pea, the finding of which would announce the king and queen of Twelfth Night. The vicar was still quite audible in his protestations that this was very much a pagan practice and not to be tolerated in a Christian home, but it was clear to Lady Westbrook that the vicar's niece would gladly gobble down the whole cake if it meant that she could be queen for the evening. Goodness knows what the young chit intended to do with that power, but Daisy guessed it had much to do with Lord Peter Martin, and was likely to cause the vicar to go into shock.

But the pea and bean, though traditional, were nothing to the other object that had been baked into the cake. Following a very different tradition, neither pagan nor Christian but very much in fashion, an emerald bracelet was hidden at the very summit of the cake, guaranteeing the serving that would contain it would go to the very woman for whom it was intended.

Daisy always liked Michael's serious little nephew. She decided she now liked him even more that he was taller and had the good sense to thoroughly disabuse Emma of any notions of bad luck attached to her.

And certainly, deciding to bake his mother's splendid bracelet into the cake was as brilliant as the bracelet itself. The years during which it had been hidden in the Pencliff safe had done it no harm, though Daisy polished it very thoroughly before drowning it in the cake batter. She only hoped Emma would not bite down too hard, for a gap-toothed bride would hesitate to smile, even in her happiest moment.

Nothing, however, would prevent Daisy and Michael from smiling at the marriage of their dearest relations. This joy, so long desired and so many times deferred, seemed the final triumph of raising two lonely children to proper adulthood. And that her Emma and his Nathaniel should finally realize they suited as no others ever could presented a prospect that was truly Elysian. Daisy was to marry Michael, Emma was to marry Nathaniel, and the Twelfth Night Cake was a masterpiece.

Truly, was there ever a better start to a new year?

EMMA PARTRICK sat alone in her darkening bedchamber, musing on the transformation of her simple white gown into her bridal dress. When she packed it for the journey to Pencliff, she only knew it would allow her to comfortably blend into the scenery and would keep her warm in drafty hallways. Now, with the addition of yards of gold trim and clusters of pearls, it would set her quite apart from scenery, and standing next to Nathaniel was likely to warm her to the very core of her being.

She scarcely dared to imagine such happiness was within her reach. They need only get through this evening's festivities, and the elegant meal, and survive the night. The vicar and their other guests would stay at Pencliff, lest a blizzard prevent travel the next morning, and the marriages would take place before breakfast.

Emma might have believed she was the only person concerned about the health and welfare of everyone involved until Aunt Daisy made it clear that she wished for the marriage of the younger couple to precede hers and Lord Michael's.

"I would first see you settled," was all the older lady said, patting her hand, but a world of meaning was contained in those few words. Tears blurred Emma's vision as she glanced at her groom, but he and his uncle seemed overly interested in the gold rings they would bestow on their brides.

By this time tomorrow, if the Fates did not conspire against her, Emma would indeed be settled.

She smoothed the creases in her silk gown for the hundredth time and reached for her elbow length gloves. Carriage wheels splashed on the gravel beneath her window, and Lord Michael's spaniel barked a greeting to each arrival. Emma heard the sound of voices, a fiddler tuning his instrument, a groom calling to another. Everyone on the estate was invited, on this Twelfth Night, to join neighbors and guests in the Pencliff ballroom.

Someone tapped at the door, but several moments passed before Emma realized the sound was closer and more immediate than the other sounds of the great house. She rose, walked across the lovely rug and opened the door to Nathaniel.

"Are you well?" she asked, a little anxiously.

He kissed her, which had the effect of reassuring her completely. "You must not worry, my dear. We shall make it to the morrow in good health and be married and have many children and even more adventures and die in very, very old age."

"Is that your warranty?" Emma asked, not entirely in jest.

"It is. And as you know, I am very rarely wrong," he said.

"You cannot say such things to me any more, for I am no longer a guileless girl idolizing an older boy." She turned back into her room and lifted her reticule from her dressing table. "I am a wise woman who idolizes a clever man. And you have utterly convinced me of the truth in the matter."

Nathaniel reached for Emma's shawl, dangling from a peg near the door, and draped it over her shoulders. "I am clever enough to know you are not at all convinced, but I promise I will do everything to keep you safe."

"It is not I who must be kept safe," she murmured, but if Nathaniel heard her, he gave no indication of it.

THE COMPANY gathered around the wide serving tables was very grand, if not quite as elevated as those who were invited to Lord Michael's gatherings on Christmas and New Year's Eve. Tradition required that every person, from the master of the house to the lowest stableboy, share dinner on Twelfth Night, dance together, and otherwise enjoy himself while on the most equitable terms. Such it was that the housekeeper might find herself in the arms of a duke, or a lady might serve lemonade to the gardener. By the next morning, all would be forgiven, if not altogether forgotten.

But for all the possibilities of mischief and mirth, Emma would not leave Nathaniel's side. She had her reasons, and they had nothing to do with the buxom laundry maid whose lace slipped down into her scanty bodice, or the gatekeeper's wife who enjoyed Lord Michael's brandy a bit too much.

Miss Cartwell abandoned her uncle to Lady Tregaris so they might together bemoan such unchecked evidence of republican ideology, and dragged Lord Peter Martin away from Miss Porter to welcome Emma and Nathaniel when they walked into the room.

"Lord Peter is so proud to stand up with you tomorrow, Mr. Evander," she said, sounding as if she had had a nip of the brandy, as well. Lord Peter, for his part, had his eyes on the laundry maid.

"Yes, it is fortuitous that my good friend can be here with me," said Nathaniel. "But of course, I might not have come to Pencliff at all if Lord Peter had not suggested it when we met in London. So, you see I owe him my present happiness."

Emma looked up at him, wondering why it would have mattered to Lord Peter if Nathaniel spent the holidays with or without his uncle, or if it had anything to do with herself.

"Of course," Miss Cartwell went on. "But as you know, Lord Peter is very considerate of family and friends. Undoubtedly, he heard of your uncle's intended nuptials and would not have you miss the surprise."

"Undoubtedly," said Nathaniel, and smiled. "I believe he heard a rumor to that effect and shared it with me. I am grateful he did so."

His arm tightened around Emma, and she decided it was not the moment to question this odd business. In fact, for all her general curiosity, she realized that with a new husband, there might be things better left unasked . . . and, therefore, unanswered. She smiled up at him.

"Will you remain in Penzance, Miss Cartwell?" Emma asked. "I believe your uncle is very pleased to have you here."

"Oh, indeed he is, for I am ever more capable than his housekeeper." She glanced at Lord Peter, whose eyes were now on her face. "But I feel a great desire to return to London. Lady Winslow is my great aunt, you know, and she has long promised to introduce me to society. Of course, I already have one or two connections."

"You shall have me among the number," said Emma.

Miss Cartwell hesitated just long enough to remind Emma that she would just be Mrs. Nathaniel Evander, and not as valuable as other connections to a young lady with high expectations. Emma laughed, also reminding herself that being Mrs. Evander would have been beyond her own expectations even a few days ago.

"Yes, I will," said Miss Cartwell. "And I am glad you find it will give you pleasure."

Emma let the subject go and was grateful for a sudden distraction at the doorway. The fiddler played a little flourish and stilled his instrument as a great cart was wheeled into the room, delivering the Twelfth Night Cake shimmering in the candlelight.

Aunt Daisy stood with her arms outstretched, waiting to receive both her creation and the expected accolades for its beauty and design.

"I have never seen her so happy," said Lord Michael, suddenly appearing at Emma's side.

"Neither have I, my lord. But it is not about the cake," said Emma as she accepted his hand. Thus she stood between the two closest men in her life, soon to be her new husband and her new uncle.

Mrs. Corcoran emerged from the crowd to the right of Aunt Daisy, holding what appeared to be a knife. Emma gasped, before she realized the silver object was nothing more than a cake server, and that the cook intended to do the honors of serving Aunt Daisy's creation. But either her enthusiasm or the brandy got the better of her because she came too close to the moving cart and tripped on the front wheel. The weight of the masterpiece propelled the cart forward, ramming it into Aunt Daisy, who stood frozen in horror.

The collective gasp in the room was more likely in response to the sight of a very large cake suddenly flying over her head than concern about a downed lady.

But Nathaniel and Lord Michael were quick to move, and pushed through the crowd with Emma fast upon their heels.

"Marguerite!" Lord Michael called, sidestepping a trail of sugar icing that now adorned the fine oak floor.

But Nathaniel, his vision obstructed by his uncle, was not quite so lucky. He stepped into the sweet mess, lost his footing, and started to fall backwards. Emma, now seeing nothing but his dark shoulders slipping down before her, rushed forward with arms outstretched, and broke his fall. Her rescue would have been flawless, but that he was much heavier than she, and they started to sink to the floor, Nathaniel's body still braced by hers.

"Oh, dear God," he said after several moments. "This might have been a disaster."

Emma looked around them, at legs and the hems of ballgowns, at lumps of cake and icing, the partridge pecking at a sugared leaf, and at one poor gentleman tripping over Nathaniel's dropped cane. "If this is not a disaster, Nathaniel, I do not know what is." And yet she clung to him, relishing the weight of his body on hers, and the good clean scent of his hair against her face.

He shifted to the floor beside her, flexed his bad leg, and laughed out loud. "I am whole, even if the blasted cake is not, and you have saved me, it seems. I say I am the luckiest man on earth."

The vicar was yelling something about saving the cake, Mrs. Corcoran was threatening an old man with her cake knife, and Lord Michael was comforting a sobbing Aunt Daisy.

"In the present company, that is saying a great deal," Emma noted soberly.

Nathaniel lifted her onto his lap, and kissed her, which said a good deal more. She was perfectly content to spend the last night of her spinsterhood in such activity, but Lord Peter interrupted them after several moments.

"I say, are there not sufficient bedrooms above stairs, old man?" he asked Nathaniel. "Or have you broken your leg again?"

"I am perfectly well, my friend, for my lady has saved me from further injury," said Nathaniel.

"Ah, then," Lord Peter said, and reached a hand down to help Emma to her feet, "have you sustained an injury by your act of heroism, Miss Partrick?"

"I have not," said Emma, as both she and Lord Peter helped Nathaniel. "Indeed, I feel better than I have in many years."

"You may feel even better after you have had a slice of cake, for everyone seems quite certain Twelfth Night Cake tastes even better when it has been tossed on the floor and splattered onto people's clothing." As if to punctuate his point, he ran a finger along Miss Cartwell's shoulder and studied a little red globule for a moment before putting it in his mouth. "Quite excellent. My compliments to the cook."

Emma looked around the room, realizing Lord Peter spoke nothing but the truth. Aunt Daisy was, as usual, making the best of a bad situation, and had the remains of the cake shoveled onto a large tray so it could be served from the table. It now was entirely upside down, and looked like nothing so much as a wide brimmed bonnet, but the large mound of sugar and flour would probably taste no different than a work of confectionary art.

"I should like a piece, Aunt Daisy," said Emma, hoping to demonstrate her confidence.

Aunt Daisy looked at her for a moment and then down at the cake, and said, "Not yet, dear. I am saving you for last."

No one else, apparently, needed to wait. The vicar, no longer concerned about pagan traditions, asked for a double portion, and Lady Tregaris scraped off all the sugared rosebuds for herself. Portions were doled out all around, until only the small circlet that originally stood on the very top of the cake was handed to Emma on a silver plate. It looked rather wretched, and had been crushed by all the other layers, but a bit of silver ribbon still poked through the icing.

The dried bean, bestowing the right of kingship for the evening, was luckily found by a gentleman. Unluckily, it was found by the vicar, who protested that he would have nothing to do with the proceedings.

However, when the queen's pea was nearly swallowed by the laundry maid and then coughed up as proof of her victory, the vicar seemed a bit more reconciled to his plight. He took the woman's rough hand, and led her to the center of the room for a dance. Neither of them seemed particularly adept at the art, but no one seemed to notice or care.

"Do have your cake, dear," said Aunt Daisy to Emma. "You will need your strength for tomorrow."

Emma, happily, knew what to expect on the day and night of her wedding, and thought it would scarcely make a difference if she ate the cake or not. She glanced at Nathaniel, who seemed more interested in her plate than in anything else.

"Well, I certainly do not need to eat ribbon," she said, using her fork to poke at the bit of silver sticking out of the crumbling cake. But it proved a bit tenacious, and then it seemed to not be a ribbon at all. In fact . . .

"I hope you are not too disappointed that you did not find the pea," Nathaniel said as Emma pulled an emerald bracelet from the cake. It was encrusted with sugar and crumbs. "This belonged to my mother, and there is a necklace as well. Perhaps you will wear both on the morrow?"

"It is beautiful, though I am not sure if I should eat it or wear it," Emma said, holding it up to the light. "It is certainly too rich for me, in either case."

"Nonsense," said Aunt Daisy. "It is precisely what you deserve. Nathaniel is a man of very refined taste, as well I know."

Both Emma and Nathaniel looked at her in surprise.

She waved off their doubts. "You have learned everything you know from your dear uncle so how could it be otherwise? In fact, just the other day . . ."

The revelation of that day was lost to them, however, as Aunt Daisy and her cake were in great demand. Lady Tregaris wished for a pea as well, and spooned through the ruins of the cake on the tray hoping to find one. Lord Peter proclaimed the cake the best he had ever eaten—and both his experience and his appetite were vast—and asked that the recipe to be sent to his own cook. The squire's wife licked the icing off her husband's plump fingers. And Lord Michael announced that they were witnessing the start of a new tradition at Pencliff.

Aside from Aunt Daisy's look of horror at that pronouncement, there was no one who thought the Twelfth Night gathering anything but the most splendid evening in the history of Penzance.

IN THE EARLY morning hours of January 6ᵗʰ, Emma Patrick turned in her lover's embrace and held her bare arm up to the pink light of dawn. She wore nothing but the emerald bracelet and the necklace Nathaniel had fastened around her neck when they retired to his bedchamber, and she decided she liked them, and him, very much indeed. In a few hours, she would be helped into her white bridal dress, but she knew everyone assembled at her marriage ceremony would see nothing but the jewels.

Aside from Nathaniel, of course, for she was now so confident in his love that she knew he would see nothing but her.

He was the only man for her. How had she not known it at once? She was sure she had loved Beaconstone, Dennis and Bart, and would always grieve the loss of them. But Nathaniel was a part of her, as no other man ever was and never could be. He understood her pain and pleasure, her doubts and hopes, her needs and desires. He knew how to make her happy.

"It is not yet morning, surely?" Nathaniel groaned, burying his face in her hair. "Did we not just go to bed?"

"It is morning, and I suspect many of your uncle's guests never found their way to bed," Emma said.

"I pity them, for it is a great comfort," he said.

"If that is your way of telling me I am as familiar as an old pillow, I shall have to do you harm," she teased, before thinking about her words. She could not have laughed about such a thing even a day or so ago.

She reached across his chest to finger the dimple in his cheek. He jumped, suddenly awake.

"Is that a weapon? What have you there?" he asked, a little suspiciously.

Her hand hovered over his face, and the bracelet glinted in the brightening sun. "If it is a weapon, you have given it to me yourself. Emeralds have sharp edges, you know."

"Which is why most women do not wear them to bed," he said, scratching his chest. "I shall have to give you cotton wool for our first anniversary."

"As you wish. But I seem to recall you asking me to wear the jewels even as you removed everything else," she said, warming at the thought.

"It was a good idea at the time." He closed his eyes as she ran her hand over other parts of his anatomy. "In fact, I have decided I like it more and more."

"Please remember that later today. I ought to find my way back to my room before our aunt and uncle decide they must each lecture us on the joys and obligations of marriage. They would not like to discover we have already read the book, so to speak."

"I am fairly certain they know where we are and what we have been doing. And are we not being married just moments before them? In that circumstance, I believe we shall have to interrupt the vicar to lecture them, as we will be the old married couple."

"So we will be," Emma said, and sighed with happiness. "And, truly, Aunt Daisy is far too busy today to trouble herself about us. She wished to festoon the breakfast parlor with ribbon and scent the room with oranges and . . . oh dear!"

"What is it? Did Peter consume all the oranges? He is a dangerous man to invite to any dinner."

"No, it is not that. It is far worse!" Emma struggled to sit up, pressing against Nathaniel's leg in the process.

He grunted. "I can only imagine. What can be worse?"

"The Christmas decorations! We were so preoccupied last night we never removed them!"

"I believe I saw the laundry woman wearing a spray of ivy like a shawl around her shoulders. She was not wearing much else."

"Dear God! The vicar will be scandalized and refuse to come to perform the wedding this morning."

"Be assured my love, if he is sober, he will come. He wore a crown of holly and could barely keep his hands off her."

Emma settled back into Nathaniel's arms. "You do not understand, Nathaniel. It is very bad luck to leave the decorations past Twelfth Night, as I am sure I told you. The tree sprites will leave the safety of their boughs and bring us nothing but misfortune for at least a year. We cannot risk it."

"I believe we already have, for it is at least six hours since the bell tolled the start of a new day, and we have both survived. I sustained nothing more than a kick to my leg, and you can only claim to have been overly loved."

Emma laughed. "Is such a thing possible?"

"No, it is not. But if we can believe it nevertheless, I would suggest that the power of being overly loved is more than sufficient to fight off the bad humor of tree sprites, or superstitious mischief, or the consequences of really bad luck. It is accomplished and Nathaniel Evander and Emma Partrick have triumphed."

237

"What have we won?" She laughed again.

Nathaniel looked quite serious, with his hair spiked about his face and a crust of Twelfth Night Cake on the bridge of his nose.

"Why, everything," he said.

OF ALL THE miracles of the Christmas season, those most appreciated by the small and weary party assembled in Pencliff's ancient chapel on the morning of January sixth were the simplest. The two grooms, uncle and nephew, stood upright and in good health at the altar. The vicar was reasonably sober, though he had to be reassured several times that the men standing before him were not a couple, and that two brides would soon be joining them. Snow fell through the night, but did not deter guests from returning to Pencliff to witness the marriage ceremony. And the ceiling of the chapel did not collapse.

For Emma Partrick, who had abandoned her childhood dreams of a splendid wedding some time after the death of her third fiancé, the day somehow proved to be everything for which she ever hoped. Her beloved Aunt Daisy would bring her down the aisle to the altar, a parent first but a bride as well. Their gowns were not at all similar, but touches of greenery added a seasonal elegance to both their costumes. Aunt Daisy rather liked the look of holly to accent Emma's emeralds, but Emma decided the bright leaves were surely her talisman of good luck, good health, and true love.

She knew a bride ought to be fraught with nerves on her wedding day, worried about the journey ahead. But Emma had already weathered several storms, and now walked slowly and assuredly down the narrow aisle, towards the one man who would provide her a safe harbor for all their life together. This she knew, as many brides did not, because of all that came before this moment, and a love that grew from a deep and abiding friendship.

Nathaniel watched her as she came towards him, looking appropriately solemn, but revealing a telltale flicker of a smile on his lips. Emma, suddenly afraid that she might laugh out loud in the sheer joy of the moment, glanced at Aunt Daisy, whose cheerful grin did nothing at all to temper Emma's feelings. She too was a bride who traveled far to reach this blessed day, and her happiness could not be contained.

The vicar looked momentarily confused as each bride went to her groom, but was urged into action by a few words from a disheveled Lord Peter, who did not quite manage to stand up with Nathaniel, and instead sat slumped in the first pew. He was flanked by Miss Porter and Miss

Cartwell, who alternately poked him in the ribs, to keep him awake. In any case, the marriage of Miss Emma Partrick and Mr. Nathaniel Evander proceeded without further incident; some minutes later, they embraced as Mr. and Mrs. Evander and stepped aside to witness the marriage of Lady Westbrook and the Earl of Bristol. The language of the second service was somewhat grander, and the vicar's voice somewhat more sonorous, as befitting such a ceremony. But he also had the advantage of an additional ten minutes to sober up.

Lady Westbrook did little to oversee her own wedding breakfast, and as the new Countess of Bristol she wisely overlooked the burned toast, undercooked eggs, and thin cream that Mrs. Corcoran prepared for the feast. The countess undoubtedly contemplated the changes she would make in her kitchen, but for now seemed perfectly content to sit with her new husband and stir her tea, and listen to stories about every other wedding in the history of Penzance. Still, she noticed when her niece and new nephew left the parlor.

Nathaniel and Emma stepped out into the winter sunshine of the new day, wrapped together in a wool blanket someone left on a chair. The footsteps of many guests, both last night and this morning, had already cleared the path, and they were able to walk some distance before Emma feared she might ruin her slippers. They stopped where they were, warm in their close cocoon, and looked towards the sea.

"It truly has been an extraordinary two weeks," Nathaniel said. "I doubt we will ever see their like."

"I hope not. But what began in misunderstanding, distrust, and doubt, has somehow emerged as a very fine thing." Emma wrapped her arm around her husband's waist. "Did you not believe I traveled to Penzance to marry your uncle?"

"No, of course not."

Emma pinched him.

"Well, yes, perhaps I did, but Peter planted that little seed in my mind. He seemed to know a great deal about you."

"He probably knew a great deal about my reputation. But nothing at all about me." She looked up at Nathaniel and saw his eyes were closed against the glare of the sun. "It is the way of the world."

Nathaniel opened his eyes. "Do you mean that rumor becomes legend, and legend becomes truth?"

"Yes, indeed. It must be the case with the stories of the ancient tree sprites that seem to have done us no harm. And did you just overhear some of the wedding stories people told to our aunt and uncle? Every one was full of mishap and misadventure. One would think it a miracle that any man and any woman ever managed to marry."

Nathaniel laughed and steered them both into a semicircle so that they were back on the path towards the great house that would someday be theirs.

"And so our story will also be told in this season for years to come, and at weddings at which the bride and groom somehow defy the Fates," he said.

"And do not forget," Emma began. Nathaniel stopped, and turned to face her.

"They must live very long and happily," she said softly, in the moment before he kissed her.

The End

Dedication

For *On the Twelfth Day of Chistmas, My True Love*

To Emma's Girls

Knowing that the name of a prophetic poet graced Public School 268 in Brooklyn, New York, We were inspired to read and write books, plays, essays, music and poetry.

And in doing so, we realized the beauty of her vision.

About the Authors

Jo Ann Ferguson has been creating characters and stories for as long as she can remember. She sold her first book in 1987. Since then, she has sold over 100 titles and has become a bestselling and award-winning author. She writes romance, mystery, and paranormal under a variety of pen names. Her books have been translated into nearly a dozen languages and are sold on every continent except Antarctica. You can reach her at her website:

joannferguson.com or by email: jo@joannferguson.com.

Karen Frisch writes Regency romances for ImaJinn Books, among them *Lady Delphinia's Deception*. With two nonfiction genealogy books in print, she began tracing her family history as a teenager and discovered she is a cousin of Edgar Allan Poe (removed by six generations). A lifelong resident of New England, she is also a portrait artist. Follow Karen on her website at:

KarenFrisch.weebly.com.

Sharon Sobel is the author of eight historical and two contemporary romance novels, and is the Secretary of Romance Writers of America. She has a PhD in English Language and Literature from Brandeis University and is an English professor at a Connecticut college, where she co-chaired the Connecticut Writers' Conference for five years. An eighteenth century New England farmhouse, where Sharon and her husband raised their three children, has provided inspiration for either the period or the setting for all of her books.